At the entrance to Macy's, Amanda paused and whirled to face Mike. "That confesssion of mine? It's this: I absolutely *love* to shop."

"That's a confession?" He scoffed. "I'm pretty sure loving to shop is some kind of girly birthright."

"There's nothing I'd rather do than spend an afternoon shopping. *Nothing.*"

With an opening like that, Mike just couldn't let it go. He captured Amanda's hand when she would have sashayed away and tugged her back beside him.

"Nothing?" he asked.

He leaned nearer so the Channel Six crew wouldn't hear and positioned his mouth against the soft skin of Amanda's earlobe—not kissing, just barely touching—and felt her fingers tighten on his at the contact. Heard her sharp intake of breath as he began speaking again. "Not even an afternoon of making love? Losing yourself in the heat, and the closeness, and the skin-on-skin touch of bodies rubbing together, lips—"

"Nope," Amanda squeaked. "Not even that."

"I have a pretty good idea how to change your mind about that 'favorite activity' thing. If you'll let me."

"Not a chance," Amanda snapped, sandals clicking on the polished floor. "This is all business between us."

"What a shame." With a wink to let her know their game wasn't finished yet, Mike smiled and followed Amanda toward the men's department. "And me with *such* a knack for pleasure . . ."

<u>BOOK YOUR PLACE ON OUR WEBSITE</u> <u>AND MAKE THE</u> <u>READING CONNECTION!</u>

We've created a customized website just for our very special readers, where you can get the inside scoop on everything that's going on with Zebra, Pinnacle and Kensington books.

When you come online, you'll have the exciting opportunity to:

- View covers of upcoming books
- Read sample chapters
- Learn about our future publishing schedule (listed by publication month *and author*)
- Find out when your favorite authors will be visiting a city near you
- Search for and order backlist books from our online catalog
- Check out author bios and background information
- Send e-mail to your favorite authors
- Meet the Kensington staff online
- Join us in weekly chats with authors, readers and other guests
- Get writing guidelines
- AND MUCH MORE!

Visit our website at
http://www.zebrabooks.com

MAKING OVER MIKE

Lisa Plumley

ZEBRA BOOKS
KENSINGTON PUBLISHING CORP.
http://www.zebrabooks.com

ZEBRA BOOKS are published by

Kensington Publishing Corp.
850 Third Avenue
New York, NY 10022

All Kensington titles, imprints and distributed lines are available at special quantity discounts for bulk purchases for sales
promotion, premiums, fund-raising, educational or institutional
use.

Special book excerpts or customized printings can also be created to fit specific needs. For details, write or phone the office of
the Kensington Special Sales Manager: Kensington Publishing
Corp., 850 Third Avenue, New York, NY 10022. Attn. Special
Sales Department. Phone: 1-800-221-2647.

Zebra and the Z logo Reg. U.S. Pat. & TM Off.

First Printing: June, 2001
10 9 8 7 6 5 4 3 2 1

Printed in the United States of America

*To John Scognamiglio
for his ongoing support, expertise,
and knack with a great title.
And to John Plumley,
who proves to me every single day
that true love really exists.*

Chapter One

If there ever was a day that called for the get-a-promotion suit, Amanda Connor figured, Monday was it. Especially *this* Monday. Unfortunately, at the moment she didn't have it. And at this rate, it looked as if she wouldn't be getting it anytime soon, either.

"Melanie, if you're there, please pick up." Scrunching her cell phone between her ear and shoulder, Amanda steered one-handed through the crawl of cars surrounding her. Phoenix rush-hour traffic. At this time of morning, a few minutes before nine o'clock, it could more aptly be called rush-hour all-you-want parking.

Ahead, sunlight sparked from the bumper of a commuter-packed SUV, forcing her to squint. She groped in the console of her cluttered Tercel for her sunglasses, still listening to the chirpy sound of her friend's answering machine message.

"So at the sound of the beep . . ."

"C'mon, Mel," Amanda muttered, drumming her

fingers on the steering wheel. "*Please* be home.
C'mon, c'mon—"

" 'Lo?" came her friend's sleep-shuttered voice.

"You're there! Great. Listen, I need the Suit. The
get-a-promotion suit. I meant to stop by last night, but
there was a crisis with one of my clients—something
about a glued-on seaweed facial and a misaligned
chakra—and I didn't have time to—"

"Hold on, hold on," Melanie interrupted. "Give
me a sec." There was a thump—probably the sound
of one of her two cats being "encouraged" from the
bed onto the floor—and then the whine of the radio
being tuned to the alternative-rock station Melanie
used to wake up to. "As usual, I'm four steps behind
you and halfway in dreamland. What's the matter?"

Amanda decided to cut to the chase. "I need the
Suit. The get-a-promotion suit."

"What for?" Melanie yawned. "You own the company, kiddo. If you want a promotion, just give yourself one."

Sure. And then she'd snap her fingers, send her
struggling start-up company, Aspirations, Inc.,
straight to the top of the most-successful-Phoenix-
companies list, and retire in six short years at thirty-
five, at which time she and the three assistants she
employed would spend their days surfboarding in
Maui.

As if.

Especially without the proven help of the Suit.

"Sure, I could give myself a promotion, but money
can't buy the kind of publicity I can get if everything
works out today. The Lotto, remember?"

A gasp. "Oh, Amanda, I'm so sorry! I completely
forgot."

"That's okay." Her heart sank a little lower. "But
my appointment with the Channel Six news execs
is in"—Amanda braked to avoid a maniacal lane-

changer in a dented Buick, then glanced at her wristwatch—"approximately forty-four minutes, and I'd really feel better if the Suit was on my side."

"Today's *really* the day? The Life Coach Lotto day? I can't believe I spaced on remembering it."

Melanie sounded repentant. Amanda felt that way, halfway into mourning for her soon-to-be-failed business. If even her best friend couldn't keep track of the publicity stunt she'd dreamed up to bolster business, how was the rest of the Valley of the Sun supposed to remember it?

She nudged the cell phone with her chin, trying to alleviate the knot of tension that had begun forming in her shoulder. Her stomach tightened, as though protesting the whole doomed venture—that, or protesting the dry half-bagel, scrambled egg white, and three-quarters of a cup of grapefruit juice Amanda had tried to pass off as breakfast this morning.

Ugh. She shuddered at the memory alone. Clearly, women's magazine diets had been invented by a bunch of masochists with antiflavor fixations. And with, obviously, no stock invested in either of the mighty double Gs: Godiva and Ghirardelli.

"Yes, today's the day," she said, shoving aside a sudden chocolate-doughnut fantasy, "and I really, really, really need the get-a-promotion suit. I'm only a couple of miles from your house right now. I can be there in less than—"

"I'm sorry, Amanda," Mel interrupted, probably recognizing the note of panic in her friend's voice and wanting to nip it in the bud. "I can't give it to you."

"It's just a loan, for Pete's sake! I'll trade you the meet-a-man miniskirt if you want, but I've got to have that suit." She glanced down at the black-on-black pants, slim-cut shirt, and slide-on mules that comprised her late-to-work emergency wardrobe. Plain and moderately fashionable as the ensemble was, it just wouldn't do when meeting the press for her one big break. "Please!"

"No, I mean, I don't have it," Melanie explained. "I loaned it to Gemma to wear to dinner with Tom's boss last week. We figured any good karma that could help Tom's chances—"

"Sure. You're right." As a longtime believer in the powers of the expensive Prada pantsuit she and her two best friends had pooled their money to purchase—and loaned among themselves, depending on whose need was the greatest—Amanda nodded. "I hope it helped. Really, I do."

Shoving back a renewed sense of panic, she mentally recalculated her route. If she merged onto the eastbound freeway and encountered nothing worse than the usual gridlock, she could get to Gemma's, retrieve the suit, and still make it to the downtown Channel Six offices in time for her ten o'clock meeting.

"Actually," Melanie said, "Tom did get a raise, a promotion, *and* some new stock options. So the power of the suit"—she lowered her voice into a dramatic, newscaster-worthy delivery—"remains unbroken."

Relieved, Amanda laughed. If she'd dieted like a crazy woman, living a nonfat, non-fun, mostly-air-and-eight-glasses-of-water-a-day existence to fit into that suit, only to discover it had somehow quit working . . . well, there was a reason temporary insanity was an accepted criminal defense.

"Okay, I'm off to Gemma's, then," she told Mel, using her knee to help steer onto the merge ramp without spilling her double latte. "Meet me tonight at Boondoggle's for a post-news postmortem?"

"Come on, it won't be that bad. The Life Coach Lotto was a stellar idea. Besides, has the Suit failed any of us yet?"

Amanda thought of the business loan she'd secured, the excellent assistants she'd hired for Aspirations, Inc., the newly-renovated office space she'd gotten at a discounted rate—all while dressed in the butter-colored, perfectly tailored Prada—and grinned.

"Nope," she admitted. "And so long as Gemma had a chance to dry-clean the thing and put it into high-security storage before the twins could get ahold of it and use it for tree-house curtains again, it won't fail me today, either." *I hope.*

" 'Atta girl. See you tonight."

"Okay. Boondoggle's at seven."

With that, Amanda signed off and tossed her cell phone onto the passenger-side seat. It rolled among her briefcase, her spilling-over purse, a clipboarded Life Coach Lotto checklist dotted with Post-it notes, and the lonely, decidedly *non*-double-G, two-and-three-quarter-inch-diameter apple her new diet allocated her for a midmorning snack, then came to rest atop the gimmicky "coach's" baseball cap she'd brought along to wear while greeting her newest client—the winner of the Lotto.

Everything really was going to be okay, she reminded herself. She was skilled, resourceful, and determined. Those qualities had brought Amanda pretty far already, and they were about to bring her and Aspirations, Inc., even further. Just so long as fate played fair and didn't hand her some kind of loser for her first winning client, things would be absolutely perfect.

She hoped.

"Look at you! Since when did you become some kind of loser? I barely recognized you!"

The statement, issued in a strident, take-no-prisoners tone that Mike Cavaco recognized only too well,

boomed inside the rolled-down window of his taxicab
and straight into his brain.

"Since when," the voice's owner went on, "did you
take to sleeping on the streets like this? For shame,
Mike."

He winced and shoved the brim of his battered
Suns cap high enough to see Myrna Winchester, his
elderly next-door neighbor, tsk-tsking from the
shopping-center space beside his cab. Behind her,
crookedly parked and looking as new as the day it
rolled off the assembly line in 1967, waited her tur-
quoise-colored Ford Mustang convertible, complete
with fuzzy dice swinging from the rearview mirror.

"I'm not sleeping in the streets," he pointed out,
trying on a grin. "I'm sleeping behind the wheel."
In demonstration, he yawned and stretched, like a
man straight out of bed—a man groggy with the
effects of too many celebratory post-game beers from
last night, too little shut-eye, and more time on his
hands than he wanted.

"At least you're not driving in that condition,"
Myrna said.

"No, I'm parked."

"I can see that. Mike, Mike, Mike. What's happened
to you? You're not even a successful taxi driver."

She looked sad to realize that fact, and the disappointment in her face got to him more than Mike
wanted. Either that or the root beer and nachos he'd
downed for breakfast weren't sitting well with him.

"Have you had any fares at all today?"

Myrna's frown said she already knew he hadn't.
Semi-affronted at her obvious lack of faith in the
neighbor she'd known for the past four years, Mike
tried to work his way into some righteous indignation
on his own behalf. Nothing happened. He ran a hand
thoughtfully over his dark, three-week-old beard,

remembered all that had happened to him since April Fools' Day, and tried again.

Zilch.

"Geez, Myrna, cut me some slack here, will ya? I'm only filling in with the taxicab gig. It's not like it's permanent or anything."

"Luckily for you." She sniffed, shifting her sack of groceries against her hip. Her blue-shadowed gaze swept over the jumbled interior of his assigned taxi, at the papers strewn on the floor of the backseat, the licorice whips slung over the two-way dispatcher's radio, and the stack of résumés and reference letters Mike unsuccessfully tried to hide beneath his elbow, then came to rest on his face.

Something in her expression, something tender and uncomfortably mushy, instantly put his guard up. But it was too late.

"Open the door, sonny," Myrtle said. "You've got a paying customer."

Mike raised his eyebrows. He nodded toward her pristine parked convertible. "You've got a perfectly good car right there."

"Pshaw. I fancy a ride, and you're here to give it. Now put those muscles of yours to good use before I break my fingernails on this door."

"Yes, ma'am." Trying to match his demeanor to her no-nonsense one, Mike eased his way out from behind the taxi's steering wheel and stepped past Myrtle to open the driver's-side rear door. He held out his hands for her grocery sack and then propped his knee on the taxi's rear bench seat while bending over to slide the groceries inside for her.

Another "tsk-tsk" from his neighbor alerted him to the fact that she'd spotted the butt-hugging rip in the rear of his favorite blue jeans. She'd probably lasered in on the insignificant mustard stain on the

sleeve of his old gray T-shirt, too. *Sheesh*. For some
people, nothing was ever perfect enough.

He levered himself back out and tipped his baseball
cap. "Your chariot awaits," Mike said, indicating the
cracked vinyl seat just beyond his outswept arm.

Myrtle didn't duck her head fast enough to hide
the smile that, for the briefest nanosecond, displaced
her disapproving frown. But even if he hadn't
glimpsed that smile, Mike would have known she
cared. Because in the space of the next hour and a
half, his convertible-loving neighbor somehow managed to find excuses for two trips downtown and one
leisurely drive to a nearby park to feed the ducks—
"Leave the meter running, sonny!"—before coming
back to retrieve her car, and that was all he really
needed to know that someone was in his corner.

It was nice. Really nice.

Especially considering how pathetically real his latest April Fools' Day joke had turned out to be.

And despite his best efforts to hide the fact behind
monosyllabic grunted answers, grouchy tugs at his
Suns cap, and a final, brief good-bye to Myrtle just
before lunchtime, Mike appreciated it. If Myrtle had
only been a restaurant owner needing to employ
about a half-dozen of Phoenix's best former food-
service workers, things would have been just about
perfect.

As it was, things were just about as *im*perfect as
you'd expect on an everyday, ordinary Monday.

And the Mondayness of the day just kept rolling
on, with the brief exception of several more 'urgent'
fares from friends who had dug up the taxi company's
number and specially requested a ride from "that
really great driver in number twenty-two."

The latest of those fares was in his cab right now,

being driven the four whopping city blocks between the mall and the nearby CheapCuts hair emporium.

"This isn't a bad job, Mike," said Rico, the impending cutee and another victim of the April Fools' Day joke that wasn't. He bounced up and down on the cab's backseat until Mike shot him a warning glance, then in his reedy nineteen-year-old's voice, added, "Sure beats slinging fries at a fast-food joint."

"Everything beats slinging fries at a fast-food joint."

Rico looked as though he'd just suggested Clearasil should be outlawed. Too late, Mike remembered where Rico had found his own temporary employment—a joint where the floors were always sticky, the burgers were always burned, and the scent of near-rancid frying oil was the closest thing to a culinary come-on.

"Hey, don't worry. We'll come up with something for the whole crew," Mike assured him. "You just wait."

Hopeful, Rico brightened up. "You've got something? Man, I *knew* you'd come through for us. I told everybody—"

"Not yet." Mike held up a hand, braking as he approached the turn-in for the shopping center that housed CheapCuts. "It might take a little time, but—"

In the rearview mirror, he saw Rico slump against the brown vinyl.

"—but things will work out. Just trust me, okay?"

"Okay," Rico said.

But in his eyes Mike glimpsed the beginnings of doubt, and it just about killed him. He needed that like he needed blackouts on ESPN, a lifetime supply of Speedos, Hair Club for Men, and another call from Heidi, the Swedish masseuse who'd dumped him when all the trouble had hit on April first. Namely, he didn't.

Hell. Were all of them starting to wonder? Or was it just Rico?

Either way, Mike couldn't do much more about it than he already had. His conscience was clear. Still, coming face-to-face with the reality of that doubt did things to him. Unprecedented things. And he didn't like it. The first thing he thought of to do about it after he'd grudgingly collected Rico's two-fifty fare—all in quarters—was equally unprecedented. But that didn't stop him.

He actually cleaned up his temporary cab. Driven by the urge to accomplish something—something *concrete*, dammit!—Mike tidied and vacuumed and polished the six-year-old hunk of junk until it looked almost like a place somebody who *didn't* know him inside and out might want to take a ride in. And that was where, tucked into the backseat cushions and squashed into the cigarette-butt-covered carpeted floor, Mike found the tickets.

All sixteen of them.

He had no idea what he was in for.

At the Channel Six offices, seated in a too-cushy chair between a freestanding southwestern bronze sculpture and a potted prickly-pear cactus, Amanda received her third piece of bad, Mondayish news of the day.

The first had been the mildly upsetting realization—discovered while retrieving her slightly-chewed Life Coach's cap from her basset hound Webster's bed and glimpsing an old dry-cleaning tag amid his collection—that she'd forgotten to pick up the get-a-promotion suit from Melanie.

The second had been the more upsetting realization—discovered while changing in Gemma's toy-strewn, vaguely diaper-scented bedroom—that even the all-the-yummy-water-you-can-drink aspects of her new diet had been only marginally enough to whittle her hips into the smallish-sized Prada pantsuit. She'd vowed then and there to discover a drop-ten-pounds T-shirt or die trying.

The third bit of bad news, just delivered by the Channel Six news "lifestyles" producer, Evan Krantz, had beaten the other two hands down, though.

"When you say, 'We don't have a winner,' " Amanda said, trying not to wreck her chances at this much-needed publicity by hyperventilating in the producer's office, "what exactly do you mean, Evan?"

"I mean, we don't have a winner."

"Don't have a winner who's telegenic, you mean? Someone who'll snag high ratings? What?"

"I mean, we don't have a winner. Period." He paused, fiddling with the stylus on his palm-PC in a way that made Amanda suspect Evan was actually playing some sort of game. On his computer, that is. And maybe with her, too.

Was this some kind of test? A think-on-your-feet quiz? Some kind of bizarre TV initiation thing, designed for media newbies like her?

Well, if it was, Amanda meant to knock his socks off.

"Nobody's turned in the winning Life Coach Lotto ticket?" she asked, just to get things straight from the beginning.

Evan shook his head. His palm-PC squeaked out a jubilant-sounding electronic accompaniment.

"That's impossible."

"I would have thought so, too," Evan said mildly. *Chirp, chirp* went his computer. "Apparently, it isn't."

"But we distributed thousands of those tickets. The In-And-Out Marts must have given away at least two thousand, all by themselves. The Lotto has been mentioned on the nightly news every day for the past month. People are crazy to win this thing, for Pete's sake!"

"Evidently not."

Amanda felt woozy. All her work had come down to this? A highly-publicized whopper of a failure? No. There had to be something she could do. But what?

From the doorway behind Evan's desk, a glasses-wearing man she recognized as one of the roving cameramen, assigned to follow her and the Life Coach Lotto winner on their adventures, poked his head inside the office.

"Evan, we're ready when you are," he said.

"Fine." Evan frowned, still not looking up. "We may be a few more minutes here."

A few more minutes. He probably meant that was all the time he'd need to dismiss Amanda, Aspirations, Inc., and every last one of her hopes of skyrocketing to the top of her field. Life coaching was a fairly new concept, to be sure. But Amanda believed strongly in its worth, and she wasn't ready to go down without a fight.

Desperately, she gulped the rest of her coffee—black, thanks, no sugar, no delicious, creamy cream—and while she waited for the caffeine to hit, Amanda looked around Evan's cluttered office, hoping for inspiration. Her gaze lit on the wall of news-broadcasting awards to her right, reminding her of exactly how popular the station was in the southwestern market. Each of those award plaques probably represented hundreds of viewers—hundreds of potential clients.

Hundreds of missed opportunities if she didn't pull this off.

"I'm sorry this didn't work out." Evan paused. Waved his stylus over the palm-PC with enough body English to make his desk chair wobble. Smirked over what had to be a victory over LED space invaders. Finally looked up and appeared to realize Amanda was still there. "Don't worry about it, Amanda. I can use the crew for a roving report on price-gouging hot-dog vendors I've had in mind."

He'd had a backup plan? Right from the get-go? A *hot-dog* backup plan?

"No! Evan, no." Plastering on what she hoped was a confident smile, Amanda leaned forward . . . well, she attempted to lean forward, at least. The fact that the cushy chair made her legs dangle an inch above the ground might have made the gesture less than impressive. "I'm sure we can still make this work. The winner is out there somewhere. We only have to—"

He shook his head. "The taping is set for today. In fact, as of"—Evan consulted his watch—"seven minutes ago, it's behind schedule. Time is money, you know."

"I know. But publicity is golden, even for a popular station like yours. We could leverage this, ramp up the public's interest even higher."

"I'm listening." Grudgingly.

Encouraged, Amanda talked faster. "Think of it, Evan. A high-profile search. An intriguing public question. 'Who's the mystery Life Coach Lotto winner?' as the catchphrase of the month." Warming up now, she spread her arms in the air, unfurling an imaginary banner. "I can just see it, emblazoned on billboards, on commercial spots, on the sides of city buses—"

"On taxicabs," Evan put in, seeming to warm up to the idea.

"Sure! Whatever you want. I'm telling you, this could work."

"Hmmm. But once you find the winner, won't interest wane?"

Evan had actually put down his palm-PC. She was getting somewhere!

"Are you kidding?" Of course he wasn't kidding.

Her mind gridlocked, and Amanda cast about desperately for more ammunition. "There's nothing the public likes better than a good rags-to-riches story. Or a remarkable makeover. Or, right now, reality TV. With this Life Coach Lotto gig, we've got all three."

"My daughter's a sucker for that *Real World* stuff on MTV," Evan mused. "And my wife can't get enough of those people on *Fashion Emergency*. You know . . ."

"It could work," she assured him, remembering all the planning meetings they'd held to set up the Life Coach Lotto. "It *will* work. Those are exactly the demographics you need to reach. You told me so yourself."

"I don't know . . ."

"You'll see." Forging ahead despite his lingering reluctance, Amanda gave a nonchalant wave and played her trump card, the angle that had gotten her in the door at Channel Six in the first place. "With my exclusive Life Coach plan, I can turn anyone into a well-rounded, perfectly-balanced example of twenty-first-century success. In just thirty days."

"Anyone?"

"You bet." *I think.*

"Even someone like that?" Wearing a crafty expression, Evan pointed out the window. The nearly floor-to-ceiling glass area encompassed most of the wall behind Amanda, and through it the busy streets of downtown Phoenix were visible in all their late-April glory.

She swiveled in her chair. Outside, the man Evan had indicated stood on the sidewalk beside an incongruously shiny taxicab, a fistful of papers in his hand, squinting up at what had to be the imposing Channel Six sign on the building. Even from this distance, Amanda could see that his Suns cap, bleach-spotted

T-shirt, ripped blue jeans, and ancient sneakers were hardly dress-for-success material.

Neither was his shaggy beard, what she could glimpse of his dark hair, or the scowl on his face. A less experienced observer might have stopped there, but Amanda also registered the slightly rounded set of his shoulders—indicating either depression, a lack of enthusiasm, or both, she figured—and the pugnacious set of his jaw—indicating that whoever the man was, he'd probably deck anybody who dared to point out either one.

Yup. That guy would be a tough case, all right.

"Sure!" Amanda said crazily, pushed beyond her usual sensible limits by the desperation of the situation and the very real danger that she and all three of the assistants she employed would find themselves out on the streets if this Life Coach Lotto stunt didn't push Aspirations, Inc., to the top of the heap. "Even a guy like that. In fact, why don't I go get him and we can get started with—"

"Oh, no," Evan interrupted. "We can't just drag in any old schmo off the street. If there's to be any hope of making the Life Coach segment a regularly-occurring feature on the Channel Six nightly news, the winner must be genuine."

Thank God. Her gamble had paid off.

Amanda hadn't believed Evan would actually take her up on her offer to make over the first ordinary Joe who came along. That certainty had been the only thing that allowed her to make such a reckless offer in the first place.

That, and the fact that the taxicab guy had already disappeared from sight.

"If you say so, Evan," she told him, inserting as much reluctance into the statement as she could.

What she hoped for in a Life Coach Lotto winner— what she *prayed* for—was a nice, semi-professional, college-educated person who was temporarily in a career-and-life slump. Someone with potential. A willingness to grow and change. And a handily telegenic, sympathetic, and allover charming personality that would gain viewers' allegiance . . . and ease Amanda's way into a ton of new clients. The last thing she needed was a grouchy-looking taxi driver who seemed as though he'd as soon crush the television cameras with his bare hands as smile for them.

Whew. Disaster averted.

Mentally congratulating herself on her quick thinking, Amanda smoothed her hand over the tailored jacket of the get-a-promotion suit. She began gathering her things. "In that case," she said, "I'll just get together with my publicist, and we'll see what we can dream up for those banners we talked about. I'd be happy to make an appearance on tonight's newscast, if you'd like, to jump-start the 'Who's the mystery Life Coach Lotto winner?' campaign."

"Hmmm. That's not a bad idea. What do you say—"

His statement was cut short by a burst of noise from the Channel Six reception area outside Evan's office. It sounded suspiciously like . . . a whoop?

Evan turned his head toward the sound. Listened. "But on second thought, I don't think that will be necessary," he finished.

An instant later, Amanda discovered why not.

"Evan! Mr. Krantz!" the receptionist shouted. "You're not going to believe this, but we've got ourselves a winner!"

Chapter Two

Geez, but that woman could whoop. Mike didn't think his hearing would ever be the same again.

Waggling his pinkie in his ear, he frowned at the long-haired, loudmouthed, forty-something brunet behind the Channel Six receptionist's desk. She'd looked as if she fit in with the subdued surroundings—a renovated mid-fifties building with marble checkerboard floors, thick-paned windows in front, and an array of southwestern artwork on the walls—but when she'd opened her mouth, the illusion had been totally shattered.

He'd heard quieter jackhammers.

"You don't understand," Mike said, waggling the fistful of tickets he'd shown her a few seconds ago. "All I want to do is return these things. Somebody left them in my cab"—he gestured outside, where his newly-spiffy taxicab gleamed in a shaft of sunlight that had knifed between the surrounding high-rises— "and since they have your station's name and address on the front, I figured—"

"They sure do!" She grinned like a loon, obviously tickled pink by that fact. "And *you've* got the winning one!"

She rose partway, her skinny backside pointing toward the skylights overhead as she jabbed him cheerfully in the midsection. Then she winked, as though the tickets were some great, terrific secret between the two of them. Even the woman's gestures were like exclamation points—sharp and mostly unnecessary in ordinary life.

Mike glanced at the nameplate atop her desk. "Look, Jennifer—"

"Jenny! Just Jenny." She giggled. "Especially for our very first Life Coach Lotto winner!"

"Okay, Jenny. I didn't win this—this *thing*, the what-chamacallit Lotto. I didn't even enter it, and I haven't been following the news lately, so I'm sorry to say I don't have a clue what it's about."

"Just Jenny" winked again. "*Sure* you don't. It's okay. You don't have to be embarrassed. Lots of people want to make changes in their lives. It's nothing to be ashamed of."

"I'm not embarrassed. Or ashamed." And the only "change" he wanted to make was to a nice, low-key, undemanding job, mostly so he could help out the rest of the April Fools' Day crew. "I just want to return these tickets."

When he'd found them, crammed in the back of his cab like that, with no idea of whom they might belong to, he thought the only right thing to do was to bring them to the Channel Six offices and let *them* handle it. Now, and not for the first time, Mike regretted his occasional Good Samaritan impulses. Didn't he have enough on his hands already?

"I picked up a few of those Lotto tickets myself." This was said in a conspiratorial aside from "Just

Jenny." "You can't win if you don't play, that's what I always say."

A bustle of movement in the offices beyond the reception area momentarily diverted Mike's attention. It sounded as though people were actually *running* back there. Dragging heavy equipment of some sort, too. He'd had no idea newscasting was such a physical job.

He looked back at Jenny. Spread the sixteen wrinkled tickets on the desk beside her quart-sized Diet Coke cup. Gave her the most patient smile he could manage. "There you go. Sixteen unclaimed tickets. Not mine. Somebody else's."

"But the winning ticket! It's right—"

Letting slip an impatient sound, Mike held up his hand. "Not mine."

"But it was in your hand! *You're* the one who brought it in!"

"And I'm the one who's leaving it here, too," Mike said. "Thanks for your help, Jenny. Have a nice day."

He turned and strode across the checkerboard floor leading outside the Channel Six madhouse, his gaze fixed on the predictable everydayness of his taxicab outside.

"You have a nice day, too!" Jenny trilled.

Mike grunted and pulled down his Suns cap in preparation for the eyeball-searing pre-noon sunlight. He put a hand to the door.

And then all hell broke loose.

Glaring electric lights blinded him. His skin, growing damp beneath his T-shirt and jeans, felt as hot as a spinner dog, rotisseried and left for an unsuspecting In-And-Out Mart customer. His head throbbed, aching with the impact of dozens of chattering voices and the click-click-click of flashes from what seemed to be a whole electronics store's worth of cameras.

This had to be some kind of damned nightmare. Scowling, Mike tried to wake himself up before it got any worse.

"Oh, look!" someone said about two inches from his right earlobe. "He's pinching himself. Isn't that cute? He probably can't believe he's the winner."

He recognized the voice as Just Jenny's. Mike blinked, and she came into view—along with the rest of the people who'd surged into the reception area a few minutes ago and, if he wasn't mistaken, had dragged him convivially all the way back inside.

He still wasn't sure what had happened. One minute, he'd been about to make his great escape, back to another afternoon of ESPN Sports Radio, with a bag of Doritos propped on his chest and a fresh supply of Twizzlers dangling from the dispatcher's radio while he waited for the occasional fare call.

The next minute, he'd found himself at the center of a media whirlwind. For an ordinary Joe like Mike, it was an unprecedented—and uncomfortable—experience.

A microphone was shoved beneath his jaw. "How does it feel to have won the new Life Coach Lotto?" the petite redhead behind it asked. "Are you excited?"

"Overwhelmed." Sourly, Mike pushed the equipment aside with two fingers.

It returned, doggedly. "And what do you think your family will say when they hear this thrilling news?"

His family. Mike had a sudden image of his parents, two brothers, and three sisters, all gathered around the big-screen TV that had been his mom's surprise gift to his dad on their fortieth wedding anniversary. The hubbub this would cause in his settled-down, close-knit family was bone-chilling.

"Look," he said—as sternly as his dad might have while telling Mike and his brothers to "quit throwing the damn baseball in the house!"—"you've got the wrong guy."

He hoped that would clear up the mistake.

He wasn't that lucky.

"Here's the winning ticket he brought in!" shouted Just Jenny.

She held it up in her red-manicured grasp. New chaos erupted as the reporters—he guessed that's what they were—jostled each other to get a clean shot of it.

"It's not mine," Mike said, but the clamor surrounding him drowned out the words.

He spotted a woman with shoulder-length brown hair heading purposefully toward him, a clipboard in hand and a lopsided coach's cap on her head. She seemed to be in charge, so Mike directed his next words to her.

"That ticket's not mine," he repeated. "I just found it in the backseat of my cab"—he gestured toward the window, beyond which his ordinary, nonpaparazzi-filled life awaited—"and thought I ought to bring it in, in case somebody had lost it."

She looked toward his cab. Returned her gaze to him. Gave a little sound that could only be described as a squeak of dismay. "Oh, no. The taxi guy."

Mike frowned. "Hey, driving a cab might not be fancy, but it's—"

"Oh, no. No. I'm sorry. Of course, you're right." Still apologizing, she drew near enough that Mike caught the mingled scents of black coffee and her subtle perfume. She patted him on the arm. "You'll do just fine."

But it was hard to miss the muttered "Oh, my God" beneath her breath.

She huddled her head close to his, their bodies

forming a cocoon of sudden intimacy amid the still-chattering media people. In her presence, Mike felt inexplicably calmer—a sensation that only grew as she flipped some papers on her clipboard and took charge of his bizarre situation.

"I've prepared a statement for you," she said, her voice low and faintly husky. "Just read it, smile for the cameras, and we'll get out of here."

"Together?" He waggled his eyebrows, trying for a little Grouchoesque humor. "Sure thing, doll."

Her demeanor turned frosty. Head cheerleader on ice. "Just read it."

Mike accepted the paper she shoved in his hand. He cleared his throat and did his best to ignore the immediate hush that fell over the waiting people. "I couldn't be more thrilled to have won the Life Coach Lotto," he began reading.

Beside him, Head Cheerleader mouthed the words, matching him perfectly.

"I'd like to thank Channel Six news"—he glanced up, realizing in that moment that those television cameras being wheeled ever-closer to catch his speech probably meant that he'd find himself on the nightly news, whether he wanted to be or not—"for giving me this opportunity to transform myself into a—"

He stopped. Read a little further, silently. "Oh, you've gotta be kidding me."

There was no *way* this little speech was helping him out of this situation. Not when it mentioned his "personal life goals" of "growth, enrichment, and balance in all things," plus a bunch of other New Age stuff that would sound about as natural coming out of Mike Cavaco's mouth as a recitation of new spring ladies' shoe styles.

"Sorry, there's no way I can say this stuff." He shoved the paper back onto her clipboard. "I'm outta here."

The shocked widening of her big baby blues was almost enough to make him reconsider.

Almost.

But Mike Cavaco was no sucker, and not even a hot-looking girl with a goofy hat and a coach's whistle slung around her neck was going to change that fact. Not even if *all* she'd been wearing had been the hat and the whistle and those sexy high heels of hers.

Automatically, the enticing image of her wearing only satiny bare skin, high heels, a whistle on a cord, and a lopsided cap filled his mind. *Wow.*

Well, on second thought. . . . No. Not even then, Mike told himself. A guy had to have his principles.

"Sorry, folks," he called out as he shouldered his way through the crowd. "Just a mistake. I'm sure Miss . . . ah—"

"Connor," she choked out.

"Miss Connor will explain everything."

All heads swiveled toward her. She winced beneath the bright lights, her pasted-on smile a little wobblier than before. Mike experienced a brief rush of sympathy for her—and then remembered the way she'd tried to trap him in the limelight with that lame speech.

"Good luck," he mouthed to her, then headed for the door.

Behind him, a man's voice rumbled over the crowd. "Amanda, if he gets away, our deal is finished!"

Mike shook his head. Poor Amanda, whoever she was. Who knew TV was so cutthroat? It wasn't her fault Mike wasn't the winner they wanted.

"Finished!" the man repeated. "Not so much as a public-service announcement for that company of yours!"

But no one seemed to be listening. The reporters' attention was fixed on the woman, who, for the moment, seemed to have regained her composure long enough to make some sort of statement. Mike glanced back. She looked perfect and polished, her wavy, shoulder-length hair gleaming in the lights and her expensive-looking suit all aglow as she spoke. Naturally, somebody who looked that good in the spotlight wouldn't understand the reluctance of a guy like Mike to jump in, too.

Her feminine voice stuck in his mind, even as he set sneaker to sidewalk once again . . . or maybe that was only the echo of her microphone-amplified voice he heard. Either way, it represented the very last thing Mike wanted in his life right now, during the worst stretch of bad luck he'd ever had: publicity.

He didn't want his family to find out about what had happened. He didn't want even more friends feeling sorry for him, calling up pity fares and giving him those sad, puppy-dog looks from the backseat of his cab. He didn't want to be on TV, and he sure as hell didn't want to discuss his personal life goals. Not even if he'd had some.

With no small sense of relief, Mike opened the driver's side door of his cab and slid behind the wheel. Automatically, he switched on his in service light, his head still buzzing with the weird experience he'd just had. That would teach him to keep up the Good Samaritan routine, he thought. Whoever had left those tickets in his backseat had a lot to answer to.

He figured that whoever the real winner was, they'd naturally turn up at the Channel Six news offices to claim their prize. No doubt, they really *would* be "thrilled to have won the new Life Coach Lotto." Whatever that was. Lately, ever since April Fools' Day, in fact, he'd been too deep in job-hunting to even crack the sports pages, much less tune in to gloom-and-doom nightly newscasts.

A tap on the cab's passenger-side window snapped

him out of his thoughts. Mike looked toward the sound.

On the other side of the glass hunched the woman, her overly cheerful grin even more uneven than her coach's cap. When she saw him looking, she gave a little wave.

Mike shook his head and shook out his keys, ramming them in the ignition with every intention of driving away.

She knocked again. "It's okay!" her muffled voice said. "You can come back inside. The reporters are gone."

He stared straight ahead, wishing she would go away.

She didn't.

Leaning his arm across the top of the steering wheel, Mike angled himself partway toward the window. He didn't want to be rude, but the woman clearly couldn't take a hint. "You've got the wrong guy. Get it? I'm not going back in there."

"You don't have to be embarrassed! Lots of men entered the Lotto."

That did it. He rolled down the window a couple of inches. "I'm not embarrassed!"

She smiled. Smiled a knowing, superior smile, one that said if he wasn't embarrassed—which, of course, he must be—he would be soon.

"I'm not," he repeated, wanting to kick himself for not revving the engine and speeding away while he'd still had the chance. Now all he could do was clench the steering wheel and match her smile for smile. "Really."

She shrugged and whipped out her clipboard. Evidently, the thing went wherever she did. "If you'll just come inside and fill out a few release forms for the station," she said, scanning the sticky-note-dotted pages before her, "we can get started. We have *a lot* of work ahead of us."

She glanced up. Through the gap in the window, her gaze swept over him, much the same way Myrtle's had earlier—and with far less approval, as a result. Unreasonably hurt by her obviously low opinion of him, Mike frowned.

"Yeah, I think I have a few fares to pick up," he said, deliberately misunderstanding her. "Good luck with your Lotto, lady."

He pulled his baseball cap down and faced the steering wheel again, preparing to put the cab in reverse and get the heck out of downtown before things got complicated.

"Wait!" she cried.

"Can't wait. Gotta go." But Mike felt himself weakening, growing curious about the desperation he heard in her voice. He knew he'd be staying in park for at least a few minutes longer.

"Just listen to me. Please." Her fingers, elegant and manicured, clenched the top of the rolled-down window.

He looked at them, taking in the contrast between her delicate lady's hands and his own big, faintly-scarred fists on the steering wheel. No doubt she wouldn't understand why that scene in the Channel Six offices had made him so antsy, so eager to get out from under the spotlight. But then, this *was* the same woman who'd used "personal life goals," "growth," and "enrichment" in the same sentence. With a straight face. With her, he could probably throw his expectations of normal people right out the window.

Reluctantly, he met her eyes. The urgency he found there weakened him still further. Dammit.

Apparently sensing a change in him, she drew a deep breath and started talking. "About the Lotto

ambush back there"—she gestured toward the
multistory building behind her—"I'm really sorry.
It's just that you were late in showing up—"

"You mean the winner was late in showing up."

"—and we were all getting a little worried. There's
been a lot invested in this already. So when Jenny let
us know about the winning ticket, well . . ."

"All hell broke loose."

That garnered a smile from her. A real smile—one
that made her suddenly seem softer and gentler and
more vulnerable than a woman wearing a pantsuit
that probably cost a week's paycheck ought to seem.
Mike smiled back.

And that was when things got *really* complicated.

"This is really generous of you, Mr. Cavaco,"
Amanda said, looking out the backseat side window
as Mike steered the taxicab through the downtown
Phoenix traffic. It hadn't been easy getting him to
agree to her plan, but now that he had, she didn't
intend to let up. "I realize this must be an inconve-
nience to you."

"Hey, it's only for an afternoon, right?"

His dark-eyed gaze met hers in the rearview mirror,
seeking another confirmation. Drawing in a deep
breath, Amanda nodded. Reluctantly.

"We won't do this any longer than *you* want to,"
she hedged. "Still, I want you to know I really appreciate your help."

He shrugged and went on driving. *Whew.* With luck,
Mike Cavaco wouldn't dig too deeply into all that she
had planned for him, and by the time he realized
the whole story, she told herself, well . . . by then he
probably would be enjoying himself too much to want
to stop. She hoped.

She still didn't understand what had finally tipped

the scales in her favor. One minute he'd been stubbornly stuck behind the wheel, refusing to do so much as look at her most of the time. The next minute, she'd smiled at him, belatedly told him her name, and he'd turned into a different, sunnier man. A man who was, all at once, perfectly willing to help her out of what he saw as a temporary jam.

It was a puzzler, all right. It was as though a simple "Amanda" had the same magical properties as a more meaningful moniker—like Rumpelstiltskin, maybe. Or Donald Trump.

Shrugging, Amanda realigned her clipboard on her lap and decided not to think about it. For whatever reason, Mike Cavaco had agreed to help her. That would have to be enough.

Besides, it wasn't as though she couldn't help him in return, she assured herself, taking another gander at her unlikely—and reluctant—winner. He was the perfect Aspirations, Inc., client. If there was ever a super-sloppy, roll-out-of-bed-and-go, prototypical bachelor, Mike was it. He was undergroomed, underemployed . . . and overqualified in only one thing.

Machismo.

She hoped she had the capability to give him the whole-life makeover he'd earned as the first Life Coach Lotto winner. The fact that he claimed to not even *want* to have won was an unexpected wrinkle, sure. But she couldn't let that sidetrack her, Amanda told herself. She was a life coach. A person trained to bring out the ultimate potential in anyone. Surely there were untapped wonders beneath the scruffy T-shirt and jeans façade of Mike Cavaco. All she had to do was uncover them.

Speculatively, Amanda looked him over again. Nice dark hair—too long and hopelessly outdated, of course, but thick and clean. That hair had potential. Wide shoulders, strong-looking hands, an athletic build . . . covered up in hideous clothes that had to have been ironed by laying them in the street and driving the taxicab over them, of course, but that could be fixed. That body had potential.

She looked at his reflection in the rearview mirror, examining his face while his concentration was absorbed in traffic. Rugged features, a straight, prominent nose, eyes she now knew could turn kind and twinkly at the drop of a hat, and a jaw . . . well, a jaw that was obscured by that hideous untrimmed beard of his. With it, Mike looked like he'd been living in a cave, emerging, squinty-eyed, every so often for beer runs and *Sports Illustrated* pickups.

So much for potential.

Of course, you couldn't judge a book by its cover, Amanda reminded herself staunchly. On the inside, Mike was probably a fully enlightened, sensitive man, completely ready for the revitalization that she and her Aspirations, Inc., staff were about to provide him.

Up front, Mike leaned on the horn. Rolling down his window with several furious, well-muscled cranks of his arm, he gestured at a driver who'd cut him off. He followed up with an extremely vivid oral description of the man's driving skills—or lack thereof— then accelerated into an impossibly tight squeeze leading toward the street they needed.

All at once, misgivings assailed her. She was a mentor, an adviser, a turbo-powered guidance counselor . . . not a miracle worker! What had she gotten herself into?

In the mirror, Mike caught her eye, his expression sheepish. "Sorry about that," he muttered. "I'm, ahhh, a little more on edge than usual today."

Yeah, right. For all she knew, Amanda realized, he was the kind of guy who dented little old ladies' bumpers for stealing a parking space. The kind of guy who got in fistfights over high beams left on a nanosecond too long. Visions of herself and her highly-touted Lotto winner hitting the nightly news as they were both dragged off to jail in handcuffs suddenly replaced Amanda's previous daydreams of business success and wall-to-wall clients.

She was halfway into a full-blown case of panic when she felt the taxicab suddenly swerve and come to a stop. An instant later, Mike's face filled her vision as he peered at her from the front seat.

His eyebrows lowered over a pair of warm brown eyes that, she was fast deciding, were his most appealing feature. His hand touched hers—which, Amanda realized, she'd clamped together in a death grip on her clipboard.

"Are you doing all right?" he asked. "I didn't mean to scare you back there."

"I'm fine."

His frown said he didn't believe her. "That bozo was about to make me miss our turnoff. You have an appointment set up, right? You would've been late if I hadn't—"

"It's fine. It's perfectly fine. Let's just go."

Outside the cab, cars whizzed past, mere blurs in her peripheral vision. Were those tears clouding her eyes? God, she hoped not. The last thing she needed was to show weakness now, especially when she was supposed to be in charge.

"Look, if there's one thing I've learned," Mike said, "it's that when a woman says, 'Everything's fine,' everything is everything *but* fine."

Amanda sniffed. "Well, I'm not like other women."

He looked her over. "No, you're sure as heck not."

For some reason, that sounded like an insult. And a curiosity-driven question, all at the same time.

"I mean," Amanda clarified, "that *I* mean it. I'm fine."

She did mean it. She really did. But a part of her

was starting to get that quivery, about-to-bawl feeling, the one she did her damnedest to keep under wraps—or at least under cover of darkness, alone in bed with nobody but an empty Ben and Jerry's carton for a witness. And so Amanda straightened her life-coach cap, drew in a deep breath, and shoved that feeling right back where it belonged—in her mental don't-go-there closet, right beside the unexpected cellulite sightings, the old boyfriend Mel and Gemma called Mr. Dingaling, and the memory of the time she'd thought nothing looked cuter on her than plat-form shoes. For six months straight.

"Look," Mike said sternly, "I am *not* a guy who makes women cry. Got that?"

She sniffed and nodded, ducking her head so he wouldn't see the tears that were about to turn her mascara into a blobby black mess.

"I mean it, now. Come on. I'm sorry about the traffic thing."

His voice was gruff. One-hundred-percent no-nonsense "you're not hurt, so walk it off" tattoos-and-tequila badass. But his touch, when he swept his thumb over her cheekbone to wipe away a tear, was unexpectedly gentle. And it was the tenderness of that touch that gave Amanda the jolt she needed to pull herself together.

It also gave her renewed hope that, in ten minutes or so, when Mike got a load of Madame Roshinka and her excellent day-spa staff of twenty-two—all with their hearts set on beginning the makeover of their lives—he wouldn't make any of *them* cry, either.

She smiled and squeezed his hand between hers, suddenly aware of the warmth and breadth and won-derful masculine feel of him. Maybe everything really would be all right. "You're a nice man, you know that?"

Mike made a face. "Hey, whatever. Just don't let

it get around, okay?" He released her and turned,
his arm spread along the back of the front seat as he
looked out the rear window to watch the oncoming
traffic. Smoothly, the taxicab accelerated into the
nearest lane. "I've got a reputation to protect, here."

The trouble was, so did Amanda. And she wasn't
sure their two reputations could exist side by side.
One way or another, one of them was going to have
to give a little.

And it sure as heck wasn't going to be her.

Chapter Three

Madame Roshinka's Rosado was a closely-guarded Phoenix secret. The day spa, tucked at the city's edge near the mountain foothills amid saguaros and vivid southwestern sunsets and housed in a renovated stucco hacienda that sprawled over a half-acre all by itself, prided itself on exclusivity, completeness, and indulgence.

It was the kind of place weary socialites went to recoup when foie-gras overload hit and nothing could restore their depleted souls like a nice algae-aloe body masque and one of the spa's exclusive vita-juice herbal drinks. It was a haven to jet-setting celebrities and the Valley's top businesswomen alike, a place where subtlety and wellness were valued as highly as time-honored spa traditions like sea salt rubs, yoga classes, and mini-nosh "meals" small enough to fit in the palm of a guest's well-manicured hand.

It was also a place where, Amanda guessed, no one had ever stomped across the tiled threshold in a pair of sneakers grungy enough to make the receptionist recoil in shock. She'd further discerned, after almost a half-hour spent at Rosado in Mike's company, that no one, from Madame Roshinka on down, had expected someone like Mike Cavaco in their midst. He'd created quite a stir.

The sound of his voice alone—deep, indisputably masculine, and just husky enough to suggest sultry, wickedly intimate nights—had been enough to draw women to the main salon area like sleek paired with silk and heat joined with touch. They clumped together in twos and threes, dressed in Rosado robes and talking quietly as they waited for the unexpected man in their midst to reappear.

With luck, none of them—including Amanda— would be disappointed.

With that thought in mind, she put her head close to the door of the changing room Mike had been assigned. Inside, she could hear clothes rustling, objects bumping against the nearest wall . . . and muffled swear words. Amanda smiled.

"Everything okay in there?" she asked.

Mike grunted in reply.

Considering that he hadn't spoken a word since she'd explained exactly what she needed him to do, she figured a grunt counted as progress. Especially now that he'd moved beyond stubbornly standing in front of the changing room with his arms crossed over his T-shirt-covered chest, glaring at the entourage they'd collected. Heartened, Amanda went on.

"Is there anything I can get for you?"

"Yeah," came Mike's reply. "A spoon."

"A spoon?" Amanda frowned. "What for?"

"To tunnel my way out of here."

She laughed. "Come on. It's not that bad."

"Ha! Easy for you to say. You're not the one with a hundred women out there, all waiting to have a look at your naked knees."

As one, the spa-goers around them pressed forward, as though eagerly anticipating that long-awaited glimpse of knobby—er, *studly* kneecaps. Still grinning, Amanda put her finger to her lips to keep the women quiet.

"Don't be ridiculous." She paused. "There are only a couple dozen women out here."

"Ha!" came Mike's muffled voice from behind the lacquered strawberry-sorbet-colored door.

"And we want to see more than your knees!" yelled an onlooker.

"Hubba, hubba!" cried another.

All the women giggled. Among them passed a member of the Rosado staff, dressed in the spa's uniform of Asian-inspired wrapped robes and matching rosy leggings, and busily handing out murky green health drinks in stemmed glasses. The staff member raised a glass in toast to the "hubba, hubba" contingent, then continued on her way.

"Don't be shy!" coaxed a woman wearing a mud facial mask and a pink belted robe. "Show us a little bum, love!"

Her suggestion was met with a chorus of catcalled encouragement. Above the din, Mike's voice rose.

"I am *not* showing you my bum!"

Stifling what could only be described as a guffaw, Amanda leaned closer to the door. Within, she heard Mike's muttered rejoinder.

"*Sheesh.* They're like a pack of ravenous wolves," he mumbled, still grumpily sounding as though he were thrashing around in his clothes. "With lipstick and Platinum cards and a pack mentality aimed at my . . . my bum."

"Mike—" she began.

"What is the *matter* with you people?" he asked in obvious exasperation. "Women are supposed to be so demure. Hah!"

"Now, hold on—"

"Wait'll the *Sports Illustrated* guy at the newsstand gets word of this. He'll never believe it."

"We're not all like that," Amanda put in, rising on tiptoes to try and peer over the top of the forehead-high changing-room door. Realizing what she was doing, she abruptly lowered again, trying to ignore the renewed cheers of encouragement from the crowd. "You can't stereotype women this way."

"You're nothing but a bunch of ogling, whistling, show-me-your-bum phonies. And *we guys* get flack for innocently watching *Baywatch*. At least those lifeguards are saving people!"

The rasp of leather against denim came from behind the door. An instant later, Mike came out with a new batch of muffled swear words. He was still struggling with the required spa-goer's wardrobe, Amanda guessed. At this rate, Channel Six would suffer a corporate takeover and go off the air before she and Mike got their Life Coach Lotto makeover story finished and taped.

For that reason only, she decided to let his ridiculous *Baywatch* remark go uncontested.

"Just come on out, *please*, Mike?" Leaning her shoulder against the changing room door, Amanda stroked the glossy lacquered wood, fancifully imagining her palm touching this side of the wood—and, at exactly the same moment, Mike's hand touching the other. "You know I wouldn't ask you to do this if I didn't really, truly, desperately need your help."

Nothing. Not even the sound of shuffling ragged denim, or a sweat sock hitting the plush carpeted floor.

"Remember what I told you about Evan, and the Channel Six deal?" Amanda went on. "I promised him you would emerge from this experience—as the

Life Coach Lotto winner—with at least a haircut and a new outfit for your trouble."

She'd actually promised Evan quite a bit more than that. In fact, if memory served, Amanda had sworn that if the producer would uphold their Channel Six news deal, she would turn ordinary-Joe Mike Cavaco into a well-rounded, eminently employable, perfectly balanced example of modern manhood. All in thirty days or less. And with on-air footage to show for it.

Amanda devoutly hoped she wouldn't live to regret that impulsive promise.

Darn it, she *wouldn't* live to regret it. No matter what.

Amanda Connor was not a quitter.

"And lunch," Mike reminded her, breaking into her thoughts with a typical guy-style concern. "You mentioned something about lunch, too. I could really go for a good chili cheeseburger. Maybe a nice Roadrunner ale to go with it. Yum."

He sounded placated. That was good, Amanda told herself. Once he discovered the light and artfully-arranged spa cuisine that was *really* for lunch, Mike might not be feeling quite so cheery.

"Does that mean you're coming out?" she asked, then added a little well-meant arm-twisting, for insurance. "We can't go to lunch until we're done here, you know."

"Well . . ."

"Woo, woo!" yelled a woman in the crowd. "Here he comes!"

Newly rejuvenated by Mike's hint that he might emerge soon, the Rosado onlookers shuffled closer in their spa-issued pink slippers. "Take it off!" yelled one, whirling a towel overhead like an overeager Chippendale's customer.

"Yes, I'm coming out. But first," Mike said, characteristically—she was learning—stubborn, "I need a pen."

Amanda was in no mood to argue. She unhooked a ballpoint from the top of her clipboard and handed it over, trying not to notice the tingly feeling that shot through her when Mike's hand closed over hers and the ballpoint slipped from her fingers.

"What's it for?" she asked as the pen vanished from sight.

Mike didn't answer. "And some paper, too," he said instead.

She shrugged and unhooked a sheet of white bond from the back of her clipboard. She fluttered it over the top of the changing-room door. "Will this do?"

"Sure." He plucked it from her hand, and it disappeared.

A moment of silence descended as all the women moved closer, curious to know what would happen next. As interested as the rest of them, Amanda put her ear to the door.

"Dear *Men's Journal*," she heard Mike say, his voice underscored by the slide of pen on paper, "I always thought these letters were fake. But something happened to me today that you've just *got* to know about. It's about women. . . ."

"I can't believe I'm about to do this," Mike muttered to himself a short while later. He adjusted the clothes—if you could call them that—that the skinny redhead in the Rosado lobby had given him to wear during his spa visit, trying vainly to cover his knees. Not that they were bad knees. Mike figured they were about as sexy as any other guy's street-hockey-scarred kneecaps were. But hey, his day was screwed up enough already.

He grabbed a handful of fabric and twisted. No

dice. It looked as if he were flashing anybody who gazed south of his strikeout zone.

Outside the little Pepto-Bismol-colored room they'd assigned him, he heard Amanda pacing, her high heels scuffing across the pink carpet as she waited, impatiently, for him. It occurred to Mike that this was a pretty funny turnaround of a typical situation. For the sake of purse-toting guys parked on uncomfortable stools outside department-store fitting rooms everywhere as they waited for their girlfriends and wives to try on "just one more cute little thing," he briefly considered camping out in there. Twiddling his thumbs. Contemplating the meaning of life. Watching his beard grow. Turnabout was fair play, after all.

But then Amanda gave one of those nervous-sounding sighs she'd been coming out with all afternoon, and he knew he couldn't do it. Feeling sympathetic toward her and her dealings with that egomaniacal producer at Channel Six, Evan What's-his-name, all over again, Mike cleared his throat and prepared to make his entrance.

"I think I'm ready," he said.

She immediately stopped beside the changing-room door. "Great! Let's get started. Helga's waiting for you in the bodywork room."

That sounded promising. How bad could bodywork be? Still . . . "Any chance the 'show me your bum' ladies are gone?"

A chorus of feminine hollers answered his question. Mike groaned.

"Not yet. You've been in there so long, I struck up a side business selling tickets," Amanda said. He could hear the laughter in her voice, and it was, Mike decided, something he could really begin liking about her. "I'm pretty sure I've almost got enough to pay the cab fare back to Channel Six. Will fourteen-fifty do it?''

"Har, har."

"Well, I had to slash prices once you said you wouldn't show us your bum."

"Very funny."

He might as well get this over with. Sucking in a deep breath, Mike opened the door and stood framed in the pink doorway. Just for the hell of it, he struck a pose.

The assembly of women fell silent. He hoped that meant they were awestruck by his appearance. He feared that meant he looked just as ridiculous as he felt. Mike slammed the door shut.

Pandemonium erupted. Women whooped and stomped their slippered feet, creating more of a gigantic whoosh sound than a respectable clamor, but being enthusiastic about it, all the same. Amanda knocked on the door, begging him to come out again.

Frowning, Mike wrenched open the door just enough to scowl out at her from behind it. "No. This is all your fault."

"Oh, Mike, come on." She looked like she was stifling a grin. "It's not that bad."

"Hah!"

"You actually look sort of . . . cute in pink."

His scowl deepened as he stared down at the signature-pink Rosado outfit, a short wrapped robe. He plucked at the gaping terry-cloth edges of the neckline. "It doesn't fit right."

She crossed her arms. "That's only because your shoulders are too broad."

"And it's too short." He gestured to where the damned thing fluttered above his kneecaps.

"Because you're so tall."

"And the belt is flimsy, too."

"You seem to have solved that problem." With a

bemused expression, Amanda looked pointedly at his waist, where Mike had buckled his ordinary black leather belt—with biker-style silver studs—atop the pink robe.

"Yeah, well . . . that other belt just wasn't doing the trick."

"You're very ingenious," she all but purred. "I'm impressed."

She looked it, too. Amanda's cover-girl blue eyes had gone all glowing and appreciative as she looked at him, and the way she gave him a slow once-over— at least of as much of him as she could see through the gap in the doorway—made Mike feel all mushy and happy and inclined to show her even more. Maybe even right down to the Bugs Bunny boxers he had on underneath the robe. But then he squinted, examining her expression a little closer, and frowned again.

"Look, lady," he said bluntly, pointing a finger at her, "flattery will get you nowhere with me. So just knock it off."

"Oh, all right. Come on." Amanda reached for his arm, as though her hundred-odd pounds of womanly self were going to drag him forcibly into the spa's main area. She stopped. Squeezed his bicep. Widened her eyes and gave a little "Oooh!"

Mike snorted, secretly pleased. Okay, maybe she did mean a *little* bit of that stuff she was saying. The funny thing was, it suddenly felt important to him that she did.

He looked into her upturned face. "Maybe later I'll arrange a private showing just for you," he said. "*Really* private."

Her mouth dropped open. Fortified by her expression, Mike winked and gently extracted his arm from Amanda's suddenly-limp grasp. Then he threw open the changing-room door, smiled at his pink spa-going fans' screaming reaction to his mini-robe-covered self, and swaggered toward Helga and the promised mysteries of bodywork . . . sneakers squeaking across the tiles all the way.

Mike didn't know how much time had passed since his grand entrance into the cotton-candy-colored world of the Rosado spa. He didn't much care, either. Alone, flat on his stomach on a padded spa table, ensconced in a pile of steaming, softer-than-soft pink towels designed to let the honey-whatchamacallit exfoliating gunk do its magic, he realized he'd never felt more relaxed in his life. Ahhhh. Sighing, he closed his eyes and surrendered to the final step in what Helga and her assistant Tiffany had called his "body-wellness bonanza."

No wonder women came to places like this. This was like the drowsy, satisfied afterglow that came after a night of wild lovemaking—without all the work. Without the hassles of making pillow talk afterward, when he was so sleepy it felt like his lips were numb. Without the "I'll call you" headaches and the "Is she satisfied?" wonderings that followed close behind. This was pure selfish pleasure, and it had unwound him in ways Mike had never experienced without the involvement of a horizontal surface—or a vertical surface, he added as a particularly wicked thought struck him—and the assistance of a sexy, willing woman.

Hmmm, his treatment-tipsy brain wondered. Speaking of sexy women . . . where was Amanda?

Shortly after she'd followed him into the marble-floored body treatment area, with its aromatherapy-scented atmosphere, dim lighting, and soft New Age music, she'd mentioned something about checking in with her staff and vanished. Now, a massage and several goopy lotion-and-potion applications later, Mike was starting to wonder if she'd abandoned him there.

Alarmed at the thought, he jerked his torso upward. A dangling seashell-shaped lamp whacked him on the forehead.

"Ooof!" Swearing, he glared up at the trio of lamps—the same trio he'd forgotten was suspended over the treatment table. Mike rubbed his head, feeling for a bruise. Instead, his fingers came away covered in the pine-tree-scented mud of his facial mask.

He still didn't know how Tiffany had talked him into *that*. Mike suspected it might have had something to do with the brain-scrambling properties of her girlish, high-pitched voice or her touchy-feely vocabulary peppered with words like "self-actualization," "hydrate," and "skintillicious." Then again, maybe he was just as susceptible to wanting to look good as the next poor schmuck.

God, he hoped not. Not even the April Fools' Day disaster should have made him sink that low. That was girly stuff.

He was a man's man. A guy's guy. A John Wayne, Clint Eastwood, "hand me that socket wrench, I can fix this," pro-football-watching kind of fella. He was only here because he couldn't stand to see a perfectly nice girl lose her TV-news deal because of him. And Mike wasn't kidding himself. That's what would have happened to Amanda if he hadn't agreed to go along with this Life Coach Lotto gig for the day.

Otherwise, he wouldn't have been caught *dead* in a place like Rosado. Mike got all the buff and polish he needed in the shower every morning, like a regular guy.

He had settled back beneath the warm towels and was midway into wondering if Tiffany would mail him some of the honey-treatment gunk in a plain brown

wrapper when the door to his right opened. Cold air
wafted over his exposed bare feet and sent a shaft of
dark hair falling into his eyes. It glued itself to the
facial mask above his eyebrow and refused to budge.

"Mike, I have some bad news," Amanda said, striding briskly—the only way he'd ever seen her walk—
into the small rectangular room. From his vantage
point, only the bottom half of her expensive-looking
pale suit jacket was visible. "It seems that—"

Mike turned his head all the way to the right and
upward, the better to look at her. Women liked eye
contact, he'd learned. And for some weird reason,
he wanted to make a good impression on Amanda.

She stopped, looking astonished. "Oh, my. Wow."

He grinned. See? Sometimes that mushy-gushy,
girly communication stuff worked, Mike thought as
he congratulated himself on remembering what
women liked. Encouraged, he decided to gaze more
deeply into her eyes.

He couldn't meet her eyes. She was too busy staring
in rapt fascination—and something irritatingly close
to amusement—at his face: his cheeks, his nose, his
forehead . . . his forehead, where the glued-on hairs
tugged painfully as he remembered them and tried
to casually sweep them aside.

His fingers touched caked-on mud. He remembered something more than needing to fix his hair
and make eye contact.

The mask.

"Dammit, Amanda!" he said, turning his head and
staring fixedly at the treatment table's padded top in
an effort to conceal as much of his mud-covered face
as possible. "Don't you know how to knock?"

"Sorry." She was stifling a giggle, he just knew it.

At this rate, she'd *never* see him as studly, date-
worthy material, Mike realized. A surge of despair
pushed through him. He *wanted* Amanda to want him.

And all the "skintillicious" exfoliating treatments in the world weren't going to accomplish that, not so long as he wound up looking like some kind of goof-ball.

"Look, can you just get Tiffany back in here, please? I'm, er, indisposed."

He yanked at the towels covering him, a few of which had shifted dangerously to the left. Somehow Helga had convinced him that the towels were adequate coverage, and he'd abandoned his boxer shorts right before the massage. Now, bare-ass naked— except for the sliding towels—and sticky with honey, Mike gazed longingly at his Bugs Bunny printed shorts, wadded in a ball on the chair just beyond arm's reach.

To his horror, Amanda picked them up. "Here, put these on, then."

"Put those down!"

She shrugged. "I just thought, if you're uncomfortable being naked under there—"

She knew. God, the humiliation. Swearing beneath his breath, Mike lowered his head to his folded arms and, momentarily encased in the safe darkness there, prayed for an earthquake. A lightning bolt. A spa-workers' strike. Anything, *anything* to erase the image of a woman he hadn't even slept with yet manhandling his underwear.

He looked up. Tried to appear menacing, which was a little tricky when covered in pine-scented goo. "Just—get—Tiffany, please," he said through clenched teeth.

Grinning, Amanda dropped his boxers. With a sort of languid grace he might have admired under less sitcom-worthy circumstances, she walked to the opposite side of the room and pushed an intercom button to the right of the door. After a brief conversation with the person on the other end, she turned to him again.

"Anyway, as I was saying—"

"You can stop staring at my face anytime now."

"Sure, sorry." Another grin.

As Mike wrenched himself to a seated position, rearranging his towels as he went, Amanda helpfully averted her gaze. She didn't even *try* to catch a quick glance at the naked rest of him, he noticed with disappointment. Not that he wanted her to. Right?

"Anyway," she went on, "we have a problem."

"The spa doesn't stock the "Kiss Me Pink" nail polish I wanted for my manicure?" Mike joked, fluttering his fingers.

"No, a real problem."

"Oookay. What's the matter?"

"It's Frederick, the hairstylist." Amanda moved aside, making way for Helga and Tiffany as they came into the room.

With relief, Mike jutted his face forward, giving Tiffany better access to remove the pine-smelling facial gunk. From the corner of his eye, he noticed Amanda watching the removal process with another one of her smart-aleck grins and gave her a glare for good measure.

"What?" she asked, the picture of innocence. "Tiffany and Helga can look at you, but I can't?"

He cleared his throat. "They're *professionals.*"

And I'm not trying to impress them.

Amanda rolled her eyes and fixed her gaze overhead on the seashell-shaped attack lamps, still talking. "Evidently, Frederick had some sort of crisis this morning—"

"The hairstylist guy?" Mike closed his eyes as Tiffany's warm terry cloth swept efficiently over his forehead.

"Yes. Something about a botched hair-color job—"

"Client-stylist miscommunication," Helga put in forcefully, starting in on Mike's honey-goo covered legs. She eased him into a lying-down position on the treatment table and went on working, wiping off the gunk with what felt like a Brillo pad. "At Rosado, we don't *have* botched jobs."

"And the upshot is," Amanda finished, sounding exasperated, "that you can't have your haircut today, Mike. I'm sorry. We'll just have to reschedule when Frederick is feeling up to it, maybe in a day or two. He's very upset."

Tiffany murmured sympathetically, obviously worried about Frederick's "crisis."

"Why not just go to somebody else?" Mike asked. "There must be more than—ouch! Easy there, bruiser!—one hairstylist in this place. It's the size of a football field."

"No one," Helga said imperiously, "is like Frederick."

"Yeah. Like, you deserve the best, Mike," Tiffany added. "Totally. What he can do with a pair of scissors and some Revlon number twenty will blow your mind."

Mike wasn't so sure he *wanted* his mind blown. "I'm not into this for more than one day," he warned Amanda. "So whatever you can't accomplish on me by five o'clock tonight . . . well, it stays undone for good."

"Mike—"

"For good!" he reiterated, throwing in what he hoped was a forceful-seeming karate chop of his hand. Things were getting out of control here, and he didn't like it.

"But if you'll only—"

"Nope."

"—just give this a chance, and then—"

"No more. I'm done."

Finished scouring him, Helga and Tiffany stepped backward. They beamed at him. "Wow, Mike," Tiffany said. "You look just like one of those male models or something."

"Yes, nice work." Helga paused in gathering up her Brillo pads to scrutinize him from toes to damp head. "You clean up pretty good. And smell nice, too. Very handsome, Mike."

Hear that? asked the look he threw Amanda's way. Sucking in a breath—the better to impressively expand his newly uncovered and exfoliated chest and shoulders—Mike decided he could afford to be magnanimous.

"Let's decide after lunch," he said. "I know the perfect place."

Amanda felt woozy. And although it might have been the sight of the metal-clad, run-down diner (*Marvin's,* she read on the sign outside) squeezed between a dilapidated instant-print shop and a Harley Davidson dealer that was at fault, somehow she suspected that wasn't it.

It was Mike.

And the memory of him on that table at Rosado, oozing relaxation and sex appeal in equal measure . . . not to mention nakedness.

Wowsers. She still felt a little scorched. And that was even after surviving another ride in Mike's Twizzler-decorated taxicab and trying to keep up her end of a confusing conversation he'd seemed especially intent on having about John Wayne movies. Amanda didn't get it.

The squeal and thud of the restaurant door opening dragged her back to the non-naked present. Beside her, Mike put his hand to the small of her back and guided her inside. The gesture felt surprisingly gentleman-like, especially for a guy whose notion of a "perfect place" for lunch involved metal siding, strange musty-spicy smells, thumping urban rock music, and lighting so dim Amanda would have stumbled on her way inside if not for Mike's steadying touch.

Trying to appear in control, she shook herself free and squinted into the gloom. She could detect shapes moving—other diners, she hoped, which would at least indicate people made it out of here alive—round, flat shapes that suggested tables and chairs, and scattered neon beer signs, but nothing more.

"Are—are you sure this is the place?" she asked, leaning closer to be heard over the *whooomp-whooomp-whooomp* of the music. "They don't look like they're serving lunch."

"Sure, they are. Marvin's makes the best lunch in town."

With an enthusiastic grin, Mike strode farther inside, tugging her along with him. Amanda's hopeful visions of having rescheduled their spa lunch for the sake of a nice quiet vegetarian bistro, with real tablecloths and a maître d' faded as her vision adjusted to the low lighting. Towed along in Mike's wake, she whipped her hips sideways between the close-packed tables, trying to avoid dragging her lucky get-a-promotion suit against their questionable surfaces. They made a circuit between two busy pool tables, then settled into a booth against the wall.

Well, Mike settled, at least. Amanda peered at the sticky-looking red-vinyl-upholstered booth in dismay and realized that the toddler-crazed chaos of Gemma's house hadn't presented half the dangers to their shared Prada pantsuit as one hour in this place with Mike would. In the end, she settled for whisking a paper napkin over the seat's cracked surface and hoping for the best.

After all, if things went well with the Channel Six news feature, she could dry-clean the Suit twice a day, if she pleased. Or even replace it with a spiffy—if nonlucky—brand-new designer suit of her very own.

"Hey, Mike!" A huge, boisterous-looking man— Marvin, she guessed—squeezed his way between the neighboring tables and came toward them. Smiling, he clapped his hand on Mike's shoulder. "Long time no see! How's it going?"

"Hey, Marvin!" After a round of rib-nudging, wink-wink introductions—Amanda had the peculiar feeling that nobody here had ever heard of a life coach and didn't believe a word of Mike's description of her job—the two men exchanged guy-style small talk about the Suns' current season, the Buick Marvin was rebuilding, and the lunch specials. Several more of their buddies joined them. Amanda spent the time surreptitiously examining the glasses of ice water a server stuck in the middle of their table, hoping against hope the glasses were clean. Did they even *have* bottled water in a place like this?

She was attempting to flag down their server and ask—he, unfortunately, seemed pretty involved in making his bicep tattoos jiggle for the amusement of a busty waitress nearby and didn't notice Amanda's arm-waving—when Mike's next words caught her attention.

"Sure, we'll take you on," he was saying. "Right, Amanda?"

She abandoned her hopes for a nice San Pelligrino. "Hmmm?"

"We'll take on Bruno and Curly in a game of pool," he replied. Mike winked at her. "Between the two of us, I think we can take 'em. Whaddya say?"

At least ten interested faces leaned closer, awaiting her answer. Looking up at the pack of tattoo-wearing, cigarette-smoking, smiling tough guys surrounding her, Amanda did the only thing that seemed reasonable.

She fibbed.

After all, if she didn't keep Mike happy, her Life Coach Lotto would be history. She was depending on the publicity it would generate to keep Aspirations, Inc., in business. To keep herself off the street. To keep her assistants employed.

Her quick backward glance confirmed that, however reluctantly, the Channel Six camera crew had indeed followed them covertly from Madame Roshinka's Rosado all the way to Mike's "perfect" lunch spot, Marvin's. The cameras were rolling. She was in all the way now.

"You bet," Amanda said. Maybe she could sneak out and buy a "how to play billiards" book while they waited for lunch to be served. "I'm game if you are."

"Great!" Mike's dazzling, happy smile almost made her bravado feel worthwhile. Almost.

But then tattoo-man returned with a plate of greasy, fried, assuredly nondietetic appetizer *somethings* and plunked them down in the middle of their table, and Amanda realized something else. Something chilling and oddly exciting and completely, crazily unavoidable.

It seemed she'd entered Mike's world this time. And she had absolutely, positively, *no* idea how to handle it.

Chapter Four

Later, leaning over the green baize pool-table top with Mike's strong arms guiding her shot from behind, Amanda decided that maybe the macho, Budweiser-and-basketball, eat-all-the-fried-foods-you-want world of Mike Cavaco wasn't so bad, after all. It positively had its good points. The steady clasp of Mike's hands on hers, for instance. The easy laughter of a bunch of guys who took life as it came. The fact that the pool table was, quite possibly, the only immaculately clean horizontal surface in the place.

Confident that the Suit would be safe, Amanda leaned a little farther over her cue, lining up her shot. She squinted with concentration.

"Keep both eyes open," Mike ordered from behind her.

She cocked her head. "How did you know I'd closed one?"

"The same way I knew you'd try to use the cue like a baseball bat and swipe the first ball in sideways."

She made a face, remembering the patient way

he'd extracted the stick from her hand. Heck, it had seemed a reasonable approach to her. "Look, I never pretended to be Fats Domino."

Across the table, Bruno guffawed. "You mean Minnesota Fats, doll."

"Whatever." They were making her all flustered. How was she supposed to concentrate—and win Mike's spur-of-the-moment twenty-dollar bet with someone named Snake—with everyone giving a running commentary? "Let's do this," she said to Mike.

"Okay." With expert touches on her forearms, her elbows, her waist, he realigned her position and gave her a few last-minute instructions. "Ready?"

Amanda gazed determinedly across the green— whoops, that was golf—at the triangle of neatly-arranged billiard balls. Then she sighted down her cue toward the one white ball they'd left out. *Visualize,* she told herself. *See the balls going into the pockets.*

Hey, positive visualization techniques worked for her clients; surely they couldn't hurt here.

"Ready," she said, and thrust forward the cue stick with all her might.

It made contact with a clunk. The white cue ball shot forward, sailing over the tidy billiard-triangle target. It missed the faux Tiffany lamp swinging over the table by inches, then arced toward a neon Coors Light sign. Reflexively, Amanda ducked.

So did about seven of the assembled he-men. She heard their biker-style, chained-on wallets and key rings jangle, the rapid shuffle of boots, and a muffled "Shit!"

A solid *thwap* sounded. She peeked upward and glimpsed a beefy, unsmiling guy with thinning hair, a handlebar mustache, and jeans worn with a T-shirt advertising a local liquor store. His tattooed arm was raised in the air, and in his fist he'd clutched the runaway cue ball.

"Power hitter," he said, nodding. "Nice try."

Amanda straightened and smiled at him. "Thank you. I'm glad you said that, actually. The power of specific encouragement is well-documented to produce positive effects on almost every study subject and has been known to—"

"Duck," Mike said from behind her.

"Huh? I wasn't finished explaining the—"

"Now." His hand spread over her head and pushed her downward.

She landed facedown on the pool table. It smelled like spilled beer and chalk. An instant later, a whoosh of air ruffled her hair, then another *thwap* came from just over her right ear.

"Thanks, Snake," Mike said, tossing the cue ball he'd just seized into the air and then catching it again. With a tug to her shoulder, he got Amanda upright again. "Sorry about that. Snake used to play ball on a triple-A team, and he likes to think he's the next Randy Johnson."

"Yeah!" yelled someone from the sidelines, hoisting a beer. "The Big Unit!"

"Hey, Snake," called someone else, "you coulda been a contenda, man."

The men nearest Snake slapped him on the back. Amanda watched, realizing with a sense of unreality that she'd just almost been brained by a person whose mother had apparently not loved him at all—to have named him after a reptile—and who had well-known "Big Unit" fantasies. Whatever *those* entailed. She didn't really want to know.

"It's all right," she said. "Really."

"I should've warned you not to hit the ball too hard," Mike said. "But you kinda looked like a light-weight to me."

Amanda grinned. Hugely. "Lightweight" was the

kind of compliment a serial dieter like her could really get behind.

"Well, I have played pool once before," she felt compelled to say. "I have to confess to a bit of experience with this."

Sure, that "experience" had taken place about twenty years earlier during an impromptu kiddie tournament in her Uncle Winston's rec room with a bunch of her Connor cousins. And she didn't really remember much about it except for the way it had degenerated into a Star Wars–style light-saber fight with the cue sticks afterward. But Mike didn't have to know that.

"Experience, huh?" He squinted at her, looking skeptical. "Then why don't we make this game a little more interesting?"

Uh-oh. "What do you mean?"

"I mean a friendly little wager."

"You already have a bet," Amanda pointed out, thinking of the twenty dollars riding on the outcome of their match with Curly and Bruno. "A bet with Snake."

"That's nothing. What I'm suggesting"—Mike leaned on his own upraised cue stick, tilting his head intimately closer—"is a wager between *us.*"

Double uh-oh. "Us?"

"Sure. Let's say, if I pocket more balls than you do, I'm off the hook for the rest of this makeover deal."

At the word "makeover," at least half of the men nearby perked up their ears. Some edged toward Mike to listen better, amused and disbelieving looks on their faces. Mike, however, didn't appear to notice their interest.

Amanda deliberated. "And if I pocket more balls than you do?"

Mike smiled, clearly believing *that* was about as

likely as wheat-grass smoothies on Marvin's menu and a clean ladies' room to boot. "Then you win an extra day to make me over," he offered.

"An extra three days." After all, she already had the rest of this day. And he'd as good as promised to go back for the haircut at Rosado, once Frederick had recovered.

"Don't push."

She narrowed her eyes. "Two days."

"Okay." *I can afford to be generous,* his expression said. *You just targeted ten percent of the neon in this place with your opening shot.*

"Done."

They shook hands on the wager. Amanda snatched the ball from his grasp and aligned it on the pool table where he'd shown her to. Then she hoisted her cue stick, visualized with all her might, and leaned forward.

"Nice tush," Mike murmured.

She levered upward. "Look, go sabotage someone else. I intend to win fair and square."

He grinned, utterly unrepentant. "It's got nothing to do with winning. I call 'em like I see 'em, that's all. You *do* have a nice tush. Round and cute and—"

Twelve guys craned their necks to see for themselves.

"—exactly the right size, I think, to . . ." Mike raised his hands, palms upward, and flexed them. With a speculative air, he looked from his big curled hands to her derriere.

Amanda refused to go where his imagination was leading them both—to the image of his hands cupping her backside. She *staunchly* refused. Unfortunately, her brain seemed to have other ideas.

It had a sequel in mind, too. One that involved getting Mike naked on Helga and Tiffany's massage table again, stripping away the towels, letting her gaze linger. . . .

"You're my client," she said crisply, interrupting herself before she could get too carried away. "I don't become involved with my clients."

She turned back to the cue ball, intent on getting the damned game over with before she found *other* parts of her body under discussion. Surely playing pool wasn't that hard, Amanda reminded herself. Especially for someone with a bachelor's degree, several years' worth of experience, her own company, and a burning need to wipe that sexy, pointlessly complimentary, machismo-filled grin off Mike Cavaco's unshaven, post-mud-masque face.

"Who said anything about getting involved?" he asked.

"You implied it." She propped her fingers on the pool table, making a bridge for the cue stick.

"I only complimented your tush," Mike disagreed. "You extrapolated from there. It was pure conjecture on your part."

Extrapolated? Conjecture? There was a disconnect here. Frowning, Amanda paused in lining up her shot. A taxi driver with a big vocabulary wasn't *necessarily* an oxymoron, but the words didn't quite fit the image she'd formed of Mike. For someone who prided herself on her expertise in reading people, the realization didn't sit comfortably.

"Enough talking," Curly interrupted. "Let's get going."

"Yeah," Bruno said, cracking his knuckles from across the table. "This isn't going to stop us from kicking your ass, Mike. Come on."

From the sidelines, Snake raised his beer. "Go, power hitter. Show 'em what you've got."

Several more men joined in the chorus, their comments punctuated with cheerful obscenities and punches to their tablemates' upper arms. Feeling increasingly on edge, Amanda nudged herself a little closer to Mike.

"They sound like they're out for blood," she whispered.

"They are. Pool is serious business at Marvin's."

"Oh, my God!"

"Don't worry," he said in the same hushed tones she was using. "You'll do fine. That twenty bucks doesn't mean that much to me, anyway. Who needs dinner *every* night?"

Aghast, Amanda stared at him. Did driving a taxi pay so poorly as that? Did he never get tips? Did he skip meals often, or did he . . . did he seriously believe she couldn't see the quiver of a smile at the edge of his lips?

She shrugged. "Not you, I guess."

"Hell, no. Just so long as I drop more balls than you do, I'll be happy as a clam."

He was impossible. There was no *way* Amanda was letting him off the Life Coach Lotto, whole-life makeover, winning-ticket hook that easily. Especially not when he obviously needed it so badly.

"You know, you might be right about that dinner thing." Just to shake him up a little, she peered speculatively at him. "You could probably stand to drop a few pounds anyway," she mused, with a jab to Mike's utterly non-existent paunch.

The crowd *oooohed*. His mouth dropped open.

Trying not to grin over his suddenly-disgruntled expression, Amanda leaned over, sucked in a breath, and took her shot. When she opened her eyes again, glossy pool balls were rolling lazily in all directions across the table. Slowly, slowly, a striped red and white one meandered toward the far corner pocket.

"Go, baby, go!" she cried, caught up in the moment.

Mike watched, saying nothing. Their audience held its breath.

The ball plunked into the pocket and rolled away into the depths of the table. It was the sweetest sound she'd heard all day.

"Yahoo!" Jubilant, Amanda threw both arms in the air, her cue stick waving madly. "I did it!"

Hey, this was fun. She could do this.

She could *win*.

"Great job," Mike said.

He obviously thought her good shot was a fluke, because he was grinning at her again despite the fact that her hole in one (or whatever it was called in billiards) meant she was winning their bet.

Mike's dark eyes sparkled at her, and his smile made a white slash against that god-awful beard. Why, oh, why, Amanda wondered distractedly, had Frederick chosen *today* to have a hairstylist meltdown? She devoutly hoped the star Rosado style-maker would recover from his hair-coloring crisis and be available later in the week.

"Thanks," she said, momentarily sidetracked from the game by an image of Mike with a decent haircut, a close shave, and a nice suit. Maybe something from a lesser-known up-and-coming designer—not too staid but tailored. Good for job interviews and less expensive. After all, after she won, she'd have two whole days to shop for suits for him and to begin on the other, nonphysical facets of Mike's makeover, too.

She could hardly wait.

After a brief, encouraging squeeze to her arm, he scanned the pool table, oblivious to her inner makeovering. "Now try to sink number six."

"The blue-and-white one?"

He nodded, and Amanda lined up another shot. She focused, tapped the cue ball with her stick, and

watched another striped ball sink beneath the tabletop, this time into a side pocket.

"Hey, I'm pretty good at this!"

"Beginner's luck," Mike said. "Keep going."

But as he watched her circle the pool table, trying
to decide from which angle to take her next shot, he
rolled his shoulders back and then frowned, looking
decidedly uncomfortable. Could it be that Mike was
worried she'd win their bet?

Amanda devoutly hoped so.

Twenty minutes later, it was all Mike could do to
keep from staring in amazement at the turn the game
had taken. Four balls remained on the table. An even
bigger crowd had shoved itself into the spaces
between the pool tables and Marvin's dining tables.
And he and Amanda were winning against two of the
biggest pool sharks this side of town had ever seen.

"I guess this just isn't my day," Curly said, straightening from the bent-over stance he'd assumed to take
his latest shot—a wobbly gouge aimed, if Mike wasn't
mistaken, directly at the green baize. He propped his
cue on the floor and made a gentlemanly gesture
toward Amanda, smiling as she passed in front of
him. "Your turn, Amanda."

"Thanks, Curly. Say, you'll remember about that
styling pomade I told you about, right? Using the
correct products is key to achieving a polished look."

As far as Mike knew, the only thing Curly polished
was his Harley. But at Amanda's words, he nodded
enthusiastically and ran his hand through his kinky
red hair as though he couldn't wait to dab on some
"pomade."

"I'll remember," he said.

Bruno bent from the waist and gestured gallantly
with one beefy arm as Amanda passed by him. "You

won't forget about my résumé, will you, Amanda?"
he asked. "Ever since my bum knee got me decommis-
sioned from the Marines, I've had a hell of a time
deciding what kind of job to get."

Mike stared at him. "You've got a perfectly good
job already. Right down the street, working at that
new club."

Amanda scoffed. "Being a bouncer in a—a—"

"Strip club," Mike supplied, grinning.

"—is hardly a career path," Amanda said. She
leaned over, checked out her shot, and then walked
farther to try another angle. A casual onlooker would
have sworn she was as familiar with shooting pool
as she was with ambushing unsuspecting cabbies for
unwanted makeovers. Glancing up at Bruno, she
added, "Stop by my office later this week, like I said.
We'll set up a series of appointments to formulate
some career goals for you."

"Great!" Bruno said, beaming. Mike hadn't seen
the big man look that happy since the day he'd signed
up for the service.

Amanda smiled back at him, and an unexpected
twinge niggled at Mike. *He* wanted to be the one
stopping by her office, not Bruno. *He* wanted, all of
a sudden, to be the one on the receiving end of those
breezy smiles and self-assured plans. Which was nuts,
of course. Because he already had been, and he'd
hated it so far. Hated it.

Hadn't he?

Swaying her hips with a seemingly unconscious
affinity for the thumping hip-hop music the guys at
Marvin's preferred, Amanda took her next shot. The
ball went wide.

The crowd of burly tough guys, neighborhood
women, and just-out-of-school slackers *oooohed* sympathetically. Marvin patted her encouragingly on the
shoulder.

Mike groaned. How had she won over this bunch so easily? They were putty in her hands, the lot of them. From Curly's pomade to Bruno's résumé to Snake's stock-portfolio problems, it seemed Amanda had the answers everyone wanted.

He hadn't even known Snake had shares in four up-and-coming dot-com companies, much less that the ex-ballplayer and part-time auto-parts sculptor was concerned about diversification.

Watching his buddies cozy up to a gorgeous, designer-clad, cool brunet with nothing more ribald on their minds than career, financial, and styling advice had been a real Twilight Zone moment. And this episode didn't seem to be coming to its surreal conclusion any time soon, either.

Bruno took the next shot and missed. Quite possibly, Mike figured, because he deliberately aimed his shot three inches to the left of the cue ball. Mike took his next shot, turned away for a bite of his chili cheeseburger and a slug of Budweiser while the ball rolled, and could have sworn, when he looked back again, that the men nearest the pool table wore identical guilty expressions.

His ball hadn't made it in. *Hell!* What was the matter with him today?

It wasn't him, Mike discovered a few turns later, when Amanda took her next shot.

"This is it," she told him, holding her cue stick over the table to measure the shot angle the way Snake had helpfully showed her. "I've got five and you've got five. Whoever sinks this ball wins our bet."

"And the game."

"Whatever." She shrugged. "It doesn't matter to me who wins the game. I'm playing to secure that makeover of yours."

A round of laughter broke out and was quickly suppressed. Suspiciously, Mike squinted at his buddies—and the onlookers—gathered around the pool table. Had someone overheard his bet with Amanda? Did they know about his makeover?

Nah, he decided. More than likely, Marvin had just told one of his patented fart jokes, and he and Amanda had missed it.

It was probably just as well. An uptown type like her would probably run screaming from the place in her three-inch heels if something so indelicate as bodily functions were discussed.

Mike straightened, thankful his blue-collar background had kept him from turning into some suit-wearing, wine-drinking, cell-phone-carrying prig—like the men Amanda probably dated. He was lucky, all right. He was proud of who he was, and he didn't care who knew it.

Watching Amanda take her final shot, he leaned one hand on the table and waited. She hit. The ball rolled. And that was when he felt it. The pool table moved.

What the hell? The tremor ended as quickly as it came. All around him, the spectators locked gazes, then looked away. Amanda's ball rolled into the pocket, and she leaped in the air with her cue stick held high, whooping it up over having won. People on all sides congratulated her. Bruno slapped her on the back hard enough to send her stumbling, cheerfully, into Curly's waiting arms for a quick consolation hug. He turned red and ducked away, leaving Amanda to talk with the rest of her newfound pool-shark fans.

"Congratulations," Mike said, making his way to the heart of the crowd after shaking hands with the challengers, Bruno and Curly. "I knew we could take 'em on."

Amanda turned, flushed and proud before him. She brushed a hank of hair from her temple and smiled up into his face, and Mike didn't have the heart to tell her what he knew was true: that they'd lifted the pool table, en masse, to make sure her balls went into the pockets.

He could hardly believe it himself. Not of his buddies, the same men who'd sat in this very place cursing ex-girlfriends, drowning their romantic sorrows in shared two-fifty pitchers, and bemoaning womankind in general. Not of Snake and Bruno and all the rest, guys he'd known half his life and had never known to be anything less than tough-as-nails badasses.

Their efforts in helping Amanda do well—and in such out-and-out blatant ways—were incomprehensible. But now, having officially won the game with his new partner, Mike could hardly turn into a poor loser and complain about it.

"Well, I wasn't quite so sure that we'd win as you were," Amanda confided, leaning close enough that he caught a hint of her light, modern-smelling perfume. "But I have to say, Curly and Bruno are being very good sports about it."

Mike glanced backward to where the "good sports" in question were quaffing fresh beers and forking over money to Snake. Every once in a while, one of them would look in Mike's direction and chuckle. It gave him a very bad feeling.

"They sure are," he said. Lightly, he slipped his hand to the small of her back, feeling the expensive fabric of her suit smooth against his palm and noticing, with pleasure, the suggestion of bare feminine curves just beneath. He guided her toward the cue-stick rack, where they could have some privacy. "And I'll try to be an equally good sport about your winning *our* bet. It looks like I'm yours for another day."

"Another two days," Amanda reminded him as she racked her cue. "We agreed on two days."

"Right."

She turned when he said it, making him wonder if she was simply intent on looking into his face while they spoke, if she didn't believe he was being a good sport about losing their bet, or if she was trying to evade his touch.

I don't become involved with my clients.

"And one of the most important things I want to do during those two days," Amanda went on, "is make sure you're healthy. All the career planning and new haircuts in the world won't do a bit of good if you don't have your health."

Mike frowned. "I don't look healthy to you?"

He raised his arm at a ninety-degree angle and squeezed, remembering the "I'm impressed" way she'd squeezed his biceps earlier. *Take that, Miss Health Nut.*

She raised her eyebrows. Somehow the gesture cast his physique and his entire fitness routine into doubt. Granted, Mike's idea of fitness consisted mostly of the occasional pickup basketball game and now and then when the neighborhood kids roped him into it, a round of Rollerblade street hockey. But that didn't mean Amanda could just dismiss him out of hand.

"All my clients receive complete physical examinations, followed by sound nutrition and fitness plans formulated especially for them," Amanda said. "It's standard procedure."

"But I don't need it."

"Hmmm." Speculatively, she looked him over. "We'll let the test results speak for themselves, shall we?"

"Tests?"

"Yes. You'll need to make an appointment to see your doctor first. It's a good idea to make sure you're ready for the physical stress of a new fitness regime before beginning."

Mike waved away the suggestion. "I can handle anything you can dish out. Bring it on."

She smiled. Enigmatically. Which only made him wonder exactly what those fitness routines of hers entailed. Aerobic-style torture? Sweaty dead lifts? Punishing wind sprints?

"If you can't get in to see your doctor on such short notice, you can see the physician I consult with for my clients. She'll work you into her schedule on an emergency basis."

"Hey," Mike said, affronted. "I am not an emergency!"

"We'll see." Amanda walked to their table, with Mike beside her, and gathered up her purse. She withdrew a business card and handed it to him. "We'll do the health-and-fitness evaluation Wednesday morning at my office, eight o'clock sharp. The address is on my card. Wear something you don't mind working out in."

"Sure." He felt vaguely steam-rollered, and wasn't sure what to do about it. Had he just agreed to a complete physical *and* a grueling series of fitness tests? Had he let himself be talked into it, the same way he'd been schmoozed out of his Bugs Bunny boxers this morning?

Had he lost his mind?

And, if so, why wasn't he more disgruntled about it?

With an efficient movement, Amanda turned, purse slung over her shoulder. Mike frowned and touched her arm.

"Hey, you're not leaving, are you?" he asked, feeling unaccountably disappointed at the idea. "What about the rest of . . ." He shrugged, giving her a meaningful look so he wouldn't have to specify what he meant aloud. "*Today?* You know."

"Yeah," put in a husky, booming voice from the

other end of the room—Bruno's voice. "What about the rest of Mike's makeover, Amanda?"

Makeover. Everyone in the place burst into guffaws. Some shouted out ribald suggestions as to what parts of Mike needed to be "made over." Others—notably Snake and Curly—pranced around the pool tables wearing imaginary bouffant hairdos and putting on pretend lipstick.

Suddenly, the reasons behind the unexpected pool-table "help" they'd given Amanda became painfully clear. *They knew.* Groaning, Mike put his face in his hands. Christ, this was worse than he'd feared. He'd never live this down now. Not the way his buddies were hamming it up.

To save face, he'd have to start dating Amanda, at the very least, he realized suddenly. It was the perfect way, the only way, out of the jam he'd found himself in. Every guy in the place would understand doing something stupid—and what was a mud masque and a honey-and-loofah body massage if not incredibly stupid?—for the sake of impressing a woman.

Yeah, that was it. Bolstered by his newfound plan, Mike put his arm around Amanda's waist and tugged her a little closer. She stiffened.

"Don't freak out because I'm holding you," he murmured in her ear. "Please. These guys are never going to let me live this makeover stuff down. I've got to have a cover."

Amanda turned her head, looking into his eyes. Her expression seemed sympathetic, and for a minute, Mike thought he was actually going to get away with it. And he did. He guessed. Sort of.

Standing with his arm still around her middle, Amanda smiled at the crowd of people. "The makeover goes on as scheduled," she began.

Everyone cheered. Marvin stomped his feet with enthusiasm.

"After all," she continued, "how else could I cozy up to a great guy like Mike?"

"Awwwww," said the crowd, just as though they'd been confronted with something incredibly sweet, like a dozen sleepy puppies. Obviously, they'd believe anything that came out of Amanda's mouth, no matter how unlikely.

"Thank you," Mike whispered in her ear, giving her a quick squeeze. "Now let's get out of here."

"No problem." Amanda led the way toward the restaurant's door, around which beams of daylight streamed into the murkiness of the interior. Once there, her smile turned unexpectedly wicked. "Next up is my special life-coach-relationships-and-emotional-attitudes questionnaire. I just know you're going to *love* it."

Awww, hell, Mike realized as the sunlight outside struck him straight in the face and Amanda's words sunk all the way in. *He'd jumped out of the frying pan and into the fire.*

Chapter Five

At Amanda's request, Mike drove them in his cab to the nearby Tempe Kiwanis city park. The Channel Six News camera team assigned to the Life Coach Lotto followed them at a discreet distance, Amanda noticed, and set up a short distance from the concrete picnic table she and Mike settled themselves on.

With a glance at the crew, Amanda fluffed up her hair and slicked her tongue over her teeth to check for wayward lipstick, unable to resist primping. This would be the first time she appeared on TV. She wanted to look good. After all, the get-a-promotion suit had no power in the beauty arena.

Satisfied with her appearance, she frowned briefly at the way Mike had plunked himself onto the hard gray concrete top of the picnic table. Since Amanda had seated herself properly on the bench, she had a terrific view of Mike's ripped-up jeans knees. And, at eyeball level, a worn spot near the crotch of his Levi's confronted her, too.

She looked away. The man had no modesty. No

style. And, she would have sworn if she didn't know better, no underwear.

And *she* had no business, as his life coach, Amanda reminded herself sternly, ogling him like this. Still, how had he managed to fade that one spot in the denim, wearing it to a paler blue that would— Amanda felt sure—feel intriguingly soft beneath her fingertips?

"If you're done getting an eyeful," Mike said abruptly, "maybe we can get this thing over with?"

Embarrassment swamped her. Amanda jerked her head upward and discovered Mike's level brown gaze locked directly on her face.

"Sure, let's get going." Heat flooded her cheeks as Amanda sorted through the papers on her trusty clipboard, looking for the relationships-and-emotional attitudes questionnaire. "Absolutely."

While she'd been contemplating the fit of his jeans, Mike hadn't even had the macho decency, she thought irrationally, to try and peek down her buttoned-up suit jacket. Sure, she wasn't *Playboy* material. Especially in the cleavage department. But was that any excuse?

Unwillingly, Amanda remembered the feel of his strong, solid arm wrapped around her waist at Marvin's. She remembered the deft curl his fingers had made at a sensitive place just above the waistband of her Prada pants. She remembered the weak-kneed sensation that had struck her when Mike had given her his first full-blown smile, after her initial pool ball had sunk into the pocket, and knew that she was treading dangerous ground.

Having a crush on a client was a bad idea. Actually acting on one would be even worse. To safeguard herself, Amanda scooted a little sideways on the sun-splashed bench, careful not to snag her suit on the rough surface.

"All right." She cleared her throat and arranged the questionnaire atop the clipboard, fastening it into place. "First, there are a few general questions about your background."

"Fire away."

"Okay. Your full name?"

"Michelangelo Anthony Cavaco."

Amanda looked up. He looked back. She raised her eyebrows. "Michelangelo?"

"Come on. It's a fine Italian name."

"Sure it is. Absolutely." She felt a grin coming on and worked to stifle it. "I'm just not sure I can call you Michelangelo with a straight face."

He smiled. "Mike is fine."

"Okay." She wrote *Mike Cavaco, nouveau Renaissance man* at the top of the page. "Age?"

"Thirty-two."

Three years older than her, Amanda calculated. A near-perfect, date-worthy age gap. Not too far apart to cause divergent worldviews and not too close together to be overly similar. Very nice. Very *inappropriate*, she reminded herself, and got down to business again.

"Siblings?"

"What about them?"

"Do you have any?" she clarified. "And how old are they?"

"Let's see . . ."

Casually, Mike leaned back, balancing himself on his splayed palms. Sunlight and shade from one of the many feathery-leafed mesquite trees planted across the park danced over his features, making him look both casual and a little mysterious. The breeze ruffled his too-long dark hair. He ticked off names and ages, which Amanda wrote dutifully onto her questionnaire, and then he summed up:

"Three sisters. Two brothers. And all of us the terror of our neighborhood growing up."

He grinned, displaying even white teeth and a surprise dimple just at the corner of his beard. What she wouldn't give, Amanda thought suddenly, to see him clean-shaven. To heck with waiting for the temperamental Frederick. She had half a mind to drag Mike home and haul out a Lady Bic razor herself.

An image of a bare-chested Mike, face lathered with shaving cream, shoved itself into her head. In her mind's eye, she sat Mike down in her apartment's tiny bathroom, moved seductively closer, and—dressed improbably in the *Buffy the Vampire Slayer* T-shirt Amanda slept in but never let anyone see—carefully dragged the razor over his whiskers.

Her imaginary Mike grabbed her fantasy butt and squeezed with both hands. Amanda hurriedly ended her reverie.

"I'll just bet you were a terror as a kid," she said, unnerved by her recurring racy thoughts about Mike. He was just a guy, just a client, right? "Were you the youngest little hell-raiser? The oldest? Or somewhere in the middle?"

"Second from the youngest. My little brother Manny was born two years after me. He saved me from being the baby of the family forever."

Four older siblings, Amanda wrote. *One younger.*

"What about your parents?" she asked. "Are they still married?"

"Forty years this past June."

"Wow." Her own parents had divorced, remarried other people, and then divorced *them,* too. Both were currently single—and looking. *Ugh.* Was there anything worse than hot-to-trot parents regaling you with stories of singles' cruises, dating misadventures, and sexual reawakenings? Just last week, her mother had actually asked Amanda if she'd found her "G-spot" yet. The mere memory of that conversation made her want to ban Dr. Ruth from the airwaves forever.

Saving her from further recollections of X-rated parental discussions, Mike said, "Yeah, it's pretty nice, actually." He tilted his face to the sky and smiled as the sun struck his cheeks and the bridge of his assertive-looking nose. "My folks have their little tiffs, like anybody else—just don't ask my dad to remember a birthday without an itemized shopping list, daily reminders, and a Post-it note stuck to his steering wheel on the big day—but for the most part, they're solid."

After consulting with so many people just like her, with multiply-divorced parents and no optimal prospects of their own on the horizon, Amanda had begun to believe that marriage really was dead.

"They're happily married, then?" she remarked, making further notations on the Relationships portion of her questionnaire. "That's good news. Research has shown that people who come from homes with stable relationships are better at making commitments themselves."

"Is that so?"

"Yes. Study after study has proved that children of divorce tend to be somewhat cynical about the future of marriage. No less hopeful but less likely to make lasting commitments."

Mike tilted his head and gazed at her with an inscrutable expression. She could have lost herself in the warmth of his eyes, in the subtle tug of man-meets-woman awareness that flowed between them.

"Which camp do you fall into?" he asked.

Gulp. "Umm, why do you ask?" she stalled.

"Because I want to know."

Of course. He *would* have a simple answer like that. Mike Cavaco was nothing if not straightforward. *And macho. And thoughtful. And currently veering ever-closer to her spot on the bench.*

In alarm, Amanda straightened, watching as he braced himself on his hand and turned sideways atop the picnic bench so that his body was lying perpendicular to hers. Below his ratty T-shirt sleeves, the sinewy muscles in his arms flexed to support him, and his thighs strained briefly beneath his Levi's. She couldn't help wondering what effect all that movement was having on that intriguing spot of worn denim she'd noticed, and wishing her Life Coach Lotto winner had been someone just a little less . . . affecting.

"Are *you* keen to commit to someone?" Mike asked. His face was nearly eye level with hers now, and he watched her intently. "Or are you the playing-it-safe type who's not interested in letting anyone get close?"

He sounded more than familiar with that second "not letting anyone get close" option, Amanda thought, unreasonably disappointed.

"How do you know I'm not already committed to someone?" she asked, folding her hands atop the clipboard in a determined effort to remain professional.

"How do I know?"

"Yes." She nodded, certain that her lack of someone to spend Sunday mornings in bed with, to share romantic dinners and weekend getaways with, and to keep her relatives' insistent "are you still single?" questions at bay with couldn't possibly show. "How do you know I don't have a husband waiting at home right now?"

"No wedding ring."

"A fiancé, then."

"No engagement ring. *Sheesh,* you're easy."

"A boyfriend!"

"Hmmm." Mike smiled. Smiled as though he had

some sort of secret, one he would be willing, if she asked very, very nicely, to share with her. And then, slowly, he ran his fingertips over the back of her hands. The gesture left Amanda utterly aware of him—of the long blunt shape of his fingers, the slightly rough texture of his skin, the heat of his touch.

"If you were already committed to someone," he said, "then you wouldn't hold your breath and go still whenever I touch you like this."

Shock jolted through her. She jerked her hands away, making the clipboarded papers flutter in the breeze. "I don't—"

"And you wouldn't watch me with that greedy expression of yours, like you're dying of thirst . . . and I'm a long, tall drink of that fancy bottled water you kept asking for at Marvin's."

Amanda sucked in a breath. *"I do not look at you that way!"*

"And you probably wouldn't have been ogling my crotch, either."

His grin widened in an especially maddening way.

"This line of conversation is irrelevant." Stiffly, Amanda rifled through her papers. "We should get back to the questionnaire."

"Sure, if that's the way you want to play it." Mike shrugged, the very picture of an easygoing, regular-Joe kind of guy. "If you want to pretend you don't have the hots for me, it's no skin off my nose."

"I do *not*— Oh, what's the use?" She sighed. "Mike, I didn't want to do this, but you're not leaving me any choice. I'll just have to level with you. And the truth is . . ."

"Yeah?"

"Well, it's that . . ." Amanda bit her lip, reluctant to do this but unable to see a better option. Quickly, she blurted out, "I'm afraid you're just not my type."

"Hmmm. Really?"

"Yes."

Technically, it was true. And as for the rest . . . well, she decided, there was no reason Mike had to know about her sudden and still-developing interest in broadening her horizons.

With a disbelieving expression, Mike frowned into the distance. He looked, oddly enough, almost as though he'd never before encountered a situation where a woman found him less than irresistible and didn't know quite how to handle it now.

The least she could do was soften the blow. Especially since she wasn't being one hundred percent on the up-and-up.

"Once I'm finished with your whole-life makeover, though," Amanda said, "you'll probably have your pick of women. I'm actually quite good at my job."

Thoughtfully, Mike stretched farther out on his side, completely relaxed, elbow crooked against the concrete picnic tabletop. He must have come to some sort of peace with the situation, because he propped his head in his hand and gave her a cheerful look.

"So, what you're saying is that you're single, right?" he asked. "Not seeing anyone at the moment? Available if I decide to ask you out on a date? I just want to get this straight."

And she'd actually *worried* about hurting this man's feelings? He was as impervious to a gentle turndown as her fat cells had become to repeated dieting threats.

Mere words failed her. *"Arrgh!"* Amanda yelled.

"Ouch!" cried a distant male voice. It came from the direction of the camera crew.

She glanced backward, where one of the sound men was yanking off his headphones and scowling at her. Cripes, could they hear this? Amanda had no idea what kind of heavy-duty microphones they had. For all she knew, the Channel Six crew had just captured the whole inappropriate—yet stimulating—

conversation on tape. The idea sobered her like nothing else.

"Sorry," she mouthed toward the sound man, and then turned back to the problem at hand.

No matter what, she could *not* have an inappropriate relationship with a client, especially one whose makeover would be so highly-publicized. Her business, her whole future, was at stake. She couldn't let her libido run Aspirations, Inc., into the ground.

Communicates quite well nonverbally, she wrote in the Notes section of the emotional-attitudes questionnaire. *Interested in forming romantic relationships. Not afraid to speak bluntly.*

Amanda glanced up, prepared to go on with the next questions on the list. She straightened her spine, opened her mouth, and said . . .

"No, I'm not seeing anyone right now."

Where the heck had that *come from?*

"Good."

Mike's smile was like that of a little boy who'd just been told the ice cream sundaes were bottomless. It charmed her in ways Amanda didn't even want to consider, especially not when she had so much at risk. Rapidly, she began firing questions at him— this time, with the non-impulsive, *thinking* part of her brain.

"What about commitment?" she asked twenty minutes later, turning to that section of the questionnaire. "How do you handle long-term relationships?"

"As carefully as possible."

She suppressed a grin. "I mean, have you had a long-term relationship? And, if so, how did you deal with it? How did it end?"

He pursed his lips, turning them downward. "How do you know I don't have a long-term relationship going right now?"

"Well, if you did," Amanda said, looking at Mike

carefully, "then you probably wouldn't be coming on to me, now would you?"

"Touché." He grinned and watched as she wrote *aware of inappropriate flirting* on the Questions page. "No, I wouldn't."

"So . . . ?"

He frowned, then admitted reluctantly, "Two long-term relationships. Mary Alice Rubens, who broke my heart after I left for school—"

"Out-of-town college?" Amanda asked, thinking how common it was for high-school sweethearts to drift apart when they left for separate universities.

"Sort of." Mike gestured with his hands, moving past Mary Alice. "And another woman who I dated seriously about two years ago. We . . . weren't headed for the same things, it turned out. We split."

And he still sounded a little raw about the breakup, too, Amanda noted. Thoughtfully, she peeked up at Mike but couldn't tell much about his feelings behind the suddenly impassive turn his expression had taken. "Her name?"

"No."

Taken aback, she put down her pencil. "What?"

"I'm not telling you her name." Pointedly, he glanced at the camera crew. "Let's talk about something else."

Hmmm. Mysterious. But Amanda had no worries. She was good at getting to know people. That was one of the skills that had led her to life coaching in the first place. She'd learn the whole story from Mike sooner or later, she was sure.

"Okay," she said, moving on to the next portion of the Emotional Attitudes section. "Next up is employment. How do you feel about your job?"

"Like I'm not going to talk about it," Mike said bluntly. He pushed to his feet and pulled his cab keys from his Levi's pocket. "Come on, touchy-feely time is over. I've gotta get back to work."

Faced with his departing self—and the brain-scrambling sight of his tight backside as Mike walked away—all Amanda could do was relent.

For now.

That night at Boondoggle's, Amanda's favorite postwork bar-and-restaurant hangout, Gemma and Mel couldn't get enough of what they quickly dubbed "Mike TV." Not long after Amanda arrived, the three of them had already plowed partway through two plates of buffalo wings, one and two-thirds rounds of margaritas, and enough questions to make Amanda feel completely backed into the corner of their usual close-enough-to-ogle-the-bartenders booth.

"And then he just dropped you off at your car outside the Channel Six News offices and drove off into the sunset?" Gemma asked. "I can't believe he wouldn't at least answer your questions about his work."

"Or about the mystery woman who broke his heart two years ago," Mel put in, pointing with her latest buffalo wing. "What do you think *that's* all about?"

"I don't know," Amanda admitted. She pushed her own remaining buffalo wing aside, trying not to think about how many calories she'd probably already scarfed down and about how blue cheese dip was definitely *not* a recommended item on her new diet. Oh, well. Tomorrow was another day. "He definitely didn't want to talk about it."

"Typical male." Mel snorted and downed another gulp of margarita. "Dead quiet about all the things that matter."

"Tom's not like that," Gemma said, staunchly defending her husband. "He talks to me all the time."

"Puh-leeze." Mel rolled her eyes. "Can we have at least *one* conversation that doesn't turn into a lovefest for your super-duper husband?"

"I can't help it if I got lucky." This was said primly, with a tidy little twist of Gemma's barely-touched margarita glass. She was the reason they'd only ordered one and two-thirds rounds of drinks so far.

"Lucky? You call being stuck at home with two toddlers and a pile of housework lucky?" Mel asked.

"Yes," Gemma insisted quietly. "In some ways. You don't know what it's like to—"

"And I hope I never will," Mel interrupted. "God willing, I'll never have to deal with rug rats of my own."

Gemma looked horrified. "Rug rats! But you just baby-sat the twins last week, and you never said—"

"Oh, Mandy and Randy are terrific, you know that," Mel said. "But you have to admit, motherhood is limiting."

"And your job at the CD shop isn't?"

"Look, I'm telling you, Gemma—"

"Now, hold on just a minute—"

"Time out!" Desperately, Amanda intervened before their familiar conflict became an out-and-out war. "We were talking about *my* problem, remember?"

"Sorry, Amanda."

"Sorry."

"Come on. I never would have told you guys about Mike if I didn't need your advice." Amanda took a sip of her margarita, working up her courage. "I think I'm attracted to him."

"You *think?*" Mel shook her head. "If you're not sure, then you're not interested. Forget about it."

"Now, that's not necessarily true," Gemma protested. "It's not always fireworks . . . *bam!* when you meet someone. When Tom and I started dating—"

"Blah, blah, blah," Mel interrupted. She gave

Amanda an earnest stare. "Look. If being with this guy doesn't make you want to find some secluded off-camera spot and boff your socks off, then he's not worth the trouble."

"Melanie!" Gemma cried.

"If he doesn't rock your world, then consider him an ordinary client and move on." Mel popped a bite of buffalo wing, chewed and swallowed, then fanned her mouth as the spicy sauce worked its magic. "I mean, come on. Surely one or more of the cameramen is cute, right? You do have options here."

"Amanda is *not* going to throw herself at the camera crew!"

"Sure she will." Mel winked. "If they're really hot."

"I think you're confusing me with *your* alter ego," Amanda said, grinning as she teased her longtime pal. "Robo-dater."

Melanie shrugged, clearly not bothered. "Hey, if the stilettos fit . . ."

"Anyway," Amanda put in, "I'm not even sure I could slip away from the camera crew long enough to—"

"—fit in a little hubba-hubba behind a bush somewhere? Sure you could." Mel waved nonchalantly. "Wear a skirt. It'll help."

Gemma choked on her margarita.

Amanda laughed. "Long enough to find *out* if I'm interested in a relationship with Mike," she finished. "I mean, whenever I get close to something good—"

"Like the ex-broke-his-heart girlfriend."

"—he clams up. I swear, he just about peeled out of the city park, he was in such a hurry to get away. Do you think he has something to hide?"

"Oh, no. No. Probably not," Gemma said, ever-faithful and ever ready to believe the best about everyone. She leaned sideways and gave Amanda a quick hug. "Maybe he just wanted to get back to work."

"Maybe he just wanted to snuggle up to Amanda," Mel suggested with a wicked expression from across the table, "and he didn't want a camera crew watching. I'm telling you, if this Mike is a guy—"

"Oh, he's definitely a guy." *A mysteriously appealing, one-hundred-percent macho, "are you seeing anyone?" guy,* Amanda thought. *And he's off-limits.*

"—then he's up for a little extracurricular 'coaching,' if you know what I mean," Mel finished. "I think you should go for it."

"He's not even my type," Amanda said. "Really. He's messy and unshaven and outspoken, and his idea of ambition is driving a cab for a living. He's still insisting he didn't even enter the Life Coach Lotto, for Pete's sake."

"She's smitten," Gemma said, her smug smile matching Mel's.

"Yup. Backseat boners, here she comes," Mel added, her tone of voice knowing. "I envy you, Amanda. I can't remember the last time I was hot for a guy so much that I'd jump him in the back of a cab."

Nostalgically, Melanie sighed. Amanda gawked at her, then made a disgusted sound, wadded up a napkin, and hurled it across the table. It bounced off Mel's head and into the lap of the man seated behind her. By the time she'd apologized for the intrusion, Mel had the napkin catcher's phone number and a date for Saturday night. She turned back to their table with a triumphant grin.

"I don't know why I even brought it up," Amanda said when their conversation had resumed. "Mike is a client, and he's not my type. Period. Working with him will *not* be a problem. I simply won't let it be."

But as Mel and Gemma both cast skeptical glances

her way, Amanda couldn't help but wonder—whether she was trying to convince her friends she wasn't interested in Mike . . . or herself?

"You've got it bad for this girl," Mike's buddy Jake told him that night at the gym. "Really bad."

"Nah."

Jake's snort of laughter destroyed Mike's carefree attitude—and his concentration. Feeling disgruntled, he set down the twin dumbbells he'd been about to heft for his second set of biceps curls.

"Okay, she's kind of a looker," he admitted. Memories of Amanda's long dark hair, big ready smile, and self-confident stance made the qualifier a lie, though, and he knew it. There was no "kind of" about it. "But this is a bad time for me to get involved with someone."

"Because of the April Fools' Day thing at the restaurant?" Jake frowned, and lay down on the incline bench, speaking between chest presses. "You've gotta get over that, Mike. It was just a job. Sure, Nickerson and the new management picked a rotten way to end it, but—"

"No, not because of that." With a grunt, Mike began a set of hammer curls. His biceps throbbed at the unaccustomed demand, but he gritted his teeth and ignored the ache. Hey, no pain, no gain, right? "It's just that . . ." *She wants to make me over.* "That Amanda is, uh, not my type."

Jake lowered his weight bar and gawked at him. "Not your type," he repeated. "Not your type?"

"Yup." With effort, Mike finished his set. "That's what I said."

"Bullshit."

Mike said nothing. He made his way past a row of treadmills packed with gym-goers and an array of weight machines in heavy use by other muscleheads like Jake while his friend trailed behind.

"Good-looking?" Jake continued. "In good shape?"

It always came down to that for Jake, a sometime waiter and part-time musician whose hobby was competitive bodybuilding and whose idea of a wild indulgence was a grilled-chicken-and-broccoli dinner *with* a plain baked potato. There were reasons Mike had come to him to help prepare for whatever fitness tests Amanda had in mind for him on Wednesday. He just hoped the routine Jake had come up with wouldn't kill him first.

"Good-looking, yes," Mike replied. "In good shape? I think so. It was hard to tell. She had on some kind of designer suit—one of those buttoned-up jobs that look kinda like a miniature man's suit."

"Well, suit or not, you at least saw her legs. Good calf-muscle development? Sexy quads? Miniskirts can—"

"Pantsuit," Mike clarified before Jake, a confirmed leg man, could go any further. "No leg action."

Jake made a face, obviously commiserating. "Too bad."

"Yeah." Mike's memory chose that moment to remind him of the feminine curves he'd felt beneath Amanda's suit jacket after their pool-game victory, though, and he couldn't work up much disappointment.

He was good at getting close to people, especially women, Mike reminded himself. That was one of the skills that had led him to a career working closely with a team in the first place. He'd learn the whole picture about Amanda sooner or later, he was sure.

Reminded by his conversation with Jake to work his legs, Mike picked up a pair of heavier dumbbells and started in on a set of squats. Beside him, Jake did lunges, moving like the well-trained workout meister he was.

"Well, you're still going to date her, right?" Jake asked.

Amid a haze of rep counting, Mike squinted at him. "Date her? Date Amanda?"

"Yeah."

"I'd have to be crazy. We're totally different."

With an amicable grin of agreement, Jake swiped a towel over his sweaty forehead and began a new lunge set. "You're going to do it anyway, aren't you?"

"Hell, yes," Mike said. "Life's too short not to try."

Chapter Six

Mike knew he was in trouble from the minute he and Amanda entered their first Life Coach Lotto destination on Tuesday morning. His suspicions only grew stronger when Amanda sucked in a deep breath, looked at their surroundings—an East Valley shopping mall—with obvious pleasure, and then turned to him.

"I have a confession to make," she said.

Immediately, Mike's brain offered up suggestions. *You really are my type, Mike. Let's go make out in the cab* was first. *I wore this outfit so you could check out my legs* was the second. And as he obligingly admired Amanda's legs—and the rest of her—in the delicately colored, floral-printed short dress and sandals she had on today, Mike was forced to reinterpret his earlier thoughts.

That hadn't been his brain talking. It had been his libido. Damn, but Amanda looked great. Fresh. Sexy. Improbably wholesome, which had never been a look Mike favored but now found he did. And, as a bonus,

Jake would have been proud of those nicely toned quads of hers.

Whereas Mike . . . well, he was too inexpert to do anything but appreciate them as a simple pair of feminine thighs that would feel terrific wrapped around his waist, hugging his hips close as he. . . .

"Mike?"

He snapped back to Earth.

"A confession?" Mike asked, scrambling to remember their conversation. He hooked his thumbs in the belt loops of his jeans, trying to ignore the way she let her gaze skitter disapprovingly past his usual Levi's, T-shirt, and sneakers getup. "What kind of confession would that be, doll? Did you get up on the wrong side of the bed and do something out of character, like double park outside the Channel Six News offices?"

He nodded toward the members of the camera and sound crews who had followed them into the mall. He wasn't sure what they planned to do with all the footage they were shooting, but they were being diligent as hell about it.

"No, that's not it." Amanda's mouth quirked into a smile. "I never park illegally."

As *if* he couldn't already tell that about her.

"Did you go a little crazy," Mike asked, "and stiff the newspaper carrier?"

"Uh-uh." She crossed her arms and waited. "He's twelve. He does a good job. He deserves a tip."

"Well, now. Let's see, here." Mike stepped closer and looked her up and down, as though gauging the secret depths of Amanda's confession. "You've got me stumped. No, wait . . ." He snapped his fingers. "I've got it. You ripped off the sacred do-not-remove tag from your mattress."

"No way!" She looked astonished. "I'd wind up in San Quentin for sure."

They both laughed.

"Then you must need to confess something completely different," Mike said, raising a hand to tuck back an errant strand of her long brown hair.

She started at his touch but didn't move away. Warily, Amanda watched his face instead. His fingers stirred up the scent of floral shampoo, and he decided the fragrance suited her. If any woman seemed pure as a daisy, it was Amanda Connor in a pretty girly dress.

"Something like . . . a hot, wild attraction for your Life Coach Lotto winner," Mike continued. "Come on, Amanda." He lowered his voice. "Tell me you want me."

To his credit, she responded with a blush and a seemingly unconscious sway toward him. To his disappointment, though, she put a lid on that reaction right away.

"I do want you," Amanda said briskly, stepping back to consult the list on her ever-present clipboard. "I want you to follow along peacefully today—"

"You actually made a list of these things?"

"—to put a damper on the flirting—"

Mike sighed.

"—and to stick to your end of our makeover bargain."

"Two days?" he asked.

"Two days," she confirmed. "Is it a deal?"

"The no-flirting thing might be tough—"

"Mike—"

"—but never let it be said that Mike Cavaco went back on his word."

Or let a good woman get away. His cover with his buddies demanded that he take Amanda on at least one official date, Mike reminded himself, or he'd never live down this makeover business. The last thing he was doing now was backing off.

"Okay." With a satisfied smile, Amanda grabbed his arm. "Then let's get started."

She strolled toward the nearest department store, reminding Mike that their mission for today was buying new clothes—or, as Amanda had put it, "Wardrobe, with a capital Wow."

He was a little afraid to find out what constituted "Wow" when it came to a few new jeans and T-shirts. But if it kept Amanda happy—and kept Mike close enough to get that date he was after—then he was all willing.

"Oh, and that confession of mine?" At the entrance to Macy's, she paused and whirled to face him. "It's this: I absolutely *love* to shop."

"That's a confession?" He scoffed. "I'm pretty sure loving to shop is some kind of girly birthright."

"No, I mean, I *really* love it. Before I became a life coach, I did a stint as a personal shopper at Nordstrom's," Amanda confided. "There's nothing I'd rather do than spend an afternoon shopping. *Nothing.*"

With an opening like that, Mike just couldn't let it go. He captured Amanda's hand when she would have sashayed away and tugged her back beside him.

"*Nothing?*" he asked.

He leaned nearer so the Channel Six crew wouldn't hear and positioned his mouth against the soft skin of her earlobe—not kissing, just barely touching—and felt her fingers tighten on his at the contact. Heard her sharp intake of breath as he began speaking again. "Not even an afternoon of making love? Losing yourself in the heat, and the closeness, and the skin-on-skin touch of bodies rubbing together, lips—"

"Nope," Amanda squeaked. "Not even that."

Swiftly, she yanked her hand away.

With disappointment, Mike let her go.

"No problem," he said as they continued into the

department store. He even managed a carefree shrug despite the nagging curiosity her continued refusals engendered in him. "I have a pretty good idea how to change your mind about that 'favorite activity' thing. If you'll let me."

"Not a chance," Amanda snapped back, sandals clicking on the polished floor. "This is all business between us."

"What a shame." With a wink to let her know their game wasn't finished yet, Mike smiled and followed Amanda toward the men's department. "And me with *such* a knack for pleasure . . ."

It was the same story at every department store they went to in the mall. Amanda would select a nice business suit, Mike would make a face, and they'd move on to the next one. After more than an hour, Amanda was frustrated, frazzled, and more determined than ever to get Mike into some decent clothes.

"How about this one?" she asked, holding up a chalk-striped gray suit with a narrow cut and razor-sharp lapels. "It's by a new-ish designer, but the style is fresh and the—"

"It looks like it would chafe," Mike interrupted, peering critically at the suit.

"I'm sure it doesn't."

"How do you know?" He reached out a hand and touched the summer-weight wool fabric. "It feels scratchy. No go."

"Come on, Mike! We've been to three stores now. You've got to try on *something*. The camera crew is getting restless."

She waved her arm toward the edge of the men's department, where the Channel Six staff assigned to the Life Coach Lotto story had abandoned their cameras and microphones for an impromptu game of cards. Evan must have assigned her a bunch of second-stringers.

Mike crossed his arms. "My jeans might not make good TV, but they suit me fine."

They fit you fine, too, Amanda thought, her gaze irresistibly drawn to the Levi's in question. Not too tight, not too baggy, they somehow managed to ride on Mike's hips with a fit that was absolutely perfect. For casual pants. Which was really the problem, wasn't it? They were here for a "wow" wardrobe, and Mike's existing jeans and "Eat at Marvin's" T-shirt with the sleeves ripped off really didn't fit the bill.

"They're great. You look terrific," Amanda agreed. She took Mike's arm to coax him toward the next rack of suits and was surprised to feel him flinch when her fingers wrapped around his bicep. "But how do you know you wouldn't look even better in one of these suits?"

Stubbornly, he refused to budge. "My uncle Alfred runs a tuxedo place downtown. Anytime I need a suit I can rent a perfectly good one."

Used rental suits. Amanda suppressed a shudder. "That won't be necessary. But every man needs a quality suit in his closet."

"Fine," Mike said. "I'll buy one and hang it up in there right away."

"You have to *wear* it. Besides, Channel Six News is footing the bill for this, remember?" Gently, she steered him closer to the rack of muted-color suits. "*You're* not buying anything today."

He stopped dead in front of a display of cuff links. "You think I can't afford a suit?"

Uh-oh. "That's not what I said. It's just that—"

"You think I can't afford a suit," Mike repeated. He faced her, intractable in his conviction—and obviously hurt by it, too. "I'll have you know, lady, that

I have enough money for everything I need. I just don't *need* one of these damned suits."

His voice had turned quiet, but there was no mistaking the heat behind it. Evidently, it radiated all the way to the card game in progress, because one of the camera guys nudged a sound man and nodded toward the cuff-link display where Amanda and her life coachee were having their stalemate.

Somehow she had to defuse Mike before he created a news story of the type Amanda *didn't* want associated with Aspirations, Inc.

She tried another tactic. "I'm sure you can," Amanda said. "And once we're done here, we'll go over your résumé together, I'll line up some job interviews, and you'll find a position that will let you buy even more of everything you need."

He glared at her. "I don't need your help getting a job."

"But that's what I'm here for. It's part of what you won. A whole-life makeover, complete with evaluations and coaching in the areas of career, appearance, fitness, relationships, spirituality, emotional health—"

"Yada, yada, yada. I don't need a suit for any of that stuff."

"Yes, you do."

"No, I don't."

"We," Amanda reminded him through gritted teeth, with a quick glance toward the Channel Six News crew, "have a deal. Remember? Two days of your full cooperation."

If possible, Mike looked even more disgruntled than before. But Amanda wasn't backing down. She came toe-to-toe with him and told herself that she wasn't at all affected by his nearness. All those theories about arguing warming up the same physical pathways that led to sexual arousal were just a bunch of hooey . . . weren't they? Sure.

"Now," she said, "either you get into one of these suits and do your best male-model imitation for the cameras . . . or we have another go-round at the emotional-attitudes questionnaire."

"*Aaack!* Not the questionnaire again." He adopted a horror-struck expression. "Anything but that!"

Amanda stifled a grin. "I mean business, buster." She selected a suit from the rack and shoved it into Mike's arms, noticing as she did that he winced again, as though the contact hurt him. Curious. But she couldn't afford to be overly sympathetic and blow her take-charge attitude now. "The fitting rooms are over there. Move it."

Mike scratched his head. "Geez, Amanda. I don't think—"

"*Now.*"

His smile made a lie of all his bad attitude from before. With a wink, Mike leaned closer, clutching the suit against his chest. "I love it when you get tough with me," he whispered. "You are one sexy lady."

She refused to blush. Refused, refused, refused.

What were the odds *that* would work?

"Distraction won't work with me," Amanda said.

Mike paused. Looked her up and down in a way that suggested he found her *very* distracting already. Smiled still wider. "Oh, yes. It will."

She crossed her arms and steeled herself against his improbable, scraggly-bearded charm. "You have till a count of three to get in that fitting room, get naked—"

"Have I told you how much I love this take-charge thing you've got going? It's really hot."

"—and get out here in that suit. One, two . . ."

"Okay, okay. I'm going." Halfway there, Mike stopped again. "But only on one condition. . . ."

"This is ridiculous, Mike," Amanda said a short while later. She stood in the middle of a cramped fitting room, staring in disbelief at her reflection in the mirror—and at the clothes she had on. Exactly *how* had Mike talked her into this again? "I'm not coming out there. Period."

"Awww, come on," came Mike's deep, rough voice from outside the fitting-room door. It sounded almost as though he were crooning to her, encouraging her, in that slow, sexy way he had, to do what he wanted. "Show us how you look. Me and the guys . . . we won't bite."

"Much!" yelled one of the cameramen.

"Rrrrruff!" yelped another.

Leave it to Evan to assign her a mostly male TV crew, Amanda groused. Somehow, while she'd been in the Robinson's-May fitting room, struggling to fulfill Mike's "one condition" of trying on appropriate suits, Mike had managed to bond with every last camera-toting, microphone-wielding one of them. By now, all of their combined masculine sympathies were firmly welded on the side of Mike—and Levi's Forever. Any minute, Amanda half-expected a full-scale, anti-wow-wardrobe protest.

"I've got *my* suit on," Mike coaxed from the other side of the door. Beneath it, a glimpse of his chalk-striped trouser legs—and the one-hundred-percent-Mike sweat socks beneath them—confirmed it. "And I already did my bit for the cameras, too. Now it's your turn."

Amanda sighed. "This is ridiculous," she hedged. "And unnecessary. If you'd just choose one of those suits I selected, we could get out of here and get on with the more important business of résumé writing."

There was a long, silent pause. Then: "Are you saying this *wow* wardrobe thing isn't important? Because if it isn't—"

"No!" she assured him hastily. "It's just that—"

"Come out, come out, come out," chanted the Channel Six crew. The sound floated down the short corridor that separated the fitting rooms from the rest of the department store, warning in its increasing volume. "Come out, *come out!*"

Feeling increasingly nervous—and more than a little disheveled—Amanda eyeballed her reflection again. She grabbed a handful of fabric and yanked it over her chest.

"This wool chafes," she complained. *Summer weight, my ass.* "It's uncomfortable."

Mike snickered.

"And the fit is all wrong," she went on. "The pants bunch up here." Even though he couldn't see her, Amanda hefted a swath of wool around her hips, frowning critically. "And the top hangs open."

"Sounds sexy."

"Hmmph. What *isn't* sexy to you?"

"Snake's mom," Mike replied matter-of-factly. "Too much lipstick, fake beachball-sized tits, perfume that makes a guy's eyes water, Janet Reno, big granny underwear, Eleanor Roosevelt . . ."

Amanda listened in astonishment. He sounded as though he had quite a few at the ready.

"Strip solitaire, tube tops worn by your single-again aunt, Queen Elizabeth, white pantyhose—unless worn with garter belts by hot, friendly nurses, of course—Dr. Ruth, parkas, orthopedic shoes . . ."

"Mike—"

"Expired condoms, women who sleep with their

cats, cats who hawk up fur balls into your shoes while
you're getting it on, socks in bed . . ."

"Okay, uncle!" Amanda cried. "I give up. You win.
I'm coming out."

"I thought so."

With a tremor of trepidation, Amanda drew in a
breath and opened the fitting-room door. Mike
stepped back to give her room, a "gotcha" smile
fixed on his face.

At her appearance, though, his smile stiffened.
Then it vanished altogether. His mouth dropped
open, and his dark-eyed gaze whipped from her top
to her bottom and then to her top again, taking in
the outfit he'd hand-selected for her to wear for her
comeuppance.

"Come out, come out!" chanted the crew in the
distance.

Resigned to her fate and determined to be a good
sport, Amanda headed toward them.

Mike stopped her. Frowned. "You're not going out
there like that."

"Why not?" Not that she really wanted to, but come
on—he wasn't even making sense. Maybe she looked
a little ridiculous, Amanda thought, but she didn't
look *that* bad. Not bad enough to cause the kind of
knocked-over-with-a-feather expression Mike had on.
"A deal's a deal. You promised to cooperate, and I
promised to wear this for at least one shot. So—"

"No, I mean you *really* aren't going out there like
that."

"What are you talking about? It's—"

"Uh-uh." Firmly, Mike grabbed her shoulders and
walked her backwards.

Amanda felt them brush past the open fitting-room
door and felt the flimsy partition wall shudder
beneath her back as Mike pressed her against it. The

vibration shimmied between her shoulder blades and made her hold on to his chalk-gray lapels for balance.

At the motion, for the first time she noticed his suit. She smiled, pleased with her choice. "Hey, you look pretty good. I'm not sure gray is the right color for you, but—"

"Shhh," Mike said inexplicably. Then, with a wild, intent gleam in his eyes and an expression of utter absorption, he wrapped his hands around Amanda's suit jacket lapels and levered himself closer, joining her against the wall. His gaze swept over her outfit once more, then came to rest on her lips. "You look . . . amazing."

"Right. In a man's suit." Amanda gestured toward the clothes Mike had chosen for her—as a joke, she'd assumed. As a taste of her own scratchy, probably chafes, definitely-not-comfy-Levi's medicine. "A suit that's too big, gapes open—"

"In all the right places." His grin turned downright wolfish.

"—is impossibly itchy, and swishes around my ankles like fur on a sheepdog." She raised her bare foot and demonstrated the droopy effect. "You can't be serious, if you—"

"Shhh. Come on, now," Mike said, shutting the fitting-room door with a backward kick. "A first kiss is a pretty big deal. You don't want to talk your way through it."

"Talk?"

He shook his head. "Kiss."

She boggled. *A kiss?* With him? He couldn't be serious! It was wrong. Out of the question. A terrible idea, although under the circumstances Amanda couldn't quite make herself remember why. Her brain had turned to mush somewhere between opening the fitting-room door and finding herself squashed against the wall with a sexy, suit-and-sweat-socks-wearing macho man, and the most she could manage was a frown of confusion.

"No," she said, surprising herself. Evidently, at least two percent of her—approximately—had her career's best interests at heart. Amanda shook her head. "No kiss. I'm not kissing you."

"You're right," Mike said, tugging her still closer with an easy gesture that made her back arch away from the wall. His expression said he knew something she didn't know . . . and he was about to share it. "*I'm* kissing *you*."

And then he did.

No kiss, Amanda tried to say again, knowing it was a bad idea, a colossally bad idea, ranking right up there with spray-on hair in a can, pseudo-chocolate-covered diet bars, platform tennis shoes, and unlimited instant store credit, but all that emerged was *"Mmmph."*

"Mmmmm," he moaned in reply, the sound a sexy rumble of appreciation and approval and anticipation of more to come. With a gesture as natural as breathing, he released her lapels to thrust his hands in her hair. His fingers twined in the strands, then his palms flattened slightly to tilt her head at a stronger angle.

His lips touched hers once, twice, tenderly, but with none of the awkward tentativeness that usually characterized first kisses. It was as though Mike had spent the entire morning contemplating exactly the right way to do *this* and had now chosen to revel, absolutely, in the pursuit of his long-awaited pleasure.

Amanda's initial reluctance was whisked away, chased by surprise and an unexpected craving to know, exactly, what this man's mouth would feel like against hers for a third time. Reality proved hot and breath-stealing, filled with the firm texture of masculine lips, deft angles, warm breath, and explorations she opened her mouth eagerly to allow.

His next moan passed over her lips, vibrated its way to all the nerve endings in her face and neck and arms. Her skin warmed. Her breath quickened. Her fingers tingled. She curled them more firmly into Mike's shoulders—when had she wrapped her arms around him, anyway?—to relieve the pressure, and experimentally flicked her tongue over the fullness of his lower lip.

Instantly, gratifyingly, Mike responded. His mouth opened to welcome her, and before she knew what to expect, Amanda felt herself swept away beneath a new deluge of sensory details. The hot, slick, vaguely minty taste of him. The tease of his beard (which she suddenly hated just a little less) prickly soft against her skin. The new-suit-mingled-with-Safeguard smell of him. The forbidden press of his body against hers, sandwiching her against the wall while his hands ran lightly along the length of her suit. Avidly, expertly, Mike somehow knew which curves were hers and which were so-called summer-weight wool.

Geez, but it was hot. Hot and dizzying and fabulous, and it all happened just fast enough that Amanda hardly had time to think and could only let herself feel and gasp and aggressively press forward, a woman of need and want.

Lowering her hands to splay them over Mike's chest, it suddenly seemed as though she'd needed to feel the solid wall of his chest beneath her palms for a very long time. Grinding her hips upward to deliver herself into his ready grasp, it all at once felt as though something important had been discovered ... and yet still remained partly buried.

Striving, *wanting*, Amanda gave herself to kissing Mike with a passion she'd have sworn was reserved for half-priced shoe sales and that ever-elusive perfect lipstick color. And he returned that passion, magnified somehow, until she felt as though their cramped fitting room could hardly contain it.

Unknowable minutes later found Mike's suit half-opened and rumpled from collar to pants legs. Amanda's suit looked much the same, gaping more than ever before and exposing a slice of bare skin and cleavage that Mike wasted no time in admiring. Breathing heavily, she hitched her too-big pants back onto her hips, where they belonged, and prepared, businesslike, to be ravished still further.

Hey, they'd found a bit of off-camera privacy, and Amanda could almost hear Mel's voice in her head, urging her to go for it. She had to agree. This hands-on approach could get to be fun. So long as no one found out.

"You really know how to make a guy feel like a hero for making the first move," Mike said, his uneven breathing matching her own. Resting his hands on the fitting-room walls beside her head, he grinned down at her, looking big and happy and remarkably cocky. "I love the way you kiss."

"I love the way you issue an invitation."

"Couldn't help it." He touched a finger to her lapel, then slid it inside to swiftly touch the skin beneath. "I've never seen a woman look more feminine, more sexy, than you do in this suit. There's no way in hell those guys outside are getting an eyeful of this."

"Ah-hah!" *So that's what the sudden backing-into-the-wall routine had been all about. Lust overload.* And after only one look. The very idea made Amanda want to strut around, feeling feminine and powerful. "The suit, huh? Go figure."

"Yeah. Go figure." Mike ducked his head and rubbed the back of his neck. "I sure didn't see that one coming."

Suddenly, he looked as perplexed as she *ought* to

have felt. But now that she'd finally figured out what had motivated him, Amanda felt about a zillion times more relaxed. She liked things to make sense. Now Mike did.

"Anyway," he continued, not looking at her, "I uh, gotta go."

He moved to open the fitting-room door. Amanda gawked at him. "What? *Now?*" *In the midst of the kissing, the touching, the getting-to-know-you talking?*

"Yeah. I'll, uh, meet up with you later for the résumé stuff." He glanced at his watch. "Say, one o'clock?"

Amanda nodded, nonplussed by his sudden change in plans but unwilling to seem bothered by his sudden retreat.

"In the meantime, just buy whatever you think would look good on me," Mike continued, clearly impatient to leave. "I think you have a pretty good idea what size."

He winked. Ducked out of the fitting room. Stuck his head back in a second later, and by now that grin of his was back in full force. "Oh, and uh, before I go. That kiss was really something. I'd say you just earned yourself another two days worth of make-overing."

"Two weeks," Amanda bargained automatically. She needed a total of at least four to effect the "new-millennium man" changes she had in mind for Mike.

"One week," he countered, his grin widening. "So long as it doesn't include any more mud masques."

"It's a deal."

Then, before she could say so much as, "Thanks for the mind-blowing kiss," Mike had opened the door and escaped into the hallway. The distant strains of the camera and sound crews' continuing "Come out, come out" chant reached her again, effectively hurling Amanda back into her usual life.

The one that *didn't* typically feature men backing her into a corner and kissing her silly.

"But what about the . . . Oh, what's the use?" Feeling ridiculous, Amanda lowered the arm she'd raised to call Mike back and sank onto the triangular seat wedged into a corner of the fitting room. She shook her head.

Scratch that "things had started to make sense" idea, she told herself. There was no way Mike Cavaco would *ever* make sense to her. Now she was sure of it.

But at least now she had another week to try and figure him out.

Twenty minutes later, Mike was waiting outside the department store when Amanda and the Channel Six News crew exited Robinson's-May, several shopping bags in tow. As they passed, he ducked behind a bushy mall plant, watching between the leaves as his life coach and her TV-happy entourage made their way to the escalators and downstairs to the exits.

Whew. The coast was clear. Hardly able to believe what he was doing, Mike grabbed his wallet and headed back into the department store with just one thing on his mind.

He'd be damned if he'd leave without that lucky gray suit.

Chapter Seven

Aspirations, Inc. (Personal Life Coaching and Career Planning, read the fine print on the sign) was wedged into the corner of a stucco-and-archway office complex in the East Valley, not far from Arizona State University. In appearance and function it was much farther away—minus one nose ring, two tattoos, and several pierced-tongue barbells—from the just-starting-out college student mind-set.

Pushing open the etched glass doors of the entrance on Tuesday afternoon, Mike was greeted with the touchy-feely New Age ambience of sitar music. He entered despite that fact and found himself in a small reception area decorated in cotton-candy colors with hints of dark blue and green, with potted plants on every horizontal surface.

The fragrances of cinnamon and dried flowers hung in the air, leaving a subtly soothing impression. Ever-present Arizona sunlight streamed across the carpet from a series of squat rectangular windows placed a few inches from the ceiling, and spotlights illuminated several framed motivational prints on the walls.

"Don't wait for your ship to come in," read one. "Swim out to it." Below its Opportunity caption, a sailboat made its way toward a vivid orange sunset. "Perseverance," read the print beside it, illustrated with a drop of water trembling at the edge of a Technicolor green leaf. "Sometimes success is just a matter of hanging on."

Touching a fingertip to the first print, Mike smiled, and an unfamiliar mushy feeling welled up inside him. It was just like Amanda, he thought, to have hung these here, where new clients would see them and be inspired. And it was just like her to have chosen these particular motivational prints, too. Like them, Amanda was both vibrant *and* more thought-provoking than he'd expected.

He'd thought he'd had her nailed before. A nice woman, vaguely out of her depth with the Channel Six Life Coach Lotto but trying hard, with a sort of plain-vanilla outlook on life and a streak of incurable bossiness.

Now, after the lucky suit ambush at the department store, Mike was having second thoughts about his assumptions about Amanda. In that suit, she'd seemed suddenly sex kittenish, in a completely unlikely way that had somehow blown all the commonsense circuits in his brain and sent him straight into that fitting room with her.

And then, to have found himself almost unable to stop kissing her—Well, it had spooked the hell out of him.

Amanda wasn't even his type. She looked like a glossed-over midwestern farm girl, complete with long dusky hair, sky-blue eyes, and a dusting of freckles over her nose. She talked like a cross between Goody Two Shoes and a sultry midnight radio DJ,

her puritanical take on things weirdly at odds with
her husky, ultrafeminine delivery. She smiled when
she saw him, bossed him around, wouldn't take no
for an answer, and obviously had an undeniable Jones
for constant bet making, judging by all the deals
they'd struck since yesterday.

No, she wasn't his type at all.

Typically, Mike liked his women long, leggy, and
willing to keep quiet during a football game on TV.
And he'd found plenty who'd fit the bill, too. At least
he had before the April Fools' Day massacre had
happened at work. With Amanda, though, he had a
feeling nothing short of full disclosure and intimate
conversation would work, whether the Cardinals were
getting their asses whupped in a crucial game or not.
She'd be a handful, all right.

Which didn't matter to him at all, Mike reminded
himself sternly. He wasn't dating Amanda. He didn't
intend to, either. At least not beyond the initial
get-his-buddies-off-his-back-makeover-cover-up date,
anyway.

Which, if he was going to have any hope of securing
it, meant that he'd better get on with his meeting
with Amanda. Striding forward, Mike headed for the
receptionist's desk at the far end of the room. Halfway
there the lights went out.

He stopped where he was, temporarily disoriented.

"Not again!" cried a feminine voice—the receptionist's, he guessed, judging by how near it sounded.
Something bumped against a hard surface, a drawer
slid open, and then a flashlight beam swept over the
room, bouncing from wall to wall. It landed to Mike's
left, illuminating a short carpeted passageway.

As though on cue, Amanda appeared within the
light. Still in her girly dress but minus her shoes and
clipboard, she looked harried. Harried and annoyed.

"Don't worry, Trish," she told the receptionist.

"It's probably just the circuit breakers again. I'll call up Louie in the building's maintenance office." She headed toward the front desk, calling over her shoulder, "Just stay where you are, Mr. Waring. I'll have this sorted out in a jiffy."

"I hope so," came a weak masculine reply.

Just as Amanda's hand hovered over the telephone, the receptionist, Trish, spoke again. "Don't bother. Louie won't deal with our office anymore."

"Oh, geez." Amanda stopped, letting her hand fall to her side. "The maintenance co-op payment again?"

"Bingo."

"Damn! I thought I mailed it already!"

"Guess not," Trish said. She didn't sound surprised. "And Louie keeps pretty close tabs on who's current for maintenance, too."

"Closer tabs than I keep, obviously." Muttering to herself, Amanda turned and headed back down the hallway. "Just keep trying, Mr. Waring," she said. "I'll be right with you."

This had the feeling of a well-practiced scenario. Still, Mike couldn't let himself stand by while there might be something he could do to help. "If you'll just point me in the direction of that circuit box," he told Trish, "I'll see what I can do."

She arced the flashlight beam over him. Snapped her gum. Shook her head. "And here I thought you were one of those unlikely big-but-scared types, spooked by the dark. Welcome to Aspirations, Inc. I wondered when you'd make your presence known. Or do you typically lurk around, spying on women from the shadows?"

"Typically, I don't have to." Squinting against the flashlight beam's relentless progress over his body and up to his face, Mike grinned. "But I do some of

my best work in the dark. If you know what I mean."
He waggled his eyebrows teasingly.

Trish snorted. "Casanova complex, huh?" She nodded knowingly and gestured toward one of the chairs.
"Amanda will straighten you out. Have a seat."

"I'm kidding." But he'd come across her no-nonsense type before. It didn't take a genius to know he had to give as good as he got. "But I've got good connections at Smoker's Anonymous and an excellent cheaper-than-dirt source for that Nicorette gum you're chomping if you'll show me to that circuit box so I can help out here."

She quit chewing and appeared to size him up. Then Trish fiddled with the flashlight, pushed part of it upward, and set it on the desktop. In the glow from its now-lanternlike light, he got his first good glimpse of his sparring partner—a thirty-something redhead with short hair, flashy clothes, and a broad lipsticked smile.

"That's not necessary," she said. "This happens all the time, and there's nothing you or anybody else can do about it. It's a delegation problem on behalf of my boss."

Amanda having trouble telling people what to do? Impossible, Mike decided. He must have misunderstood her. "Delegation problem. Meaning . . . ?"

Trish jerked her thumb backward, toward the passageway where Amanda had disappeared. "Meaning, Amanda ought to delegate half the stuff she forgets to do to *me*, and refuses to. She's got to take care of every last thing herself. By now, for instance, she'll have sweet-talked Louie into helping us out. *Gratis*, at least for the time being. Amanda's a whiz at persuading people to do what she wants."

"You don't have to tell me," Mike agreed. *I'm the guy who wound up wearing pink clothes, being stripped of both his sense of beauty-treatment-free dignity and his underwear, and being sized up for future makeover night-mares, all at Amanda Connor's insistence.* "I've been on the receiving end."

"Join the club, dreamboat." Trish popped her gum again, then smiled. Mike had the feeling she'd gone a few rounds with Amanda, herself. "Anyway, Louie doesn't stand a chance. Soon as the boss gets him on the phone, he caves, no matter how many times this happens. Any minute now, we'll find out. . . ."

One of the lights on the fancy phone system at Trish's elbow blinked out. A few minutes later, the receptionist raised her watch and counted. "Four, three, two. . . ."

The overhead lights came on, blinding Mike with their sudden intensity.

"Problem solved," Amanda said, striding back into the room with a self-satisfied expression. "I forgot to tell you, Trish, about my next appointment. As soon as I finish up with Mr. Waring, I'll—" She stopped, seeing Mike for the first time. "Oh. You're already here."

And she didn't look too thrilled about it, either, Mike noted. The prick to his pride made his voice a little rougher than usual when he replied.

"Sorry, did I interrupt your wheeling-and-dealing hour?" he asked, gazing pointedly at the newly functioning lights. "I know you drive a hard bargain, but I hope Louie didn't have to agree to a honey-whatchamacallit treatment, too."

"Of course he didn't." Amanda drew herself up—less loftily than usual, thanks to her missing high heels—and looked wounded, wounded enough to make him ashamed of having risen to her bait. "Where Louie is concerned, a sea-salt scrub would be a lot more effective."

"Where you're concerned," Mike said, still feeling the sting of her less-than-happy-to-see-him greeting, "paying for maintenance service on time would be a lot more effective, I'll bet."

"For your information, this was a temporary glitch. I have no trouble at all making ends meet."

"Sure." He swerved his gaze to hers and held it. "Sort of like me, huh?"

The way Amanda had doubted his ability to pay for a damned suit at the department store still rankled, and Mike wanted her to know it. Just because he didn't wear designer shoes and a flashy gold watch didn't mean he couldn't take care of himself—and the people who were depending on him.

"No, not like you at all," Amanda shot back. "*I* happen to be meaningfully employed."

Ouch.

Dismissively, she turned to Trish. "I'll be finished with Mr. Waring in a few minutes. Please add Mr. Cavaco here to the schedule—and book two additional daily appointments for him for the next three weeks."

Without a backward glance, she strode down the passageway again. In the distance, he heard the muted sounds of Amanda speaking with her client, then their conversation was drowned out by the thunk of Trish's appointment book hitting the desk.

"Two appointments a day, huh?" she said as she turned the pages, asking him for the correct spelling of his name and then writing in twice-daily entries. "Wow. You must *really* need help."

Mike quit staring after Amanda and forced himself to focus on the receptionist's chatter. "Yeah, maybe I do. She thinks I'm her Life Coach Lotto winner."

"You're not?" Scribble, scribble. "I saw on the news you had the winning ticket." She tilted her head upward, scrutinizing him. "Yep. Tall, dark, and yummy. In a scruffy sort of way, that is. You're the winning-ticket man, all right."

"Somebody left it in my cab by mistake. I was trying to return it. For some reason, I—"

"Just couldn't say no to Amanda?" With a shake of her head, Trish wrote in a few more appointments. "Don't worry. We've all been there. You'll get used to it."

"Like hell I will," he protested, but the receptionist only chuckled and went on writing.

Left to cool his heels until his unwanted life coach found room in her busy afternoon for him, Mike knuckled up the brim of his Diamondbacks cap and scratched his head, unreasonably needled by Amanda's dismissal of him. And puzzled by his quick-and-dirty response to her earlier, too.

It wasn't like him to be so quick off the cuff with a cutting remark. But then, times had been tough lately, what with his trouble finding spots for his April Fools' Day crew and this unexpected—not to mention downright discombobulating—makeover thing. And Amanda *had* provoked him first. Fighting back was a time-honored male instinct.

Hell, he figured it probably had begun way back when the first caveman accidentally bumped into another caveman. Instead of both caveguys apologizing—the way their nearby cavegirlfriends undoubtedly urged—they'd progressed from "Oh, yeah? Why don't you watch where *you're* going?" all the way to beating the mastodon-flavored stuffing out of each other. It was the way of men. You didn't back down. You didn't take advice. And you didn't show weakness, no matter what.

Those were values Mike took seriously. But on the other hand, guy-style logical thinking and masculine codes of honor didn't necessarily mean squat to the average "tell me how you *feel* about this" woman. Chances were good Amanda didn't have the first idea what she'd done to provoke him.

The truth of the realization hit him all at once. To hell with waiting obediently in the reception area like some dumb puppy on a leash, Mike decided. The thing to do was go enlighten Amanda. *Right now.*

"Mike, I can't talk with you right now," Amanda said, feeling her neck cramp as she craned her head to look up at him. From her lotus-position spot on her office floor she could just barely glimpse the doorway where he'd poked his big shaggy head inside. "I'm busy."

"You don't look busy." He obviously wasn't going to go away quietly, as she'd hoped. "You're just sitting there on the floor. Hey, Mr. Waring."

Both men nodded at each other. "Hey," said her client, opening his eyes and temporarily abandoning all the hard work they'd achieved so far during this meditation-focused session. "How's it hanging?"

Amanda boggled. Thin, reserved, stressed-out plastics-company bookkeeper Mr. Waring coming out with something like "How's it hanging?" What the heck was this *power* Mike had over people that made them abandon their perfectly good, ordinary personalities—not to mention their anti-client-kissing policies—and come over to the dark side?

"Low enough to keep my boys cool and happy," Mike answered, coming all the way into the room.

Both men guffawed. Amanda rolled her eyes.

"You can't stay here," she told Mike, leveling him a no-nonsense look. "There are plenty of seats in the reception area. I'll be with you in a few minutes."

"That's quite all right, Ms. Connor," Mr. Waring interrupted, rising from the yoga-style sticky mat adjacent to hers on the floor. His comb-over flopped back and forth as he moved. "I'm afraid I'm a lost cause with this meditation practice, anyway."

"No! Of course you aren't a lost cause," Amanda reassured him. Originally, Mr. Waring had come to her for help securing the promotion he hoped for, but after a series of meetings, greater aspirations had emerged, personal serenity among them. All in all, she felt quite proud of the progress they'd made. "Meditation doesn't come easily to all people, it's true. But with your stress levels, I really believe you can benefit from this."

"Thanks, but . . ." Mr. Waring winced as he adjusted his eyeglasses, fogged up from the deep-breathing techniques she'd been showing him. "I'm finding it very hard to focus today. Perhaps it's the tax forms for the new Plastics-doh shipment that are bothering me, but . . ."

He trailed off, with several more comments about work stress and his supposed inability to meditate. Frustrated, Amanda sent a nanosecond's worth of *Now look what you've done* in Mike's direction.

He only gave her a placid look and sat down in the nearest chair, his bent knee propped on his leg and his hands folded over his flat, T-shirt-covered midsection. He'd chosen, Amanda noticed, *her* chair. It felt as though he'd staked a claim on her, in some prehistoric, holdover way, and her feelings tumbled all over themselves in reaction to it. She didn't know whether to be amused or annoyed, flattered or angry.

Settling for all four at once—hey, she was a new-millennium, multitasking woman, wasn't she?—Amanda marched to her desk and grabbed Mike's bicep. "Don't worry, Mr. Waring," she said as she hauled Mike to his feet and started hustling him toward the door. "As soon as I get Mr. Cavaco here settled, then we'll sit back down, focus on your mantra, and everything will be fine. You'll see."

"I don't know . . ."

"Trust me." Amanda grimaced and put both hands

on Mike's broad-muscled back, intending to push him forcibly out the office door if necessary. Beneath her palms, she felt sudden resistance.

"Don't do it, Waring," Mike urged. "It's a trap. I trusted her and wound up with no underwear, covered in honey, with three dozen screaming women lining up to look at my knees."

Mr. Waring's mouth dropped open. Amanda gave an extra-hard shove.

Not budging, Mike looked over his shoulder at her. "You should be grateful I didn't warn him about that touchy-feely questionnaire of yours."

"Q—questionnaire?" Mr. Waring gulped.

"Or that little wagering problem you've got going. You know, Gambler's Anonymous probably has a chapter in Phoenix. You could—"

Amanda quit pushing. He was too much.

"You're like a child, you know that?" Mike turned to face her, his eyes sparkling, but she refused to be wooed. "You just can't stand it when you're not the center of attention."

"Sure I can. You're the one who turned the spotlight on me, trying to make me leave," he replied, exasperatingly. With an expansive gesture, he motioned toward the sticky mats on the floor and nodded encouragingly to Mr. Waring. "I'll be perfectly happy to wait on the sidelines while you two finish your meditation."

She folded her arms. "That's impossible."

"No, it's not."

"I'd prefer you leave."

"If you're such a pro at this stuff, what's wrong with my watching? You'll be too focused to be disturbed, and maybe I'll discover a deep-seated interest myself. I might even become, you know, enlightened. Or something."

Amanda cocked her head and looked at him skeptically. She wasn't buying this, of course. But on the other hand, a guy like Mike probably had a lot invested in not embracing change. If this whole macho routine was only a front—and come on, it *had* to be, to some extent—maybe this would be a way to drag Mike painlessly out of his comfort zone. A life coach had to be willing to adapt her techniques to suit her clients.

Especially if she hoped to win a recurring spot on the Channel Six nightly news by turning one Life Coach Lotto–winning ordinary guy into a well-rounded, perfectly balanced example of modern manhood—also known as the challenge of a lifetime.

Still: "You'll disturb Mr. Waring."

She looked to her client for confirmation. Unfortunately, he'd adopted Mike's wide-legged, tough-guy stance and was staring at him as though he planned to memorize every word that came out of his mouth. With Mr. Waring's talent for detail, he just might accomplish it, too.

"Nah," Mr. Waring said. He hooked a thumb in his belt loop, à la Mike, although the gesture lacked some of its élan when paired with sharply creased permanent-press pants. "He won't bug me."

Victorious, Mike raised his eyebrows at Amanda. "See?"

"No," she insisted.

He sighed. "I'll bet you ten bucks you can't meditate with me in the room."

"Twenty."

"Fifteen."

"You're on!" Amanda cried. "Watch out, buster."

Ohmigod. What had she just done? Had Mike actually goaded her into *betting* on meditation practice? Covering her face with her hands, Amanda took a few deep breaths and then plopped, barefoot, onto her sticky mat. What was done was done. There was no way she was quitting now.

Amanda Connor was not a quitter.

She rearranged her dress to cover her knees, then repeated her earlier instructions to Mr. Waring, who lowered himself onto the mat beside her. Assuming their cross-legged positions, they both closed their eyes and began to meditate.

Just as she let her eyes drift shut, an image of the way Mike had looked a few seconds earlier floated across her consciousness. All rugged angles and impervious self-confidence, he'd been leaning against the office doorjamb, watching, waiting, planning another kiss, one just like the one they'd shared before. *Mmmmmm* . . .

Yikes. *That* wasn't part of the Sanskrit phrase she used for meditation practice! Breathing in again, Amanda gently turned her focus toward her mantra and started over.

"I just realized what the problem is," Mike interrupted.

Her budding serenity scattered, just like anti-kissing self-control in the face of an appealing man, an empty dressing room, and an unexpected off-camera opportunity.

She murmured a request for quiet.

"What mantra is Waring using?" he insisted, his now-lowered voice closer, as though he'd moved beside her.

She cracked open one eye. He *had* moved beside her. Near enough to set her sense of professionalism ajangle. "What mantra?" she repeated.

"Yes, what mantra." Mike's mouth straightened, and he angled his head toward her. "And don't look at me like that, either. I didn't just crawl out from under a rock, you know. I understand what a mantra is. Even taxi drivers can comprehend meditation techniques."

Before she could reply, Mr. Waring did. "My mantra is *Om Namah Shiviah*. It means 'honor the self' in Sanskrit."

"No wonder!" Mike pushed himself upward and strode toward Mr. Waring. He hunkered down in front of him. "That's a noble sentiment and everything, but I'm not surprised you can't focus on it for more than, oh, five seconds at a time. What you need is—"

"Mike! That's enough," Amanda said sternly. "Mr. Waring, ignore him. He doesn't know what he's talking about."

Her client looked from her to a self-assured-seeming Mike and then back again. He frowned.

So did Amanda.

"Okay, okay." Holding up both hands, Mike stood again. "You don't want my help. I'll butt out."

"Thank you."

Mr. Waring drooped, seeming dejected. Determined to bolster him with the proven techniques she'd used time and again with her clients, Amanda gently touched his shoulder. "You can do this. I believe in you."

"I'll try." He straightened his back and arranged his hands, index fingers and thumbs touching, atop his knees.

"Good," Amanda murmured. "Now, just let go."

"And," Mike advised, "picture a naked woman."

With a flash of his good-natured smile, he ducked out of the office at last, leaving her alone with her client. Tamping down her aggravation at Mike's misinformed guidance, Amanda glanced at Mr. Waring to make sure he hadn't been disturbed.

Oddly enough, he looked absolutely serene.

In fact, in all the weeks she'd been working with him, she'd never seen a more beatific smile on his face.

Chapter Eight

Mike was flipping through a woman's magazine, morosely eyeballing articles like "Are Your Thighs a Turnoff?" and "The New Love Games: Fifty Ways to Make Your Next Date Sizzle" when Amanda finally saw fit to sashay her way into the reception area and rescue him from the pathetic dearth of useful reading material. With his brain still buzzing with numbers thirty-four and sixteen, he watched her say good-bye to Waring.

On his way out, the guy gave Mike a just-us-guys grin and a two-thumbs-up salute. Evidently, taxi-driver mantras worked just fine with *some* people. After all, the right picture *was* worth a thousand words.

Amanda had a brief, heads-down conversation with Trish, the receptionist, then took a client's phone call. Five minutes later, she ushered Mike into her office and shut the door behind them both.

He turned to face her, wanting to clear the air between them before their scheduled résumé-writing session began. "Look, about the way I snapped at you before," he began, rubbing the back of his neck with his hand. "I didn't mean to hurt your feelings or anything—"

"It's over with. Forget about it."

She caught his disbelieving look.

"Really," Amanda said. "We both said things we didn't mean. Part of the growth you'll experience as an Aspirations, Inc., client is due to letting go of the past. Just consider this an example of that practice."

Could it *be* that easy? In his experience with women, probably not. But Mike was willing to try.

He shrugged and crossed the room, his workout-stiffened muscles protesting each movement. *Damn that Jake and his get-ready-for-Amanda's-fitness-tests workout routine.* At this rate, he'd be ready to cry uncle at the first bicep curl she suggested. It was embarrassing. But proving her wrong about his supposed lack of fitness was more important than mere physical comfort, and besides, by tomorrow the soreness would probably be gone, right?

Trying not to wince, Mike eased into the nearest chair and made himself comfortable for whatever résumé-writing tortures Amanda had in mind. He didn't know how he was going to satisfy her in that department, especially without spilling the beans about the "Incident." There was no way in hell he was allowing his personal failings to wind up on TV for the amusement of millions. But now that he'd agreed to help her, he wasn't about to cut her loose. Not so long as Amanda still needed him.

"Before we get started on anything else and before the Channel Six crew gets here"—she stopped beside him, digging into the handbag she'd grabbed from atop her desk—"I owe you this."

Mike frowned at the fifteen dollars being thrust in front of his nose. He gently pushed the money back toward her. "No, thanks. It was a sucker's bet. I shouldn't have made it."

That seemed to make her even more insistent. "Take it. Go ahead. I lost. I couldn't meditate with you in the room. I was . . . distracted despite my best efforts. I don't know what happened."

"I do," Mike said. "You were thinking about that kiss, the one in the dressing room." Memories of it whisked through his mind, a Technicolor remembrance of a warm, willing Amanda, two pairs of ready hands, and a kiss to end all kisses. "I, uh, guess I ought to apologize for that."

"Hmmm. Apologize, huh?"

"That's what I said."

Slowly, Amanda lowered all the way into his line of vision until she came face-to-face with him. Her formerly rueful, bet-losing expression had changed, he saw. Uh-oh. Mike could feel it coming—a whopper of a chewing out from a woman with something big on her mind.

"You bet you ought to apologize," she said with, to his confusion, the beginnings of a smile on her face. "You ought to apologize for not finishing the job while you had the chance and the privacy to do it."

"Finishing the— Wha—?"

Mike shook his head. He could have sworn Amanda had just admitted—if he wasn't mistaken—to being mad that he *hadn't* done a more thorough job of kissing her earlier. *Nah, that couldn't be it.*

He was still trying to process that decidedly unexpected piece of information when he felt her hands clamp purposefully onto the sides of his face. At the contact, Amanda winced, made a funny face at his beard, and then moved her hands up to his ears instead. Mike couldn't object much when she used them to gently tug him forward, toward the edge of his chair. She was, after all, getting ready to kiss him. Any idiot could tell that much, and Mike didn't consider himself an idiot.

Especially when it came to women.

Especially, strangely enough, when it came to *this* woman.

"Allow me to show you," Amanda murmured, "in contrast to your masculine approach, how a *woman* goes after what she wants." She paused. "First she moves directly toward her target."

Her flowery dress billowed slightly, pushed outward by the movement of her thighs as she came nearer, almost straddling him with her knees on the edge of his office chair.

"Direct," Mike repeated, raising his hands to her hips. Now his grin matched hers. "I like direct. A lot, so far."

"Then she focuses on her target." Her gaze dropped to his mouth and held. She licked her lips, as though she couldn't wait to taste him again. "And thinks about her goal."

He squirmed, his trusty Levi's suddenly failing him in the comfy-fit department. "Focus is good," he managed.

"I think so, too." Speculatively, Amanda looked him over. "You can take notes on all this, if you like."

Her overly innocent expression was distinctly at odds with the sultry squeeze of her thighs against his jeans-clad knees. For the life of him, Mike couldn't figure out why she insisted on talking at such a moment, but he did his best to play along.

"Um, notes," he said, shaking his head. "Maybe later."

"All right. Now, where was I?" She paused, a goddess surveying the mortal she'd selected to grace with her presence.

"Focusing." Would panting destroy his aura of

cool? Mike hoped not, because soon he wouldn't be able to help it. "Goal."

"Ahh, that's right. My goal." Another pause, while she leisurely ran a fingertip over his lower lip. "Next, she allows the anticipation to build," Amanda went on, locking eyes with him. "Because she knows that anything worth having is worth waiting for."

The room whirled, all the furnishings going out of focus as everything lost significance beyond the woman in his arms. He suddenly felt in over his head, or maybe that was head over heels, and the realization should have sparked some reasonable concern in him, Mike realized dimly. Because he'd never fallen this hard, this fast, for any woman. And he had no intentions of doing so now, either.

Whoop, whoop, went the warning sensors in his head, but by now his body was rapidly gaining the upper hand, and Mike ignored them.

"And then," Amanda whispered after a long, excruciatingly anticipation-filled moment, "she makes her move."

And blows his mind, Mike thought silently, crazily, as her mouth met his and their kiss began.

"Mmmmm," he moaned, loosening his grasp on her hips to slide his hands upward, everywhere. She felt soft and wonderful and right, with just enough aggressiveness to take charge and exactly enough cooperative spirit to leave him feeling as though they were in this together.

Together, together. The thought tumbled in his mind, initially alarming but fast growing into something Mike figured he could really get behind. The kiss deepened, as though they'd practiced merging lips and bodies and souls for years and years and were merely refreshing their memories. Panting, Amanda tilted her head and lunged toward him again, this time pinning him against his chair. The rough tweed fabric bit into his back. The womanly, perfectly curved reality of Amanda kissing him awakened his front.

It wasn't enough. Mike wanted more, and he reached for it, bringing Amanda still closer until she *was* straddling his lap now, and as they went on kissing, it occurred to him that they really wouldn't be close enough until they'd shed at least a few kinds of clothing.

He was about to suggest exactly that when he felt Amanda's hands on the bottom hem of his T-shirt. Mike almost pulled back, so uncanny was the synchronicity of his thoughts with her actions. But then Amanda wiggled and tightened her grip, and he forgot what the problem was altogether.

She twisted on his lap and pulled the fabric upward, pausing momentarily to ogle his midsection in a gratifying way that let Mike know her "drop a few pounds" crack at Marvin's yesterday had only been a tease.

On second thought, thank you, Jake, for those million or so crunches. They must have already started working their magic.

With a cute little frown of determination, Amanda wrestled his T-shirt upward and threw it onto the desk behind her. Then she leaned forward, ready to— Mike could only hope—kiss her way over more of him.

Suddenly there was a rapid knock. A jumbled conversation outside followed, then the door burst open beside them. Lights swept over him and Amanda both, and Mike imagined he could hear handheld cameras whirring as they recorded every incriminating moment of their chair-top sprawl.

A sideways look confirmed his worst fears. Naturally, the Channel Six crew had chosen exactly this moment to turn up. The way his month had been going, he should have known this was way too good to last.

Mike wanted to groan. Instead, he looked up at Amanda and thumbed away a pale pink lipstick smudge on her chin, hoping to cheer her up in the face of their combined doom.

"I'll bet," he said in a low voice, "that you can't talk your way out of this one."

Her eyebrow raised. "Double or nothing?"

Mike nodded toward her desk, where the fifteen bucks at stake peeked out from beneath his discarded T-shirt. "Sure. At this point, I can't think why not."

"Okay, then." Determinedly, Amanda straightened on his lap and prepared to confront their reality-TV nemeses. "You're on!"

Helplessly, Mike grinned and shook his head. Those were beginning to be the words he most dreaded hearing from her.

It would have been the same for any sane man.

"*Yoga?*" At the mere mention of the word, Melanie burst out laughing, slowing the stride of the post-work walk she and Amanda were taking through the Arizona Center, an open-air downtown Phoenix shopping mall located near Mel's eclectic CD Swap music shop. "You actually told them that Mike had pulled a muscle practicing a yoga pose in your office . . . and they *bought* it?"

"What can I say?" Amanda shrugged modestly, brushing a lint ball from the T-shirt she'd put on with her track pants and sneakers. "I guess I have a talent for improvisation."

"You?" Mel chortled again. "Honey, you couldn't improvise your way out of a pair of stilettos with a shoehorn. No, the fact that this yoga story went over was sheer luck, believe you me."

"Maybe." Amanda grinned. "But it was all I could

come up with. The sticky mats were right there, and Mike looked reasonably limber—"

"Hubba, hubba."

"—and in the end, the Channel Six News crew thought it made a pretty good story, believe me."

She could still remember the smirks on their faces as she'd recounted to the crew how Mike had pulled a shoulder muscle halfway through the downward-facing dog asana and had required her assistance to massage away the pain. Her story had neatly explained away both Mike's bare-chested condition and her own lap-straddling position, and she'd barely had time to finish it before the camera and sound guys had been off and running, ribbing Mike about his "injury."

"What did Mike have to say about all this?" Mel asked.

"He wasn't thrilled, believe me." Her off-the-cuff alibi had been a hit with everyone except her star client. "As he put it, not only was he now labeled as a guy who did yoga—"

"Wuss material, for sure."

"But—hey! That's what Mike said!" In astonishment, Amanda gawked at Melanie, striding beside her as they rounded the corner of the nearest boutique and started their second lap. "He growled something at me about how I'd branded him with a wuss workout. I can't believe this!"

"Well, it's true. It is a wuss workout."

"It is not. Yoga can be very physically demanding."

"So can straddling hunky new clients in your office, I'll bet."

"Mel!"

With a non-repentant grin, her friend picked up the speed, forcing Amanda to keep pace past the calorific allure of the gourmet coffee shop and bakery. By the time they'd left the dangers of white chocolate macadamia-nut cookies behind, Amanda was out of breath, and Mel was puffing. Literally. Melanie was never far from her Marlboros and refused to quit despite Amanda's best efforts. Today she'd tried hiding the cigarettes underneath her discarded life-coach cap, but Mel had only given her a knowing look and swiped them back.

"I was hardly thinking of Mike as a client when I tackled him like that," Amanda explained primly. The lingering soreness in her inner thighs testified to how rare an experience it had been for her and reminded her of exactly how emboldened, how seductive, and how *alive* her encounter with Mike had made her feel. "I don't know what came over me. There's something about him that's just so . . ."

She sighed, unable to put her feelings into words for possibly the first time in her life. Looking into Mike's eyes today, it had seemed as though she'd known him forever. *Would* know him forever. And in light of that fact, finishing what they'd begun in the Robinson's-May dressing room had felt absolutely right. At least for the moment.

After their close call with the unexpected arrival of the Channel Six crew, though— Well, now Amanda wasn't so sure.

"He's not even my type," she told Mel as they sprinted up the stairs to the Arizona Center's second level. "So far we don't even have much in common."

"Except lust."

"We don't tend to communicate very well."

"Except nonverbally."

"And we live in two different worlds. You know, I'm getting the impression that Mike doesn't even *want* to quit driving that taxi of his. Can you believe that?"

"Sure." Mel took a contemplative drag on her Marlboro, then went on swinging her bent arms in the power-walker's stride they used on their frequent mall hikes. "I can believe it. Look, the explanation for all this is simple, kiddo. It's the lure of the forbidden. You're not supposed to have Mike—"

"He's my client!" Amanda protested. "My most public client ever! Of course I can't 'have' Mike."

"So you want him twice as much. Forbidden fruit syndrome. Remove the mystique and this little fling of yours could be over with before it begins."

Amanda wasn't quite convinced. After all, there was that mysteriously powerful attraction between her and Mike to be considered. Still listening, though, she followed Mel past a shoe store and a kiosk selling buy-it-and-wear-it hair extensions.

"You know, if you want, you can toss him over to me." Her friend threw a wolfish smile over her shoulder. "I'd be glad to take care of Mike for you."

Mel was only kidding. Amanda knew that. Their friendship was too sacrosanct to risk over an obvious gaffe like one of them dating a man the other had kissed. Twice. Open-mouthed. Still, nonserious as Mel's comment had been, it put an unwelcome frown on Amanda's face. Mike with another woman? *Grrr.*

Which was ridiculous, of course. If Mike wasn't right for her, why not let him loose?

Because you want him, that's why, a part of her insisted.

She barely recognized that part of her—the foolish, pie-in-the-sky, love-at-first-sight, true-love-exists romantic part that existed, way down deep, inside her. Until this moment, she'd believed that fanciful, hopeful streak of hers had gotten buried beneath dating one too many guys like the ones Mel and Gemma had dubbed Hoover Lips and Mr. Happy Pants.

Now that it had resurfaced, Amanda knew beyond a doubt the only smart thing to do would be to bury it again. Really deep this time. Where the vulnerability it caused wouldn't touch her.

Somehow, though, she couldn't.

But that didn't mean she had to admit it. "You're my friend, Mel," she joked. "I can't stick you with a guy who thinks shaving is an afterthought and dressing up means throwing on the Levi's with the smallish holes."

"Very magnanimous of you," Mel observed wryly. "In that case, maybe you're stuck. Unless you're a forbidden-fruit woman to him, in which case . . . I dunno. That could complicate things a bit."

Was she Mike's forbidden-fruit woman? *Urgh*. That didn't sound very positive, never mind the fact that *he* was probably her forbidden-fruit man. If clandestine attraction was all that lay between them . . .

"Actually," Amanda admitted, not ready to confront the whole FF question, "there's something else. Something you don't know."

"Oooh, I'm intrigued," Mel said, widening her eyes beneath her rat's-nest, fashionably mussed black hairdo. "You haven't had a secret since you confessed to making your first visit to Madame Roshinka's." She grinned and tossed her Marlboro butt into a nearby ashtray. "I've never seen anyone stammer quite so hard over the words *Brazilian bikini wax.*"

Amanda blushed and strode steadily onward. Maybe confiding in "Motormouth" Mel wasn't the smartest idea. Over the years, she'd more than earned her nickname. But Gemma had already phoned to say she'd be late meeting them for their nightly walk— something about the twins and a bucket of wallpaper paste—so Amanda really didn't have much choice. And she *had* to get this off her chest.

"It's about what happened later this afternoon, after the yoga-pose incident," she began.

"I'm all ears." *Right up to the four studs in each lobe.*

"Well, it's about Mike's aptitude testing. It's a vital first step in determining career goals—and then writing a résumé—because applied properly, aptitudes are a client's strongest tools, enabling him or her to reach their utmost potential with a job that they'll—"

"Hon," Mel urged, "cut to the chase. We only have two more laps to go."

Amanda decided to sum up. "I started out with eye-hand dominance tests, which were typical. Right hand, right eye, no sign of color blindness."

"Terrific. He'd make a boffo interior decorator. So what?"

"Wait, there's more. Next up was inductive reasoning. Strong, but I'd have expected that. Doctors, lawyers, and mechanics—"

"And taxi drivers?"

"—typically score well in that area because they have the ability to arrive at general principles from a set of specific facts."

"Ordinary English, please," Mel prompted, bracelets jangling as she put both hands to her head. "You're talking to someone who spends all day with alternative music playing at work. Loudly. *Really* loudly."

"Okay. Anyway, I went through the rest of the tests, right? Number memory, analytic reasoning, tonal memory, pitch discrimination, silograms, spatial-relations tests, ideaphoria—"

"Hey, that would be a great name for a band!"

"—and so on." Amanda gave her friend a quelling look. "There was some useful information, of course, but it was the final test that really got to me."

"Final test?"

"Yes. The tactile-receptors test."

"Your idea of 'ordinary English' is obviously different than mine," Mel said.

"*Touch*," Amanda specified. "The final test measured Mike's sense of touch." Slowing her pace slightly, she described the process she'd been through with Mike, then summed up.

"So what you're saying," Mel said when she'd finished, "is that this guy's sense of touch rates off the charts?"

"In a simplified way, yes. But—"

"Your forbidden-fruit fella is a supersensualist," Mel announced matter-of-factly.

"Well, I, uh, wouldn't interpret the results quite like—"

"Sure you would." Mel stopped, scrutinizing her. "You already have!" Laughing, she started walking again, leaving Amanda to scramble behind. "If I know you, you couldn't take your eyes off him all the rest of the afternoon. Especially his hands, I'll bet."

"Bet? No way," Amanda said rapidly. "I've gotta quit."

Mel looked at her quizzically. "Who said anything about making a bet?"

"You did."

"No, I—"

Just then, Gemma breezed up, clad in a coordinated purple windsuit and sneakers. Her pants legs were covered in small white handprints.

"The wallpaper paste. The twins," she said when she noticed her friends' scrutiny. "Don't ask. So, what'd I miss?"

"Three turns around the mall, one near-miss diet disaster at the Smoothie stand, twelve cute guys," Mel offered nonchalantly, "and one tiny news item: Amanda's making plans to boff her Life Coach Lotto winner."

"Mel!" Amanda cried.

Curiously, Gemma turned her gaze to her friend. Amanda wanted to walk right through the concrete underfoot and emerge on the bottom floor, where Melanie's "news items" couldn't touch her.

"Well, the path to true love has taken stranger twists," Gemma said with a shrug. She picked up the pace, obviously determined to drop those last five posttwins pounds. "I say, go for it, Amanda."

Mel and Amanda both gawked. *Go for it?*

If Amanda didn't know better, she'd have sworn Mike's come-over-to-the-dark-side powers of persuasion had somehow touched Gemma, too. Otherwise, something really strange was going on.

"No, no, no, and maybe," Mike said, adding a paper to the pile at his left elbow with each word. The stack had already grown discouragingly damned big, and it had only been a few weeks so far. "No dice with this batch, but I'm not giving up."

The dozen or so people assembled with him in the back room at Marvin's grumbled their understanding. A few yelled out encouragement: "Go get 'em, Mike!"

"There are other restaurants in Phoenix," Mike said. "I'll—"

"Nickerson's probably blackballed us all," Jake interrupted, inciting a round of yeahs from the prep cooks and dishwashers at his table. "We'll never work in this town again."

"I'll never afford a baby-sitter again," said Tracy, a late-twenties blonde holding a squirming toddler in her arms.

"I'll have to take that job in the school cafeteria," added Doris, the dark-haired woman beside her. "Hair nets. No cigarette breaks. Mystery meat. Ugh."

"I'll flip burgers at Mickey D's forever," put in Rico, frowning disgustedly as he snaked his hand toward Jake's bottle of beer.

"Hands off that Budweiser, junior," Mike ordered, nodding toward Rico. Grinning, the kid withdrew his hand and went back to nursing a Coke. "And as for the rest of you"—he spoke loudly, to be heard over

the increasingly noisy conversations going on—
"don't worry. I got us into this, and I'll get us out of
it."

"It's not your fault, Mike," said the Monroe sisters,
loyal to a fault. "You didn't mean for this to happen."

Mike couldn't listen. Sure, he hadn't meant it. But
it had happened all the same. And he wasn't about
to shrug off his responsibility toward his team.

Not after April Fools' Day.

"The fact is, it did happen," he said. "Nickerson
gave us the boot."

"Bad-tempered S.O.B.," muttered Jake.

Holding up his hand for quiet, Mike went on. "He'll
regret it. If he hasn't already. This is the best damned
team in town, and I'm going to keep looking until I
find someone who recognizes it."

Someone who's willing to take the whole *team.*

Someone who doesn't insist I'm "overqualified."

"Maybe we ought to split up," said one of the
Monroe sisters. A former busboy near her nodded.
"It's great that you want to do this for us, Mike,
but—"

"No buts. I'm close. I can feel it."

All around him, heads nodded. His friends and
former coworkers kept their faces turned toward him,
their gazes locked trustingly on him, and Mike knew
he couldn't let them down.

"Who's with me?" he yelled, thrusting a fist upward.

"I am!" shouted more than a dozen voices.

Their vote of confidence was clear. Mike only
hoped he could live up to it.

By the time Mike got home that night, it was beyond
"last call" and as dark as the inside of a refrigerator
with the door closed. Head buzzing, he made his way

carefully inside and flicked on the living-room light switch.

Hell. Incandescent lighting was way overrated.

He winced and swerved to the left, thinking that maybe those final beers—and the margarita chasers—with Jake, Rico, the Monroe twins, and the rest of the team hadn't been such a brilliant idea. At the rate he was going—ultra-slow-mo—he'd make it into bed by about six A.M. Unfortunately, moving any faster made it seem as though the room were Tilt-A-Whirling around him.

In the bedroom, Mike toed off his sneakers and kicked them into a darkened corner. They sailed past his bureau and the straight chair beside it, briefly calling his attention to the stack of folded—and now unneeded—uniforms on the chair seat.

He stared at them, frowning. An uncomfortable sensation poked at him, as though the Tilt-A-Whirl feeling had returned—except he wasn't moving this time. It wasn't that he was *worried* about finding a new gig for his team, Mike told himself, turning away from the stack. Not exactly. It was just that—

In the act of tugging off his T-shirt, he paused, his attention blissfully diverted. A scent wafted up from the laundered-a-thousand-times cotton fibers crumpled in his hands, a fragrance both new and alluringly familiar, sweet and spicy.

Amanda.

The scent was her perfume, rubbed onto his shirt during their office-chair encounter today.

Amanda. At the remembrance, Mike felt woozier than ever. Then he felt something else, too. Something mysterious and indefinable, kind of like the workings of his beer-benumbed fingers on his Levi's fly buttons right now.

There was something about her. Something he liked, maybe could even lo— He stopped himself in mid-thought (mid-*dangerous*-thought) and finally succeeded in wrenching off his jeans and underwear. Naked and newly resolute, Mike headed across the bedroom toward the bathroom.

He had a date with a razor. A rendezvous with some shaving cream. And a suddenly intense urge to rediscover life without an inch of whiskers all over his jaw.

Not that any of that meant, Mike told himself savagely as he stared into the mirror and unsteadily lathered up with Gillette Extra Foamy, that he was softening up toward Little Miss Yoga Pose. Not one damned bit.

Mike Cavaco was his own man, and that was that. He was a damned good taxi driver, a whiz with a razor, a soon-to-be-in-demand employee of some—Awww, hell, he was also about to pass out.

Thud.

Chapter Nine

Waiting for Mike to arrive for his Wednesday morning fitness-evaluation appointment, Amanda sat at her desk with the phone cradled to her ear, simultaneously counseling a client and trying to slice her allotted sixty-calorie apple into the maximum number of pieces.

If she closed her eyes, she could almost pretend it was the cinnamon-raisin bagel with maple cream cheese she'd been craving since restarting her diet yesterday.

"I understand that you're upset, Mrs. Neubaum," she said into the receiver. "Anyone would be. But I'm sure that once the peanut butter is removed, the piano will be good as new."

She cocked her head, listening to the elderly woman describe the latest roadblock in her goal of becoming a professional concert pianist. Originally, Mrs. Neubaum had come to Amanda for help organizing her grueling canasta schedule—and her closets—but after a series of meetings, much greater aspirations had emerged. In all, Amanda felt quite proud of the progress they'd made.

"Maybe I should just get rid of it," Mrs. Neubaum said, speaking of the piano again. "It's a lot of trouble to keep dusted, and with this latest peanut-butter problem—it was extra-crunchy, you know—"

"Nonsense! You're on your way, Mrs. Neubaum. You wouldn't want to abandon your dreams now, would you?"

"Well . . ."

As her client went on, puffing into the phone while she scrubbed off the peanut butter her grandson had crammed into the keys "to see if the music would stick," Amanda murmured encouragingly. She believed in Mrs. Neubaum's potential, even if Mrs. Neubaum herself wasn't quite convinced. Yet.

Finishing her phone call, Amanda went on to take several more, all from current clients. Some had been rescheduled to accommodate the brouhaha surrounding the Life Coach Lotto winner and needed reassurance. Others had good news to share. A few more needed pep talks, an important part of being a life coach.

Providing pep talks, cheering clients up when they felt discouraged, was one of the aspects of her job Amanda most enjoyed. There was nothing like the feeling she got when she successfully turned around a client's perceptions and prepared them to meet the challenges ahead. It was exhilarating, enriching, more mood elevating than the phenylethylamine in chocolate.

Mmmm, chocolate. Morosely, Amanda picked up a paper-thin green apple slice and stared at it. *It's good for you,* she reminded herself. *Crisp, vitamin-packed, fat-free, low-calorie, high-fiber . . . boooring.* Her inner-rebel kicked in and snapped the apple slice in half.

Hey, now it was *two* slices. A bonus. She could—

No, this would never work. She wanted a bagel with cream cheese, and nothing else would do.

Unfortunately, in an effort to bolster her shaky motivation, she'd put on her "skinny" suit this morning, a pair of mercilessly tailored cream-colored pants with a matching jacket. She'd even tucked in the lightweight knit-silk sweater she had on underneath. At this point, deep breathing was difficult. Eating an entire cinnamon-raisin bagel would be impossible.

Damn.

Amanda was picking up the phone to call Gemma for a dietary commiseration fest when Trish buzzed in.

"Mr. Hubba Hubba on line two," she said.

"Who?"

"Mike Cavaco. The Yoga King." Trish gave a muffled feminine snicker. "Next time he gets stuck, let *me* unkink him, will ya?"

Fat chance. "Sure, Trish. If you think you're up to it."

"Meow! What's got you so cranky?"

Amanda laughed. One thing was certain about Trish. She gave as good as she got. "My diet. My taste buds got wind of some French fries at lunch on Monday, and things haven't been the same since."

"Tough break," Trish said, her voice crackling over the intercom. "Try sex. It'll burn calories."

Amanda glanced at her thighs. "Not enough calories."

"Maybe. But after all that whoopee, who will care?"

With another laugh, Amanda signed off and prepared to take Mike's call. She sucked in a deep breath. Cleared her mind of all Trish-generated sex-related thoughts. Definitely did *not* pursue the intriguing mental image that popped into her head of Mike's big, strong, tough-guy hands and the ultrasensitive, supersensitizing touch capabilities that went with them.

She should have known that was too ambitious.

As soon as she heard his voice, Amanda was in over her head. Her heart thump-thumped like a lovesick cartoon character's, and this after only a couple of days. What would she feel like after a whole week?

"Hey there, doll," Mike said in response to her hello. He sounded slightly hoarse and vaguely muddled, as though he'd just gotten up. At nearly ten o'clock? "I've got bad news."

Her insides flip-flopped. "Bad news as in 'I broke my leg playing street hockey and I can't be on TV anymore?' " *Might as well get the worst-case scenario out of the way first,* she figured. "Or bad news as in 'I'm running ten minutes late for my appointment'?"

"I'm not coming for my appointment."

"What? You have to! The Channel Six News crew will be here any minute now, and I—"

"Sorry. It's out of the question."

"Mike, I don't understand. Do you have to work today, is that it?"

"Nah. My shift doesn't start until three."

"Then why . . . ?"

"I'll come in tomorrow instead."

"But your fitness tests are all scheduled for today. My on-call physician gave her approval to start, and I—" Amanda's chest tightened, threatening to cut off her breathing. "God, Mike, *please* come in. I'll look like an idiot in front of the camera and sound guys if you don't."

Especially after yesterday's yoga-busting fiasco.

"It's impossible," Mike said. It sounded as though his mouth were working in slow motion. "We'll do it another day."

Balling her fist, Amanda stared at the neatly arranged apple slice mound she'd made. The last thing she needed in this day was one *more* piece of frustration.

"Please, Mike. Whatever's going on, we can talk about it," Amanda coaxed.

Sometimes clients got cold feet. They got close to their ideal, life-coach-encouraged life, and the unexpectedness of it all made them freak out. It happened. She wouldn't have expected it with a self-assured guy like Mike, but . . .

"Really, Mike," she pleaded. "I—I need you here."

"You need—" His voice broke off. "Awww, hell. Hang on."

There was a scraping sound, then a whoosh on the other end of the receiver. Amanda heard the phone joggling against Mike's cheek as he moved. He was getting up! He was coming! Thank God.

She imagined him reluctantly getting out of bed, naked and glorious. Did he even sleep naked? Amanda didn't know, but in her mind's eye, he most definitely did. She saw Mike walking across the floor and then stretching in a shaft of morning sunlight as he held the phone to his ear, his muscles flexing and releasing in a subtly sexy show of male strength. *Mmmmm.* All at once, Amanda wanted to squeeze magically through the phone and emerge on the other end. She wanted to spread her hands over Mike's chest, his shoulders, his arms. Yearned to explore the firmness of his backside and the taut lines of his thighs. Ached to expose those towel-shrouded parts of him she hadn't yet glimpsed and test the theory Mel and Gemma put forth about the size of a man's nose and its relationship to the size of his . . .

"*Gaaaah!*" yelled Mike. The phone thunked onto something hard.

Amanda yanked her receiver away from her ear,

frowning at the echo that had burst into her eardrum. So much for her flight into Fantasy Mikeland.

"Are you all right?" she asked. "What happened?"

"Nothing."

"You sound sort of shook up."

"Who me? Nah. I'm fine. Fine."

A long pause followed. Amanda said nothing at first, afraid to disturb the delicate agreement she'd forged with Mike about coming in for his appointment. When it went on a bit longer, though, she couldn't resist.

"Look, if you want me to," she began, "I can come to you. My test equipment is portable, and the fitness evaluations can be done almost anywhere. I have your address on file, so I could just—"

"No!" Mike sounded panicky. "No! You can't come here."

"Why not?"

Did he have a woman with him? All at once, Amanda felt depressingly sure he did, although why that would make him actually scream out loud, she couldn't imagine.

And didn't want to.

"It's no trouble," she continued briskly, determined to breeze past this little hitch in her fantasy scenario. "I can be there in twenty—"

"No! Really. You, uh, don't have to do that. Do *not* do that."

"I want to." And the more Mike protested, the more *strongly* she wanted to. It was client cold feet, Amanda told herself. It was practically her duty to go to Mike's house and talk him down.

"Amanda, I've gotta go," he said suddenly. "I'll see you *tomorrow*." His emphasis on the word *tomorrow* was obvious.

A click sounded in her ear. Amanda gaped at the phone. He'd actually hung up.

He wasn't coming. And she wasn't supposed to go to him.

What now?

The intercom squawked into the room. "Heads up, Amanda," Trish said in a low voice. "The Channel Six guys just arrived."

Trailed by a cadre of camera people and audio operators, Amanda strode across the paved center of Heritage Square, a group of historically restored Victorian houses in downtown Phoenix. On weekends, the area was often filled with arts-and-crafts merchants and visitors waiting to tour the homes, but at ten-thirty on a Wednesday afternoon, the only inhabitants seemed to be Amanda and the Life Coach Lotto crew.

The soles of her sneakers squished against the pavement as she left the parking garage behind and headed toward one of the houses. A faint spring breeze, scented with equal parts car exhaust and paloverde blossoms, lifted her hair from her shoulders. The strong April sun beat steadily on her head and shoulders and sparked off the ornately painted address plaques affixed to each house.

Most were public buildings—historical museums, gift shops, and small restaurants. Their brick-and-gingerbread faces hid furnishings both authentic to the late-nineteenth-century period during which they'd been built and relevant only to modern times. It was a charming square, but surely this couldn't be where Mike lived?

Had he deliberately led her astray? What *was* behind his insistence that she didn't come to his house?

Amanda stopped beneath the fluttering leaves of a cottonwood tree and double-checked her Cavaco file. She squinted at the ironwork street sign to her left, marking the nearest traffic-prohibited intersection. *Hmmm, curious.*

"Hey, an espresso shop!" bellowed one of the camera guys, pointing toward a red brick converted house on the corner. Its Café Crema sign swung on painted pickets in the grassy yard.

In a flash, the entire crew headed for a caffeine fix, leaving Amanda to find the address she sought on her own.

It took nearly two minutes of knocking before anyone came to the door. If Amanda hadn't been so certain this was the place—for instance, if Mike's Twizzler-decorated taxi cab hadn't been parked out front—she would have thought she had the wrong house. As it was, the red-brick, gable-roofed converted carriage house had been tricky to find—tucked behind the other houses in the square, as it was—and she'd almost overlooked it.

With any luck, the Channel Six News crew would have just as much trouble tracking down the place. If Mike *did* have a woman in there with him, the last thing she needed was for the whole sordid incident to be caught on tape. It would effectively put the kibosh on the Life Coach Lotto . . . and, if she were honest with herself, it would put a few new cracks in her heart, too.

Amanda was glancing over her shoulder, checking to make sure the crew hadn't caught up with her yet, when the door creaked open.

One-half of Mike's face greeted her through the six-inch gap he'd created. At the sight of her, his visible eyeball bulged. "Oh, no. It *is* you."

"Hi! I decided to bring the fitness tests to you. Never let it be said that Aspirations, Inc., leaves their

clients in the lurch!'' Determined to be chipper even
if it killed her, she hefted the canvas bag of supplies,
from which a jump rope, a chrome-plated barbell,
a tape measure, and other assorted accoutrements
protruded above the Life Coach Lotto logo. "The
camera crew is right behind me, so we'd better get
started."

She nudged the door with her knee, intent on
getting inside and clearing out Mike's mystery woman
before the camera and sound guys arrived. Expecting
the thick-planked wood to swing open so she could
troop inside, Amanda frowned in confusion when it
remained stationary. Her client, as it turned out, was
still holding the door mostly shut.

From behind it, Mike scowled. Or at least the visible
half of his face did. "Go 'way. We'll do this
tomorrow."

"But—"

"I told you not to come today."

"I had to! How else would I have made your life
goals happen? This is a necessary step in the—"

A muffled noise from within made Mike look away.
Clamping her mouth closed, Amanda tried to identify
the sound, but couldn't. Probably the trampling of
stiletto-clad feet as Mike's woman-of-the-moment
scrambled to put her clothes back on, she decided
sourly. It was probably tough to find your panties
when they'd been ripped off in the heat of passion.

Not that Amanda would know anything about *that*,
of course.

But a part of her—a teeny, tiny, *insistent* part of
her—was beginning to want to find out.

"Look, I'm sorry," Mike said, breaking into her
imaginings of the torrid, movie-style lovemaking he
probably enjoyed on a regular basis. "But I can't do
this today. I'll, uh, call you."

I'll call you? Amanda gaped in disbelief.

If she wasn't mistaken, she'd just been dumped—
and worse, with the oldest, lamest, most singularly
untrue phrase in the male lexicon.

"Hey!" she protested. "I'm a life coach, not a girlfriend. You can't just shut me out like this!"

"Watch me," Mike said, clearly distracted by the
source of the sound he'd heard earlier. Then, spreading his palm against the door, he gave a push to close
it.

Amanda shoved her foot into the narrowing gap,
door-to-door salesman style. If he thought he was
getting away with this, he'd better think again. She
was a life coach, and a life coach never gave up on her
clients. Not even when they gave up on themselves.

The door rebounded off her foot, inflicting mini-
mal damage to her new cross-trainers. Whew. Filled
with determination, she grabbed the door's edge and
prepared to wrestle it out of Mike's grasp.

It swung easily.

Frowning in confusion, Amanda gave it a tentative
shove. The old-fashioned door opened all the way,
revealing the carriage house's interior and the back
side of Mike's retreating self. Wearing nothing but a
pair of boxer shorts imprinted with yellow smiley
faces, he hurried toward a bamboo-and-wicker accor-
dion-style floor screen at the far edge of the room
and disappeared behind it.

Probably to go tend to what's-her-name, the sexpot
who'd prevented him from keeping his appointment,
and who obviously didn't care about Mike's Life
Coach Lotto–entrant desire to improve himself.

Left alone, Amanda clicked the front door softly
shut behind her and lowered her Life Coach Lotto
canvas bag to the floor. The space surrounding her
was open, with no visible interior walls. Furniture
groupings defined a living room and sitting area—
clustered around a huge TV set with video-game con-

trollers clumped in a heap at its base—a dining area, a peninsula, and a cooking space. Beyond the living room, light shining on the ceiling visible above the folding screen indicated another area, probably the bedroom.

Hubba, hubba, her inner Trish piped up. *The bedroom.*

Shaking her head, Amanda moved farther inside, caught between curiosity about the place where Mike lived and urgency to find out what, or who, could have possibly been important enough to call him away from the door like that.

Naturally, since she was a woman, curiosity won.

Hey, near as she could tell, there was only the one front door. Mike and his mystery woman weren't sneaking past without Amanda noticing them, anyway. And home visits were, she assured herself, an important diagnostic tool when dealing with clients. You could learn a lot about someone by examining where they lived.

The decor was one hundred percent Early Bachelor Pad. An overstuffed sofa covered with a purple Arizona Diamondbacks throw. A scarred square coffee table stacked with issues of *Sports Illustrated,* paperback books, and a crumpled Doritos bag. Gigantic stereo speakers. A round fifties-diner-style chrome dining table, complete with four matching orange vinyl-upholstered chairs and a poker-chip centerpiece. A tired-looking spider plant, which seemed to be gasping for air, next to a framed southwestern print.

Overall the effect, especially when set against the carriage house's oak plank flooring, old-fashioned wainscotted-and-whitewashed walls, and mullioned windows, was eclectic. Eclectic and messy. Messier, even, than Mike's taxicab. She wouldn't have thought it was possible.

All except for the kitchen, that is. There the appliances were pristine, the countertops free of empty

snack-food bags and soda cans. Green leafy plants
bloomed on the windowsill, and a crock of cooking
utensils stood guard over a fancy cooktop. A tall bottle
of imported olive oil gleamed in the sunlight, and
as she walked toward it, Amanda detected the faint
aromas of garlic and coffee lingering in the air.

This was a room that saw frequent use, she thought,
running a hand over an eight-inch-tall plant with soft
leaves roughly the shape of pine needles. She fingered
one of those leaves, wondering about a man who
couldn't be bothered to buy new Levi's, even when
his current pairs were all but turning into Swiss-cheese
denim, yet who obviously nurtured a whole row of
thriving plants in his kitchen.

Smiling, Amanda pondered the meaning of that
tidy line of plants nestled securely in their terra-cotta
pots. Clearly, Mike had mastered the first third of
the commitment triumvirate: houseplants. Once he'd
moved on to caring for a pet, he'd be ready for the
third step: committing to a woman.

*C'mon, Lassie. Benji. Puppies on the doorstep. Anyone.
Let's move this man along!*

She wondered if Mike knew exactly how telling his
green thumb was. After all, no woman in her right
mind would become seriously involved with a man
who couldn't be bothered to at *least* look after something green, inanimate, and undemanding.

Stroking the spiky leaves again, Amanda felt her
grin widen until it was huge and silly and lovestruck.
The contrasts in Mike intrigued her. The occasional
glimpses of tenderness in him touched her. The trouble was, what the heck was he *doing* over on the other
side of the room-divider screen?

Cocking her head, Amanda listened.

"Come on," he coaxed in a low voice. "Just go *in*
there."

Sounds of a slight scuffle followed.

"I'll be back to get you as soon as I can," he continued when the scrabbling had ended. He sounded out
of breath. "I promise."

Promise. Humph! Motivated by Mike's spectacular
ability to sound so sincere one moment—and bail
out with a mere *I'll call you* the next—Amanda headed
toward the sound of his voice, straightening the
untucked Life Coach T-shirt and track pants she'd
changed into for Mike's fitness tests as she went.
Together, they comprised her don't-mess-with-me
wardrobe. Equipped with them, she figured she could
handle whatever her clients dished out.

"Mike?" she called. "Your front door was still
open—" A little embellishment of the truth didn't
hurt, right? "—so I came on in."

The scuffling sounds increased. "Come *on,*" Mike
urged his mysterious companion. "For once in your
life, just—be—cooperative."

It sounded as though he were speaking through
gritted teeth. Now Amanda felt almost sorry for the
mystery woman she'd become sure was on the receiving end of all that scuffling and pleading. Sure, she
didn't like the idea of another woman in Mike's life,
but this was going a little too far.

She rounded the folding floor screen, prepared to
really let him have it. Instead, at the sight that greeted
her, Amanda could only stop and stare in puzzlement.

On his hands and knees, Mike was using his shoulder to push an interior door closed. The two-inch-
wide view of what lay beyond it revealed a slice of
jumbled clothes, a brightly-lit dangling light fixture,
and several empty plastic clothes hangers. A closet.
That glimpse quickly vanished as Mike gave another
shove.

Inside, someone pushed back, making those scuffling sounds she'd heard. Leveraging himself against
the slick wood floor with some difficulty, Mike

abruptly switched directions, grunted, and bumped the door all the way shut with his hip.

He collapsed in a heap, the weary droop of his head an incongruous contrast to his yellow smiley-printed boxers.

Nice legs, Amanda noticed unwillingly. *Sinewy, solid, embellished with a nice amount of dark, manly hair. Also, nice bed,* she continued, gazing rapidly over the rumpled bedclothes, bureau, chair, and other bedroom furnishings. *Big and comfy and—*

"I hope you don't mind my barging in like this," she made herself say before she could get any more carried away with mentally tucking herself in with Mike between the blue-checked sheets. "It's just that we have work to do and not much time to do it. You might not realize it, but you're in the throes of goal-achieving cold feet. You need my help."

As *if* that explained her presence in his bedroom.

It did, however, provide her with a cover story. And that was all Amanda really cared about at the moment. That and finding out who was hiding—however unwillingly—in the closet.

At Mike's side, something smacked into the door. The wood shuddered. He gave it an exhausted shake of his head, then looked up at her at last.

"You just don't give up, do you?" he asked.

She got her first good look at his face, and gasped.

"Don't say it," Mike warned. "Just don't say it."

Unfortunately, Amanda was about as cooperative as his unwilling closet inhabitant. She gawked at him uninhibitedly, then raised a pointing finger.

"What . . . what happened to your face?" she asked.

He shrugged. "It's nothing a little time won't cure."

"You mean you intend to walk around like *that?* In public?"

She boggled. He shrugged again.

He didn't really have a choice. Mike had discovered that much this morning while on the phone with his ultra-persistent, won't-take-no-for-an-answer life coach. He'd dragged himself out of bed, wandered into the bathroom clutching the cordless, caught a glimpse of himself in the mirror, and . . . well, at this point, let's just say he felt lucky to have covered the whole damn thing as well as he had.

So far.

"I thought I might, yeah."

He wanted to casually raise his hand and stroke his jaw in a carefree, action-hero kind of way, but his inability to flex his biceps made a gesture like that impossible. Since waking up, he'd barely been able to move, although he had mastered a sort of shuffle to get around with. He couldn't even raise both arms to shoulder height without feeling as though they might just give up and snap off.

Damn Jake and his workout plans! He never should have gone back for an emergency follow-up workout yesterday. Two days in a row had obviously wrecked him.

"But Mike," Amanda said, gazing at him with a frown, "half of your beard is gone. Just . . . gone. *Half* of it. Not that I'm not in favor of losing the facial fuzz—"

"Hey!"

"—but I'm not sure that's the best way to go about it. Are you?"

Geez, he hated hypothetical questions. Especially the girly version, which tended to be geared toward trapping a guy into an admission he'd regret. Should he agree with her and risk explaining what had really

happened? Or disagree and risk making Amanda
think he was blowing off her expertise altogether?

Torn, Mike hesitated. This was one of those trick
questions, to be sure. Kind of like "Do these pants
make my butt look big?" He was sure to lose either
way.

"Ummm," he vacillated. "Well . . ."

"You can't," she insisted. "I'll call Frederick at
Rosado right away. Maybe he can fit you in." Amanda
scrabbled at her waist, obviously intent on using her
cell phone to call the fancy hairstylist at the Pepto-
Bismol Pink Palace. "This is an emergency, after all."

Mike couldn't take it. It couldn't really be that bad.
Could it?

"I like it," he fibbed, crossing his arms and jutting
his half-hairless chin into the air. He really hadn't
been too steady with the razor last night, or maybe
he had up until he'd passed out. He couldn't remember for sure. "It makes a statement."

She scoffed and began dialing. "I don't think you
want to say what that's saying."

"Yes, I do." Slowly, painfully, he got to his feet
and put a hand over hers, stopping her emergency-
hairdresser 911. "Don't worry about it."

As soon as he could move normally, he'd take care
of it himself. Maybe in another, oh, week or two.

Amanda stopped. Looked at him closely. "You're
wincing. Is something wrong?"

Damn. "Nothing you need to worry about."

"But Mike, I want to make sure you're okay."

She gazed into his eyes, giving him a one-two punch
of baby blues . . . big, compassionate, and bluer than
the bedsheets on the mattress behind them. She cared
for him. Really cared for him. Could that face-saving
date he needed be that far away?

"You're my Life Coach Lotto winner," Amanda
continued. "It's my job to make your whole life as

terrific and high-achieving as possible. And you can't do *that* looking like *that*."

His dreams of caring crashed and burned.

"Look," Mike blurted, "for the last time, I didn't enter your damn contest, and I had that winning ticket by mistake. By mistake. Get it? One of these days, the real winner is going to turn up and—"

"It's all right." She patted his arm, making his bicep throb anew. How could a mere two consecutive days of strength training have had this humiliating effect on him? "You don't have to be embarrassed. Lots of men entered the Lotto."

"Arrgh!"

He was saved from having to say anything more articulate by a whirlwind renewal of effort behind the closet door. Thumps reverberated through the bedroom, chased by Amanda's horrified looks toward the now-bulging (he'd swear) wooden door. Then, just when things ought not to have gotten any worse, they did.

His unwilling captive burst open the door.

Chapter Ten

"Cupcake!" Mike yelled. "Stop!"

But it was no use. With typical feminine independence, Cupcake hot-footed it out of the closet and headed at warp speed straight toward Amanda . . .

. . . who squealed with delight.

"A dog!" she cried. "You have a *dog*, not a woman. Oh, thank God. No stilettos, no heat-of-passion panties, no secret life-coach saboteur. A dog! Oh, Mike!"

His mind locked onto the relevant-seeming portion of that statement. "Panties? Huh?"

"A dog!" she breathed, enraptured by the sight of the pooch trotting in her direction. "That's *wonderful*."

Mike frowned, completely at a loss.

As though it had been preordained by some twisted sense of fate, his scruffy-looking, impossible-to-hide dog leaped joyfully toward Amanda. In turn, Amanda crouched down in her T-shirt and track pants and gleefully accepted an armful of poodle. Yes, poodle.

In a frenzy of joy—now that she'd joined in the

party at last—Cupcake wagged her way up Amanda's body. The dog licked Amanda's chin, inciting a round of riotous laughter, squirmed happily in Amanda's arms, and generally acted in the completely un-cool, totally unrestrained way Mike always *wanted* to act when he was around his new life coach but couldn't.

When he'd worked up the sense of detachment he needed to face Amanda again, Mike cleared his throat. "Cupcake, come," he commanded. "You'll get Amanda all hairy, you fur ball."

"It's okay. I don't mind."

He watched her ruffle Cupcake's floppy ears, nuzzle her curly poodle fur, and coo in baby talk to the dog. All at once, a suspiciously warm and mushy feeling flooded through him.

Amanda hadn't laughed at him for his dog, Mike realized. She hadn't made fun of Cupcake's runtiness, frou-frou poodle haircut, or puffy tail . . . or, worst of all, the bubblegum-pink nail polish his nieces had swabbed on at the last Cavaco family get-together. Instead, she'd embraced Cupcake in all the dog's innate weirdness, and it was almost as though Amanda had embraced him, in turn.

Hell. He could really fall for a woman like that. Not that he planned to, or would, Mike hastily assured himself. He was interested in Amanda strictly as a makeover cover-up excuse. But, hypothetically, he might have fallen for her. As in, right at that very moment.

As though alerted by his thoughts, Amanda glanced up, a radiant smile on her face. That smile was suspiciously at odds with the misty look in her eyes, but Mike figured he'd never really understood what made her tick in the first place . . . so why should this be any different?

"Plants *and* a dog! You've reached phase two," she murmured inexplicably, ducking her head as she scratched Cupcake between the ears. Her goo-goo-eyed gaze met his again. "A dog!"

He couldn't for the life of him understand the significance. But Amanda seemed happy, and that was enough for now. Especially since she also seemed distracted from the problem of the missing half of his beard.

"She seems to like you, too," he pointed out. "Usually Cupcake pees on strangers."

Amanda looked horrified. She hugged the dog to her chest, ramping up her cooed praise. "She was probably scared or nervous. Weren't you, Cupcake? Yes, I'll bet you were."

She raised her head and cast squinty, suspicious eyes at Mike. "What kind of people do you have over here, anyway?"

He shrugged. "Normal people."

She made a skeptical sound.

"My family. My friends. My team."

"Team? The guys from Marvin's, you mean? I still owe Snake that portfolio review, as it turns out."

An uncomfortable urge to unburden himself to her began in Mike's chest and quickly spread upward, threatening to choke him if he didn't just say the words. *Tell her,* it demanded. *Tell her about April Fools' Day and your team. Tell her!*

But he couldn't. Confiding in anyone felt like a weakness, one Mike couldn't give in to. So instead, he knelt beside Amanda, knees threatening to buckle the whole way, and gave Cupcake a few "I'm sorry about the closet incident" pats.

"Just some people I work with sometimes," he said.

Her expression made it obvious that Amanda thought he'd meant a team of taxi drivers he worked with occasionally. For the moment, Mike let her believe it.

"Cupcake seems like a great dog," Amanda said a

few minutes later, still cradling the poodle in her lap and pointedly trying not to stare at Mike's demi-beard. "Why'd you try to hide her?"

"Some of my dates laugh when they see her," he said matter-of-factly. "They seem to think a guy like me ought to have a Doberman or a pit bull, or something. So when Cupcake here trots out . . . well, it ain't pretty. I think it, uh, hurts her feelings."

"Awwww." Looking crestfallen, Amanda hugged the dog tighter. "Poor Cupcake. I guess the collar doesn't help, then?"

She snagged her thumb beneath it, a black leather number studded with tough-looking silver spikes. Mike touched it, too, and their fingers met. Lingered. Clasped.

"Nah," he said, finding it weirdly difficult to speak due to the warm, tingly feelings spreading from the places their skin touched. "Frankly, I think it's over-compensating."

She laughed. In response, Mike gave Amanda the smile that had been building inside him ever since he'd seen her welcome his froufrou dog and felt his heart expand even further.

"So, uh, since you've already seen Cupcake and everything," he began, staring fixedly at their fingers intertwined beneath the dog's leather-and-studs collar, "I guess it's safe to invite you over here more often."

What? his inner commitment-phobe screamed. *More often? What are you saying?*

Amanda froze beside him, her formerly stroking fingers stilled. The air between them seemed to grow thick with tension—that or expectation. He hoped it was expectation.

"Like, for dinner sometime," Mike continued, his heart galloping into some kind of unnatural hip-hop rhythm. If he hadn't known better, he'd have thought he was nervous. Which was ridiculous, of course. Mike Cavaco didn't *get* uptight talking to women. Ever. At all. Right?

"Tonight, even," he choked out. "How about it?"

No, you numbskull! the buttinsky in his brain shouted. *It has to be a public date, something the guys at Marvin's will see.* But waiting for Amanda's answer, Mike couldn't quite bring himself to quibble over details. So they started out with an ice-breaker dinner at his place. Big deal. They could always go out some-place public—like Marvin's again—later on. The guys would see them together, Mike would drop a few hints about how he'd agreed to the makeover thing to get on the good side of the hottie he was dating, and his reputation would remain intact.

Yeah. Now that he'd stepped into the abyss, the whole thing started seeming like a terrific idea.

Unless she said no.

Her gaze met his. She looked reluctant. A little sad. And his heart lurched.

"You know I can't date you, Mike," Amanda said gently. She withdrew her fingers from his and gave Cupcake another pat before rising to her feet. "A life coach can't become involved with her clients."

"Fine." Mike struggled to stand as well, muscles screaming. He was glad Amanda wasn't looking at him. It would have been embarrassing to have her witness him biting his lip to keep from crying out like a baby. "I quit. There must be a runner-up who can take my place."

A faint smile touched her lips. "Nice try, Casa-nova."

"I'm serious."

"Don't be. Don't put me in the position of choosing between you and my Lotto, Mike, please."

She walked across the room, her sneakers squeak-ing against the hardwood floor. Cupcake followed, tail wagging more slowly as the mood between Mike and Amanda turned more serious.

"You won't like the choice I make," Amanda said.

She'd choose the Lotto. Mike knew it, had known it, had probably even sensed it right from the start. So why hearing her say so out loud now made him ache even more than he already did, he couldn't have guessed.

"Hey, it's just dinner," he said, striving for a light-hearted tone.

"If Channel Six got wind of it," she protested, "my chances for a weekly news spot would be over with."

"And you want that spot." It wasn't a question.

She nodded. "Truthfully? My company isn't doing so well. Without the publicity a weekly feature would bring . . . I don't know if Aspirations, Inc., can survive. We'll all be out on the street. Me, Trish, my other two assistants. They're all depending on me."

Amanda turned her back to him again, grasping the polished wood of the mission-style footboard on his bed. "I dragged them into this venture with me, and I won't let them down. *I won't.*"

He couldn't help but respect her for wanting to take care of the people who worked with her. Wasn't that exactly what he was trying to do himself, for his team? But still, Mike Cavaco wasn't a quitter. And he wasn't convinced that a simple dinner for two would be tantamount to a ticking career time bomb for Amanda, either.

"While you're so busy," Mike said, "watching out for your team—"

Her head came up, as though she'd sensed the connection behind his inadvertent slip. *Team. Damn.* He didn't want her to know about that. Didn't want the *rest* of the world to know about it, either, via the soon-to-be-aired Life Coach Lotto broadcasts on the news. Hurriedly, Mike continued:

"—who's watching out for you? Who's making sure *you* get what you need?"

"I'm perfectly capable of getting dinner on my own, thanks," came her breezy reply. "Take-out Thai food might not be the most nutritious or low-cal on the planet, but it's—"

"That's not what I mean."

Amanda sighed, absently watching as Cupcake attacked a wayward corner of the bed's comforter and worried it with sharp canine teeth. "I know. Look, you can't change my mind about this. It's impossible. No matter how much I . . ."

Wish you could, Mike finished silently. *No matter how much I wish you could.*

"No matter how much," she said softly, "I wish things were different."

Had she just admitted what he thought she'd admitted? Mike took a step closer, ignoring the persistent throbbing in his quadriceps.

"You wish things were different?" he repeated, a smile starting someplace inside him. This was all the chance he needed, wasn't it? "You wish—"

"But they're not," Amanda cut in, looking vaguely panicked. A knock at the carriage house's front door punctuated her statement and made them both turn their heads toward the sound. Raised voices followed. "That's the camera and sound crew. Fully charged on triple mochas, I'll bet. I gave them the address. I'd better—"

"Amanda, wait."

"—go let them in to set up." She turned, heading resolutely toward the dividing floor screen. At the edge of the wicker and rattan that served as his bedroom "wall," she paused and glanced backward, her gaze dropping gradually lower. "While I'm doing that, you might want to put on some pants."

"Huh?"

"Linda, the video operator, collects things with those yellow smiley faces on them."

Hands on hips in a frustration-filled pose, still wanting to get a straight answer from her about that "wishing things were different" business, Mike looked down at himself. Several dozen yellow smiley faces grinned up at him from his boxer shorts.

Yikes. He'd forgotten how he was dressed—or undressed, as the case was. Lunging toward the bureau as Amanda left the bedroom, trailed by Cupcake, he dragged out a pair of Levi's.

Mike tugged them on his muscle-stiffened body as rapidly as possible, which wasn't very rapidly at all, given the complete lack of cooperation from his muscles. He figured they had to be on strike by now, or something, because they sure as hell weren't working the way he was used to.

Conversation filled his living room as the Channel Six News crews lugged in their equipment and began setting up. Any minute, he half-expected Linda the Smiley Collector to peek around the dividing screen, spot the yellow smiley faces still visible between his partially-buttoned fly, and—

A female head popped around the screen's edge.

"Gahh!" Mike yelled.

It was Amanda. "Don't worry, Smiley Man. Your secret's safe with me." As though she'd guessed what he'd been thinking, she gave him a sassy grin as he hurriedly finished his fly buttoning. "Unless you refuse to shave off the other half of that beard, in which case all bets are off."

Beard? Hey, that gave him an idea. Sure it was a little devious, Mike decided, but everything was fair in love and war, right?

Besides . . . *she wished things were different.* If that wasn't a nugget of encouragement for a guy to grab onto, Mike didn't know what was.

"Actually," he said, working to shove some reluctance into his voice, "I can't shave it off. Sorry."

Amanda's eyes widened. "What do you mean, you can't? There's only half a beard there! The Channel Six crew cannot film you like that. Our segment for today will be shot! Evan will kill me for wasting crew time."

Mike shrugged. "Like I said—sorry."

"You're doing this on purpose." Narrowing her eyes, she stepped all the way around the screen and stopped in front of him, arms crossed over her chest. At her feet, Cupcake flopped onto her haunches, her brown doggie eyes filled with an equally accusing look.

"This refusal to shave and go forward with your life plan is simply part of those client cold feet I told you about," Amanda continued. "Don't worry about it! Those feelings of anxiety will go away when you take action toward your—"

"In the first place," he interrupted before she could psychoanalyze him further, "I started shaving off my beard for you. Because you didn't like it."

Her mouth snapped shut. Cupcake cocked her head.

"I didn't finish the job yet, is all." Mike tried not to smile at the surprised—and if he didn't miss his guess, pleased—look on Amanda's face. "A killer round of margaritas sucked away some of my motivation last night. And as for today—"

He raised his arms to chest height, unable to prevent a wince at the resulting pain in his overworked muscles.

"—well, my arms aren't functioning so great right now. I can't reach my face. That's why I can't shave off the rest of my beard."

Amanda glanced from his arms to his chin, to her own track pants and T-shirt. Comprehension swept over her features.

"You practiced for the fitness tests, didn't you?" she asked.

"No!" Mike grimaced and put his arms down. Hey, maybe he could still bluff his way through this. Maybe she'd believe he'd had some freak margarita-lifting accident or something. "Heck, no. Who, me? Practice? Why would I need to—"

"Arrgh! Men!" she cried in evident frustration. "I'm going to have to start issuing a warning sheet and a bottle of Ibuprofen to every new macho wanna-be who signs up for life coaching."

"Macho wanna-be?" While launching this little scheme, he sure hadn't anticipated *that* little ego dent. "Macho wanna-be? Hang on there!"

"It's true." Amanda's eyes shone, probably with amusement. "You were afraid of looking weak in the fitness tests, so you boned up on your technique. It happens all the time."

Cupcake thumped her tail on the floor in agreement. He should have known the two females would side against him. But there was still a chance this whole mess could be salvaged.

"Look, I can take on you and your fitness tests anytime, lady," Mike told her, painfully standing straighter. "Anytime."

"Good!"

"Fine."

"Excellent." Her triumphant expression foretold an expected victory. "Then today works for you?"

"Uhhh . . ." *Hell.* He'd painted himself into a corner with that one. But no one called Mike Cavaco a wuss and got away with it. "If you want, yeah."

He could have sworn he heard his muscles whimper.

All at once, Amanda's gaze softened. She stepped closer and put one hand on his shoulder. "Come on, Mike. You don't have to. I was only making a point about—"

"*I will.*"

She shook her head, blowing out a great gusty sigh. "Not with that half-beard, you won't. We're taping a segment of the Life Coach Lotto, not America's Funniest Home Barber Disasters."

As though the matter were settled, Cupcake got up and pattered into the living room. Mike watched the dog go, knowing he was close to victory.

"What do you suggest we do about it, then?" he asked, refraining, with difficulty, from grinning like an idiot. A getting-his-way, *non*-macho-wanna-be idiot.

Amanda frowned at his face and assumed the manner of a person taking on a difficult task. "Well, I guess I'll just have to shave off the second half of your beard myself before anybody else sees you."

Bingo.

Leaving him no time to gloat, Amanda shoved Mike with both hands across the bedroom and into the bathroom. "Sit down and wait for me in here, and whatever you do, don't come out! I'll be right back."

She couldn't *believe* she was doing this. Which she'd have to admit, if Amanda were honest with herself, was becoming a running refrain in her encounters with Mike. She still wasn't quite sure what to make of it.

Despite her hasty explanations to the Channel Six crew—who'd lapsed immediately from their setting-up tasks into a rousing card game on Mike's kitchen table in typical work-avoidance mode—Amanda wasn't sure this was such a brilliant tactic. Unable to reveal the beard-fragment fiasco, she'd told the crew she wanted one run-through of the fitness tests with Mike in private. A rehearsal, so to speak. They'd agreed. Anything for an easier taping. And now, here she was . . .

Shaving Mike. Sheesh. As if *that* would help her retain her increasingly difficult to manage life coach's professionalism. After all, you couldn't get much more intimate than standing over a seminude man in a tiny room, stroking something sharp over his chin.

Directing her attention with difficulty onto the hot tap water flowing over her fingertips, Amanda tried to push away the image of the shaving-Mike fantasy she'd entertained earlier. But now that it was about to become reality—almost—it proved extremely reluctant to go. Instead, her mind served up tantalizing glimpses of broad bare shoulders, tawny skin, naked male muscles, and . . . whoops. That was reality.

Maybe some Zen-style focusing on the present moment, on the here and now, would help her. Determinedly, Amanda centered her thoughts on her physical environment.

Okay, it was hot. Steam filled the bathroom. The mingled reflections of her (readying a warm washcloth) and Mike (waiting on the closed lid of the room's only seating area) gradually misted, then disappeared altogether into the droplets of moisture on the mirror. It was as though they were alone together in a world of slick tiles, running water, and pristine surfaces.

Alone. Seductively and dangerously *alone.*

Trying to clear her head, Amanda sucked in a breath of moist, soap-scented air. Her hair clung to the sides of her face, and when she leaned over to check the water temperature one last time, her ponytail swung over her shoulder and then lay there, all perkiness gone from her 'do thanks to the heat.

"Do you ever wear your hair down? I'd like to see it."

Mike's voice startled her into dropping the washcloth. New beads of water splattered her T-shirt, too, making it stick to her skin in places.

When she looked at him, Mike's gaze leisurely slid away from those very stuck-on places.

"Sometimes," Amanda replied, concentrating on wringing out the steaming terry cloth again. She carried it the few steps to where Mike waited and gingerly lay it over the remaining half of his beard, keeping her hand steady to hold the cloth in place. "Not usually when I'm working, though."

His fingers fastened over her wrist. Eyes closed, Mike angled his head closer to her forearm. His nose nudged at the underside of her wrist, surprising her.

He inhaled deeply. "You smell good. Perfume?"

Shakily, Amanda nodded. If one touch of his skin against hers made her feel this on edge, simmering with anticipation, she couldn't help but wonder what would happen if they got even closer.

"I like it." Slowly, Mike's eyes opened. With unabashed appreciation, he looked at her. "I'll bet you put it everywhere. Your ankles. Behind your knees. Between your thighs."

As though his rumbling voice had the power to caress her, heat swept into the places he'd mentioned. Pressing her thighs together, Amanda forced herself to think of nothing but getting through the job she'd agreed to. A simple shave.

"Pulse points," she explained. Maybe injecting a little science into the discussion would cool things off somewhat. "Perfume goes on all the places where your—"

"Pulse beats. I know. Behind your ears, at the base

of your throat, between your breasts ... on your wrist." Plucking aside the warm washcloth with a careless motion, Mike bared his face and her palm at the same time. Hot, damp whiskers moved over her skin. His lips touched her wrist.

Amanda's pulse doubled.

Crazily, she wondered if a rapid heartbeat made perfume smell stronger. Maybe that explained the dizziness that swept through her, briefly, before she regained her wits.

Another kiss. Mike's murmured voice followed, a sound of approval and curiosity. With a parting stroke of his thumb, he released her hand.

Her whole body leaned nearer, wishing he hadn't.

Outside the closed bathroom door, in the carriage house's living room beyond, the muffled voices of the Channel Six crew upping the ante in their poker game reminded her of what was at stake. She had to get Mike ready for their next on-camera appearance. *And fast.*

Before she gave in to the sensual, mist-shrouded atmosphere that swirled between them and lost her resolve altogether.

Mike smiled up at her. Wordlessly, he handed her the washcloth, as though they hadn't just shared an electrified, dangerous moment.

His lips were soft, Amanda found herself thinking, disjointedly, as she plunged the terry cloth into the stream of hot water again. Soft but firm. Warm. What would they feel like against her mouth ... again?

Their kiss in the Robinson's-May dressing room had been impetuous, fueled by curiosity and given license by opportunity. They'd been attracted, Amanda told herself. None of the crew had been in sight. They'd acted on impulse and had stopped almost immediately.

Surely she could manage the same trick again. Right?

Right, jeered her inner-cynic as Mike shifted in his seat and her stomach pitched with excitement, her thoughts instantly leaping toward another kiss. This from the same woman who jumped Mike in her office chair and did her best to finish what he started.

Clearly, Amanda could not be trusted—when given the chance—to not taste her forbidden-fruit man.

But Mike could probably still resist. Right?

"If I thought I could stand up without breaking something," he said, his voice steady amid the drip-drip of the hot water, "I would kiss you again."

Oh, God.

"I've been wanting to," Mike continued, "ever since you cooked up that yoga excuse in your office. You were standing there, explaining all about downward doze lasagna—"

"Downward dog asana," Amanda corrected, stifling a grin.

"—and all I could think about was the feel of you. And that little moan you gave when that kiss really got going. And how soon I would be able to touch you again. And it's been making me crazy."

Her grin faltered, chased away by the serious tone in his voice. He meant this, she realized. And she wasn't quite sure she was ready to face up to the significance of that.

"Obviously, you were already a little crazy," Amanda tried, unsteadily wringing out the washcloth and slapping it over the remaining half of his whiskers again. "Otherwise we wouldn't be dealing with this beard issue right now."

"Misdirection won't work." Mike's voice was matter-of-fact. So was his demeanor when he nodded toward the can of shaving cream on the vanity. "Neither will this shave job without some of that."

Hurriedly, she snatched the can and shook it. Mike watched her efforts, his eyes sparkling.

"What?" she demanded, undone by the constant *wanting* she felt . . . and by Mike's unfailing ability to destroy her efforts to ignore it.

"I was just thinking," he said. "If I had you around to shake that can for me like that, I'd probably shave morning, noon, and night."

His gaze fastened tellingly on her breasts. All at once, she felt every last jiggle created by her vigorous shaking. The soft abrasion of her breasts rubbing against her cotton bra and T-shirt seemed twice as heightened; her rapidly-puckering nipples felt twice as sensitive. And Mike, damn him, knew it.

His appreciative smile told her that much.

"You're beautiful," he said. "No, don't lob that can at my head. We still have a job to do, remember?"

His kid-in-a-candy-store expression dared her to come closer and finish that very same job. Never one to turn down a challenge, Amanda did.

She squirted out some thick, menthol-scented shaving cream onto her fingertips and began smearing it over Mike's beard. His jaw felt strong, his skin and beard decidedly masculine. His body radiated heat. If she concentrated, she figured she could convincingly pretend that touching him didn't affect her.

Maybe.

But not so long as he didn't cooperate, darn it! Mike clasped his hands lightly around the backs of her thighs, just above her knees, and guided her nearer into the spread vee of his legs. Left standing there, Amanda pressed her knees together, trying to keep her nylon track pants from getting on a more intimate basis with his Levi's.

It didn't work. She and Mike were closer than a candle and a flame, and all she could think about was finding out exactly how hot the fire could get.

"Anyway," he confided in an as-I-was-saying tone as he lowered his hands to his knees again, "since I'm not one hundred percent up to par on the kissing routine today, we'll have to make some adjustments."

Don't ask. Just don't ask, she ordered herself, instead leaning sideways to pick up the razor—a blue disposable Bic exactly like the one in her shaving-Mike fantasy. Probably a detail like that was *not* some kind of sign, right? *Do not ask!*

"Adjustments?" she asked. *Arrgh!* Evidently, her brain was no more obedient than her raring-to-go libido.

"Mmmm-hmmm."

He closed his mouth and puckered sideways, forming a smooth runway for her efforts with the razor. She carefully swiped away a swath of foam and beard and then rinsed off the razor for another go.

"I've been sitting here thinking about it," Mike told her as she leaned forward for a second pass. "And the way I figure it is, anything you want me to kiss, well, you'll just have to put it close enough for me to reach."

Her brain offered up several thrilling possibilities. Staunchly, Amanda tamped them down and prepared to pretend she'd rather shave him than undress him. That she'd rather stroke a razor over his jaw than stroke her hands over his shoulders, his chest, his lean stomach, his—

"You'll have to put it," he clarified helpfully, with a devilish lift of his eyebrows, "at mouth level."

Amanda froze and glanced downward, seized by a sudden hunger for forbidden fruit. Directly in her line of vision, her breasts thrust themselves toward Mike, a few inches from his face. Obviously, her body was sexually psychic and had guessed what he'd been about to say.

A close shave was overrated, Amanda decided, hurling the razor into the sink beside her. It landed with a splash, sending water droplets bouncing over her arm and shoulder and ponytail and probably ruining her hairstyle still further . . . but by then she'd lunged on top of Mike, unable to resist any longer, and she didn't mind a bit.

Chapter Eleven

Mike was pretty sure he'd wound up in hell. He didn't know how it had happened, since he generally tried to be a decent guy and couldn't remember the last time he'd done something truly wrong (like ignore a nice girl's come-hither smile or blow off an NBA playoff game to watch *Antiques Roadshow*). But he knew he was in hell all the same. Because Amanda was on his lap, kissing him in ways he'd only dreamed of being kissed by her . . . and he couldn't do a damn thing about it.

He tried raising his arms to hold her close. His muscles locked up in protest, stiffer than . . . well, *almost* stiffer than everything south of his smiley boxers' waistband. He tried cupping her breasts, but his biceps refused to allow any upward movement. He tried nuzzling her, desperate to take what she was so eager to give, but all he wound up with was a mouthful of T-shirt lint.

It was enough to drive a man insane.

Mike groaned and gazed up at her through sad,

needful eyes, his useless arms unable to progress any higher than her hips. As though sensing his frustration, Amanda smiled and leaned back. A few seconds later, her Life Coach Lotto T-shirt landed atop the discarded shaving cream can.

He took one look, and groaned louder.

She clapped her hand over his mouth, smearing off the remaining shaving cream in the process. The sudden motion made her breasts jiggle against his chest, and only the wispy barrier of her extraordinarily sexy plain white bra separated them. Needing to touch her was going to kill him. It was as plain as that.

Mike knew it for sure when she unclasped her bra with her free hand and shrugged it off. The tangle of fabric and thin straps landed atop the shower rod and dangled there, taunting him. Irresistibly compelled, his whole body tightening with anticipation, Mike looked at her again.

His next groan was still louder, even muffled as it was—quickly—by her hand.

"Shhh," she whispered, seriously sexy in her remaining track pants and sneakers. Somehow, the clothes Amanda still had on only served to heighten the . . . well, the amazing sheer nakedness of the rest of her, Mike decided. "We have to be quiet. The crew is only a few feet from the door, remember?"

As though it came from far away, Mike registered the clank of poker chips hitting his kitchen table, followed by murmured voices. The Channel Six News crew. Oh, yeah. *Great.*

Whatever, a part of him screamed. *Amanda wants you!*

He nodded and kissed her palm. She grinned and removed it. "And we only have a few minutes, too," Amanda warned, "so we'd better make this quick."

"Quick. Yeah." The words were a near groan.

Lowering herself onto his lap again, she kissed him. Her scent surrounded him, part fresh, clean perfume and part warm woman. Her softness covered him, skin rubbing on skin as her breasts dragged back and forth over his bare chest. The sound of her rapid breathing mingled with his own panted breaths, combining with the drip of hot water and the rasp of track pants against denim to create a symphony of wanting. Shifting slightly, Mike angled his head and gave everything he had to their kiss. It was all he could do; aside from his lips, his body was pretty well nonfunctional.

"*Mmmm.* This is more like it," Amanda said.

She raised her head, and her seductive smile made Mike long to haul her back down again for another round. Unfortunately, he couldn't. Damn it.

"You're incredible," he gasped. "But I—I—"

"Shhh. I know. You already told me. Mouth level."

Still on his lap, she grabbed hold of his shoulders and arched her back. At the motion, her breasts rose higher. Their softness thrust toward him, irresistibly full and tipped with taut pink. Hungrily, Mike ducked his head and accepted what she'd offered.

Just as he'd dreamed, Amanda tasted sweet and hot, and he couldn't get enough. By the time he'd kissed his way to her nipples and felt them tighten against the moist heat of his tongue, he was ready to scream with need. Amanda clutched his head to her, twisting her fingers in his hair and telling him, in panted whispers, exactly how much she wanted him.

With difficulty, Mike gave her one last kiss and then leaned back. Against his shoulders, the porcelain commode lid felt hard and icy, but he didn't care. Not when the rest of him still blazed heat.

"Lean down," he said, watching as Amanda did exactly that, letting her long, wavy ponytail whisk over his shoulder. Her face neared his, and in her eyes he glimpsed the same wildness that twisted through him. "Give me your mouth. Your tongue. I need—"

She did. The kiss was fierce, their mouths and tongues and breaths coming together in a naked avowal of the desire they shared. Amanda writhed against him, her hands everywhere as she explored from his head to his chest and lower. When she came to the waistband of his Levis, they broke apart.

"I need you," she whispered. "Please, Mike. *Now*. We don't have much time."

"Ahhh, Amanda." He tried to raise his hand to stroke her face, to hold her while he rode the wildness inside him, but his muscles shrieked pain instead, and his arm locked up halfway there. Feeling defeated, Mike closed his eyes.

She mistook his withdrawal for surrender, and levered herself upward, yanking at her track pants. Her hair swirled around them both, whipped back and forth by Amanda's frantic movements. The air between them stirred. He heard the fabric rustle, felt as much as imagined the slide of it against her legs, moving lower . . . lower . . . revealing more of her as it puddled around her ankles.

The muffled thud of kicked-off sneakers hitting the wall was followed swiftly by the swish of her pants following. At the sound, Mike couldn't help but open his eyes again. And seeing Amanda there, wearing nothing but a pair of skimpy white panties and an endearing expression of mingled vulnerability and determination, was nearly his undoing.

"It's crazy," she said, her shoulders pushed back proudly. "I feel as though I've known you forever . . . but only partway. Let me—let me know you. Completely."

He couldn't refuse. He couldn't. Mike wanted her too much, and suddenly it felt as though he'd waited far too long for this moment to arrive. The Tilt-A-

Whirl sensation returned, more dizzying in its intensity than last night, and somehow he knew the only thing that could set his feet on solid ground again was loving Amanda.

"Come here," he said, and smiled at the wonder in his heart when she actually did. "Let's get better acquainted."

She smiled at that massive understatement, and Mike wondered if she knew how important this joining had become to him. It was as though only loving Amanda could ease the urgency inside him, only being with her could make him whole . . . and the realization of those truths would probably have sent his bachelorhood-loving self screaming into the hills if Mike hadn't reassured himself so quickly that he couldn't possibly be falling for her this hard, this fast.

Amanda straddled him, her panties more of a tease than a barrier as she lowered herself onto his lap again. Mike gazed at the delicate, darker-shaded triangle visible behind the fabric, marveled at the contrast between her feminine strength and his suddenly helpless masculinity. Heat seared between them. His body leaped at the contact, straining to be free, and it was all he could do not to go crazy in that moment.

Their next kiss was tender, sweetened with new discovery and heightened by the knowledge that this time, at least, nothing could stop them.

Nothing, that is, except Mike's damned nonfunctional muscles. Groaning with effort and frustration, he tried to hold her close and managed to successfully clasp both hands around her hips. *Hurray!*

"Ahhh, you feel amazing," he breathed, spreading his palms and fingers over her curves. "So soft. So good. So—"

"Mike, you're gritting your teeth," she interrupted, pushing out the words between panted breaths. Amanda stopped moving suddenly, examining his expression through troubled eyes. "You're sweating, too. What's the matter?"

"Nothing," he ground out. Surely sheer force of will was enough to make his muscles obey him. It had to be. "Hot in here."

"No, it's not that." Her voice lost a little of its panted edge and turned slightly more concerned. She smoothed her hand over his tense forehead, her touch a worried inquiry. "You're—you're hurting."

"I can take it." Mike grunted the words, desperate to reassure her. "No problem."

"But—"

He kissed her, trying to tell her without words that it didn't matter, that he'd have crawled over a thousand broken beer bottles and margarita glasses, would have braved another visit to the Pepto-Bismol Pink Palace or any other torture, just to make love to her. He thought he'd made his case pretty well, too, until he finally raised his head and witnessed the results.

As though nothing had happened, Amanda sucked in a breath and went right on talking. "But you're hurt! I forgot about your overtraining, forgot about the fitness tests, forgot about your poor, sore muscles."

She gazed down at him with what was probably meant as empathy but which only felt like a gigantic hunk of unwanted pity. At the sight of it, Mike wanted to open the commode lid, flush himself down, and disappear for good.

"I'm fine," he said roughly. Then, when she remained unmoving, more urgently. "Please, don't stop. Don't stop. I need—"

But it was too late. The spell was broken, and so was the atmosphere of uninhibited closeness between them. With evident regret, Amanda pushed herself upward and reached for her clothes. Her bra dangled teasingly in front of his face, then was whisked away as she put it on.

"I can't," she said softly. "I can't take advantage of you like this. You can't even hold me."

Mike glared at his stupid, nonfunctioning arms.

"And I can't stand to think I'm hurting you. I'm sorry."

He didn't know what to say. Even as he sat there in his tiny, steamy bathroom, she moved farther and farther away from him. Their closeness was pushed away with every new piece of clothing Amanda put on.

She sat on the edge of the bathtub to lace up her sneakers, her dark ponytail brushing his Levi's-covered knee. Tenderly, Mike lifted the silky strands of her hair in his fingers, running their softness over his knuckles . . . and wishing he had the authority over his muscles to reach higher and loosen her hair all the way.

But he couldn't. Dammit. Mike frowned, wanting to break something to ease the frustration he felt. The medicine cabinet looked like a likely target. He'd never been particularly keen on it, anyway.

"Awww, hell, Amanda." He'd never disappointed a woman like this, had never wanted more to know the right things to say, now that he had. "I—"

"It's all right." Briskly, Amanda stood, and her hair slithered from his grasp as rapidly as she'd escaped from his arms. "I'll finish that shave job." Her gaze dipped in an evaluating fashion over the straggly remnants of his beard, then zeroed in on the shaving cream. "We'll go tape our next Life Coach Lotto segment, and we'll do this later. Okay? Okay."

Privately, Mike had his doubts about that. But ten minutes later, uninterestedly clean-shaven and properly dressed, that's exactly what he and Amanda headed out to do.

They should have known their efforts were jinxed, though. The minute they stepped out of the bathroom, the shuffling of poker chips at the kitchen table abruptly stopped, and after the silence that followed came a yelp of surprise. Mike and Amanda rounded the wicker-and-bamboo floor screen to see the entire crew stifling huge grins and one of the camera operators glaring down at Cupcake.

The dog gave a tentative tail wag. Then she shook herself and trotted happily toward Mike, leaving behind a suspiciously large wet spot on the video guy's pant leg.

"Cupcake strikes again," Amanda said. "You'd almost think she knew we didn't want them around, wouldn't you?"

To Mike's mingled relief and chagrin, they rescheduled the fitness tests for the following Tuesday. Amanda cooked up a story about having decided to involve Mike's friends in the health-and-fitness routine she was devising for him, rattling off some mumbo-jumbo about "environmental factors" and "group-support theories" and, unbelievably, the Channel Six crew bought it. Even more unbelievably, Amanda managed to persuade Bruno, Snake, and Curly to join in her scheme, too.

Mike still didn't know how she'd done it. So far as he knew, his buddies got physical for nothing short of a hottie in a short skirt—say, chasing down the blonde at the end of the bar before she vanished into the crowd and got away. But today, he'd already witnessed Bruno doing one-arm push-ups, Curly hoisting his massive self daintily across a balancing beam six inches off the ground, and Snake standing flamingo-like on one foot to test his flexibility.

Through all this, Amanda stood off to the side of

the East Valley park they'd gone to, making notes on her ever-present clipboard, patiently explaining each fitness test, and occasionally blowing her coach's whistle. The fact that she looked outrageously cute in a pair of shorts, another Life Coach Lotto logo-emblazoned T-shirt, a baseball cap, and sneakers, might or might not have had something to do with the impressive morale of his friends . . . but it sure as hell had an effect on Mike.

He would ace these fitness tests, or die trying. Somehow, he had to impress Amanda. Accomplishing that had begun to feel increasingly important to him, and after yesterday's steamy-bathroom debacle, Mike figured he had plenty of lost ground to make up for.

Now that Bruno, Curly, and Snake had quit ribbing him about his new clean-shaven, sans-beard look, he might have a chance at it, too.

The four of them jogged around the perimeter of the park, each unwilling to slow down and have the worst timed rating on the one-mile run. By the time they finished their third lap and neared the picnic ramada where Amanda and the camera crews were working, Mike was seriously sucking wind. Not that he'd admit it.

It was possible, he thought, that all the miserable couch-potatoing he'd done after the April Fools' Day incident—not to mention all the time he spent lounging in his taxi these days—hadn't done him any favors in the muscle-bound-and-macho department. Feeling grumpier than ever and with a sneaking suspicion that maybe he *did* need some coaching help, Mike kept on running.

He caught Curly ogling Amanda's legs as they passed and whacked him upside the head, Three Stooges style.

"Hey! In your dreams, meathead," he growled between breaths. "Let's show a little respect, here."

Curly grinned, his red hair neatly shellacked to his

To start your membership, simply complete and return the Free Book Certificate. You'll receive your Introductory Shipment of 2 FREE Zebra Contemporary Romances. Then, each month as long as your account is in good standing, you will receive the 2 newest Zebra Contemporary Romances. Each shipment will be yours to examine for 10 days. If you decide to keep the books, you'll pay the preferred book club member price of $10.75 – a savings of over 20% off the cover price! (plus $1.50 to offset the cost of shipping and handling.) If you want us to stop sending books, just say the word… it's that simple.

If the Free Book Certificate is missing, call 1-888-345-2665 to place your order.
Be sure to visit our website at www.kensingtonbooks.com.

BOOK CERTIFICATE

Yes! Please send me 2 FREE Zebra Contemporary romance novels. I understand I am under no obligation to purchase any books, as explained on this card.

Name _____

Address _____ Apt. _____

City _____ State _____ Zip _____

Telephone (____) _____

Signature _____

(If under 18, parent or guardian must sign)

Offer limited to one per household and not valid to current subscribers.
All orders subject to approval. Terms, offer, and price subject to change. Offer valid only in the U.S.

CN061A

Thank You!

ll..l.l...lll.....ll.l.l.l..l.l..l..l.lll.l..l..lll.l..ll...l

Zebra Contemporary Romance Book Club
Zebra Home Subscription Service, Inc.
P.O. Box 5214
Clifton , NJ 07015-5214

scalp with the styling products Amanda had recommended. "What's the matter? She's cute."

"She's your coach," Mike said, pumping his arms harder.

"She's your coach, too," Curly protested. "I don't see *you* having any problems with checking out her legs."

Snake and Bruno nodded as they jogged. "Yeah, Mike," Snake panted. His thick silver wallet chain jangled in time with his strides, accenting his cut-off jean shorts and Harley Davidson T-shirt "workout gear." "He's right."

"That's different." As a group, they weaved around an arrangement of playground equipment and emerged into the open again. Mike frowned. "I'm, uh, only in this Lotto thing to help out Amanda. As a friend."

Bruno chortled. He was the only one of them, Mike was pretty certain, who still had the breath for such a maneuver.

"Sure, Mike," he said, picking up the pace.

They all groaned and reluctantly matched his superhuman ex-Marine speed.

"Yeah, right," Snake added when they'd found their rhythm again and were running past a group of picnic tables. "You want to be the friend who gets a lot friendlier. *If* you know what I mean."

It didn't take a genius to know they'd jump to exactly that conclusion. Mike had been counting on it.

"Well, hell," he said, trying not to think about the fact that his chest felt like it might explode from lack of oxygen. After all, this makeover cover-up thing was starting to pick up speed. "Of course I want to get friendlier with Amanda. Why else would I go to a damned spa for her?"

They all nodded. Their instant acceptance of his alibi was reassuring—until the next question came.

"So," Curly said, "if you're so cozy with Amanda, how come we haven't seen you guys actually out on a date?"

Damn. "I'm, uh, stillworkingonit," Mike replied.

"Huh?" came his way in three-part stereo. Three puzzled faces turned toward him, jogging up and down in his vision as they continued running. The finish point was just ahead, but Mike had never felt further from being where he wanted to be.

"I'm still working on it," he gritted out, more slowly this time. "It turns out Amanda has this policy about not dating her clients."

"Awwww," moaned Bruno, Curly, and Snake in unison.

Mike glared them into silence.

It lasted all of ten seconds.

"That's too bad," Bruno volunteered. "Shame you didn't know about that policy thing before you started in on your *makeover.*"

All three of them tittered. Actually tittered. If Mike hadn't been feeling so pissed at them, he might have found their descent into girlyhood amusing. As it was, he only scowled.

At his side, Snake waved for the cameras. Then he nudged Mike, his grin widening. "Hey," he suggested, "don't worry about it, dude. Maybe Amanda hasn't gone for the 'before' you, but there's still a chance she'll go for the 'after' you, right?"

They all collapsed at the finish line, laughing like idiots. Walking away from them, feeling his heart rate gratefully plummet, Mike snatched up his plastic squeeze bottle from the sidelines and squirted some water into his mouth. *Maybe she'll go for the "after" you.* Ha!

Dousing Bruno, Snake, and Curly with the

remaining thirty-odd ounces in his bottle in an impromptu water fight probably qualified as a pretty juvenile act. Small comfort, too. After he'd done it, though, Mike had no regrets.

Especially not when Amanda whipped out a portable blow-dryer from her magical Life Coach Lotto canvas bag, somehow secured power for it, and insisted on having the Channel Six stylist give each dripping, disheveled man's hair the "complete camera-ready treatment."

It only got better, too. Every last minute of his buddies' "makeover" was caught on tape.

Chapter Twelve

"I'm glad you came in to see me today, Howard," Amanda said the following Wednesday, a week and a half into the Life Coach Lotto project. From her cozy office chair, where she always felt most competent and in control, she smiled across the desk at the man seated opposite her. "I think we accomplished a lot together."

"Sure did, Power Hitter." He squared up the paperwork in front of him and returned her grin. "Sure did."

She cleared her throat and gave him a disapproving look. "I thought we'd agreed you wouldn't call me that anymore."

"I thought we'd agreed you'd call me Snake, like everybody else," he returned, polishing his nails on the edge of his Harley Davidson leather vest and then straightening the matching black-leather-pants coverings layered atop his jeans. With them, he looked sort of like a latter-day western outlaw. "Howard is a

wuss name. A guy named Howard probably does . . .
I dunno, *yoga* or some shit.''

He caught her expression. "Pardon my French."

What was *with* these guys and their antiyoga fixation? If you asked her, Amanda figured the whole lot
of them could use a little Eastern-style balance in
their lives.

But she recognized a losing battle as well as any
woman. And this one wasn't worth wasting energy
on.

"Okay," she agreed. "Snake it is, then."

"Righteous."

"But only if you follow that stock-diversification
advice I gave you," Amanda added, sitting up straighter
and tapping her desktop calendar blotter with a pen.
"And start following that high-fiber diet I told you
about, too. After a few days, those digestive problems
you mentioned will be a thing of the past."

"Awww, hell," he muttered, looking pained. "I
can't. The guys would laugh me out of town the first
time I whipped out a bran muffin."

"Well, fruits and veggies are a nice option, too."

He grimaced. "Are you sure T-bones don't have
fiber?"

"Positive."

If possible, Snake's face drooped even further.

"And," Amanda went on, writing a few names and
phone numbers on a piece of paper, "I want you to
consider contacting the art dealers I mentioned about
arranging an exhibit of your auto-parts sculptures.
Here's the list."

He took it and stared at the names doubtfully. "I
dunno, Power Hitter. My sculpting's just for the hell
of it. It's not—"

"Come on, now," Amanda interrupted gently.
"Abstract, modern pop art is really booming right

now. It would be a shame to let your potential go to waste.''

Originally, Snake had come to her for help in managing his financial portfolio, but over the course of their first life-coach meeting, greater aspirations had emerged—acclaim as a sculptor, among them. All in all, she felt quite proud of the progress they'd made— or would make soon.

Snake folded the list and tucked it into his leather vest pocket. "I'll think about it."

"You have to do more than think. You have to act!" Amanda urged, a sense of purpose sweeping through her on Snake's behalf. "You can do it, I know you can! I believe in you."

He frowned, looking skeptical. *Dream-realization jitters,* she diagnosed. They struck many of her clients when they got their first real sense that their goals might be within reach. A little time—and a little taste of success—would cure them.

Having encouraged Snake as much as possible for now, Amanda buzzed Trish on the intercom and asked her to set up a series of biweekly appointments for him.

"I can't make it this Friday," Snake interrupted as she and Trish discussed the schedule. He shook his head. "That's when I'm judging the big arm-wrestling match down at Marvin's."

"Arm-wrestling match?" Amanda asked.

"Yeah. This time, Mike's going up against Curly."

She gulped, imagining huge, kinky-haired Curly squashing Mike's hand in one meaty fist. Not that Mike was a weakling, by any means, but Curly was roughly the size of a Buick, with arms to match.

"Course, with Mike as reigning champion," Snake went on, "Curly's got a tough row to hoe. Personally"—He leaned forward conspiratorially and winked—"my money's on Mike. You coming down to Marvin's to watch?"

Camera-free time with Mike. Her pulse quickened. But no, Amanda reminded herself as she finished setting up future appointments via Trish. She couldn't get involved with a client. Especially not one who intrigued her as much as Mike did. They'd already taken their relationship much too far, and she had to put a stop to it. Now.

No matter how much Mel and Gemma had cheered her news of the forbidden-fruit man nibbles she'd had. No matter how much she herself had loved them.

She absolutely could not go down to Marvin's to cheer Mike on. He'd infer from her presence that she wanted more involvement between them. (*You do,* her conscience reminded.) He'd think she couldn't stand to be apart from him. (*Increasingly true,* her libido jabbed.) He'd believe that he was coming to mean so much more to her than their professional relationship implied. (*He does! He does!* cheered her heart.)

No, if she were smart, she wouldn't go down to Marvin's on Friday night. She wouldn't see Mike any-place where the mushy, yes-there's-love-at-first-sight part of her could take hold.

Still, when Mike was so obviously overmatched, would a harmless, well-meant, teensy-weensy vote of confidence and encouragement hurt? After all, encouraging people was her business, for Pete's sake!

"Sure, I'll be there," she said quickly, raising a fist in a cheerleader's gesture. "Go, Mike!"

As soon as Snake left, Amanda was on the phone with Gemma. Her friend's usual commonsense advice was weirdly lacking, though, leaving Amanda gaping at the phone held at arm's length while Gemma nattered on about not missing any "unexpected opportunities."

Shaking her head, Amanda returned the receiver to her ear. Something was definitely going on with steady, sedate Gemma.

"If you're already hot for this guy," Gemma was saying, "and your heart is telling you to go for it—"

"I can't listen to my heart!" Amanda cried, breaking in before she heard something truly impossible, like *Go ahead, fall in love with Mike.* "This Lotto is my big break. I've got to listen to my head!"

"What does your head know that your heart doesn't?" Gemma argued. "If Mike is the man for you, a part of you knows it, and you can't deny it forever."

"I have to," Amanda moaned. "Somehow! It's just that every time I'm around Mike, it's like some *other* part of me takes control, and I can't stay away. It was hard enough when he had that scraggly beard. *And* the half-beard. But you know, it doesn't even matter to me now that he's clean-shaven. I wanted him before, and I want him now. Why can't I convince myself to just stop it?"

"True love," Gemma suggested, sounding like her real self at last. "You're falling in love with Mike, and what he looks like doesn't change that."

Amanda considered the idea, and a new surge of misery engulfed her. *Maybe it's true.*

"No, no, no!" she protested, arguing with herself as much as with Gemma's idea. "Mike Cavaco is the worst possible person for me to fall in love with. It can't be true!"

"Sure it can," Gemma insisted. "I think it already is."

And the only thing worse than hearing reliable, sensible Gemma say something like that was the realization that Amanda had next. It *was* true. *She was falling in love with Mike.*

Determinedly, Amanda put her new, terrifying real-izations behind her and got on with her day. Just because she was falling head over heels for a guy who was probably completely wrong for her, who was her opposite in almost every way, and who possessed none of the necessary ambition that was such an important part of her life, well . . . that wasn't any excuse to throw in the towel, was it?

No. She'd muddle through somehow, Amanda promised herself. Possibly by never calling up her friends for love-life advice ever again.

By the time Bruno arrived at Aspirations, Inc., late that afternoon for the résumé-writing session they'd arranged, she felt so grateful for the distraction he offered that she all but lugged him into her office by force.

"Bruno!" she cried, leaping up when he stuck his head inside the door. "I'm so happy to see you."

"Uh, likewise."

Compliantly, he let himself be led as Amanda grabbed him by the arm and marched him into her office. Her fingers didn't fit all the way around his massive, Marines-honed bicep, and she gave a moment of thanks that *he* wasn't Mike's opponent.

No. She wasn't going to think about Mike. *Or* Friday's big off-camera opportunity to see him. And she sure as heck wasn't going to give in to the Snoopy-dance impulse she felt whenever those two things crossed her mind.

"What kinds of life goals can I help you out with?" she asked, retreating to the other side of the desk to take a seat. "Running a marathon? Getting a master's

degree? Starting your own frozen yogurt shop?
They're all very popular!"

Beneath his growing-out GI haircut, Bruno wrinkled his forehead. "Uh, I guess. But I only came here
for help with my résumé. Remember?"

Amanda tried not to feel let down. Brainstorming
a new approach to Bruno's résumé might not be
challenging enough to provide quite the distraction
from forbidden fruit she needed right now. But she
did want to help him, so she nodded.

"That's right. Of course. Sorry, I just get carried
away sometimes, wanting to help my clients."

She smiled at him. He smiled back.

"I don't even like frozen yogurt, anyway," Bruno
said.

"Me, neither. I'm a Chunky Monkey girl all the
way. Never mind." Getting back on track, Amanda
relaxed in her chair and requested the completed
job-history-and-skills questionnaire she'd given Bruno
during their original meeting.

Looking relieved, he handed it over. She reviewed
it, noting several impressive areas of expertise—and
one small glitch.

"This looks great," she began. Bruno beamed.
"I'm not sure, though, that your work as a Tops 'N
Tails bouncer ought to be included on your new
résumé."

"Why not? I do a good job watching out for the
girls."

"Well, another . . . *sort* of employer might frown
on a, a—"

"Strip club," Bruno supplied.

"Right." Her face heated despite the air-conditioned temperature in her office. "Anyway, let's just
leave that part off for now, all right?"

With a little less enthusiasm than she'd have liked, Bruno agreed. After further conversation, Amanda discovered why.

"So that's why I like working at the Tops 'N Tails so much," he was saying, looking at her with a self-conscious expression. "They're all so nice about the karaoke thing."

"So what you're saying," Amanda summed up, "is that you feel best when you're up onstage, performing?"

"Well, I, uh . . ."

"Maybe your true calling is as a singer!" she cried, thrilled to have finally glimpsed Bruno's secret life goal—the thing she could most effectively help him accomplish. "Of course! It's perfect! Now, here's how we can go about chasing that dream."

She outlined several steps he could take between now and their next life coach meeting, all geared toward achieving his hidden ambition to become a performer. Sure, Bruno had originally come to her for help in creating a new résumé, but now that their meeting had revealed even greater aspirations—fame as a professional singer, among them—Amanda couldn't wait to get started. She felt quite proud of the progress Bruno had made already and told him so.

"Awww, thanks, Amanda," he said, presenting her with a view of his cropped hair and newly-pink scalp as he looked downward. Who'd have guessed a tough guy like Bruno was capable of a blush? "I dunno about this singing idea, but hey . . . now that we've spent a little more time together, at least I know why Mike said all that stuff about you."

"Stuff? About me?" Her attention perked up one hundred percent, the way her libido seemed to at the merest touch from the man in question. "What kind of stuff?"

"Well, I was pretty shocked, to tell you the truth," Bruno began, and then he went on, hesitantly, to elaborate.

By the time he'd finished, Amanda was feeling pretty shocked herself.

"I can't believe this!" Mike yelled, slamming on the taxi's brakes. In the far corner of the grocery-store parking lot—he, Bruno, and Snake had been in the midst of making a beer run before tonight's poker game—the cab hurtled to a stop. He wrenched his arm onto the front seat and swiveled sideways to glare at Bruno, seated next to Snake in the cab's backseat. "*You told her what?*"

"That, uh, Amanda was the first woman you'd thought about getting serious over," Bruno said. "The first woman since the Swedish masseuse, anyway—"

"Inga?" Mike sputtered. "You told her about Inga?"

"—and that, as her friend, I thought she had a right to know how you felt about her," Bruno continued with exaggerated innocence. "That's all."

"Oh, man." Snake chortled. "Women eat up that friendship stuff with a spoon. They love it."

Along with Snake, Bruno nodded. As though Mike intended to charge them all for a pre-game drive to Safeway, he blinked up at the meter and started counting out the fare with large, patient fingers. He handed it over.

The motion kicked Mike into gear again. Snatching the money, he hurled it into the backseat, where the dollar bills Bruno always paid with—shared tips from "the girls" at work—fluttered onto his friends' shoulders and laps.

"But I never said that!" he shouted.

Bruno shrugged, placidly gathering his scattered money. "She especially liked the celibacy part."

Celibacy? Mike was afraid to ask. But he couldn't help it. He just couldn't.

"What celibacy part?" he asked, drumming his fingers on the steering wheel. Maybe the motion would relieve his urge to wring Bruno's miserable, interfering neck.

"Your new celibacy," Bruno replied. "That you started after Inga left until you found a woman who really, uh, I think I said, 'spoke to your inner heart.' "

"Whoa. That's beautiful, dude," Snake said, shaking his head in apparent awe.

"Thanks. Got it from a vitamin commercial."

They both guffawed.

For a minute, Mike could only stare at them in horrified amazement. Then he found his voice again. "But I'm not celibate!"

Sure, it had been a while since he'd cozied up to a woman. All his good-time girlfriends had seemed to discover "other interests" after the April Fools' Day incident, and Mike had descended into the realm of the unshaven, unappreciated, and temporarily unemployed. But that didn't mean he'd become a born-again virgin, for Christ's sake!

"I dunno, Mike," Bruno said, shaking his head. "Amanda seemed really touched by that part. You saving yourself for the perfect woman. Her maybe *being* that woman. . . ."

"It's genius," Snake said. He gave Bruno a grudging look of respect. "Celibacy. Man, no woman could resist. She'll be on him like glue on a stamp. If you know what I mean."

Bruno chuckled.

"Like chrome on a Harley," Snake mused, dreamily. "Like suds on a beer."

"Snake—" Mike warned.

"Lipstick on a collar," he went on.

"Snake!"

"Painted Elvis on velvet." A low, appreciative chuckle emanated from the backseat. "Man, oh, man. That office chair of hers looked pretty comfy to me, *if* you know what I mean."

"Shut up, Snake!" Mike yelled, venting some of his irritation by twisting off the taxi's ignition and wrenching out the keys. He refused to think about the memories culled by Snake's assessment of Amanda's office chair or the new ones sparked by a similar seated position he'd taken in his small, steamy bathroom just a couple of days ago.

"Come on, Mike," Bruno began in a placating voice. "He's just—"

"And *you.*" Mike rounded on his crew-cut-wearing friend again. "Dammit, Bruno! You said you were just going in there to work on your résumé. So far as I know, that résumé of yours does *not* include a futz-around-with-Mike's-love-life section! I was going to ask Amanda out for this Friday, but now—"

"Oh, yeah," Snake interrupted, "speaking of this Friday, you can't. You have an arm-wrestling match at Marvin's. Eight o'clock. Amanda's going to be there, so don't blow it."

"Don't blow *what?*"

"An arm-wrestling match," Snake repeated. "At Marvin's. Friday. Against Curly."

"Ten bucks on Curly," Bruno chimed in.

Mike glared him into silence.

He turned to Snake. "I do not have an arm-wrestling match. No. You wanted stock-portfolio advice from Amanda, not a promise to watch an event that's not even happening!"

"She wanted to come. If you don't ever see her, how do you expect to date her?"

"I see her all the time." Grinding his teeth, Mike fought an urge to stuff both his matchmaking "buddies" in the trunk for the drive home. "Not that it's any of your damned business."

"Yeah," Bruno put in, nodding. "That's right, he sees Amanda a lot. For his *makeover.*"

Masculine titters filled the cab. Mike was really beginning to hate the *M* word.

Plucking a Lucky Strike from the pack in his vest pocket, Snake shrugged. "Sissy stuff. What you need is something manly to impress Amanda with. Like arm wrestling."

"Arm wrestling with Curly isn't manly," Mike protested. "It's hand-and-finger suicide. Ten-digit Russian roulette! Have you forgotten that I *need* my hands to do my *job* with?"

"But you don't have that job anymore." Bruno frowned in obvious puzzlement. "So what difference does it make?"

Sure, bring that up, Mike thought. *As if he didn't have problems enough right now.*

"I plan to get another job just like it," he gritted out. "Soon. In the meantime—"

"In the meantime, he's hot to score with Amanda," Snake explained to his backseat neighbor, lighting up his Lucky Strike. "Which is why we're helping him. Not that I can blame you, Mike. She's—"

"She's *not* going to be the subject of this discussion," Mike broke in, scouring them both with a menacing look. He snatched the cigarette from Snake's mouth and crushed it in the taxi's ashtray. "Or any other discussions, either. Got it?"

They both nodded, suitably chastened. For a whole five seconds. Then Bruno chortled and nudged Snake with his elbow. "Jake was right. Mike's got it bad for Amanda, doesn't he?"

At the mention of his trainer friend's name, Mike's muscles seized up in remembered agony. He'd done pretty well on Amanda's fitness-evaluation tests, especially once she'd dosed him with anti-inflammatory ibuprofen and given him a few days to recover. The ultrahealthy (low-fat, high-fiber, low-sugar, high-yuck) diet she'd suggested afterward would be impossible to swallow, of course. It was way too light on Frosted Wild Berry Pop Tarts, not to mention Twizzlers, and—

"Looks like it," Snake agreed. "Jake sure called it. Head over heels, I think he said."

"Yeah. Worse than Inga, don't you think?"

"Maybe . . ."

Speculatively, they both glanced at him, as though sizing up the likelihood of his, say, proposing to Amanda via JumboTron at the next Diamondbacks game. For an instant, Mike bought into the fantasy. Did Amanda even like baseball? If she didn't, a ball-park proposal would never go over very—

"Dammit, you two! Knock it off!" he yelled, abruptly wrenching himself from the on-bended-knee scenario he'd been imagining. "From now on, just stay out of this thing between me and Amanda. *Out of it.* Got it? It's none of your damned business."

"Okay, Mike."

"Sure thing. Whatever you say."

"Noses out of it," Bruno elaborated.

"No matter what," agreed Snake.

They folded their arms and smiled at him, looking fairly cherubic, at least for a Harley-riding auto-parts sculptor and an ex-Marine strip-club bouncer.

"Good luck," they said in unison.

As *if* that would work, Mike thought, glaring once more at the innocent-looking duo in the backseat before shoving the keys into the ignition again. The way his luck was running, he'd have the whole gang at Marvin's running around matchmaking between him and Amanda before the week was out.

Oh, the horror of it.

Chapter Thirteen

On Thursday, Mike survived a couple of grueling job interviews, several fares from hell on his taxicab shift, a six–zero blowout in the Padres versus Diamondbacks game broadcast on the radio . . . and a crazy, nearly overwhelming urge to drop by Amanda's office and finish what they'd started. He hadn't seen her since the fitness evaluation tests and the diet-advice session that followed, and not knowing where he stood with her was killing him.

By the time he drove up to his parents' place in the southeastern Phoenix suburb of Mesa, jockeyed for a parking spot on the crowded street, and eased out of his cab into a rapidly darkening evening, the last thing he wanted to do was attend the biweekly Cavaco family dinner.

Grumpy, disheveled, and itching to swap the khaki pants and knit shirt he'd dragged on for the job interviews in favor of a pair of Levi's and a T-shirt, Mike slammed shut the driver's-side cab door and pocketed his keys. He squinted through the deepening twilight, following the spill of streetlight to the front door of the house he'd grown up in.

The two-story split-level house still looked as Brady-Bunch-meets-the-eighties as ever. Its light tan paint job was peeling in spots, its la-di-da desert landscaping was getting a little thirstier than it ought to be, and his mom's cheerily lewd yard gnomes were as off-color as always. But the music and laughter and conversation coming from inside still gave him exactly the coming-home feeling he always expected, and his dark mood lifted as he started up the cracked concrete pathway.

The front door opened partway there, flooding the quiet street with newly-amplified classic rock. Five little girls of varying ages appeared in the passageway and squealed when they saw Mike. Three seconds later, he was bombarded.

"Unca Mike!" cried his youngest niece, running on her chubby three-year-old's legs to lock her arms around his knees. "You here!"

"Yay! Uncle Mike!" yelled two more voices, these filled with the squeaky enthusiasm only seven-year-old twin sisters could manage. They put a wrist lock on him, each grabbing an arm and jumping up and down.

"Uncle Mike! We thought you'd never get here!" His eldest niece, too cool to actually jump up and down at the advanced age of twelve, contented herself with slugging him on the shoulder. "We've been watching for like, you know, hours."

His fifth niece, six years old and too shy to speak, only stood there on the sidewalk, gazing up at him through shining eyes. Then she, too, tackled him hard enough to punch the air from his stomach. Mike stumbled backward, off-balanced by the usual onslaught.

His sister Kimberly passed by the open front door,

looked out, and rescued him a few minutes later. "Off, you little hooligans," she said, peeling away her own twins as well as the other three girls with a good-natured grin. She sent them inside with threats of needing someone to dust "Grandma's hundred-piece assortment of collectible plates" before dinner and then turned to Mike when all the girls had scattered.

"So," she said, dragging him inside the mayhem of the Cavaco clan, "where's your girlfriend, huh? When are you going to bring someone over for dinner?"

Thoughts of Amanda immediately pushed their way into his mind. Then he imagined polished, ambitious Amanda in the midst of his laid-back, unpretentious family and hurriedly turned his thoughts away. He'd make a better match pairing off Cupcake with the amorous AKC-registered weimaraner down the street.

"Kim, I'm not seventeen anymore." With a nod of greeting, Mike accepted a bottle of Budweiser from his younger brother Manny in passing and took a slug. "I'm not gullible enough to tell you about my dates."

"*Hmmph*. Give a guy one little piece of misguided advice—"

"You told me to give my prom date a set of socket wrenches instead of flowers!"

"—that happens to be a little bit unique—"

"She broke up with me. For the rest of the year, every girl in school called me Socket Man."

"—and what happens? He never forgives you." With an overly-disappointed shake of her head, Kimberly looked him up and down. "Little brothers."

"Big sisters."

"Hey, now that we've identified everyone," said another of his sisters, Amy, joining them with a drooling baby nephew on her hip, "whaddya say we get on with dinner? I'm starving."

Mike agreed. After the day he'd had, he figured he could use some good eats and a little relaxation. He headed for the warm, sprawling kitchen that was the center of the house, prepared to do his part for the sake of a decent meal.

On the way there Susan, his third sister, grilled him about why he was so dressed up, "all but wearing a tie!" His mom buried him with hugs and haircut advice, exclaiming all the while about how "spiffy" he looked without his beard.

His dad threw an arm over his shoulder and gave him a complete overview of the Suns' chances in the upcoming basketball season. Brian, his older brother, nodded hello and then went on leading the multitude of Cavaco offspring in a rowdy game of Pin the Tail on Grandma's New Blue Jeans.

Above all, the big-screen TV blared, the stereo at the other end of the house blasted classic rock, and laughter ruled. By the time Mike finally made it to the kitchen, his beer was gone, he had two nephews trailing his heels and one riding piggyback, one of three cats was rubbing his ankles, something he thought was bubblegum was stuck in his hair . . . and his smile was authentic.

He was home.

Dispatching some of the kids to lug in the supplies he'd brought from his taxi—"and get some Twizzlers for yourselves, too!"—he settled in to work. Things were already in progress, and when he entered the kitchen, Amy looked up from the lettuce she was tearing into a salad bowl.

Then she asked the question he'd been dreading and blew his newly-happy mood all to hell.

"How's work these days, Mike? Luke and I brought the kids in last week, but I guess we missed your shift."

Uneasiness settled in the pit of his stomach. Trying to shake it off, Mike dragged out a cutting board and selected a heavy chef's knife from the block beside the stove. He shrugged.

"I haven't been on at work much lately," he said, partly truthfully. "No biggie."

"Oh. Well, maybe we'll catch you next time."

"Sure." *Tell her,* urged his conscience. *Tell them all about April Fools' Day!* But he couldn't. Seeing the disappointment on his family's faces would have killed him. "Maybe next time."

Amy murmured agreement and moved on to slicing radishes. Left momentarily alone at his end of the counter, Mike frowned down at the cutting board and wanted to smash it over his forehead. Maybe that would knock some sense into him.

Maybe then he'd be able to find a way to tell them all what had happened.

But for now, he just couldn't. They'd all been so proud when he'd gotten the job in the first place. Hell, he still got woozy just thinking about the Cavaco celebration that had followed his hiring. So long as he could duck around the truth with stories of missed shifts, helping a buddy with his part-time taxi driver's job, and taking a few days off . . . well, he would. It was as simple as that.

Sure, when the Life Coach Lotto segments started to air—after his whole-life makeover was one hundred percent complete—that would probably complicate things a little. But Mike still thought it was pretty likely the real winner would turn up eventually and the Channel Six execs would scrap *his* participation faster than you could say breach of promise. The segments he'd taped would probably never even air. So what did he have to worry about, really?

The answer was brought home to him a few minutes later. A weird dinging sound made him jerk his head up from the dinner preparations, and all around him, the Cavacos nearby did the same thing.

"What was that?" asked Brian, now wandering through the kitchen in search of a nephew's lost Binky.

"I dunno." Amy looked up from her salad bowl, frowning. "I don't think I've ever heard it before."

More puzzled murmurs followed. Then the sound came again, echoing all through the house.

"It's the doorbell!" cried his Mom. "It's been so long since anybody used it, I didn't recognize it."

Mike shrugged and selected a green bell pepper from the pile at his elbow, then went on chopping. Anybody who knew the Cavacos realized they had an open-door policy for friends, neighbors, and family. Nobody but a door-to-door salesperson would have rung the doorbell. His mom's nonstop conversation would probably keep the poor schmo occupied for the next half-hour, easy.

The sound of voices—feminine voices—emerged from the hubbub surrounding him, gradually growing louder. A minute later, one voice emerged over all the rest.

"I told her she didn't have to ring the doorbell," his neighbor Myrna Winchester was saying as she entered the kitchen with her orthopedic shoes squeaking, "but she insisted. I couldn't talk her out of it."

Ha, he thought, still chopping. Whoever had come with Myrna sounded an awful lot like Amanda—stubborn, determined, and outspoken. Anybody who'd go head to head with Myrna had to be.

And then . . .

"Mike!" Amanda cried, coming into the kitchen with various members of the family trailing her. "I'm so glad I finally caught up with you. I've been looking all over for you!"

Busted was his first thought. Somehow, Mike thought crazily, Amanda had divined the lack of wheat germ and grapefruit in his dinner menu and had come to crack her life coach-slash-nutritionist's whip.

Her smile, though, when he turned to look at her, was breathtaking. And not at all censorious. Mike could only assume she had some other purpose for being there, which left him with nothing to do but boggle at her unexpected appearance. Mixing Amanda with his family put a big chunk of his life completely out of context, and he hardly knew how to react.

Oblivious to his surprise, she strode toward him, dressed casually—for her—in a short dark blue skirt, buttoned-up patterned shirt, and bare legs. Her strappy sandals clicked against the linoleum. Her clothes fit close against her body, and on anyone less wholesome and polished looking than Amanda, the effect might have been too much. As it was, Mike had trouble taking his eyes off her.

Yes, she looked that terrific. Damn, was he in trouble.

"I'm sorry to track you down like this," she continued to say, "especially after office hours."

Office hours. Another few words and she'd reveal the Life Coach Lotto makeover routine. Mike would never have another moment's peace. Ever. He dropped his chef's knife with a clatter.

Farther down the kitchen counter, Amy gave him an inquisitive look over her ever-larger bowl of salad. "Office hours?"

"It's okay." He interrupted Amanda at the same time, pointedly ignoring his sister as he wiped his hands, and then took Amanda's arm to draw her closer. "I don't mind."

Amanda's bemused gaze took in the apron tied around his middle, the checkered towel he'd tucked into the waistband to wipe his hands on, and—he thought—the bubblegum in his hair.

"Yes, I know that you're not big on formalities," she said, lips quirking as she tried to hide a smile. "You look cute in yellow ruffles, by the way."

"Har, har." Mike made a face and steered her into a semisecluded spot near the refrigerator. He could feel her staring at the brown leather deck shoes he'd worn with his dressier clothes today and knew there'd be a boatload of questions to answer about that later, too. "You're not big on surprises yourself," he pointed out. "Yet here you are."

He raised his eyebrows, hoping like crazy that her presence there didn't involve anything related to Lotto. A crucial need to visit Frederick, Tiffany, Helga, and all the kneecap oglers at the Pepto-Bismol Pink Palace, for instance. Or a sudden, irrefutable yen to examine his so-called quest for personal enrichment. If it did, Mike figured he just might crack.

"Yes. Well. It's just that I really need to talk to you," Amanda explained, dragging her gaze upward from his telltale shoes. "And I didn't think it could wait. It's about the—"

"Hold on." Before she could finish saying *Life Coach Lotto* and drag him into a fresh purgatory of makeover jokes—not to mention unwanted inquiries into his until-now unknown state of partial unemployment—Mike grabbed a spare longneck Bud from his passing brother. He opened it and thrust it into her hand, using the motion to lean closer, surreptitiously.

"Ixnay on the Ottolay," he said through the corner of his mouth. He made a ref's *no good* gesture with his hands. "Nobody here knows about that." The eager, get-ready-to-promote light that came into her eyes scared the hell out of him, and he hurried to add, "And I want to keep it that way."

She looked deflated. "Why?"

He frowned. "I just ... do, that's all. That's enough."

"No, it's not. These are the people you love." Amanda's expansive, spread-arm gesture encompassed the melee surrounding them, including the blasting music, laughing conversation, and screaming, running, rowdy rug rats of all sizes. She set down her beer and continued. "Their support is very important to the development of your personal-growth plan. I can't believe you haven't shared any of this with them."

Now she seemed hurt. Hurt and disappointed. In him. Feeling like a regular heel, Mike fought an urge to envelop Amanda in a big hug . . . and then tickle her into looking less glum. He figured it would probably work, too. At least until she recovered well enough to grill him about career goals or pretzel him into a yoga pose like poor meditation wanna-be Mr. Waring from Aspirations, Inc. He had a feeling nothing could keep Amanda from her chosen path for long.

"You don't have to look at me like I have two heads," he complained, growing increasingly bothered by the fact that he was cornered. "I'm not a big talker, that's all."

"It's not just talking! It's *sharing*. Sharing your hopes, your dreams, your successes and failures."

Failures? The whole idea was a nightmare.

"Then the people you love, and who love you, can support your growth," Amanda continued urgently. She gave him a serious look. "You have to share, Mike. Honest."

"*Have* to share?" He winced, remembering, all of a sudden, why he hadn't brought very many women to the biweekly family dinners. Moments like this were why. Awkward moments when a woman tried to make him do something he didn't want to do.

Share his failures? Share his ups and downs, warts and all? With the people whose opinions mattered most to him?

Not just no—hell, no.

"It's good for you," she added with that air of authority she carried around with her like an extra-lavish purse. "You'll like sharing once you get used to it. You can start today."

He'd rather clip his toenails with a weed whacker.

"To tell the truth," Mike said, trying to appear saddened himself at the revelation to come, "the Cavacos aren't all that big on sharing. We're not a real sharing kind of bunch. So 'sharing' this kind of thing with them would really not be—"

He paused as a small hand tugged at a corner of his apron. Looking down, Mike spotted two of his nieces standing at his side.

"Unca Mike," said the three-year-old. "Here."

Her chubby fingers held aloft a cookie studded with M&M's. It was missing several kid-sized bites.

"It's your favorite kind," explained the seven-year-old twin standing beside her. "We're sharing it with you."

He knew his part in this long-standing ritual, designed by his mother to improve her grandchildren's manners. Mike accepted the cookie with profuse thanks, popped it into his mouth—inciting shrieks of excitement from his nieces about his bulging cheeks—and then chewed and swallowed, rubbing his belly with overplayed enjoyment. *"Mmmm, mmmm, mmmm.* Thanks, girls."

They ran away laughing, doubtless to swap Grandpa's beer with Alka-Seltzer or play hide-and-seek with one of his brothers' car keys. Still grinning at their mischievousness, Mike turned to face Amanda.

She'd crossed her arms over her chest. Her expression was a knowing one, and it made him start to sweat.

"What?" he asked.

"Cavacos don't share, huh?" she asked. "Not ever?"

"Not the way you mean it," he said rapidly. "Uh-uh. We're not some touchy-feely bunch of—"

"Hey, Mike!" interrupted his mom, gesturing him to the other side of the kitchen, where a group had clustered around the big, farm-style rectangular table. "Come on over here and give Mrs. Winchester a hug, will ya'? The poor dear came all the way across town with your friend Amanda, and you haven't even said hello."

Beside his mom, his next-door neighbor Myrna Winchester waited for him, she of the on-demand taxi rides and vintage Mustang convertible. She spread both arms outward in an expectant way that pretty much sealed his fate. "Come on, sonny!" she boomed. "Give me some sugar."

Beside him, Amanda smirked. "Not touchy-feely, huh?"

Mike scowled. "Okay, whatever. You obviously have some women's intuition thing going on here"—*or, more obviously,* she'd seen through his flimsy excuses.—"to have picked up on all this. But you don't know the whole story. You've gotta trust me. Just don't say anything about the Lotto. Not now."

"But—"

"No. You won't like what happens."

Her eyes widened, then narrowed swiftly as comprehension dawned, or so she thought. "Are you threatening me? Are you saying you'll quit the Lotto if I tell your family about it? Is that it? Why, you rotten—"

And miss being around Amanda? Mike thought. *Not a chance.*

Not that he'd reveal as much to her.

"Hey, I still owe you a few days on our last bet, remember?" he said instead. He ducked his head, rubbing the back of his neck with one hand. "I'm not a welsher. I'll stick it out."

"Good," Amanda shot back. "Because *I'm* not a quitter."

Suddenly, relief poured through him. Smiling at the sensation, Mike raised his hand to stroke her cheek.

"I know that," he said. "Against all reason, it's one of the things I love most about you."

Then he winked, turned toward his obligatory hug with Mrs. Winchester, and headed across the kitchen.

He was halfway there before he realized what he'd just said.

Chapter Fourteen

Love? Mike *loved* her?

Or, at least, loved things about her? Wow.

Still reeling at the thought, Amanda watched him cross the kitchen and give Mrs. Winchester a hug. He grinned as the elderly lady ruffled his hair and tsk-tsked over its unfashionable length, offered her a compliment on the way her brilliant blue eye shadow matched her vintage handbag, and was rapidly drawn into conversation with the many Cavaco women gathered around the table.

Left momentarily alone, Amanda wandered to the kitchen counter. She gazed at the dinner preparations going on, at the cutting boards, bowls, piles of colorful chopped vegetables, and everything else, and in them she saw the cooperation of a family that enjoyed being together. A family that helped one another.

In contrast, the infrequent meals Amanda shared with her parents usually took place in restaurants—separately. Divorce and fine dining didn't really mix, they'd all discovered through trial, error, and a number of inflated bills for broken dishes. She had no brothers or sisters. And while Amanda loved her parents, they were really too wrapped up in their individual quests for new people to date to become very involved in their daughter's life.

Not that she had it so bad, Amanda reminded herself. They all cared for one another—after a fashion—and she also had Gemma and Mel as her secondary family. Trish, too. But looking at the happy, chattering Cavacos all around her did something to her—something uncomfortable and unfamiliar. Seeing them together filled Amanda with . . . Well, it felt a lot like *longing*. Which was a strange emotion to experience when you made it your job to tell other people how to manage their lives.

Surely she didn't need a dose of her own advice?

From across the room, Mike glanced back at her. *It's one of the things I love most about you*, she read in his eyes. A thrill raced through her, combining with the adrenaline rush searching all over town for Mike had given her to create a sort of high-voltage *yes, yes, yes* cocktail. Amanda grinned goofily. Maybe falling for Mike wasn't wise. But it sure was exciting.

He turned back to his conversation. "So Amanda was waiting at my place when you came over to walk Cupcake?" he asked Myrna.

"Sure was, sonny. Course, at first I thought she must have the wrong house—nice girl like that looking for you," Mrs. Winchester said. "No offense, but ever since you started that taxi-driving job, you've been looking a little scruffy around the edges."

"There are more important things than personal appearance," Amanda put in gently. The group at the table faced her. "Not that *your* personal appearance didn't grab some attention on the way over, Myrna. I thought we'd have a whole caravan of eager fellas

following your convertible all the way here, judging
by the honks and waves you were getting."

Mrs. Winchester primped, fluffing up her white
hair. "It's all in the attitude, dearie."

They'd made quite a pair, Amanda felt sure. She,
frantic to find Mike and talk to him about Bruno's
revelations. Myrna, calmly sympathetic and more
than ready for a road trip in her turquoise Mustang.
She had been the one to reveal Mike's typical Thurs-
day-night whereabouts. As Mike's longtime neighbor
and a frequent guest herself at the Cavacos' get-
togethers, Myrna Winchester had known exactly
where to go. Once they'd finished walking Cupcake
together, they'd headed out.

"Your . . . friend seems very resourceful," Mike's
mother said. She gave Amanda a curious, friendly
look. "I can't believe you haven't mentioned her to
us by now, Mike."

She raised her eyebrows toward her son. Meaningfully.

Mike looked cornered. "I was going to, Mom."

"When?"

"Uh, well, uh—"

Amanda couldn't take it. Obviously, despite his bravado, Mike was a terrible and reluctant liar, and in
this instance, telling the truth about her would mean
revealing the whole story about Mike TV and the
Lotto, too. He looked so uncomfortable, actually
stammering out a reply, that she stepped around the
kitchen counter and extended her hand toward Mrs.
Cavaco.

"I'm Amanda Connor," she said formally. "I
haven't known your son all that long, but I can see
where he comes by that personal charm of his." She
couldn't help but smile. "I'm pleased to meet you."

Rather than shake her hand, Mrs. Cavaco used it
to tug her forward for a big hug while she cried out

a welcome. Taken by surprise, Amanda could only stand there for a second. Her own family wasn't—to put it mildly—made up of huggers. Awkwardly, she raised her arms and gingerly patted Mrs. Cavaco's back.

A pace behind his mother, Mike stood staring, openmouthed, at the pair of them. Then he snapped his lips shut and shook his head. By the time Amanda felt she'd started getting the hang of the whole hugging thing, introductions were being made all around. Before long, she found herself invited to dinner and in the midst of the preparations.

She stood at the counter now with her own cutting board, trying to follow Mike's instructions amid all the noise and confusion surrounding them. Frowning in concentration, Amanda watched as he demonstrated the proper way to pinch cilantro sprigs from the lacy-leafed plant in its terra-cotta pot on the countertop and showed her how to chop the pungent herb. Then she listened as Mike described the vegetables they'd be using in the spicy chicken-chipotle chili.

"All these veggies! And here I'd thought you'd forget your healthy new diet the instant you walked out of my office." Amanda beamed at him, pleased to feel she was making a positive difference in his life. "You looked so forlorn at the idea of life without Cheez Whiz."

"I am forlorn." Grinning, Mike opened a drawer and withdrew a pink frilly apron identical in style—if not color—to his. Before she could so much as take a step backward, he'd wrapped it around her waist and was busily tying the strings. "I'm downright brokenhearted."

"*Awwww.*"

She was close enough to feel the heat of his body, close enough to smell the bubblegum in his hair. His strong arms pinned her in place, and Amanda submitted willingly, enjoying the flex of his forearms against her waist. Their bodies nearly touched, and she looked up from contemplating the broad, solid wonderfulness of his chest to find him looking at her with something suspiciously close to tenderness in his gaze.

Oh, she was done for. Mush, mush, mush in this man's arms . . . and it was all Amanda could do not to blurt out the reason why she'd come before she forgot what it was altogether.

To buy herself time, she smoothed out her apron and took a step back. "Brokenhearted is a pretty strong word, especially when it comes to Cheez Whiz," she said lightly. "Are you sure you don't mean—"

"Amanda," Mike interrupted, all teasing gone from his face as he watched her move away, "about what I said before . . ."

Oh, God. That's one of the things I love most about you. He was going to elaborate! Her insides whirled with anticipation. Trying to seem composed, Amanda picked up her chef's knife and stared, unseeing, at the pile of onions awaiting her. "Yes?"

"Well . . ."

"Go ahead." *Before you drive me crazy with waiting!*

"I didn't meant to be, uh, misleading about the whole sharing-and-touchy-feely thing," Mike said, rubbing his hand over the back of his neck. "You deserve the truth. You just surprised me, is all. I'm sorry."

Disappointment surged through her. Pushing it back, Amanda grabbed an onion and balanced it in the center of her cutting board. "Is that it?"

Silence. "Uh, sure. What else would there be?"

Talk. A budding relationship. Total honesty. Love! Obviously, Mike's whole-life makeover hadn't progressed to the point where he was comfortable with those

things, though. Maybe she was misleading herself.
Maybe.

"Forbidden fruit," she said, skewering him with a
no-nonsense look. "There might be forbidden fruit."

He scratched his head. "Forbidden fruit?"

"Yes," Amanda said, thinking of her conversations
with Mel and Gemma on this very topic. They'd all
agreed that Mike was her forbidden-fruit man, which
probably made her his forbidden-fruit woman.
Couldn't he see that? "Sometimes, when you're not
supposed to have something, it makes it all the more
desirable. When really you might not be hungry for it
at all. See?"

"Not really."

She sighed and tried again. "Take this red pepper,
for instance." She plucked one from the bowl and
lofted it in her hand. "If someone told you that you
could never, ever, under any circumstances, taste this
crisp, juicy, delicious red pepper, wouldn't that make
you want it all the more? Forbidden fruit?"

Mike wrinkled his forehead. "But a red pepper is
a vegetable."

"Arrgh!"

As though sensing this was important to her, he
hurried to explain. "Forbidden vegetables, I don't
get. And when I want something, I take it. So—"

"Unless it's forced on you," Amanda interrupted,
feeling increasingly crazed by their whole situation.
"Unless it sits you down in a tiny, steamy, intimate
room and has its wicked way with you."

Mike jabbed the flat of his palm against his ear, as
though checking his hearing. "Huh?"

"Me! Me! I'm your forbidden fruit! And I had my
way with you in spite—in spite of your celibacy vow."
This was what she'd sought him out to tell him, what
she'd searched for him to apologize for, and now

that the moment had finally arrived, Amanda wanted
to all but yell out the words.

"Oh, Mike! My only excuse is that I didn't know,
but that's paltry in the face of your commitment to
waiting for your inner heart to speak. Bruno told me
the whole story, and I'm sorry, so sorry, to have put
your celibacy vow at risk. I swear it will never, ever,
happen again."

Beside her, Mike muttered something that sounded
very much like "I'm going to pound Bruno." Then
he gently eased the chef's knife from her grasp—
dimly, Amanda realized she'd been waving it around
in her usual speaking-with-her-hands way—and set it
on the counter. He placed both hands on her shoulders.

"I. Am. Not. Celibate," he said.

She gasped. "You mean that *counted?* In the bathroom? Even though we didn't . . . ohmigod! Mike, I
had no idea, no idea at all. I'm so sorry. This has
probably set back your spiritual growth by who knows
how much."

Amanda moaned and stuck her head in her hands.
Mike peeled her fingers away and shook his head.

"I've never been celibate. Bruno made it up. Forget
about it."

She tried to smile. "Oh, it's nice of you to want to
make me feel better. Really. But as your life coach,
I honestly think—"

"I'm telling you the truth. And even if I had a
celibacy vow—*which I don't*—there's no one I'd rather
break it with"—Mike emphasized his point with a
slow stroke of his hand over her cheek, then a swift,
surprising kiss—"than you."

"Awwww." *Geez, he was sweet sometimes.* But still . . .
"Really, if there's anyone who can understand the
importance of making a potentially life-altering personal choice, it's me. I respect your decision, Mike.

You don't have to worry that I'll think less of you, somehow, because you've decided to become c—"

"Arrgh! I'm not celibate!" Frowning, he fisted his hands, then gently bopped them in the air, obviously frustrated. His voice was low and insistent when he continued. "I love making love. I love everything about it. The closeness, the feeling of skin against skin, the discovery. The sounds . . . moans and whispers, bedsprings creaking, bodies coming together. The sense of urgency and the smell of musky sheets. Seeing a woman entirely naked for the first time—"

Mike's direct, dark gaze met hers, and she knew he was speaking of them, together, of what he hoped would come.

"—and knowing how good we're about to feel. And so much more. Making love is like getting an amazing new present, all wrapped up in mystery and shiny bows, except I get to open it over and over again . . . and I get to share it, too. What could be better?"

"Ummm." She should have been able to think of something, Amanda knew. But now that the time for a reply had come, she found herself too mesmerized by the images he'd drawn to think of much beyond candlelit rooms, tangled sheets, slow-moving bodies, and mingled sounds of passion. "Better?" she parroted.

"Nothing could be better," Mike answered, completely certain.

Sometime during his explanation, he'd tangoed them both across the room, backing her up against the refrigerator's cool surface in the relative privacy of its little alcove. Now he joined her there, pinning their bodies together. He tilted his hips forward and used one big palm to cradle her jaw.

His other palm flattened beside her head, spread along the freezer door. Slowly, he kissed her, and the heat he generated could have defrosted an entire SuperChiller, all by itself.

"So if you're asking if I'm celibate, the answer—for the last time—is no. I can think of a few ways to demonstrate my commitment to anticelibacy to you"—his grin was devilish, anticipatory, and predatory—"but only about half a dozen of those ways would involve standing up like this. And none of them could properly take place at a nice family dinner."

A moment of expectancy swelled between them. So did heat, curiosity, and a growing sense of being attuned to something larger and more reckless than either of them. The mixture felt intoxicating, too tempting to deny.

"Hey, who's hungry?" Amanda asked, increasingly inclined to believe him about the noncelibacy thing—and increasingly aware of the devilish grin bubbling up inside her, as well. "I've always felt that meals were overrated, anyway. At least as far as dating is concerned. You know, the traditional dinner-and-a-movie first date, where you're both so—"

"So unnecessarily talkative?"

"Ummm—"

"Mmmm-hmmmm." And then Mike was there, pulling her all the way into his arms, kissing her in a way that made her feel as though her toes weren't even touching the linoleum anymore, and it was all Amanda could do to kiss him back. The distant commotion receded still further, and everything narrowed to the press of their bodies, the pounding of her heart, the song in her soul.

They broke apart, and Amanda sucked in a breath. "You know, I knew you'd scored high on the tactile-receptors test and all, but *this* . . . well." Feeling shaken, she drew a hand through her hair, trying to straighten the partially-upswept strands. "This is something else again. Wow."

"I like to think it's the two of us together that makes it so amazing," Mike said, his expression uncharacteristically wistful. Then he seemed to come to himself and frowned. He stuck a finger in his ear, waggled it as though he needed to check his hearing, and cleared his throat. "That, or the aphrodisiacal qualities of those forbidden vegetables you were talking about."

He waggled his eyebrows meaningfully toward the red peppers on the counter, several feet behind them.

Amanda laughed, not buying into his forbidden-vegetable excuse. Obviously, tough-guy Mike had an inner core of marshmallow fluff, and he didn't want her to know exactly how much of a big softie he could be. Privately, she found his unabashed mushiness incredibly endearing . . . but if he wanted to pretend he owed it all to rogue veggies, who was she to disagree?

"Wait'll you get to the broccoli," she growled with mock ferocity, dragging him closer by his shirtfront. "It'll knock your socks off."

"If you want me undressed," he said with a grin, willingly letting himself be dragged, "you only have to say the word. I've got a land speed record inside me just waiting to get out."

Amanda raised her eyebrows. "In the naked-in-under-sixty-seconds category?"

"Sure. Your wish is my command."

"Then c'mere," she murmured, enjoying the giddy feeling that being in control of six-odd feet of Chippendale-worthy, competitive-speed-stripping male gave her. "And let me tell you about the forbidden rutabagas. I've heard they're out of this world."

She initiated the kiss this time, but Mike was a wholehearted participant. Their joining was even better than before, sweetened with tenderness and filled with an exhilarating sense—for Amanda, at least—that she'd finally met her match.

Here was a man who wasn't threatened by her expertise, who didn't bolt at the mention of sharing and meditating and trying the seaweed body wrap. Sure, Mike hadn't leaped at the chance to experience those things, but he hadn't refused, either. And that showed there was hope for a future between them.

Didn't it?

Mike was willing to change, and she was willing to help him with that change. Along the way, she was willing to stick her toes into the sloshy waters of his ordinary-Joe, unpremeditated, Budweiser-splashed lifestyle, no matter how little it suited her. Mutual giving. Compromise. That was all they needed to begin a relationship.

Wasn't it?

That, and a healthy dose of attraction, Amanda decided, smiling anew as their matching aprons touched and she detected a distinct rise beneath Mike's yellow ruffles. At the contact, she deepened their kiss and buried her fingers in his still-needs-a-cut hair, letting herself be swept away.

For too long, she'd been constructing her life with all the expert-approved tools, Amanda mused, following her expertise and instincts to build a business of her own and credentials she could be proud of. But it had all come at the expense of *this*. Love. Risk. Excitement.

Not to mention pulsating, red-hot whoopee.

Didn't she owe it to herself to delve beyond the initial differences between her and Mike and find out what might happen?

Sure she did. And she owed it to Mike, too. After all, without him (and his winning Life Coach Lotto ticket), the burgeoning growth in her life wouldn't have been possible at all. Now that it had begun, it was time for a salsa-spicy, macho-sexy, "come on and live a little" mini-sabbatical.

In the spirit of her new resolution, Amanda wrapped her arms around Mike's neck and lost herself to their next kiss. Its intensity pounded through her, making her head spin and her pulse roar in her ears, making her breath quicken and her senses go numb to everything except the man holding her in his arms.

Maybe that was why she didn't hear Mike's brother Manny approach until he was right beside them, noisily clanking his empty Budweiser bottle on the countertop in an obvious effort to gain their attention. And more than likely that was why the importance of Manny's next words didn't quite hit her the way they should have.

At least not at first.

"Hey, Chef Mike!" he said, slapping his brother on the back. "How about you quit sticking your tongue down your girlfriend's throat for a few minutes—"

Amanda felt Mike's body tense against her, doubtlessly because of Manny's crude turn of phrase. (Was she ever lucky *he* hadn't been the Cavaco to bring in the winning ticket!) Uncertainly, she took a step back.

"—and get busy with that dinner you promised?" Mike's expression hardened. "Get lost, Manny."

"Hey, you're the one with the fancy schmancy foodie education, not me," Manny said with a shrug. "If I thought *I* could make sense of that mess over there, I might do it. But if it's not a hot dog in a pan of boiling water or a bowl of Rice Krispies, it's too tough for me."

Gently, Mike edged Amanda a bit to the side, as though he wanted a wide berth in which to take a swing at his younger brother. Then, with an impatient jerk, he opened the refrigerator, withdrew a fresh bottle of beer, and shoved it into Manny's hand. "Beat it."

"But—"

"You're right. You owe Amanda an apology first."

Manny looked puzzled. "Hey, it's no big deal. I was only kidding. It was the hunger that made me do it."

Giving her a grin that suddenly made him look every inch a teasing Cavaco male, Manny clutched his abdomen as though the chicken-chipotle chili delay were a mortal danger.

Mike stepped closer to his brother, his stance unaccountably rigid. "Say, 'I'm sorry, Amanda.' "

"I'm sorry, Amanda," Manny dutifully replied, "about the tongue thing. It was out of line." *There. Happy now?* asked the look he shot Mike. "But if my brother would jump into Chef Mike mode and stay there, none of this would have happened."

He leaned forward and winked, speaking directly to Amanda. "Don't worry. This isn't serious. He gets a little temperamental when one of us invades his kitchen, is all."

A sense that she was missing something here niggled at the back of Amanda's mind. She glanced from Manny to Mike, noting Mike's increasingly thunderous expression, but didn't have a clue what to make of it. Maybe this was typical sibling rivalry, par for the course among brothers. As an only child, she had only textbook examples to go by.

Despite Mike's efforts to physically nudge him out of the kitchen, Manny kept on talking. His beer-scented breath washed over her, along with his next words.

"We shoulda all gone down to his restaurant." Manny belched, looked surprised, and then sloppily made his way across the kitchen—with liberal help from Mike. "He's never got himself slapped up against the fridge with some hottie while he's there. All business. Chef Mike. That's him.''

And all at once, just like that, Amanda realized what had been bugging her. The missing puzzle piece dropped into place, and she couldn't believe she hadn't guessed the truth until now.

She glanced toward the countertop, taking in the precision-cut vegetables diced into individual prep bowls. Toward Mike's aproned waist, where the folded kitchen towel he'd tucked there swung with practiced expertise. Toward the pot of cilantro on the countertop that was, Amanda noticed belatedly, exactly like the pots of herbs (for that must be what they were) in Mike's spotless carriage-house kitchen.

Gathering steam, she thought back to Mike's reluctance to discuss his career plans. His occasional references to his "team." His aptitude testing, which had revealed strong hand-eye coordination, huge amounts of creativity, leadership ability, and a surprisingly thorough knowledge of mathematical and chemical principles.

Bingo. The answer was plain.

"Mike!" Amanda cried. "You're a chef, aren't you?"

He blanched.

"And not just any chef, either," she continued, gleeful to have the mystery solved at last, "but an unemployed, making-dinners-for-his-family, needs-a-hot-new-job chef! Hallelujiah. This could *not* get any better."

"Oh, God," Mike muttered, shaking his head. "I was afraid you were going to say something like that."

Chapter Fifteen

Driving across town after dinner that night, with Amanda beside him in the taxi's front seat, Mike thought back with affection on the halcyon days—okay, the halcyon twenty minutes—when his biggest problem had been convincing Amanda he *hadn't* taken a vow of celibacy. Compared with what had followed, persuading her he was still interested in general hanky-panky had been a walk in the park.

Damn Manny and his big, fat mouth.

Feeling a crimp in his neck, Mike loosened his white-knuckled grip on the steering wheel and used one hand to liberate a Twizzler from the bunch dangling from the dispatcher's radio. Wordlessly, he offered one to Amanda.

She made a face. *Oookay, fine.* Not good enough for her, he guessed. Defiantly, Mike chomped down on the strawberry strand he'd selected with deliberate relish and went on driving.

Streetlights whipped through the darkness, striping the dim seclusion of the taxi's interior with bright flashes. Cars raced past, lightly spattering the wind-shield with spray from the road. It had rained an hour or so before, and the whole world smelled wet and clean.

At his side, Amanda folded her arms over her chest. She waited.

Still hoping to dodge this whole thing, Mike bit one end of his Twizzler to hold it in place and method-ically folded the rest into his mouth, accordion style. When he'd closed his lips on the whole bundle, it popped open inside his mouth, skewing his cheeks at crazy angles. Bugging out his eyes in mock surprise, he looked sideways at Amanda to see if she'd gotten the joke that never failed to crack up his Cavaco nieces and nephews.

Stone-faced, she crossed her legs at the knee. And waited.

His mood plummeted. Chewing his Twizzler wad with somewhat less enthusiasm, Mike noticed the way her dark skirt slid upward, baring several inches of curvy, feminine thigh. And swore that no matter how much of herself Amanda flaunted in front of him, he damn well wasn't going to apologize for what had happened tonight.

He was taking her home, wasn't he? Wasn't that enough?

Hell, yes.

Amanda cleared her throat. Stared outside as the Tempe city library slid past, followed by the highway overpass and several blocks of lighted office buildings, landscaping, and traffic. And waited some more.

Mike went on chewing his Twizzler gob. It clumped together in his mouth, superpseudostrawberry and sticky-sweet. Upon reflection, he decided he should have packed some steel wool to scour it from his molars once he'd finally worked it into a swallowable size. He still didn't know where the stupid urge to make Amanda laugh had come from, anyway.

Beside him, she swung her foot methodically up and down, making her strappy sandal dangle and then flop back in place. *Whup, whup, whup,* it went against her heel, the very sound a recrimination. If Amanda thought a mere annoyance like that sound was going to make him buckle . . . well, she'd better think again.

Mike Cavaco was made of sterner stuff.

He was pissed at her, plain and simple. She'd had no right to show up at his parents' place, make his whole family love her, and then blow his carefully-constructed April Fools' Day cover-up to smithereens with one gee-gosh-golly "You're out of work!" exclamation. No right at all.

His gaze wandered, all by itself, back to her thighs. Mike gave himself a mental wallop and stared at the road, instead. So what if looking at Amanda made him feel all gushy and sentimental inside? So what if thoughts of her, in his arms again, dominated every other brain wave he had?

That didn't mean he was going to apologize. Hell, no.

They passed a shopping center, a Starbucks, and a taco stand. At the stoplight, Mike's attention swerved—completely independently of the apology issue—to Amanda's upper half. Specifically, her breasts. She'd dressed for the unpredictable late-April weather in a skirt and buttoned-up shirt with elbow-length sleeves, but one of those buttons had somehow communicated to him that it had come unfastened, and he felt compelled to check it out.

He looked. *Yup.* The fourth button from the top had escaped from its place, revealing a glimpse of bare cleavage and the lacy top edge of a bra.

His groin tightened. His memory gave him a steamy-bathroom-style poke, designed to call up the last time he'd seen Amanda in her bra . . . and not much else. His mind started whispering something about making amends.

Maybe an apology wouldn't be the end of the world. In the murky lighting, Mike couldn't be sure, but he was growing more and more convinced that Amanda's angry-lioness expression had eased. The timing was looking good. Hell, he'd probably get some kind of female-approved brownie points just for initiating things.

Torn, he drummed his fingers on the steering wheel. At the sound, Amanda glanced over.

It was all the encouragement he needed. Squinting toward the streets ahead with what he hoped was every appearance of noncaring, Mike made the first magnanimous gesture.

"Is that your street up there?" he asked, nodding north.

Amanda snorted and turned away again. She was still waiting, he could tell. "The first one on the right," she said neutrally, "after the next light. The Mesquite Bosque apartments."

He glanced at her profile. It reminded him of the severe expressions worn by the nuns who'd taught him back at St. Anthony's school. *Sheesh!* Couldn't she recognize a simple almost-apology when she heard one?

Mike tried again. This time, he ramped up all the way to a crystal-clear semiapology. "Nice apartments," he said. "The little crosshatches on the stucco really add a good, uh, element of—"

"Come on, Mike," Amanda interrupted, turning to face him again. "It would have come out eventually. You know it's true. You couldn't have kept your job situation a secret from your family for very much longer."

Relief flooded him. As long as she was talking, there was hope she wasn't mad at him anymore. Paradoxically, though, Mike realized that *he* was still pissed and not ready to let go of it, either.

"Says who? I was doing a pretty damned good job of it. Until you came along."

Her sigh was muffled by the squeal of tires on wet pavement as he turned into the apartment complex's parking area. "I told you before. I didn't mean to break the news so indelicately. How was I supposed to know you'd kept your family in the dark about your job situation *and* the Life Coach Lotto?"

On those final words, her voice cracked. Amanda hastily shut her mouth and blinked, pointing toward an available parking space in the nonresident section. Feeling like a regular heel, Mike parked the cab and switched off the ignition. He pocketed his keys.

In the silence that followed, the only sounds were the pings of the engine cooling and the drip of collected rainwater from the parking ramada onto the trunk hood. Mike flung off his seat belt and twisted the steering wheel in his hands, working his cupped palms back and forth to release some of the tension he felt.

For a few minutes longer, Amanda waited. And then time ran out. She unbuckled her seat belt and gathered up her things.

"Thanks for the ride, Mike," she said.

Panic seized him, but all he could manage was a strangled sound. "Wait."

"What for?"

"I'm sorry."

The full-on, deluxe treatment succeeded where the others hadn't. With her fingers on the door handle, Amanda paused. "For what?"

Momentarily stymied, Mike stared at her. He'd

apologized. What more did she want? "For not apologizing sooner?" he guessed.

A faint smile touched her lips. "I'm sorry, too."

And then she got out of the taxi.

Keep walking, Amanda told herself, brushing past the wet leaves of tropical-style landscape plants that jutted at irregular intervals into her apartment building's curved walkway. *Just keep walking.*

A soggy, low-growing palm frond snagged her handbag. Struggling to free it, she heard footsteps clomping up behind her and knew that if Mike had followed her, making her great escape wouldn't be as easy as she'd envisioned.

He was ashamed of his participation in the Lotto. Her greatest achievement—her final hope for the resuscitation of Aspirations, Inc.—and he hadn't been able to look his family in the eye and tell them about it. The memory of it still lodged in her heart, like a painful, stubborn—damn this palm tree!—bruise that wouldn't heal, and knowing that about Mike, Amanda didn't see how she could possibly go through with the rest of their time together.

At first, she'd thought he was simply embarrassed about the physical makeover. Men could be touchy about appearance issues. But then—

"Amanda, hold on." Suddenly Mike was there, not touching her, only standing in the darkness with her purse in his hand. Somehow he'd freed it. He watched her intently. "Don't go like this."

"Like what?"

He silently offered her handbag, and she accepted it, feeling the warm imprint of his fingertips on the leather. An urge struck her to caress that spot, to soak up the heat she'd hoped would be hers tonight, but Amanda resisted.

"Like you can't stand the sight of me anymore," Mike said. "Like I'm somebody you don't know anymore. We both know that's not true."

"Do we?" she asked. "How well do I really know you, Mike? It turns out you have an entire career path I knew nothing about." *And shouldn't*, a part of her jibed, *a professional life coach like me have been able to pick up on a major detail like that?* "You have some kind of culinary whiz-kid past that was surely relevant to your goal setting."

"My mom tends to overplay that child-prodigy stuff," he interrupted, rubbing the back of his neck with one hand. "It doesn't mean that much."

"And even after everything that happened tonight, I *still* don't know how you lost your job."

Despite the semidarkness surrounding them, broken only by lighted apartment windows and low landscaping lights, she saw him flinch. Instantly, Amanda's heart softened.

"It hurt me that you hid your involvement in the Lotto," she said quietly. "Are you ashamed of working with me?"

"Hell, Amanda. If I was, do you think I'd still be here?"

Thinking over all she knew of him, she answered: "No."

"I told you before, that wasn't even *my* winning ticket. I found it in my cab. I only went through with this thing because of you. Because I wanted to help *you.*"

"Then why . . . ?" Tears choked off her voice, and she shook her head, unable to go on. In spite of that fact, somehow Mike knew what she meant.

"You started psychoanalyzing me in front of my whole family, that's why!" he said. "Right there at the kitchen table, between the chicken-chipotle chili and the chocolate-chip cookies, you started in on fear of failure, fear of success, and all that other mumbo jumbo. What was I supposed to do? Just sit there and take it while you dissected me like some kind of damned project? *Is that all I am to you?*"

"You implied that I was a glorified school counselor!" she cried, going toe-to-toe with him. "You made them all think I was some kind of New Age flake."

The memory alone made her mad, and she pierced him with an unswerving look. "You told them my specialty was inciting kneecap-ogling mobs and making ex-Marines cry with fitness tests from hell!"

He gave her an uncomfortable *so what* sort of look.

"That stuff about Bruno wasn't even true, and you know it," Amanda said, slicing her palm through the air. "He never cried."

"Hey, you didn't see his face when you suggested he include ballet stretches in his workout routine," Mike said, cocking his head. "There were tears there."

"No, there— Oh, what's the use? The point is, your family hates me now!"

"They don't."

"They do."

"Nah," Mike said. "I was too late for that. They already loved you." He sounded disgruntled, and a bit awestruck, by that fact. "My mom has never hugged one of my girlfriends. They usually get a handshake and a twenty-point quiz."

"Mike—"

"And my niece had already dragged out a clipboard from somewhere, pretending it was one of your relationships-and-emotional-attitudes questionnaires." His smile flashed in the darkness, warming her in spite of her befuddled feelings. "You, Ms. Connor, were a hit."

"With everyone except you," Amanda pointed out.

"Hey, you dropped a big bomb tonight." He shrugged but still didn't touch her. "It took me a while to recover. My family wasn't exactly, uh, happy about my job situation."

His *lack* of a job situation, he meant. Empathy tugged at her. Unemployment was especially tough on men, who tended to identify strongly with their success at work. Sure, his part-time taxi driving helped pay the bills—and helped out a buddy, who, as Mike had explained, had broken his leg and needed someone to pick up his shifts—but it wasn't, couldn't be, the same for Mike as excelling at a job of his choosing.

In retrospect, she wasn't surprised he'd hidden it from his family. Their good opinions doubtless meant a lot to him and were too important to risk. But she was surprised, and disappointed, that Mike had hidden it from her—a professional, trained to deal with situations exactly like his.

"I was trying to help." A raindrop fell from the queen palm to her right, and Amanda felt cold wetness slide down her scalp. Lowering her voice so that her neighbors wouldn't hear them, she said, "I was interested in your past, in how all this happened. But you're so damned closed-mouthed that I—"

"Fine. The short version." Mike paused, sucking in a breath as though to gather his courage. "I love to cook. Some kids like cars, some like drawing, some like computers. I like cooking, and have ever since I was old enough to hold a wooden spoon."

Amanda pictured a mini-Mike, complete with apron and oversized wooden spoon, standing on a stool to bake something. The image made her smile. She wanted to touch him, to let him know she understood. His stiff posture warned her away.

"My grandparents ran a coffee shop when I was a kid, and I got started there, helping out," he continued. "Pretty soon I was reworking the whole menu. Business tripled."

"Because of your revamped menu? Wow. How old were you?"

"Sixteen." Hurriedly, he went on. "After a food critic from the *Republic* reviewed some of my specialties, a resort in Scottsdale offered me full tuition to culinary school."

"Culinary school?"

"Le Cordon Bleu. In Paris."

Amanda gaped. He said the name of the world-famous cooking academy as though it were no big deal, and with an impeccable French accent, too, she noticed. With new curiosity, she listened further.

"In return for coming back to work at the resort when I finished my training. I did."

"At sixteen?"

He shook his head. "Among other things, Le Cordon Bleu requires a high school diploma for admission. By the time I doubled up on classes, went to summer school, and graduated high school early, I was seventeen. Nearly eighteen after nine months at Le Cordon Bleu."

Still very young, Amanda thought. "And then you went to work for the resort?"

"For a couple of years at least. That was all I could take of being the resident oddity. I bailed for a series of new jobs, building my team as I went." Mike's expression softened, as it always had at the mention of his "team." "And years later, everything was coming up roses, at least until earlier this month."

"When I came along with the Lotto." Amanda's spirits sank. She hadn't known he was that unhappy taking part in her whole life makeover scheme.

"No. When April Fools' Day happened."

"You lost your job on April Fools' Day?" It had to be a joke. But the way he squinted into the distance, taking in her apartment complex's three-story stucco buildings, lush landscaping, and distant turquoise swimming pool without really noticing any of it, told her it wasn't. "What happened?"

Mike's gaze returned to her. "Something that won't happen to you, not if I can help it."

"Huh?"

"I heard that goon at Channel Six threatening you that day, Amanda. Telling you that if I walked, your chances with the station were zilch."

"Evan? But he—"

"He would have done it, and we both know it," Mike said. "Look, I know what's at stake for you here. We'll work this out somehow. Don't worry."

His hand touched her cheek, the backs of his fingers skimming over her skin in a caress as gentle and heartfelt as a bedroom whisper. Despite her mixed-up emotions—or maybe because of them—Amanda felt comforted by the gesture.

"I'm impressed by everything you've done, Mike," she told him softly, grasping his hand in her own. She squeezed. "You've got talent—and the guts to choose your own path. I respect that."

His gaze swerved away, caught with compelling interest—again—on the view surrounding them. Amanda wasn't fooled. Marshmallow Mike was struggling to get out. It wouldn't be long before tough-guy Mike couldn't contain him anymore.

"And I know we can do some fabulous things together!" she went on, feeling better now that they'd cleared the air between them. "This opens up a whole new avenue of opportunity for you. Just think: Chef Mike, the talk of the town."

Picking up speed, Amanda imagined publicity appearances galore, featuring Mike as the hot nouveau chef of the moment. Interest in cooking and all things culinary had soared lately. FoodTV dominated

cable channels. Chef Emeril Lagasse routinely sold
out his live, arena-style cooking shows. Themed restaurants drew dating couples, families, and singles
alike in record numbers. The timing was perfect.

"I can see it now," Amanda said, raising her hand
as though showing Mike his name in lights. "A Cavaco
cookbook. A line of yellow ruffled aprons with your
autograph stitched on each one."

She expected him to crack a smile at that at least,
but he didn't. So she plunged onward: "Cookware
endorsements—those are very lucrative, you know.
Your own brand of gourmet sauces and condiments,
à la Newman's Own. It'll be terrific, Mike!"

He shook his head. "Amanda—"

"Okay, okay," she said, assuming his visible reluctance was due to some specific part of her developing
plan. "Maybe we'll have to ditch the condiments, but
a knockout *puttanesca* sauce would be amazing, and
hugely profitable for you, I'll bet." Already dreaming
up packaging ideas, Amanda went on. "I know originally you came along for the ride just to help me
out, but now . . . now we've discovered much greater
aspirations. I just know we'll make great progress
together!"

Amanda beamed at him, caught up in the dreams
of success she'd spun on Mike's behalf. She wished
he would at least look at her. *Something.* "You'll be
the fresher, sexier, more exciting Galloping Gourmet
of the new millennium. You'll be absolutely unstop-
pable."

She paused, thinking for a moment. "Do you have
any objections to posing shirtless, say, for a promotional cooking calendar? Because I've always thought
shoulders were a wildly underrated part on a man,
and yours . . . well, they're fabulous. Like sexy icing
on top of a sexy cake."

At that, Mike did look at her, albeit in a resigned

sort of way. And then he grinned. "I've never thought of myself as a sweet treat before, but if you're dead set on the idea . . . who am I to argue?"

Amanda's smile widened, too, and a sense of relief poured through her. They'd gotten past this. They'd maneuvered over the first bump in their relationship. And from here on out, things could only get better.

"I'm *so* glad you're with me on this idea, Mike. Honestly. You don't know what a relief it is to— *mmmph!*"

She had to quit talking, because his kiss cut off her words and scattered her thoughts. One minute, she was standing there feeling puddled rainwater soak into her sandals and squish against her toes, shivering against a sudden breeze that shook the wetness from the leaves surrounding them, and bubbling over with enthusiasm for this new vision of Mike's whole-life makeover. The next minute, warmth swamped her as Mike fastened his hands around her arms, hauled her up against his body, and lowered his mouth to hers.

He tasted of need and lingering traces of chocolate-chip cookie, of want and of luxurious, slow, thorough exploration. His left hand dropped to the small of her back, guiding her with splayed fingers into the closeness he meant to give. His right hand cupped her jaw and held her still, possessively ensuring that she would remain steady for his kiss.

As *if* she'd have wanted to leave. Giddy with sensation, Amanda gave herself to the moment, not caring when her handbag fell from her fingers to the gritty pathway beneath their feet, not bothered when a new burst of rain-scented night air rustled the purse-snatching palm fronds and sent them slapping against their bodies. All that existed was this. Mike. This place, this feeling, this *need* that tugged her under with all the momentum of a roller-coaster car on a wild, steep track. All she needed was to stay in his arms, and if she did, Amanda suddenly felt certain, everything would begin to make sense.

When he raised his head, she gasped. "Wow, Mike, I—"

"Uh-huh. Enough talking." Still holding her close, Mike demonstrated his loyalty to the strong-and-silent school of thought with another, even hotter, kiss.

It was as though he'd started all over again at ground zero, as though her garbled words had disturbed the romantic momentum he'd had going and he needed to begin again . . . even more slowly this time. His mouth opened against hers, his lips and tongue doing unbelievably erotic things, and there wasn't a single thing Amanda could do except luxuriate in it. Giving herself over to the sensation, she clung to Mike, trying to tell him with her hands and hips and mouth how much she loved . . . this.

And loved him. Amazing as it was.

He moved his lips from her mouth to her neck, then lightly tugged at her sensitive earlobe with his teeth. He kissed away the lingering ticklish sensation that resulted and gradually made his way to the other side. Grasping his head in her hands, Amanda sifted soft strands of thick hair through her fingers, imagining the contrast of Mike's dark hair against her skin. Where she was light, he was dark. Where she was delicate, he was strong. Where she ached . . . God, she hoped he did, too.

"Don't you think that—" she began.

Mike kissed away the words.

"—someplace indoors—"

How did he *do* that little nibble trick on her lower lip? Every nerve ending in her body shimmered, nearly setting her off course. Shivering with pleasure, Amanda grabbed double fistfuls of Mike's hair and gently yanked his head upward.

"—would be better for this encounter?"

He looked dazed. Blinking, Mike went on stroking his hands up and down her back and hips. His attention wavered from her face to the areas he was touching, and the expression of intense absorption on his face was more flattering than a thousand *you look nice*s would have been.

She had to seize control now, Amanda decided. Otherwise, she just might yield to the invitation in his gaze and try for a tryst beneath the bird-of-paradise plant to their left.

"Inside?" she tried again. "My apartment?"

This time, Mike heard. To her surprise, he looked as though he were thinking something profound in reply, as though sonnets and ballads were zipping through his head and then, inexplicably, getting stuck just behind his lips.

At long last, he replied. "Yes."

A *whoopee!* shot through her. Trying to play it cool, Amanda contented herself with snatching up her handbag, grabbing Mike's hand . . . and beating the land speed record for the hundred-yard-apartment-121B dash.

Chapter Sixteen

He couldn't fight it anymore, Mike realized as the door shut behind him and Amanda, and enclosed them in the softly-lit, potpourri-scented intimacy of her apartment. He just couldn't.

Sure, tonight's debacle had been a blow to his pride. And knowing that Amanda knew about his April Fools' Day failure—if not in detail—might ordinarily have turned down the heat on his libido. But with Amanda in his arms, eagerly kissing him back, somehow Mike felt as though things might turn out okay.

He'd only begun kissing her in the first place to shut her up. He wasn't proud to admit it, but there it was. She'd been all bubbly and excited, running on about kooky monogrammed aprons and outrageous Hunk-of-the-Month foodie calendars—starring him!— and Mike had been at a loss as to how to stop her before she got too carried away.

So he'd kissed her.

The only trouble was, he'd liked it so much he

hadn't wanted to stop. Neither had she, judging by the vise grip she'd had on his head while he'd been exploring the luscious softness of her neck. And *now* look where they were.

Actually, Mike didn't want to look. He registered the shadowy outlines of a typical one-bedroom apartment, furnished with pillow-adorned furniture and other typical girly-style stuff, and then got back to what really mattered.

Amanda.

He took her in his arms, kissing her toward the solidity of the closed door behind her. A thud followed as her purse hit the carpet. Moving together, they backed up against the door; he felt the wood shudder beneath the impact. Her clothes were damp impediments to the warmth of her skin beneath. As sure as he tasted coffee and chocolate still lingering on her breath, Mike knew he'd see the garments gone before long.

Moaning, and obviously not to be outdone in the first-move department, Amanda took his head in her hands and kissed him back. She tunneled her fingers through his hair, arched her body against him, and gave a purely-Amanda hip wiggle that let him know she wouldn't be averse to seeing his clothes gone, too.

The sound of their breathing filled the room, harsh and fast and punctuated by whispered promises that Mike hadn't even known he had in him. Promises to love. To dream. To remember. Spurred onward by those thoughts and others more carnal, he gave over to the feel of Amanda pressed against him, to the glide of their mouths and the heavy beating of his heart.

"Can I get you something?" Amanda asked between gasps, vaguely gesturing toward the far end of the apartment. "A cup of coffee? A—a cookie? I don't think I have any beer, but I—"

Mike grinned at her unfailing show of good manners. No wonder she'd become a life coach, with *do the right thing* imprinted on her soul the way it was. He shook his head with a murmured "No, thank you" and went on with what he'd been doing.

Her hands clasped over his, stopping his progress down her shirt buttons. "I should at least let you sit down. The sofa is right over—"

"All I want is you."

"Oh, but I'm sure you'd be more comf—"

"You." Mike squeezed her hands and gave her what he hoped was a reassuringly lascivious smile. "Preferably naked. Here, let me demonstrate."

He tugged his knit interview-going shirt from his pants, whipped it over his head, and tossed it away. It landed with a small *thwap* atop an end table, covering the girly decorative objects beneath it.

She gaped at his naked torso with a satisfying amount of *hubba-hubba* interest. Smiling, Mike struck a macho pose.

"See?" he asked. "Easy as pie. Now you try."

Only a moment's hesitation followed. Then, with trembling fingers Amanda unfastened the rest of her shirt buttons. Seconds later, the garment flew to join his shirt.

"Good thing I'm wearing my no-second-thoughts bra," she volunteered as she tucked her fingertips into his khaki-pants waistband and dragged him closer again. Her sassy smile was indecently sexy. "Otherwise, I might not have had the guts to do that."

No-second-thoughts bra? *Don't ask,* Mike commanded himself; instead, he focused on the wonderful curves offered up to him by that same mysterious lace-trimmed and satin-cupped bit of feminine magic.

Did bras possess superpowers? He'd almost have believed it, given the reaction his body was having to the sight of Amanda wearing hers.

Superpower-endowed or not, that bra would have to go, of course. Later. Right now, Mike had other things to think about. Like the wonderful, warm weight of her breasts in his hands as he cupped her. The erotic pucker of her nipples, covered only in a fragment of sweet-scented satin, nudging against his palms. The sweep of her breath across his naked chest as Amanda nuzzled him from collarbone to shoulder and back again.

Her hair fell over his skin, a thousand sleek dark kisses. Her murmured words eased into his heart, telling him she wanted him, needed him . . . cared for him. Like a runner at the end of a race, Mike felt his legs tremble, felt his knees threaten to buckle at the first swirl of Amanda's tongue against his chest, the first faint bite of her teeth against his neck, the first touch of her hands on his fly.

The rasp of his zipper filled the space between them.

Hot, heavy, pulsing, his body ached to fill that space. Gasping for breath, Mike flicked open her bra with his thumb and let the wisp of smooth fabric fall away. The motion revealed skin that was smoother, still, with a taste . . . a taste as indescribable as the sensation that filled him when he lowered his head to her breast and kissed her there. Ahhh, but he needed this. Needed *her*. And nothing, not even that weird snuffling sensation near his left foot, was going to . . . .

Waitaminute. The snuffling continued, strangely familiar. Mike felt his pants leg being pushed to and fro with blunt but gentle pressure, then a sigh filled the room. With a mental shrug, he chalked up the disturbance to Amanda and her Amazing Animatronic Shoes (or whatever nickname she'd devised for them), and went on loving her.

Long minutes into his quest to kiss every golden, occasionally freckled inch of Amanda's beautifully naked skin, the snuffling returned. Then a heavy weight suddenly settled atop his left shoe.

He looked down. Sprawled muzzle first on top of his interview-going deck shoe was the most doleful-looking, energyless basset hound he'd ever seen.

"Uh, hey, there," Mike said by way of a gruff and reluctant greeting. It was, after all, tough to seduce a woman with sixty pounds of canine slumped across your shoe.

Amanda looked down, too. "Oh, look! He likes you." She gave a little jump and squeezed Mike's arms with happiness. "That's Webster. My dog. He's probably just now made it out here from his doggie bed in the hallway."

"Huh. Some watchdog, if this is his way of confronting an intruder. What's he going to do, slobber me to death?"

"Don't be ridiculous." Amanda grinned fondly down at the dog, then up at him. "You're not an intruder."

Mike snorted.

With what must have been an enormous effort, Webster summoned all his strength and wagged his tail. Once.

"He's a good dog," Amanda went on. "He just doesn't like to rush into things, that's all."

Neither do I, said her newly serious expression. She gazed at him with eyes gone wide and blue and slightly less dreamy, and it took every ounce of strength Mike had not to remind her that he'd been waiting for this moment almost from the instant he'd laid eyes on her. All the time they'd spent together since then had done nothing but make the yearning he felt even worse.

"If you don't want this, Amanda," he said, tucking a silky hank of hair behind her ear, "tell me now."

The moment that followed turned into two. Then three. To Mike, it felt like an eternity. With unwanted clarity, he recognized the ticking of a clock someplace in the apartment, the green glow of a microwave control panel reflected in the glass of the framed print beside the door, the pulse and ache of his body beneath the now-tight-fitting Snoopy boxers he'd chosen to wear with his formerly loose fitting khakis.

"I do want this," she said at last. "Please."

To prove it, Amanda pressed upward against him, delivering herself once more into his waiting hands. Her kiss deprived him of both oxygen and the will to be gentlemanly, all at the same time. All he wanted was this woman. This moment. Forever.

They careened across the living room, drunk on lust and just coordinated enough to sidestep a now-snoring Webster—who'd obviously decided Mike was no threat, and, furthermore, didn't have any hidden Milk Bones in his shoes. Stumbling over God only knew what, Mike and Amanda kissed and touched and somehow made their way to the sofa, collapsing on its comfy chenille cushions in a heap. Mike felt something lumpy gouge his back, dragged whatever it was from the sofa's depths, and tossed it onto the floor. Ahhhh. That was better.

On top now, straddling him, Amanda bent over to kiss him. Her bare breasts dragged across his chest, inciting every nerve ending in his body to sit up and cheer. Mike buried his fingers in her hair, found the clip that secured it, and released it. Handfuls of brunet softness were his reward, and he held back the strands just long enough to whisper against Amanda's mouth how incredibly beautiful he thought she was.

Her reply was a sigh and a reinvigorated interest in kissing her way down his body. He writhed beneath the soft press of her mouth, needing to touch Amanda at the same time. No pleasure was too great to give her . . . no moan was heartfelt enough to express all the feelings surging through him. She slid her hands leisurely down his abdomen, past his hips, all the way to his opened fly. Khaki and cotton parted at her touch, elastic obligingly expanded, and when at last her fingers closed over him, a wave of tenderness and need gripped Mike unlike anything he had ever felt before.

Forcing himself to go still beneath it, he indulged in the stroke of her palm against his hardness, in the perfect pressure of her fingertips along the length of him. Groaning, he watched Amanda's face as she explored his body and knew that if he did nothing else right with his life, he would give her everything he could tonight.

There would never be a better time than now to begin. Gently, Mike covered her hands with his and urged her upward again, softening his change of venue with a long, hungry, can't-get-enough kiss. And it was true, he realized as he cupped her breasts and kissed her there, as he circled his thumbs around her taut nipples and then tasted their heat, as he urged Amanda onto her back beneath him. He couldn't get enough. Not of this woman.

The thought might have stopped him, might have scared him with its (let's be honest here) utter significance, had Mike not been faced with the lush softness of sweet, semi-clad Amanda beneath him. As it was, rational deliberation fled at the first arch of her hips under his stroking hands. He dipped his palms to her thighs; they trembled. He inched her skirt upward with his hands, watching as more and more of her was revealed. Half-crazy with wanting, Mike ducked his head to her torso and kissed the bare skin just above her skirt's waistband.

Amanda squirmed and squealed, clutching at his shoulders.

He paused. Braced himself on his forearms. Looked up through the hank of hair that had fallen into his eyes and raised his eyebrows in question.

"Your hair tickles," she explained. A small hip wriggle served as punctuation.

"You want me to stop?"

"God, no." Her voice was husky. Alluring. Nearly as incredible as the feel of her body against him in the dimly lit room. "Don't *ever* stop."

"Mmmmmm." Mike trailed his tongue along her torso, making his way upward. He delved his hands beneath her, felt the cottony press of the sofa cushions against the backs of his fingers, and found her skirt zipper. The muted hum of it unzipping was, quite possibly, the most promising sound he'd heard all night.

"I don't plan to stop," he murmured, now working the fabric that separated him from Amanda's rocking hips all the way down her legs. "At least not until you're hot and trembling. Limp with satisfaction. Smiling with the knowledge that twice is nice and—"

"Twice?" The inquiry teased him as much as her bare toes did—when had she slipped off her sandals, anyway?—as she deftly shoved off his shoes. They plunked from his feet to the floor, loudly colliding with something there in the dimness. "Only twice?"

"Three times. Four times. Anything you want." Feeling breathless, Mike kissed her as he dropped her skirt onto the coffee table beside them. "Anything, everything, for you."

"It's enough to be with you," Amanda said, all seriousness in her murmured words. "That's all I want."

With a rush of affection that made his hands shake, Mike tweaked her ear and gave her a smile. He couldn't speak. Not when emotions swirled through his mind, and his body urged him onto an entirely incoherent course. Instead, he lowered himself again, savored the warm press of their bodies coming together, and then remembered what had changed and levered himself upward again. After all, Amanda was wonderfully close to naked now, and he didn't want to miss a thing.

Merely looking at her, lying all goo-goo-eyed and gorgeous in nothing but a pair of wispy pink panties, was enough to make his heart rate triple. Hardly able to form the words he needed, Mike ran his hands over her body, tracing the triangular outline of the satiny fabric still hiding her from him.

"Awww, Amanda," he whispered. "You take my breath away."

She smiled and turned her head sideways, her knees rising against his as though to automatically shield her nakedness from his view. Flinging one arm over her head, Amanda peeked at him through the gap made by the crook of her elbow.

"Lucky thing I'm wearing my antiembarrassment panties," she said, unbelievably earnest, "or I couldn't stand to hear a compliment like that."

She still couldn't. Who did she think she was kidding? Even in the terrible lighting—a pale glow that came, Mike saw now, from the over-the-stove light in the apartment's kitchen at the far end of the room— he saw the blush rise in her cheeks.

"I'll bet you look cute even when you're embarrassed," he said, knowing damn well that she did. "Maybe even *especially* when you're embarrassed."

"*Mmm-hmmm.* And when I'm naked, too. Don't forget that."

"*Oh, I won't.*"

And to prove it, Mike started all over again, kissing her slowly before moving on to nibble her earlobe, nuzzle her neck, and indulge himself in a head-to-toes exploration of Amanda's body. Their lovemaking was tender and lighthearted, hot and irresistible, and by the time he'd changed positions again (and found himself on his knees at Amanda's feet), Mike knew he would never be the same after having experienced it.

"Let me love you," he said, rising on his haunches in front of the sofa. Amanda perched on the cushion before him, wonderfully sans panties now and evidently suffering no late-onset embarrassment at the lack of them. She swept his hair from his face and smiled dreamily as he grasped her knees in both hands and hoarsely repeated his request. "I need to taste you. Let me love you, right now."

She sucked in a breath, but his gentle pressure on her knees met no resistance. Inch by inch, Amanda's legs spread wider until she was sexily and completely revealed to him . . . or would have been, had the lighting been better. Wildly excited, Mike reached for the table lamp he'd seen silhouetted beside them.

And with no warning at all, Amanda froze up.

Let me love you, echoed temptingly in her head, but at the same time the lamp on the end table flared into life. *Dammit.* Amanda felt her body go rigid.

As light filled the living room, she squeezed her eyes shut. This was it. The end. But not for the reasons Amanda might have expected, given their intimate position and the even greater closeness that awaited them. This wasn't about wanting to hide her not-a-size-two body. It wasn't about worrying that her lipstick was nonexistent and her hair was a mess. It was much worse than that.

No, what Amanda worried about was this:

With the lights on, Mike would see the Slob-o-Rama that was her apartment.

He'd see that the things they'd tripped over on the way to the sofa had been kicked-off shoes, video rental boxes left where they lay, and still-being-read paperback novels. He'd realize that the thing jabbing him in the back had been a month-old fitness contraption she'd bought at the onset of her current dieting frenzy with hopes of finally achieving thinner thighs and bounce-a-quarter-off-them abs.

He would understand that no matter how together and competent she seemed while at Aspirations, Inc., Amanda Connor was nothing but a desperately rushed, inherently disorganized, completely incurable *slob*.

A slob who couldn't even—and this suddenly took on momentous importance, given what she now knew of Mike—cook a decent meal in her tiny Lean Cuisine-littered kitchen.

Her cover would be blown. The gig would be up. Mike would know the truth about her, be understandably disillusioned and disappointed by her obvious lack of perfection, and invent some excuse to leave before the tower of unrecycled newspapers near the kitchen dinette toppled over and crushed him beneath their East Valley headlines.

With a terrible sense of foreboding, Amanda held her breath. Briefly, she considered flinging herself wantonly over the whole awful mess in a bid to distract Mike from the truth. She could have pulled it off. Her diet had been mostly working—despite a few cheeseburger and chocolate-chip-cookie detours—and even though she didn't have an ideal figure . . . hey, it was the only one Mike was naked with right now, wasn't it? That had to count for something.

But before she could move, Mike did. She felt the

subtle pressure of his grip on her knees change as he turned his head to gaze around the room. Bravely, she cracked open one eye.

His perusal was blessedly quick. "Hmmm," he said. "Cozy."

Cozy? Her heart jolted in shock. She must have misheard him.

Mentally, Amanda began preparing a heartfelt speech about how she *never* had anyone to her apartment if she could help it, about how even Mel and Gemma preferred to meet at Boondoggle's rather than risk navigating the dangerous clutter of makeup and hairstyling products littering her bathroom, about how her mother had always nagged her to clean her room and even at the age of eight those directions hadn't stuck.

But before she could say a single word, Mike smiled at her in an endearing, melt-your-heart way, with those warm brown eyes of his shining in the lamplight . . . and went back to kissing her knee.

Dumbfounded, Amanda watched as Mike made his way from the inside of her knee to her inner thigh. The ends of his hair swept along in dark counterpoint to his ever-moving mouth, and as near as she could tell, he was completely absorbed in making sure no portion of her anatomy went unexplored.

Or unkissed.

His murmured words of approval made their way up to her, spoken against her bare—and increasingly tingling—skin. Mike must have shaved before the job interview he'd mentioned, Amanda realized dumbly, because his cheeks and jaw (while handsomely angular and masculine and appealing to a degree she couldn't believe she hadn't noticed sooner) were smooth against her sensitive thighs. Tentatively, she stroked her palm over the crown of his head.

The motion elicited an encouraging moan, and a

new sweep of his tongue over the freckle halfway between her knee and the outer edge of . . . well, of the hot, wet, aching place she hoped Mike would make his way to soon. Closing her eyes, letting her head fall back against the sofa cushions, Amanda did the only thing that seemed reasonable, given the amazing circumstances.

She enjoyed herself.

She enjoyed the slow, sexy glide of his tongue against her. Enjoyed the teasing play of his lips over every sensitive inch between her thighs. Savored the sound of Mike's moans as he loved her, and did her best not to scream aloud as he discovered those especially responsive places . . . and paid them each due attention.

Biting her lip, Amanda held his head lovingly to her. She quivered, driven nearly to madness by the pleasure, the overwhelming feelings of affection and need, that filled her. When at last Mike proved his mastery of her body, holding her open to him with both strong hands on her hips, and the first incredible waves of her orgasm took her, Amanda did scream aloud, calling his name again and again. Loudly. Hoarsely. Helplessly.

And when he soothed her afterward, she nearly wept at the tenderness in his voice.

Oh, but she'd fallen for him so hard, Amanda realized as she drew him up to her and they cuddled together afterward. Despite the warnings of her nagging commonsense side, she'd found herself swept up in the way being with Mike made her feel. Happy. Secure. And oh, so ready for more.

"Something's not right here," she said, panting the words as her heart rate gradually slowed. As he'd promised, her body did feel limp and wonderfully satisfied, but now she ached for more. "Here I am, naked and grinning like a goofball"—Mike's smile matched hers as he cradled her head in the crook of his arm and kissed her—"and you're still wearing some clothes."

With pretend scorn, Amanda eyeballed his khaki pants, trying not to appear distracted by the expanse of lean abdomen visible above his opened fly. She shook her head at his socks. Felt her attention being drawn to the perfect balance of brawny chest, wide shoulders, and strong, lean-muscled arms that Mike displayed so confidently and happily beside her and refocused her attention on her mock reprimand.

"You'd better lose some of those clothes," she said. "I won't be responsible for any damage I might cause ripping them off you myself."

His grin widened, as though she'd just admitted, aloud, the hidden urge she felt to stroke every part of his body. To kiss him up one side and down the other. To discover what, exactly, lay behind those remaining clothes. Amanda guessed that in a way, she had.

And now, awaiting his response, she squirmed in anticipation.

Mike leaned forward obligingly. An instant later, his socks sailed through the air and landed beside Webster's chew toy on the floral-upholstered side chair.

He settled back into position, bare toes waggling, both arms spread along the back of the sofa in a posture that definitely invited her further perusal. "How's that?"

"Not good enough."

"Oh?" His eyebrow rose. She had no idea how he could appear so unruffled, especially considering the massive erection tenting the front of his boxer shorts and pants. "Why not?"

"Because you're still wearing"—Amanda pinched

a bit of khaki between her fingertips and waggled it—"these."

"You know," Mike said, appearing uncommonly thoughtful, "these pants *do* feel a little snug."

A little snug? she thought, gaping as he rose to his feet and demonstrated his cooperation with a slow striptease. She was surprised he'd ever fit all that behind a mere zipper in the first place. Amanda sat up attentively as his pants landed atop her fitness gadget and Mike stood almost bare before her.

She was dying to touch him. More than likely, the way she'd just licked her lips had already clued Mike in to that fact. In keeping with her resolve to get him completely naked, though, Amanda only gazed up, up, up, past his thighs, his hips, the evidence of his need for her, his chest, his shoulders—whoops, her attention had strayed downward again—his chest, his shoulders, and all the way to his face.

The loving expression she saw there perfectly matched the emotions filling her heart. She didn't know when she'd last felt so full, so free, so joyous. *Never* sprang to mind, and Amanda knew that no matter what else happened this night, she would not be the same when it ended.

"Never mind," she croaked, barely able to speak for the caring that overflowed inside her. "I think I can take it from here."

The sudden touch of her hands on the waistband of his boxers made Mike's knees wobble visibly. Amanda might have felt a burst of feminine pride at that fact, had she not been too busy to consider it beyond the initial recognition of it. As it was, she soon had her hands full with the inspiration that struck her next, and she couldn't seem to think straight while she leaned forward and took him in her mouth to carry it out.

At the first sweep of her lips and tongue along the

smooth, hard length of him, Mike's guttural exclamation vibrated all through his body. Amanda felt it, and the need behind it was echoed low in her belly. Eyes closed, she pleasured him freely, loving the wildly aroused feel of him, the masculine, musky scent of him. Again and again she kissed him in the most intimate of ways until his hands tangled in her hair and his thighs trembled against her seeking hands.

Suddenly, Mike urged her upward. He flattened his palms against her face and kissed her deeply, their mouths warm and needful. "Your bedroom," he gasped. "Where is it?"

Dizzy with wanting, Amanda gestured toward the hallway. "That way. But I—"

He didn't wait for a more detailed explanation. With astonishing strength and steadiness—given his helplessness at her hands just moments earlier—Mike swept her into his arms and strode toward her bedroom. The nightlight she kept in the hallway showed the way. The usual mess cluttering the floor seemed to leap sideways at his determined advance, making way for them. In her bedroom at last, Mike laid her on the bed's dark-softened comforter and followed her down.

The embrace of pillows and smooth cotton met her back; hot, hard man pressed against her front. Panting, Amanda guided him to her, and in that one motion of her hands against his taut, firm-muscled behind, she realized that she simply couldn't wait any longer.

Between kisses and renewed caresses, Mike murmured his need for her. Amid stroking and begging and incoherent cries, Amanda agreed. When finally he began teasing her, coming inside her partway only to retreat and then move forward again, it was more than she could stand. She gritted her teeth and resorted to brute force.

The upward tilt of her hips created a powerful thrust that joined them together so perfectly, so deliriously, that Amanda wanted to cry aloud with the wonder of it. Mike made love to her with a surety and a passion that seemed to cocoon them both in a world of pleasure and togetherness forever.

"Ahhh, Amanda," he groaned, "I can't wait anymore."

"Don't. Don't," she whispered back. *"Be with me."*

And he was. As the tremors shook him, as ecstasy overtook his final, steady thrusts, Mike matched his gaze to hers, forehead to forehead. Looking deeply into each other's eyes, they found the kind of union that neither had dared to dream of . . . and even as they fell back against the wild, tangled bedclothes, breathing hard amid the beating of their hearts, Amanda and Mike refused to look away.

At least they did—until round two began, of course.

Chapter Seventeen

Amanda was awakened the next morning by several unprecedented things. The first was the scrumptious smell of something delicious cooking—in *her* kitchen!—for breakfast. The second was the gentle loft of a brilliant orange bird-of-paradise blossom hitting the pillow beside her. The third was the gruff, toe-tingling sound of a male voice speaking to her from the other side of her bed.

She turned her head to see the fourth and most welcome unprecedented waking-up thing of all: the sight of Mike, tousle-haired, smiling, and only partially dressed in his wrinkled khaki pants from last night, bearing a plate of breakfast.

"You wake up as beautifully as you snore," he said. "Sit up and have something to eat."

Amanda swept a hank of snarly hair from her eyes and found herself not believing him about that "beautiful" stuff, considering the circumstances. Nevertheless, she sighed happily and boosted herself into a sitting position, helped by Mike's arranging of the pillows at the headboard behind her.

So what if his hands wandered a little in their execution of the task? So what if the food got a little cold while they reminded themselves of the pleasures of last night? Breakfast in bed wasn't truly romantic without a little woo-woo to go with it, Amanda figured. And besides, she *was* wearing a little something— nothing, actually—which could be construed as an invitation to the ogling and stroking that followed.

Thirty minutes later, she'd finished the tomato, basil, and feta cheese omelette that Mike had somehow coaxed out of her malfunctioning kitchen and was twirling the flower he'd brought her with a bemused smile on her face.

"That was amazing," Amanda said. "I had no idea those ingredients could be combined into something so delicious."

Mike beamed beside her. He'd stretched out on top of the comforter, barefoot, his head propped in his hand, to watch her devour the meal he'd made.

Now, he shrugged. "It's all in the happy feelings the cook has while he's preparing the food," Mike told her. "When I cook, I think about balancing the flavors, the textures, the colors, the temperatures— all that stuff—of course. But I also think a lot about how the person who eats it will feel when she tastes it. How much *pleasure* it will bring her. How much she might remember it and want to experience it again."

"It's sharing," Amanda mused, thinking that she'd finally had a glimpse into what made Mike the man he was. "Isn't it?"

"It's loving," he replied. "Simple as that."

Yeah. Simple. At his sudden mushy declaration, they both immediately found other items of compelling interest in the bedroom to look at. The nightstand, piled with books, and the breakfast tray he'd brought. The bureau, spilling over with panties and bras. The closet, bulging with clothes that looked as though they might go on strike if any more garments tried to join them in the minuscule space.

Everything that had separated her and Mike until now came crashing back into Amanda's consciousness, like an unwelcome and unwanted houseguest, and no matter what she did, she just couldn't give those thoughts the boot. No doubt, it was the same for Mike.

Why else would he have pretended such overwhelming interest in the one-thousand-proof feminine, framed print of a kitten (given to her by her grandmother, which was why it remained there) hanging on her distant bedroom wall? Surely he didn't have that much of an affinity for fuzzy white kitties, fields of yellow daisies, and butterflies.

"Anyway, thanks for breakfast," Amanda said briskly.

"So, I guess I oughtta take care of that tray," Mike said at the same time, reaching across her body for the china-laden breakfast tray on the nightstand.

They both smiled. The awkwardness between them eased a little . . . possibly helped along by the brush of Mike's forearm across her breasts as he balanced the tray in midair. With telltale dexterity, he flexed his fingertips to swoosh it overhead, simultaneously getting to his knees atop the mattress. A moment later, he was standing in front of the window again, the world's sexiest bedside waiter.

Amanda yawned, then carefully set aside her flower and pushed back the covers. "I need a shower."

"I need to tell you about April Fool's Day," Mike said at the same time.

They froze in place, Mike looking as though he couldn't believe he'd actually said those words aloud—Amanda feeling as though she didn't dare move, for fear that he'd change his mind about confiding in her.

Then her professional training kicked in, and she made herself continue getting out of bed. Men were often perfectly willing to have a heart-to-heart, she reminded herself. But they didn't necessarily want to do it counselor-and-client style, with both parties staring earnestly into each other's eyes for hours on end. They wanted important conversations to seem . . . almost incidental. A by-product of a really urgent tag-team oil change or an inarguably necessary auto wash-and-wax.

"Great," she said, dragging on a short green robe from the chair beside her bureau. Belting it, Amanda swung her tangled hair behind her shoulders and strode barefoot toward the hallway. "Why don't you tell me about it while we do the dishes? We'll need *some* distraction, after all."

Happily, her tactics worked like a charm. Ten minutes later found her and Mike up to their elbows in soapsuds, with plates and pans and silverware gradually progressing from Amanda's washing side of the sink to Mike's rinsing side. As they worked, he talked.

"I'd been working at Cucina Amore for a little over a year when this happened," he was saying, mentioning a popular Italian eatery in downtown Phoenix that was a lunchtime favorite with the staff at Channel Six and other local businesses. "My team had joined me by then, too."

"All of them?"

He nodded. "At the risk of sounding like some kind of culinary prima donna"—Mike quirked his lips and arranged another dish in the drainer—"I only took jobs at restaurants that would hire everyone on my team. I'd worked with them. I trusted them. And they were—are!—damned good, from Rico, the prep cook, to Doris and Tracy, the waitresses, and all the rest."

"You're loyal," she observed. "Nothing wrong with that."

Mike snorted. "Tell that to the people I've been interviewing with over the last three weeks. *Nobody* wants a ready-made team. That, or they seem to think I'm 'overqualified' for every position, which destroys everybody's chances."

"Maybe you ought to consider breaking up the team," Amanda ventured. "And maybe you *are* overqualified. After all, Le Cordon Bleu training is—"

"No." Mike scowled into the running rinse water. "And I don't care about being overqualified. I just want to work someplace where my family can come to dinner without feeling out of place. Someplace where blue-collar, everyday-Joe-type Cavacos won't stick out like a sore thumb. That's not too much to ask, dammit."

His loyalty to his family was endearing, if a little (and Amanda couldn't help but think this, with her life coach's background and new knowledge of Mike's past) misguided. Surely the Cavacos could learn to love dining at any kind of restaurant, from the lowliest dive to the poshest resort. Couldn't they?

Privately, Amanda thought they could. Typically, though, Mike was obviously trying to protect the people he loved. He was trying to guard them from hurt feelings and—more than likely—empty wallets. She had to respect him for it.

But she couldn't resist one teeny-tiny caveat. "You're right, Mike. A job that appeals to you isn't too much to ask." *And I can find you one, too,* she thought excitedly. *New-millennium, super-sexy Galloping Gourmet, here we come!* "Still, I'm sure your family wouldn't want you to hold yourself back on their account. They seemed like generous, open-minded people to me. If you shared your concerns with them—"

"Look, do you want to hear this or not?" Mike interrupted, giving her a harsh look over the slowly deflating soapsuds. He clenched his fingers on the pan he'd been rinsing and stared down at it. "Because I haven't told anybody about this April Fools' Day thing. After last night I thought, maybe . . . well, hell. I don't even know why I brought this up."

Because you want to share it with someone who's close to you, Amanda finished silently—hopefully—for him. *Because you know I'll be there for you.*

But she couldn't hop on board that train of thought for long because, suddenly, Mike looked miserable. Out of his element, unusually self-conscious, and endearingly determined to do what he thought was the right thing. His gruff, frustrated-sounding rejoinder made Amanda want to hug Mike's worries right out of him—that, and get started on finding him a new position right away.

Obviously, Mike *needed* something new. Something better. But for now, she only murmured an apology. Invited him to continue. And gently pried the drippy nonstick omelette pan from his grasp before he snapped off the plastic handle in aggravation.

"So what happened on April Fools' Day?" she asked quietly. "What changed?"

"Me," Mike replied, seeming to come to himself again as he accepted the next pile of cutlery from her soapy hands and rinsed it. "To make a long story short, I decided it would do everybody some good to cut loose on April Fools' Day. Cucina Amore had just been taken over by new management, the restaurant staff was worried about their futures, and I hated seeing everybody upset that way."

"Understandable." *For a big softie like you.* "So what did you do?"

Mike ducked his head. His mouth quirked, briefly, into a playful grin. "I changed the menu," he said. "A simple gag designed to cheer up the staff. I'd dated the woman who ran the printing shop where our menus were made up, and I convinced her to create an . . . uh, alternate version."

Amanda ignored the hot streak of jealousy that shot through her at the mention of Mike's old girlfriend. Okay, she *mostly* ignored it. Pretending the spatula she was scrubbing was the printing hussy's head probably didn't count. Right?

"A bogus April Fools' Day menu, huh?" she asked, edging herself near enough that her hips touched Mike's companionably as they worked. "That sounds pretty harmless."

"It might have been," he agreed, "*if* I hadn't already been having sort of a . . . run-in with the new management at the time."

"Uh-oh."

He nodded. Grimaced in remembrance. "Let's just say that Nick 'Nicky' Nickerson and I had different ideas about what made for a good restaurant."

Amanda hid her hilarity at the manager's redundantly redundant name behind a commiserating look for Mike's troubles with the man. The last dish was rinsed and put in the countertop drainer. With a practiced flip of his wrist, Mike whipped a kitchen towel from its place on his shoulder and began drying. Amanda settled atop the counter to continue their conversation.

"He didn't like the joke menus, then?" she asked.

"To put it mildly. But he was the only one who didn't. They were a big hit with the staff. I've never seen my team so eager to deliver orders to the kitchen before." The playful grin returned to Mike's mouth, bringing a sparkle to his brown eyes and etching his features with the good humor she'd become used to seeing in him. "The name of the place—Cucina Amore—"

"Kitchen of love?" Amanda translated.

"Mmm-hmmm." He waggled his eyebrows and looked around, as though she'd suggested inaugurating *her* kitchen as the same. "Anyway, that was the inspiration for the menu. The regular menu items were written in Italian, with English descriptions."

Amanda nodded, familiar with the tongue-twisting convention. More than once she'd been compelled to attempt completely inaccurate foreign-language pronunciations in restaurants throughout the Valley—all for the sake of a mere bite to eat.

"So on the bogus menu," Mike continued, "we, uh, took some liberties with the Italian names of the menu items."

Now his grin had widened completely, like that of a rascally boy who knew he'd been naughty . . . but wasn't sorry to have done it, only to have been caught.

"Liberties?" She had a pretty good idea where he was going with this. "Such as?"

"Sausage and Peppers Lust-ica," he replied, ticking menu items off on his fingers as he went. "Linguine Alla Kiss-me-o. Cannelloni a Porno."

At her openmouthed expression, Mike looked chagrined. "Okay, so it was a little juvenile—"

"A little?"

"—but it was *really* funny. You should have seen the number of orders for Tortellini Di Feel-me-up—"

Amanda clapped her hand over his mouth before he could finish. He peeled her hand away, and the last syllables of the pasta dish's ribald name emerged.

"—io."

"That's terrible," she said, shaking her head and grinning a little in spite of herself. The image of pretentious Cucina Amore patrons ordering heaping plates of Linguine Alla Kiss-me-o *was* a little funny.

She wondered if that particular dish had come *sans* garlic.

"It was a *joke*," Mike said. "Just a little something to brighten everybody's mood after the management takeover. And then . . ."

"And then?"

"And then I was in the midst of telling Nick 'Nicky' Nickerson why I refused to cook in a clown suit and bright pink toque as part of his idea for a revamped circus-themed restaurant when Doris came around the corner and put in for a double order of Tortellini Di Feel-me—"

Her hand was almost fast enough to stop him this time.

"—up-io," they said in unison when Amanda had removed it.

He winked.

"Nicky heard what she'd said and marched into the dining room for one of the bogus menus," Mike said. "By the time he'd recovered from his apoplectic fit, I was fired, Doris and the Monroe twins were fired, Jake and—"

"Your whole team?" Amanda asked, aghast.

He shook his head. "No. Not all of them were fired."

"Whew."

"Some of them quit in solidarity with me and the others. Like Rico, the prep cook. Rico's a stand-up guy."

"Oh, Mike." She opened her arms to him, and when he didn't move forward for the embrace she offered, Amanda grabbed the kitchen towel in his hands and used it to drag him closer. She hugged him into the vee of her legs, their heads nearly level because of her top-of-the-counter position. "No wonder you love them so much. They're not just a team. They're your friends."

He cleared his throat. "Nobody said anything about love," he said gruffly.

Amanda's smile was hidden from him as she kissed the warm skin at his temple. "Nobody had to." *You big marshmallow.*

"But I have a few thoughts on love*making* if you want to hear them." Mike waggled his eyebrows, giving her a hopeful, mock-lecherous look.

"I'd love to hear them." She leaned back in her best interested-listener pose, hands propped on the countertop behind her for support. "Fire away."

His mouth found hers, teasing and nipping and reminding her of all they'd shared last night. Then his fingers found the belt of her robe and deftly untied it. "Actually it's more of a visual-demonstration thing. C'mere and I'll show you."

Laughing, Amanda did . . . and boy, could that man "demonstrate."

By the time Mike had showered (at length and with a beautifully soapy Amanda for company), shaved (with a pink Bic), dressed in yesterday's clothes (wrinkled, but who cared?), and slid behind the wheel of his taxi for the drive home, he felt a thousand pounds lighter. Telling Amanda his deep, dark April Fools' Day secret seemed to have lifted a weight from his shoulders he hadn't even been fully aware of carrying. He still couldn't believe he'd confessed his big failure . . . and survived.

Whistling as he drove, Mike rounded the corner leading to downtown Phoenix's Heritage Square and his carriage-house home. He squinted against the late-morning sunlight sparking from the cars surrounding him, aware of the cheesy grin on his face and the punch-drunk feeling of happiness in his heart.

You were right, Jake, he thought, giving his trainer

buddy a mental high-five. *I am crazy about her. And I don't mind a bit.*

He'd be seeing Amanda again, too. They had a life-coach session scheduled for after lunch during which she planned to complete several phases of his personal-growth plan. The very phrase "personal-growth plan" still scared the bejeezus out of Mike, but after the amazing night he'd just had, he figured he could survive anything.

Good thing, too, because he never had completed that emotional-attitudes questionnaire of hers. *Ugh.*

After checking with the docent at the Heritage Square offices for the list of maintenance work he performed around the square in exchange for reduced rent on his house, Mike got out his keys and walked up his front steps. Automatically, he double-checked the converted carriage house's Victorian-style façade. As a part-time caretaker, he was responsible for keeping its outside looking as historically authentic as possible, and he took the obligation seriously.

Everything checked out. Still whistling, Mike opened the door to Cupcake's frantic, joyous barking and spent a few minutes lolling on the floor with the dog. He couldn't resist telling her all about Amanda. Cupcake wagged her tail with appropriate enthusiasm and licked his face to let him know she approved. Either that or she sensed that he'd been making omelettes and was hoping for leftovers.

Ten minutes later, dressed in clean Levi's and a Marvin's T-shirt, Mike sat on the edge of his unslept-in bed and laced up his sneakers. His gaze fell on the shoes' tattered, grass-stained uppers, reminding him of the fitness tests that had caused the extra wear in the first place. His muscles ached in remembrance.

You know, tomato, basil, and feta cheese omelettes probably didn't fall into the Recommended Healthy

Foods category of Amanda's diet plan for him, Mike
reflected. Especially not after you added the buttered
toast. Holey jeans and sneakers assertive enough to
walk on their own probably didn't play into the
résumé-worthy look she'd been going for with that
suit. And he hadn't actually practiced any of the yoga
poses she'd so earnestly recommended to him—not
even Warrior II, which sounded like an action movie
and was vaguely macho enough for consideration.

Sneakers tied, he sat back. Also there was no way
in hell, Mike considered further, that he was going
to pose (brandishing a whisk and not much else)
for the kind of "sexy chef" calendar Amanda had
suggested so eagerly last night.

He pursed his lips in thought. The truth was, short
of a shave, he hadn't really changed at all in the
nearly two weeks they'd been working together on
the Life Coach Lotto. And what's more, he honestly
didn't think he needed to *do* any real changing,
either. After all, he hadn't even entered the Lotto in
the first place. Some other poor schmo had and then
lost his ticket.

Was this going to be a problem?

Nah, Mike told himself, striding into the kitchen
to grab his keys from the hook beside his imported
extra-virgin olive oil and a stack of *Bon Appétit* back
issues. Amanda knew he wasn't up for a permanent
lifestyle change. There was no way she seriously
expected him—regular-guy Mike Cavaco—to become
the new Galloping Gourmet or whatever other crazy
chef-related ideas she'd cooked up last night. That
had to have been simply the excitement of the
moment talking.

Right? Right.

Reassured, Mike scrubbed a hand through his
messy, nearly shoulder length hair and then headed
out the door. At long last, things were going his way

again, and he couldn't wait to share the good news with Bruno, Snake, and Curly.

Share, share. He was firing up his taxi's ignition before the reality of what he'd thought finally caught up with him. *Share the good news.* Making a face, Mike gunned the motor and peeled out onto the street.

Nobody was changing him, he vowed, spooked by the whole experience. *Nobody.*

"Trish, keep Mrs. Neubaum on hold a few minutes longer, would you please?" Amanda asked, yelling down the office hallway to the front desk.

Less than a half-hour had passed since she'd arrived at Aspirations, Inc., freshly-showered, blow-dried, dressed in her cutest make-your-man-drool miniskirt, heels, and V-neck black sweater, and ecstatically post-tête-à-tête. But that blissed-out mood had rapidly evaporated, and already she was up to her eyeballs in emergencies. Frankly, Amanda was unable to cope with another one right this second.

"Tell her that the Magic Marker stripes her niece put on the piano will probably come off with a little bit of Windex and some elbow grease."

"Gotcha, boss."

Feeling frazzled, Amanda sucked in a deep breath and prepared to console Mr. Waring on line two. It turned out that his supervisor (the head of the accounting department at the plastics company) had walked in on Mr. Waring in mid-yoga, reverse-triangle pose and had immediately filed sexual-harassment charges. Evidently, the fact that Mr. Waring had changed into spandex yoga togs and had been pointing his newly flexible butt toward the cluster of secretaries' cubicles hadn't helped matters any.

"I don't know why this is happening to me now," Waring said to her on the other end of the phone.

"I tried to share my sense of relaxation and enlighten-ment with Ms. Ketchum—"

"Your supervisor?" Amanda noticed the third phone line light up and winced.

"Yes. But that's when she started dialing human resources to request the sexual-harassment complaint form. I can see that perhaps leaving my office door open during yoga practice wasn't the best decision," Mr. Waring went on. "But my fifteen-minute morning break is mine to do with as I wish, and I resent the fact that—"

"Maybe we should talk this over in person," Amanda suggested, feeling her head begin to throb. The ener-gizing eucalyptus aromatherapy candle she'd lit hadn't done a thing so far, and she was beginning to seriously crave a jelly doughnut to see her through. She flipped the pages in her day planner. "I don't have any more appointments available this week, but—"

"All booked up with your Lotto winner, right?" Waring accused, a clear tsk-tsk in his voice. "I'm *never* able to reach you when I need to these days. You're getting out of balance, Ms. Connor."

"Possibly," Amanda snapped, driven to the brink. This was the third such complaint she'd heard today about her time-consuming efforts on behalf of the Life Coach Lotto. "But at least *I* know enough not to squeeze myself into spandex, Mr. Waring. No one looks good squished into skintight clothes, with the possible exception of Batman."

A gasp came through the phone. "I see. If *that's* the way you feel about it, I don't think there's any reason—"

Immediately, Amanda felt contrite. "Wait a minute, Mr. Waring. I'm sorry. Terribly sorry. That was out of line. I don't know what I was thinking."

"I'll say. Batman wore a *rubber* suit."

She sighed, massaging her temples. Her ten-thirty appointment arrived while Amanda was still apologizing to Mr. Waring, and by the time she'd reassured him sufficiently to hang up, all the phone lights were blinking, and Trish was standing in her doorway with a fistful of pink message slips.

It was too much. Groaning, Amanda folded her arms atop her desk blotter and thunked her head down on top of them. "I can't do it," she cried to Trish. "Everybody wants something from me, and there just isn't enough of me to go around."

"Not since that new diet of yours," Trish said loyally. "It's working like a charm. That, or all the energizer-bunny-style whoopee you've been having is burning more calories than industrial-strength Tae-Bo. You look great."

"I feel lousy."

It was true. Satisfying her clients made Amanda happy. When she helped them, quite simply, she felt as though she'd done something worthwhile. She felt as though maybe her slob-o-rific personal habits didn't actually doom her to a life of never achieving good things. She felt *needed*. But *not* satisfying her clients—as was the case today—made her miserable.

Raising her head again as Trish left, Amanda spotted something orange flutter to the desktop. She picked it up. A fragment of bird-of-paradise blossom. She'd tried to wear the flower Mike had given her in her hair this morning and had only succeeded in arriving at her office—apparently—decked out in what looked like misguided confetti.

Now her slobbiness was following her to work! Was there no end to the depths to which she would sink?

Evidently not, Amanda discovered when she'd taken all her phone calls, juggled her appointments, and explained twelve separate times why the Life Coach Lotto had to temporarily take precedence in her schedule. Because, as she hung up the phone for the last time and prepared to meet with Mike, Amanda spotted jelly-doughnut icing globules decorating her shoes. And papers strewn from one end of her office to the other. And doodles covering her usually-pristine desk blotter.

As though suffering from the unprecedented disarray, her potted spider plant (said to be unkillable by non-green-thumb-endowed owners) drooped dispiritedly over her framed photo of her, Mel, and Gemma at the Grand Canyon late last year. And when Trish brought her a cup of coffee from the office pot, Amanda reached for it and saw a whole contingent of white Webster hairs stuck on the sleeve of her sweater.

Arrgh! There was no doubt about it now. She'd officially become an at-work slob as well as an at-home slob! Aghast, Amanda put down her coffee cup and tried to pull herself together.

So she'd had a tough morning. So she'd totally slobified her office in the space of an hour and a half. Was that really so bad? Did that *really* mean she was doomed?

Amanda wasn't certain, but it sure as hell felt like it.

Clearly, she had to put a lid on this. She had to reassert control. The mess-o-rama surrounding her—and her dissatisfied, emergency-ridden clients—proved that much. But since she couldn't do a thing for her other clients until she'd assured Aspirations, Inc.'s future via the Channel Six Life Coach Lotto segments, the answer was clear. Now, more than ever, she had to make sure Mike was a success. He was, after all, her last hope.

Digging out her Rolodex from beneath a jelly-splattered "How to Find the Job of Your Dreams" pamphlet, Amanda got down to business jotting down contacts for Mike's supersuccessful, megasexy, Galloping Gourmet–worthy chef future. Now, she vowed, there'd be no stopping her.

Chapter Eighteen

They were back at the Pepto-Bismol Pink Palace.

Mike wasn't too happy about it, either. Striding through the East Valley spa's marble-tiled hallways beside Amanda, dressed once again in the requisite pink Rosado robe, he tightened his leather belt atop the terry cloth and grimly followed the uniformed spa employee ahead of them.

Where she was leading them, Mike didn't know. He didn't especially want to find out, either, but he had a feeling he was going to, whether he wanted to or not.

If he'd known that Kneecap Oglers Central was on the agenda for today, he might have done things differently. For one thing, he might have worn a less breezy pair of boxers. His balls were all but shrinking at the sustained contact with potpourri-scented air and New Age music. It was damned emasculating. For another, he might have actually looked harder for a pair of sweat socks without holes in the toes.

As it was, he was stuck. So Mike merely strode forward with his bare toes scrubbing against the insides of the unlaced sneakers he'd insisted upon wearing, and tried not to be aggravated at Amanda.

She'd ambushed him, plain and simple. He'd been all hepped up, prepared (as well as could be expected) for a grueling touchy-feely Q and A session about his dreams, his past relationships with Inga and all the others, his ambitions, and his secret terror of grown women who kept stuffed animals in their cars . . . and then Amanda had gotten a telling gleam in her eyes, cut their questionnaire session short, and hustled him here.

To Pretty Pink hell.

"Frederick will be *so* delighted to see you today," said the ultra-groomed blonde spa employee ahead of them. She paused before a series of three closed doors and beamed at him and Amanda. "We showed him your 'before' photo, Mr. Cavaco, and he's been *itching* to get his hands on you ever since."

Someone in the Channel Six remote crew tittered. The camera and sound people had materialized at the spa entrance when they'd arrived there just before noon, and they'd dutifully trooped down the Rosado corridors right along with Mike and Amanda, equipment in full *embarrass Mike* mode.

"Mike can't wait, either," said Amanda. Her pumped-up enthusiasm warned him that something dire was at hand, but he didn't know what. "We're very happy Frederick could fit us in."

She jabbed him in the ribs with her elbow.

Mike rubbed his side, a few inches above his low-slung leather belt. He shot her a glare.

Amanda sent back a furiously pantomimed display that, from behind the spa employee's back, was clearly meant as a request for him to say something.

"Yeah," he muttered reluctantly. He did want to

make Amanda happy, after all. "I can't tell you what this whole experience means to me."

The buffed-and-polished blonde nodded. "Very good. Frederick *does* like to see the proper quality of . . . oh, shall we say, obsequiousness? . . . in his makeoverees."

"Makeover," said someone in the sound crew. "Huh, huh."

That was just about enough. Mike turned to confront the jerk, but an instant later, Amanda had grabbed his arm and was dragging him through the now-opened doors into a room chock-full of marble, mirrors, gleaming chrome, tropical plants, and unidentifiable bits of beauty equipment. It was as though Bob Vila's work shed had exploded and been reassembled by a cadre of pink-loving teenage girls with a Beauty Shop Barbie fixation.

"Frederick will see you now," said Ms. Obsequiousness, bending low—yes, actually bending—and sweeping her arm sideways as though she were introducing a reclusive dignitary.

Mike looked past her fingertips, squinting against the glare coming from the mirrors-and-chrome overload. Then he spotted him—Frederick. It had to be. The stylist had a welcoming smile on his face and a wild, creative glint in his eyes that probably didn't bode well for Mike.

He also had a diminutive espresso cup in his hand and an overall look that Mike could only describe as coffeehouse Amish—head-to-toe black clothes, lean build, aggressively trimmed pointy beard, slicked-back dark hair in a three-inch ponytail, and narrow black-framed glasses. Mike was still trying to get his bearings when Frederick set down his espresso cup and joyously clapped both hands together.

"Mike!" he cried. "Dear, dear Mike. Come in, come

in, to my little abode. I will make you *très magnifique*, never fear!"

Mike balked. He didn't want this guy's version of *très magnifique*. It probably involved lots of black, several pairs of pointy-toed shoes, and a steady diet of organic Costa Rican coffee. But he could hear the camera crew making surreptitious chicken noises behind him, and Amanda was watching him with her hopes in her eyes, and he couldn't stand to disappoint her.

"All right," he said, squaring his shoulders. "Let's get this haircut over with."

After all, how long could it take? A few snips, a quick buzz around the neck and ears, and *bam!*—he'd look like his old self again. Easy as pie. Even if it *was* happening in a place that looked like something out of *2001: A Froufrou Spa Odyssey*.

Robe flapping, Mike advanced on the pink upholstered salon chair Frederick had staked out. His squeaking sneakers attracted smirks from the spagoers already in mid-makeover, and he scowled them into looking away. He couldn't remember the last time he'd felt more conspicuous. More uncomfortable. More likely to boycott Channel Six programming for his entire life.

"Oh, it's not *just* a haircut," gushed another spa employee, this one a twenty-something brunet with a pixie haircut and alarming red lipstick. She set him down and displayed her teeth in a not-quite-smile. "First, Frederick always does a thorough consultation with his new clients."

A consultation? More talk. *Ugh.* Clenching his hands on the chair's bubblegum-colored armrests, Mike tried not to let his reluctance show. What would they talk about, anyway? The dearth of quality barristas at Valley coffeehouses? How hard it was to keep your goatee pointy?

Not freakin' likely, Mike thought.

Frederick materialized in front of the chair, looking as excitable as Cupcake with a new squeaky rubber T-bone.

"Espresso? Cappuccino? Iced chai latte?" he asked. "No? Sure? Supersure? All righty, then. Let's get started."

Frederick futzed around the chair's perimeter, examining Mike from all angles and making occasional exclamations below his breath. An assistant dogged his steps, scribbling down his cryptic comments (Wax! Glaze! Baliage! Volume!) as they moved. At the edge of the hubbub, Amanda hovered, looking like a proud parent on the first day of preschool. She crossed her arms and bit her lip, awaiting the verdict.

"*Looove* the look," Frederick said, gesturing with beringed fingers toward Mike's spa robe, belt, boxers, sweat socks, and sneakers combo. "Very original. Very witty. Very "macho meets manicurist," wouldn't you say? And those *legs!* My God! Delicious."

Startled, Mike yanked at the hem of his robe. Was this guy checking him out?

"Oh, we're going to have a marvelous time together, Mike. Really marvelous," Frederick was saying now, apparently oblivious to his client's growing alarm. "The next— Oh, what would you say, Geneva?"

The red lipsticked assistant scrutinized Mike, then scribbled something else on her clipboard. "Three hours."

"The next three hours are going to be *such* fun!"

Three hours? God only knew what they'd accomplish on him in that much time. Mike bolted.

The next thing he knew, vinyl hairstylist's capes were flying in his path, the Channel Six cameras were whirring, and Amanda was calling his name. Mike found himself slammed firmly back into the salon chair before he'd so much as achieved blow-dryer-worthy escape velocity.

Above him, Frederick removed his hands from Mike's upper arms. The *stylist* had been the one to tackle Mike into his chair?

"Impressive, no?" he asked, preening. "I train with Sven at my club in Paradise Valley. It's all about light weights and high repetitions." He mimed some rapid-fire biceps curls. "Strength without bulk. Lift and repeat. The results are a*maz*ing."

He was doomed. Doomed, Mike realized. Amanda was perfectly willing to offer him up as a sacrificial lamb to the gods of style (seeing that he'd been subdued, she'd already moved on to making calls on her cell phone), and there wasn't a damned thing he could do about it.

Scary-Lipstick Girl peered critically at Mike's forehead. "Shall we start with the unibrow problem?" she asked Frederick.

The stylist leaned closer, giving Mike a strong whiff of some expensive piney-smelling cologne. He poked a finger in the center of Mike's forehead.

"I don't know. The brows *do* need some work, but—"

"I do *not* have a unibrow!" Mike said, shoving away Frederick's hand. "There's nothing wrong with—"

"Oh, but of course you couldn't be expected to realize it," interrupted the blond spa employee who'd led him into this mess. "It's just like the pedicure problem. Nobody wants to admit to a Cro-Magnon-style unibrow, any more than they want to show off their bunions."

Mike followed her gaze to his sneakers. Inside them, his toes curled from the disapproving chill of her scrutiny. Did spa employees have X-ray vision or what? He didn't know exactly what a bunion was, but he figured he ought to be at least old enough to gum his food before it became a concern.

"I'm pretty sure I don't have—" he began, but

Frederick cut him off by lifting hanks of Mike's hair in his hands and clucking with disappointment.

"What we need to do here," he said, "is find something that will fit in with your lifestyle. Something *different,* of course. Why don't you tell me a little bit about yourself, Mike? Hmmm?"

While Mike hemmed and hawed, reluctantly disclosing his temporary taxi-driver job ("So gritty!" exclaimed Frederick delightedly), his weekend street hockey games ("Oooh, sporty!"), and his need for something wash-and-go ("Just a *few* products won't hurt"), the stylist perched himself atop the counter at his station, crossed his legs, and listened avidly. Beside Mike's chair, Geneva took notes. When Mike had come to the end of his brief spiel, Frederick and Geneva looked at each other. They smiled conspiratorially.

"The works," they said in unison.

Awww, hell, Mike thought. *The works.* Whatever that involved. Gritting his teeth, he clutched the salon chair's armrests and prepared for the worst. At this point, he just hoped he could survive with his dignity—and his Mickey Mouse boxers—intact.

"I'd say things are going swimmingly for you," Gemma told Amanda a short while later. She forked a bite of arugula into her mouth and chewed thoughtfully. "It sounds like you're making amazing progress with Mike."

"Things are going pretty well," Amanda agreed. *Now. Now that she'd discovered the hook of the century for her Lotto winner . . . and had fallen in love with him, too.* "He's in good hands with Frederick and Geneva."

Once she'd realized how much media attention she'd need to launch Mike's sexy new-millennium Galloping Gourmet gig, Amanda had decided to step up the remaining physical part of his whole-life makeover. She'd been lucky that the star stylist had been willing to fit Mike in today.

Since leaving Mike in preshampoo and condition, she had been lunching on one of Rosado's four garden patios with Gemma and Mel. And during the past half hour, Amanda had told her friends everything. With the exception of the more *personal* details from last night. Amanda wasn't the kiss-and-tell type.

Well, okay. She was the *kiss*-and-tell type, but that was as far as it went. After all, a girl had to have some secrets, and there were some aspects of her night with Mike that she still wanted to hold close to her heart and just *savor* for a while longer.

At Mel's elbow, a uniformed male spa employee stopped to inquire about their meals. Mel gave him a saucy up-and-down perusal, then suggested he check back with her later on. "In case I find an appetite for a little something sweet."

"You're incorrigible, Mel," Amanda said, laughing. "Look. The poor guy is so shook up, he almost ran into the cactus gardens."

They all watched as the flustered employee swerved to avoid a potted prickly pear at the Saltillo patio's edge. With a quick glance back at Mel, he assumed a dreamy look and then was forced to skip sideways to miss the stone fountain in his path. Barely visible on the other side of the mist and tinkling water, he hurried off.

Mel shrugged and lit a cigarette. "What's the use of playing hooky from work if you don't get a little nooky while you're at it?"

Gemma choked on her iced tea. "Mel!"

"What?" Mel blew a smoke ring and pushed away her plate of mostly-eaten Caesar salad. "Like you and Tom have never had a nooner?"

Amanda stifled a grin at Gemma's shocked expression. Then she looked on with more interest as Gemma's cheeks reddened. "Gemma?"

"Well, there *was* that time with the Victoria's Secret leopard-print chemise . . ." Gemma wiped her mouth with her napkin, looking embarrassed.

"The make-your-man-an-animal chemise?" Amanda asked, shoving away her own mostly-eaten field greens with grilled maple-sesame salmon. "Gemma, you wild woman!"

"Yes, well. Tom is always extremely supportive of my attempts to liven up the—"

"Screw supportive!" Mel cried, leaning forward and hooting with delight. "Did he throw you down and go for it or not?"

A nervous titter escaped Gemma. She nodded.

"Way to go!" Amanda said encouragingly. For someone like Gemma, dressing especially to entice her husband was a major step.

"We're, um, working our way through the animal kingdom," Gemma explained shyly. She tucked in another bite of arugula and stared at her plate while she chewed. "I just bought a zebra-print bra. And last week, Tom brought home a bearskin rug for after the twins went to sleep."

"Hubba, hubba!"

Gemma flushed. A soft smile tilted her lips upward.

"Damn." Shaking her head, Mel ground out her cigarette and looked at Gemma. "I am *so* envious of you right now, I can hardly stand it. The men I meet think brushing their teeth before a date is a big romantic gesture. I can't imagine any of them dragging home actual animal skins for me."

"Well," Gemma said, "it was actually synthetic. Not that big a deal."

With a smile for Gemma's obvious bid to downplay her marital adventures, Amanda gave Mel's arm a reassuring squeeze. "Hey, hang in there. You'll find your perfect Mr. Caveman eventually."

"Har, har. Easy for you to say. *Your* dates come straight to you," Mel said. "Whatever happened to that 'no dating clients' policy you had, anyway?"

"I decided it was like having a 'no dating men shorter than me' policy," Amanda said lightly, unwilling to think about her relationship with Mike in those terms and even more unwilling to consider what might happen if Channel Six got wind of it. "It took too many men out of the running."

The three of them laughed. Then, having saved calories by choosing salads and iced tea for lunch, they waved over Mel's favorite spa guy and ordered a Sinful Triple Chocolate Delight. With three forks.

As long as she was breaking her own rules, Amanda figured, her diet ought to be first on the chopping block. But she'd barely had time to let the first bite of creamy dark chocolate mousse melt on her tongue before her cell phone rang. Hastily wiping her lips, she answered it.

Seven minutes later, Amanda hung up to face her friends' semi-accusing stares. They'd obviously heard her end of the conversation.

"That was Evan," she explained as she tucked the phone back into her handbag with shaky fingers. "The lifestyles producer from Channel Six. He's, uh, been screening the raw footage from the Life Coach Lotto."

"And?" Mel demanded.

"Well . . ." Amanda felt her lower lip wobble, and she hurriedly sipped some iced tea to hide that telling weakness. She gulped in a breath, trying not to panic and fall apart. "He thinks it needs more drama. Or it won't hit with viewers."

"What?" Mel was clearly indignant. She'd actually

put down her forkful of Sinful Triple Chocolate Delight. "I don't believe this."

"Believe it." A deep sigh welled up from inside Amanda. Why this? Why now? "He—he said he might not air the life-coach segments at all. He has this hot-dog-vendor exposé already in the can, and he—"

She broke off, unable to go on. *Replaced by a report on crooked wiener hawkers.* It didn't get any lower than this.

"Oh, Amanda." Gemma gave her a quick hug. "What are you going to do?"

"I—I don't know," Amanda confessed. Her voice squeaked with misery. "It hadn't even occurred to me that Evan might not like what we've done so far."

"What do you mean, you don't know?" With an abrupt gesture, Mel waved her arm in the air. "You heard her, Gemma. She's going to do all that chef stuff with Mike. Public appearances. Calendars. Cookbooks. You were just talking it up with Evan, Amanda!"

She had. In a fit of desperation, she'd blabbed to the lifestyles producer about Mike's Le Cordon Bleu training and then had run several promotional ideas past him. Evan had seemed very receptive, even so far as to suggest a joint Channel Six and Rosado–sponsored cooking appearance on the station's morning show. But still . . .

Gemma looked concerned. "I don't know. Shouldn't you check with Mike first before making those kinds of plans?"

Yes, said Amanda's conscience. "He'll be fine with it," said her desperate side, which obviously felt more vocal today. "Mike has gone along with everything so far, hasn't he? This will simply mean a few tiny adjustments to our remaining schedule."

Amanda seriously hoped she sounded more confident than she felt. She also hoped that Evan hadn't meant the final comments he'd closed their conversation with—the ones about how, if Amanda didn't pump up the drama on the Life Coach Lotto (with, for example, a Mike Cavaco cookbook featuring its author in a sexy toque-and-not-much-else pose on the cover) and make the life-coach feature a ratings magnet, her chances at a weekly spot were finished.

She *needed* that spot. Needed the exposure it would gain for Aspirations, Inc., and the assurance that Trish and her other employees—who had clients of their own—would still have jobs a few weeks from now. If the Channel Six deal fell through . . . well, Amanda just couldn't allow that to happen.

"Don't worry, you two," she told Mel and Gemma, grabbing their hands for good luck and forcing a smile. "I'm as sure of Mike's success as the Next Big Thing—chefwise, that is—as I am of our ability to polish off the remaining two billion calories in this Sinful Triple Chocolate Delight."

Amanda straightened her shoulders and picked up a fork, determined to go forward if it killed her. No matter what happened, she wouldn't let down the people who depended on her. Her staff. Her clients. Herself.

Forks also in midair, Gemma and Mel gave her joint skeptical looks. "Are you sure?" Gemma asked.

"Have you ever known me *not* to be sure about something?"

"Not something work-related," Mel admitted. "You're a never-say-die, superbionic workaholic when it comes to the well-being of your clients."

"Well, then. There you go."

Amanda dug into the desert and realized with amazement that her appetite was actually gone. Funny, she'd tried diet after diet when all she really needed was a daily dose of disaster to make her urge to splurge disappear. Nevertheless, she raised her chocolate-laden fork and moved to make a toast with it, as though it were a glass of champagne.

"To Bruno," she said, doggedly returning to the subject of work, bionic or otherwise, "who has his very first professional singing engagement at Gemma's parents' anniversary party tomorrow night!"

"Hear! hear!" her friends chorused, hefting their forks in a touching show of camaraderie. If she was willing to move forward, the feeling from Mel and Gemma obviously was, then so were they.

"To Snake," Amanda added, "whose sculptures will be publicly displayed for the first time ever at the Kugelhoff gallery downtown next week!"

"Hurray!"

"And to Mike," Amanda finished, feeling a helpless smile light her face at the thought of him as she recapped her congratulatory toast, "who's destined to be Phoenix's answer to Emeril Lagasse, the Galloping Gourmet, and Hunk of the Month, all rolled into one!"

"Hurray! Hurray!"

They all downed their dessert bites, happily discussing their approval of everything that Amanda's clients had accomplished. No sooner had the taste of chocolate left their palates, though, than Mel turned in her patio seat and pointed toward something moving past the spa windows to their left.

"Don't look now," Mel said with a wry twist of her lips, "but I think your galloping Hunk of the Month just sprinted past wearing nothing but undies and a headful of highlighting foil. Look."

They did. Amanda was out of her seat before her napkin hit the table.

Chapter Nineteen

"Amanda!" Mike said, spotting her out of the corner of his eye. "In here."

Help, he wanted to whimper. But there was no way he'd sink that low. Not even after all he'd been through at the hands of Mr. Coffeehouse Amish and his evil assistant, Red Lipsticker.

Mike Cavaco was tougher than that, dammit. Despite the incident a half-hour ago with the highlighting goop.

There was a clatter of high-heeled shoes against the glossy floors as Amanda stopped and turned around. Moments later, a gasp let him know that she'd reached the room he'd been sequestered in . . . and she'd seen him, too.

"Oh, Mike." She dropped to a crouch beside the pink über-Barcolounger the spa employees had urged him into, her expression sympathetic. "Are you all right?"

He grunted, not trusting himself to speak. The foil things in his head were piercing his scalp, the fumes from the Revlon number twenty were making his eyes water, and he was still a little out of breath from his futile sprint through the Rosado hallways.

Also, the pedicurist was listening in from her stool between his bare feet, and he was afraid to find out what she'd do to him with all her pointy beauty instruments if he complained. So instead, Mike stared stoically ahead at a *Do It Yourself Feng Shui* poster on the opposite wall and nodded.

I'm okay. Not counting the poking, the prodding, and the in-depth discussions about my pores.

Amanda stroked his shoulder. "Well, it looks like everything's going according to plan," she said encouragingly.

At the heartening note in her voice, Mike relaxed a little. Once he'd raised his gaze from the welcome and sexy sight of her legs—bared to mid-thigh in her short skirt—though, he noticed Amanda's lips twitching, a sure sign she was holding in a smile. At his expense!

"Sure," he groused. "Everything's going according to plan. *If* the plan is to turn me into a girl. Ouch!"

He glowered at the pedicurist. In retaliation, she broke out something that looked like a miniature power circular sander and flipped the "on" switch with obvious relish. Then she guided the buzzing instrument toward his poor defenseless feet. Feeling a whimper coming on, Mike clenched his gloved hands (smeared with Apricot Oil Cuticle Enricher, part of his manicure) on the Barcolounger's sides.

"You're very masculine," Amanda assured him, giving him a wink that reminded him pleasantly of last night and diverted his attention from what was going on below his ankles. "No amount of beauty treatments could change that."

"Ha!" interrupted the pedicurist. "Maybe. *If* he'd let us perform the treatments. It took two facialists, one jujitsu instructor, and an aromatherapy counselor to get him in here so I could do my job. He bolted in the midst of phase two."

At the mention of phase two, Mike's scowl deepened.

"So *that's* why you were running through the hallways." With a sideways nudge of her hip, Amanda encouraged him to scoot over. She perched on the edge of the beauty Barcolounger, her nearness somehow soothing his rattled nerves. "Mel and Gemma and I were wondering about that. We saw you through the windows facing the patio, and—"

"They tried to wax my chest!" Mike exclaimed.

The horror of it still gave him chills. He clapped his hands over his torso, unable to actually feel the smattering of dark chest hair beneath his palms (thanks to the stupid manicure gloves), but he knew it was there. That was enough.

"That's phase two," he told her. "Wax. My. Chest!"

This time, Amanda did laugh. "So? Male models do it all the time. You might have liked the look."

The pedicurist agreed with a nod.

Mike shuddered. "Do you have any *idea* how much that would hurt?"

"Poor baby," muttered the pedicurist.

He shot a glare at her. As though she hadn't goaded him into it in the first place, she blithely massaged pale green goo into the soles of his feet and didn't look up.

"Do *I* have any idea how much waxing hurts?" Amanda asked. Pointedly, she raised her leg, then gazed at the skirt-shrouded junction of her thighs. "Yes. Yes, I do."

Mike thought about it for a minute. Considered exactly how Amanda had looked last night, wonderfully naked and nicely groomed. Realized with new insight exactly what she must have endured—*and where*—to achieve that tidy look, and grimaced.

He suddenly had new appreciation for all that women went through to look beautiful.

"You didn't think we were born with a neat little landing strip down there, did you?" Amanda added, raising her eyebrows.

"I didn't think about it. I only enjoyed it." And, starting now, he'd be sure to give some extra TLC to all those affected areas. "But from now on, if you don't want to—*ouch!* What the hell was *that?*"

He jerked away from a sudden pain south of his ankles. From her stool, the pedicurist blinked innocently. A short rectangular thing dangled from her fingertips. "All this talk about waxing reminded me," she said. "I forgot to do the tops of your toes."

"Ow, ow, ow." With growing comprehension, Mike examined the rectangular thing. Those brown flecks glued to one side of it had to be hairs—*his* hairs—ripped from the tops of his toes!

Before he could so much as cry uncle, the pedicurist slapped another rectangular strip onto his left foot and then wrenched it off. Not even knowing it was coming made it hurt less.

Feeling tears sting the corners of his eyes, Mike blinked fiercely. He looked to Amanda to back him up on the sheer monstrosity of this, but she seemed unconcerned by what had happened. Maybe all women were closet masochists, he decided. Why else would they subject themselves to bikini waxes?

"Unsightly hairs tend to grow at the tops of each toe," the pedicurist explained, "and on the very top of the foot. One benefit of our pedicures is removing those hairs."

"But I'm a guy!" Mike exclaimed. "I'm *supposed* to be hairy!"

"Not *that* hairy," muttered the manicurist.

"Tell that to the people who make those rotary nose-hair trimmers," Amanda put in, shuddering. "They might disagree."

"Arrgh!" Everyone here was insane. Even Amanda.

"Say, where's the Channel Six crew?" she asked then, evidently only just now noticing that they were alone in the room with Nurse Ratched and her demonic pedicure tools. "They followed us into Frederick's salon, so I figured they'd be taping this, too."

"They did. For about two minutes." *Starting shortly after the pink-wearing linebackers had gotten him into the Barcolounger.* "Then they decided they had enough torture footage—"

The pedicurist scoffed.

"—and went to get some shots of the Rosado grounds."

"They went to the *More Sensual Sexuality* seminar in the Gecko room," the pedicurist informed them. "It's very popular."

"Well, I guess it's no worse than poker," Amanda said.

She shrugged, the motion drawing Mike's attention to the enticing curve of her breasts beneath her close-fitting lightweight black sweater. He wished he and Amanda were alone again. Holding hands while watching TV. Moaning while making love. Even delving deeper into the relationships and emotional attitudes questionnaire. Anything would be better than this.

He hoped she knew he was doing this for her. Mike swore he'd never have endured this kind of humiliation for anything less.

As though she'd sensed the mushy direction of his thoughts, Amanda leaned closer. Her face neared his, almost at kissing distance, and Mike was suddenly filled with anticipation. Gloved hands, tinfoil hair, bizarrely hairless toes, be damned. He'd kiss her and feel like himself again. He inhaled, subtly moving his head forward in readiness for the kiss.

"What's that stuff on your eyebrows?" she asked.

Damn. "Eyebrow dye." Feeling disgruntled, Mike folded his arms over his chest and watched Amanda examine his forehead from all angles. She raised a fingertip toward him as though tempted to touch the purplish glop Geneva had smeared on him but lowered it at the last minute. "Frederick said my eyebrows were too dark to go with my new hair. You know, after the lowlights, baliage, and glaze get applied."

Which made him sound more like a cabinet in need of heavy-duty refinishing, Mike thought grumpily, than a man.

As though that actually made sense, Amanda nodded.

He had to make her see reason. "They plucked my eyebrows, too. In the middle. And a bit below the arch." He couldn't *believe* he actually knew the terminology. *Hmmph. Stupid unibrow obsession.*

No sympathy was forthcoming. Feeling increasingly discontented, Mike upped the ante.

"The spa doctor tried to give me some over-the-counter pain reliever first, but I said no." He cleared his throat gruffly and tried to look appropriately macho. It was tough to pull off while wearing a tinfoil Medusa look. "Didn't need it."

He'd already decided he'd kill the pain later, the respectable, manly way. With Budweiser and a basketball game.

"Good for you." Amanda patted his glove, clearly unconcerned.

Weren't women supposed to be the caregivers in relationships? He'd thought he'd seen something like that while surfing past Oprah the other day, but it may have been a delusion. After all, he found it hard to believe he might actually have paused the remote on the *Oprah* show in the first place, much less remembered the topic under discussion.

"We only offer pain reliever to the men," the pedicurist supplied. Clearly, she had trouble minding her own damned business. "They've usually never been tweezed before. And the sound of crying disturbs the other spa visitors."

"I told you before. My eyes were watering from the hair-color fumes!" Mike said hotly.

"Mmmm-hmmm."

"It's all right," Amanda said. *Pat, pat.* "I know how you feel. I look like I've got two caterpillars over my eyes if I don't keep on top of things with my Tweezerman."

Okay, Mike decided. Sympathy was worse.

"All finished!" the pedicurist announced. Getting heavily to her feet, she gallumped to the Rosado intercom and spoke into it. When she'd finished, she said, "I hope the results meet with your approval."

Pursing her lips, Amanda peered solemnly at his feet. She gave a two-thumbs-up sign.

Mike didn't dare look. Besides, he figured there was still a chance he could grab Amanda, sneak out the back way—he hadn't yet tried running past the patio onto the championship golf course and disappearing into the sand trap—and end this nightmare right now.

He got to his feet. So did Amanda.

As they neared the doorway, someone entered it. Someone with dark pixie hair, high-gloss red lipstick, and a clipboard.

"Gahh!" Mike yelled.

"Jeez, are you ever jumpy," Amanda said, nudging him with her shoulder. "It's just Geneva."

Right. That's what the problem is.

"Yes, I've come to take you to your next stations." Geneva consulted her clipboard. "Finishing the eye-

brows, finalizing the manicure, and then off to shave
therapy."

"Hold on," Mike said, retrieving his shoes and
sweat socks from beside the pink Barcolounger.
"Where, *exactly*, do you plan to shave me?"

A guy couldn't be too careful in a place like this.

A small smile. "Your face, of course. I'll be taking
care of it myself, since it's my specialty. We use a
straight razor for extra precision—and that good old-
fashioned touch."

Yikes. The image of Geneva wielding sharp instruments near his face wasn't one Mike wanted to contemplate. However, Amanda chose that moment to
tweak his whiskers—sixteenth of an inch long, though
they were—in a clear *take-'em-all-off* gesture. There
was nothing to do but suck it up. Be a man.

So he did. And, amazingly enough, Mike found
the experience surprisingly comfortable—unlike the
haircut that followed.

With Amanda watching every I-can't-believe-this-is-
happening moment, Mike sat in the salon chair he'd
begun in, adjusting his short spa robe for maximum
Mickey Mouse coverage as he did. Then a third assistant removed the folded tinfoil squares from his head,
rinsed out the hair color, and applied the glaze.
Finally, Frederick himself stepped in, turbocharged
on espresso and wielding his stylist's shears in a wild
Edward Scissorhands style that made Mike close his
eyes and use every ounce of concentration he had to
remain still.

He was pretty fond of his ears, after all.

Baliage and brief blow-drying came next, interspersed with frenetic applications of seven separate
styling products. Mike figured so much styling gunk
should have weighed his head down, but when Frederick pronounced, "Ta da!" and stepped back, he real-

ized that he'd never felt lighter from the shoulders up.

Magazine pages ruffled as Amanda set aside the *Entertainment Weekly* she'd been reading. The subtle tap, tap of her heels warned him she was headed his way. Wanting to see what fate awaited him before she got there, Mike opened his eyes and peered into the mirror.

Boggling, Mike blinked and looked again.

He looked like a new man. A different man. A man with tousled, precisely-cut glossy brown hair. An ultra-close shave. Eyes that sparkled with surprise beneath perfect (enhanced) tough-guy eyebrows. And an over-all polish that came from having been worked over, shined up, and catered to by professionals for the better part of an afternoon.

He couldn't believe it.

With a dramatic swish, Frederick swiveled the chair to face Amanda. She stopped dead, her gaze traveling from Mike's chest to the top of his head and back again. Suddenly, it mattered desperately to him that she approve of his new look.

Mike cleared his throat. "Well?"

Moments ticked past with all the speed of a baseball rain delay. Beneath his pink spa robe, he began to sweat.

"Oh, Mike," Amanda finally said. "It's . . . you . . . I . . . Oh, my God." She waved her arms, still staring. "You look *amazing*."

"Like a male model, no?" asked Frederick, beaming.

"Like a dream," Amanda told him.

Getting up from the chair at last, Mike smiled. He liked the sound of that "like a dream" business. And as long as that was how Amanda saw him, whatever it took to get there was all right by him.

Especially since this *had* to be the last phase of his

makeover. Now, he thought with relief, he was finally done.

This is never going to end, Amanda thought a week later, rolling over onto her back and staring up at the ceiling in Mike's bedroom. The tangled linens all around her were proof of the wildly enjoyable hour and a half she and Mike had just spent together, but now that their impromptu lovemaking was over with, she was beset with doubts all over again.

Mike was never going to pose for the chef calendar. He was never going to dazzle the Channel Six execs with a dramatic life change, courtesy of Aspirations, Inc. Not if he kept avoiding the necessary preparatory steps.

And *she* was never going to get out of bed again, not if he kept up that delicious kissing maneuver he'd been demonstrating behind her right knee.

With a regretful sigh, Amanda grabbed Mike's ears and urged him upward. He rose, with visible reluctance and a teasing grin.

"What's the matter?" he asked. "Scared to find out if the third time's the charm?"

His cocky smile dared her to go for the gusto— three toe-curling, mattress-clutching, wahoo-screaming orgasms in a row. With difficulty, Amanda resisted the challenge.

"No," she said. "I'm scared to find out that you're as irresistible as I think. At this rate, we'll never get anything done."

"And that's a problem because . . . ?"

"Because I really need to get this press release finished."

"Press release, schmess release." Mike made a face. "All we really need is love."

She smiled as he levered himself up beside her.

Amanda had to admit, Mike really did look incredible.
His new haircut emphasized the rugged line of his
jaw, the angles of his cheekbones, and the dazzling
width of his smile. It made the melting brown of his
eyes twice as prominent . . . twice as affecting. And
minus his beard, he seemed utterly au courant and
completely professional looking—exactly the sort of
man she'd always imagined herself with.

Funny thing was, none of that really mattered to
her. She'd been wild for him before the Rosado transformation, and she still was. The only difference was,
in the days since the first night they'd spent together,
Mike had felt free to suggest numerous close encounters of the *very* best kind, and Amanda had felt free
to take him up on those suggestions.

Right in the midst of preparing a press release for
the upcoming personal appearance she'd scheduled,
for instance.

But now that was all behind them.

"Let's get back to this," she said, grabbing her
clipboard from the bedside table. "My philosophy is,
the best way to get the publicity you want is to design
it yourself. So we're back to question number—Rats.
Now where's my pen?"

As Mike propped up the pillows against the headboard, Amanda clutched a sheet to her naked self
and looked for the pen she'd been using—before
Mike had suggested a line of questioning of a more
personal nature.

Do you like the way this feels? she remembered him
saying, a Dolby Surround memory complete with the
husky, sexy edge to his voice. *And this? And this?*

Oh, yessss . . .

Shaking herself out of her romantic reverie,
Amanda angled herself sideways and looked under
the bed. At her movement, Cupcake jumped up from
beside the nightstand and licked her face. Webster—

who'd become fast friends with Mike's lovable poodle
from their first bark-and-sniff meeting—managed a
lift of her muzzle and a tail thump. After a few pats
for both dogs, Amanda got back to searching.

"Ah-hah!" Triumphantly, she returned to an
upright position, pen in her grasp. "Found it."

"Mmmm. I found something, too." From behind,
Mike cupped her breasts in his hands, tenderly stroking as he pulled her down onto the mattress again.
With his teeth, he grasped the sliding edge of the
sheet and tugged it lower still. Seconds later, his
mouth was on her nipples, making her forget everything. Everything . . . except the clipboard that was
jabbing a rectangular-shaped dent in her derriere.

"Ooof." Squirming out of reach, Amanda gave Mike
a conciliatory kiss and fished out the clipboard.
"Sorry, but we really ought to get this done. Honest.
We need to develop your media persona before my
meeting with Evan at Channel Six tomorrow, and—"

"Enough said. Fire away." Mike held up his hands
and reluctantly settled back into a more businesslike
position.

Well . . . as businesslike as a man could be, wearing
nothing but skin and sporting a sheet-tenting woody
that probably rivaled her clipboard for hardness.

"Okay." Blowing out a deep, regretful breath (she
really did want to try out that hardness-comparison
test, now that she'd thought of it), Amanda raised
her pen and read the next question. "Have you had
any unique or exciting experiences? What was your
most thrilling moment?"

"Hmmm. Does that thing we tried with the Redi-
Whip count? Because as far as unique and exciting
goes—"

Amanda felt herself flush and gave him a playful
whack.

"Okay. Non-X-rated moments. I get it." Mike furrowed his brow and thought it over. "I went bungee jumping once. Scaled Squaw Peak. Rollerbladed past a contingent of Nude Seniors United at Mission Beach in San Diego. Tried my hand at surfboarding. Does any of that count?"

"That's more than enough." *Enjoys sports*, she wrote on her rough-draft planning paper. "Now, what about the future? Where do you see yourself in five years?"

"Five years? That's easy." With an absolutely matter-of-fact honesty, he looked her in the eye. "I see myself with you."

"Oh, you won't need coaching for *that* long." Amanda waved her arm dismissively. "You've made terrific progress already. A few sessions to eradicate your Twizzler fixation and we'll—"

"No. *With you*. As in, together."

She stopped dead, her Bic poised atop the clipboard. Her heart pounded. Trying to sound as though his answer didn't matter desperately to her, she asked, "Is this some kind of test? An is-she-a-commitment-hound quiz? Because I have to tell you, Mike—"

"It's not a test. It's the truth." He ducked his head and rubbed the back of his neck, staring at the rumpled comforter. "I want to be with you, Amanda."

Excitement sizzled up her spine. *He wanted to be with her!* Still, a girl couldn't be too careful. Not when her heart was at stake. "Be with me? As in . . . ?"

"This." He came closer and nuzzled her neck. "That." He kissed her lips. "Some of these." He trailed those kisses down to her breasts again, sliding the sheet lower once more, and stroked his hands over her hips. From there, Mike waggled his eyebrows. "Whaddya think?"

I think it's not enough. Not if he meant having a wild, between-the-sheets-only relationship, which, given the remarkable things he'd begun doing to her body while awaiting her answer, seemed a reasonable conclusion. It wasn't enough if the crazy, jittery, head-over-heels feelings she'd been having were really what Amanda thought they were.

Love.

No, if this was love, then love*making* by itself would never be enough. But despite all that, Amanda couldn't commit to anything more, not with the future of her career still so uncertain.

She wouldn't come to Mike unless she could stand on her own two feet while doing it. She refused to be dependent on him. Refused to ride his chef-of-the-moment coattails like some modern-day June Cleaver. But only time would tell if she could really pull off the miracle of business survival she needed. So she tucked away her fears for now and grasped the moment as it came.

"I think," Amanda replied, smiling to chase away her worries, "that this time might be better spent doing a little in-depth analysis of your, um, *interpersonal skills.*"

Grinning more widely, she set aside her clipboard. Then, with loving hands, she tugged Mike back up to meet her. With a kiss, she tried to communicate all the longing she couldn't express aloud. Her joining with him was deep and heartfelt, and when it was over with, Mike smiled back.

"Awww, Amanda. You always know what I need," he murmured, stroking her face with one big hand. "Always."

She closed her eyes at the caress of his fingertips, wanting to imprint the memory of his touch forever. Suddenly melancholy, Amanda tilted her cheek more fully into his palm.

"I only hope," she said, "I can give you what you want."

"Oh, *you can.*" Mike's smile broadened and turned wicked. He braced himself on his forearms above her, deliberately allowing their bodies only the faintest, most anticipation provoking contact. "You can give me what I want. Absolutely."

Silently, Amanda shook her head. She couldn't. Not if what he wanted—obviously—was a casual relationship and not if she had to come to him as a failure. The failure she would inevitably be if the Life Coach Lotto didn't make it on the air.

"Don't believe me?" His kiss was as light as a dream. "I'll show you how. Come here."

She did, knowing full well that he'd misunderstood her. She didn't have the heart to correct him. For now, Amanda decided as she wrapped her arms around his middle and gave herself over to the warm weight of his body against hers, she'd just have to show her love for Mike by doing what she did best:

Making his life into the finest, most life coach approved, one-thousand-percent satisfying experience it could be.

And then some.

In the meantime, though, there was that little matter of finding every last one of Mike's erogenous zones to attend to. *Yum . . .*

Chapter Twenty

"I heard Nickerson's clown theme didn't go over very big at the restaurant."

In the dimness of Marvin's, Mike turned at the sound of Jake's voice. He'd arrived at the diner just minutes earlier, ready for a meeting with his team, and the place was buzzing with conversation, music, and the clatter of dishes.

"Yeah?" Mike asked, leaning against the edge of Jake's booth. He couldn't help but feel a low-down sense of satisfaction that the man who'd thrown their lives into turmoil on April Fools' Day was having troubles of his own. "Where'd you hear that?"

"From one of the new waitresses he hired," Jake said. Grinning, the part-time trainer hefted his bottled water and glugged some down. "I train with her at the gym. She said Nick 'Nicky' Nickerson is scrambling to come up with something new. I guess customers thought the circus theme was a real joke."

Mike wasn't surprised. "I could've told him that.

People go to restaurants to be entertained, sure. But if the food isn't good—"

"And how could it be, without you?" Tracy asked loyally, edging past him to slide into the booth opposite Jake.

"—then ambience doesn't matter."

"Hey, clown noses aren't ambience," Jake grumbled. "And he wanted everybody wearing them, from the waitstaff on down."

"Tell me about it." Nodding, Rico joined Tracy.

They bent their heads to look over the latest batch of snapshots of Doris's grandchildren, pushed across the table to them by Doris herself. She was seated next to Jake, eyeballing his bodybuilder's plate of plain grilled chicken and green beans with suspicion. To Doris, no meal was complete without bread.

Mike accepted a beer from a Marvin's waitress, tucking a tip into her palm as he did. After taking a swig, he leaned over Tracy's shoulder to look at the photos. Seeing Doris's grandkids grow from tiny, wrinkled newborns to chocolate-smudged toddlers was secretly one of his favorite parts of his get-togethers with his team.

But tonight his mind wandered. He found himself wondering if Amanda wanted kids. Found himself wondering, further, what those kids might look like. Would they be freckled and gorgeous, like Amanda? Or dark and scruffy and take-life-as-it-comes, like him?

Like him? Whoa! Was he, bachelor extraordinaire and subscription-carrying member of the Maxim reader list, really thinking along those lines—marriage, kids, a house in the 'burbs? Mowing lawns and burping babies and introducing little Michelangelo Jr. to all the Cavaco family traditions?

Well, Amanda probably wouldn't like the wedding-night tradition, where all the Cavacos crammed into the honeymoon suite and offered ribald Italian-style marital advice, Mike thought, but yeah . . . he actually was thinking along those lines. Forever kind of lines. With Amanda. Something about her brought out all the mushiness inside him, and he'd discovered he really didn't mind it all that much.

In retrospect, Mike realized that was what he'd been trying to communicate to Amanda in bed yesterday. He'd been trying everything he could think of to let her know how he felt about her.

No matter how she'd tried to turn their time together toward Life Coach Lotto business, he'd made sure to connect with her on a personal level. No matter how she'd talked and laughed and squirmed away, he'd made sure to follow . . . and to love her. With his hands and his mouth and every part of his soul, he'd made love to her as often and as well as he could. Because that was all he really wanted to do.

He only hoped she'd gotten the message, because Mike didn't consider himself a real verbal kind of guy.

But then, what man was? He'd read somewhere that the average woman spoke seven thousand words in one day, the average man, only two thousand. That didn't leave a lot of room for diversity. Most of those typically hard-rationed male words, Mike was willing to bet, dealt either with sports, the hot-looking babe across the street, cars, gadgets, or work.

Speaking of work: "What's up with the latest batch?" Rico was asking, nodding toward the stack of papers in Mike's hand. "Any luck?"

Everyone quieted. For Mike, the pressure mounted.

"Well . . . there's a possibility of everyone getting hired at a new truck stop that's opening up off the 303, outside Sun City West," he said. He cleared his throat, uncomfortably aware of how few options he was really offering them. "It's not fancy, but they're staffing from the ground up. Also, I hear rumors of a

sushi bar opening up near the new Chandler Fashion
Center mall. If everybody bones up on their nori rolls
and wasabi, we could—"

"Mike, wait," Tracy interrupted. She looked at
everyone assembled there at Marvin's, as though con-
firming something with each person she touched on,
and then took a deep breath. "We think maybe it's
time for us to . . . split up."

Split up? He felt punched in the gut. Plain as that.

Jake jumped in. "Yeah, Mike. I mean, you've been
great and all, doing all the legwork, trying to nail
down another gig for us. But we're all adults. We can
find new jobs on our own."

"It's not your responsibility," Doris piped in, carefully tucking her grandkids' pictures into their photo-
processing envelope. "You've been wonderful to try,
but we've all been talking about this—"

Damn. He knew he shouldn't have taken the time
for that second pass through his hair with the
extrahold Redkin Rewind styling paste the Rosado
staff had sent him home with. He'd only wanted to
look nice for Amanda . . . but his preoccupation with
her and with changing himself into something he
wasn't for the sake of the Life Coach Lotto was obviously beginning to take its toll on the rest of his life.
Case in point: His team was dumping him.

"—and we think," Doris continued, her eyes kindly
and experienced behind her plastic-framed glasses,
"that it would be better for all of us if we split up
and took whatever jobs we could find. All by themselves, my husband's retirement checks don't quite
keep us in the style to which we'd like to become
accustomed"—a wobbly smile quirked her lips—
"and, well, we just think it would be for the best."

He couldn't speak. Mike could only stand there,
clutching the useless reams of restaurant leads, the
stacks of résumés, and the culinary-related newspaper

clippings he'd been hoping would eventually lead to new placements for everyone. He could only stare blindly at everything he'd assembled with hopes of replacing the jobs his stupid April Fools' Day stunt had lost for his friends, and know that he'd failed.

Failed.

He looked at his friends. Familiar faces stared back at him, some with tentative smiles, some filled with what looked like pity. A few people looked away altogether.

Feeling the old sense of defeat surge up inside him, Mike released it in the only way he knew how. He took action. He set his unwanted Budweiser on the table, not caring if anyone saw the way his unsteady hand made the bottle wobble. He took one last look around, shaking his head. Then Mike Cavaco did the one thing he'd never done.

He walked out on his team.

"Mike, wait!" Tracy cried from behind him. "Please don't take this the wrong way. We only mean . . ."

Without stopping, Mike held up his hand, and she fell silent. "It's fine," he rasped. "See you around."

And then he was gone.

Things only got worse in the coming days, and the lone bright spot was Amanda. With her by his side, Mike felt better. Happier. More optimistic. She made him laugh, and she made him feel good, and during their private time together he discovered a softer side to her that he didn't think she let many people see. Amanda trusted him enough to let loose her clipboard and be vulnerable, and he loved the glimpses he had into her funny, generous, and caring nature.

Their relationship moved along at warp speed. When they weren't "on," when they weren't in client-

and-coach mode, being with Amanda was like lolling around in the sunshine—warm, bright, and good for the soul.

The rest of the time, though, was a whole lot shadier. Mike spent part of his time in his taxi and the rest of his time being prepped for, drilled on, and lectured about his upcoming personal appearances. By the time Coach Amanda finished with him each day, he felt as though he'd been put through the ringer. And the fact that none of the restaurant-job leads he'd pursued had panned out didn't help matters any, either.

He'd be damned if he'd go back to one of the Phoenix area's fancy southwestern resorts, places where his former whiz-kid past would be the talk of the *cuisiniers* and Cavaco family–style hijinks would be frowned upon. Hell, his dad didn't even own the kind of clothes a person needed to get into one of those hoity-toity restaurants. And his mom would leave in tears, the way she had when the sommelier at his last resort restaurant had mocked her request for pink champagne instead of the more sophisticated Krug 1989 Clos du Mesnil.

No, Mike wouldn't consider another resort. But restaurateurs at other, less upscale places typically cut his interviews short, saying that his Le Cordon Bleu training made him overqualified. No one wanted to take a chance on a chef who might become bored or temperamental or make radical changes in the kitchen. It was as though they expected him to dish out pâté de foie gras instead of hamburgers and Gruyère-potato gratin instead of French fries.

There had to be some kind of middle-of-the-road option. But as the final week of his month-long Life Coach Lotto whole-life makeover approached, Mike still hadn't found it.

Amanda, however, had kept herself plenty busy.

Sometime between preparing Mike, trying to keep Aspirations, Inc., in good repair despite more missed co-op payments (negotiations with the maintenance man, Louie, were ongoing), and shuffling appointments with her existing clients, Amanda had lined up Mike's debut personal appearance as the "hotter, sexier, new-millennium Galloping Gourmet."

It was to be a cooking demonstration at AJ's, a gourmet food store in the East Valley, benefiting a local charity and cosponsored by Channel Six and Rosado. She'd made him review his proposed menu four times. She'd second-guessed his choice of ingredients. She'd changed her mind about the table decorations and the Life Coach Lotto banner on a daily basis. And, worst of all, Amanda had arranged for him to tape a segment on Channel Six's morning show to promote the event, which was how Mike found himself running late on a Tuesday morning, jockeying for parking in a crowded downtown lot, and hurrying into the Channel Six offices.

He pushed open the door and strode across the checkerboard tile in the renovated fifties-style building where his adventures had begun. "Just Jenny" was still behind her reception desk, and she gasped and giggled when she saw him.

"I just can't *believe* you're the same guy," she cried when she'd settled down enough to squeal out the words. Excitedly, she stood up behind her desk and made a circle in the air with her arm. "Go on, show me all of you."

Reluctantly, Mike took off his baseball cap and turned around.

"Ooooh!" Jenny clasped her hands to her ample bosom and sighed. "You look fabulous. Like a new man. See? What'd I tell you? Winning the Life Coach Lotto has been good for you."

Her words reminded him that the winning ticket

hadn't actually been his. On that day almost four weeks ago, Mike had only been turning in what he'd thought had been a lost ticket. Was it too late now for the real winner to turn up?

Before he could pursue the thought any further, Amanda emerged from the interior of the station, dressed in a pale pink skirt and a matching sweater. Her hair was upswept into full-business mode, and she was carrying her clipboard again, but no amount of carefully-assembled professionalism could make Mike forget what her lips tasted like without that rosy lipstick or what she sounded like while laughing over one of his jokes.

He smiled as she neared him. Her heels clicked over the tiles, echoing the quickening beat of his heart. Something in his face must have given his feelings away, because "Just Jenny" craned her neck to look, and then sighed.

"Hey," Mike said when Amanda reached him. "Fancy meeting you here." He flipped his Diamondbacks cap back in place and squeezed her free hand, still smiling.

"You're late. And where's your suit? Oh, God!" Looking panicky, Amanda took in his board shorts, T-shirt, and sneakers. "I'm sure I told you to wear a suit!"

He shrugged. "I must have forgotten."

"Mike!" With an increasing edge of despair, she let go of his hand and grabbed the edge of his T-shirt sleeve, tugging as though venting her frustration on the innocent frayed cotton. "How am I supposed to make this appearance a success if you won't even cooperate?"

"Hey, I'm here, aren't I? Come on, it's not that bad. It's a morning show, not the Oscars. Bleary-eyed viewers who haven't even had their morning cup of Joe yet aren't going to care if I'm not *QG* material."

"That's *GQ,*"Amanda shot back, obviously harried. "And no, they might not care, but I will! There's a lot riding on this, Mike."

"I know. Why do you think I'm here?" Surely the Channel Six morning-show hosts—and their viewers—cared more about what he had to say than what he looked like . . . didn't they?

Obviously, Amanda didn't think so. Muttering to herself, she tightened her grip on her clipboard and then dragged him by his sleeve toward the back of the station. With a final doff of his cap to "Just Jenny," Mike let himself be led.

"It's a good thing I thought about this possibility," Amanda told him when they'd reached a conference room located off the central Channel Six hallway. She hurried to a rack at one end of the room and plucked something from it—a men's dress shirt and suit on a hanger, Mike saw. "Here," she said, thrusting the clothes toward him. "Put these on."

"Here?" He gazed around the room, which had three windows with views of the rear parking lot, a long conference table littered with hairstyling products and men's shoes, and a full-length mirror propped against one wall. "Now?"

She kicked the door closed. "Yes. Here. Now. Hurry!"

Amanda's hands against his shoulders urged him toward one corner. Tapping her toe, she waited for him to change, tsk-tsking over his Roadrunner boxers as she did.

When he'd finished, she stood on tiptoes and straightened his suit lapels. Inspired by a thousand and one cheesy movies, Mike jokingly clasped her hands and raised them to his lips for a kiss. Before he could finish his romantic gesture, though, Amanda gawked at his hands and jerked them down to waist height.

She turned them over in her palms. "Geez. What did you do with these hands, anyway?"

"You."

The "very funny" face she made told him his double entendre wasn't appreciated. "Your manicure is ruined."

"You didn't seriously expect me to walk around with shiny buffed fingernails all week, did you?" Mike was sure his expression of distaste matched hers. "It's unmanly."

Sighing, she snatched his baseball cap from his head and tossed it onto the conference table. Then she advanced on him with a tube of gel and a can of hair spray.

"What did you do to your hair?" she asked peevishly, raking her sticky gel-covered hands through the tousled strands. "It looks like you slept in it."

"I did."

"And your face! When was the last time you shaved?" She pinched his jaw between her thumb and forefinger, scrutinizing his ten A.M. shadow.

Mike squeezed out an answer from between his mashed cheeks. "Um . . . yesterday morning?"

He hadn't really had the motivation to continue with his super-spiffy male-model routine. Not after what had happened with his team abandoning him. After all, he was pretty sure it was the Lotto makeover's fault, since it had consumed all his time and energy— time and energy he *should* have been spending on fixing his April Fools' Day disaster.

"Yesterday?" Amanda cried, horror-struck. "You haven't shaved since *yesterday?*"

"Look, it's not the end of the world," Mike said, trying for a joke to lighten the mood. "Maybe I'll resurrect the scruffy look. I'll be a trendsetter."

"Aspirations, Inc., is not about scruffy. It's about

success and achieving goals and working toward a dream," Amanda said, painstakingly ticking off each item on her list. "It's not about scruffy, scaly, and, and— Oh, my God. Is that a *blue* tinge on your teeth?"

"Blueberry pancakes. I took my nieces out to IHOP for pancakes this morning." Seeing her dismayed expression, he hurried to add, "Don't worry, the blueberry tint comes off after a couple of—"

"*Arrgh!*"

Suddenly, Amanda fisted her hands on his lapels and thunked her head onto his chest. Then she did it again and again, as though beating her head against the proverbial brick wall. Mike would have liked to think he had abs of steel (thanks to Jake) and a chest like a rock (didn't every guy?), but still . . . this couldn't be good.

"Amanda, Amanda, stop." Gently, Mike captured her head in his hands to make her quit. He smoothed tendrils of hair back from her cheeks and spread his fingers over the freckled softness of her skin. "Calm down. Please. Shhh. Everything's going to be okay."

She sucked in a miserable, shuddering breath. Then she thunked her head down again and sniffled against him, wrinkling his stand-in dress shirt and suit front.

Mike didn't care. This was obviously some workaholic woman's meltdown. He didn't have to understand it to want to help. In his arms, Amanda's body gradually eased as he went on stroking her back with long, even pressure, and by the time a few minutes had passed, her posture had lost some of its peanutbrittle stiffness.

Relieved, Mike smiled as he rested his chin against the crown of her head. "Okay, now," he murmured, still encircling her in his arms. "What's the matter?"

* * *

"What's the matter?" In astonishment, Amanda raised her head from Mike's shirtfront. She couldn't believe he was asking such a thing. *"What's the matter?* How can you ask that, what's the matter?"

Before answering, he pried her fists from his lapels. After the clench she'd had on them, they looked like a couple of gray wool ruffles.

"I can ask that because I'm worried about you," Mike said. "I want to help."

"Help? Ha! You might have started by showing up here ready for your taping!"

"I *am* ready."

Sure he was. Now. Now that she'd broken out her emergency supplies. She should have known this would happen. After all, Mike Cavaco appeared to be missing the ambition gene or whatever it was that kept people like her moving forward while people like him . . . turned up for a TV appearance wearing beach clothes and ratty sneakers.

Stomping toward the table, Amanda grabbed a balled-up pair of gray men's dress socks. She hurled them at Mike.

He caught them, looking surprised. "Hey! What's your problem? I'm only trying to be nice."

"My problem," Amanda said, picking up the nearest size-eleven black oxford and testing its weight, "is that I have a lot depending on this Life Coach Lotto in case you didn't notice. And, for all intents and purposes, *you* are the Lotto. If you blow it, my career is toast."

Fourteen ounces, she estimated, peering thoughtfully at the shoe. Exactly the right weight to knock some sense into running-late, messy-as-he-ever-was Mike Cavaco. Hadn't all her coaching had any effect on him whatsoever?

"I'm not going to blow it." Mike came forward, a be-patient-with-the-crazy-lady expression on his face. "The morning-show people want to talk to me about my career as a chef, right? Well, I know about that backwards and forwards. No problem. So you don't have to worry."

If there was anything Amanda hated, it was being told not to worry when the circumstances clearly called for a total anxiety-fest. If Mike knew what Evan had told her this morning about how important these personal appearances were to the future of the Lotto . . . but she couldn't tell him.

Knowing that the entire future of Amanda's hoped-for weekly news features—and the survival of Aspirations, Inc.—depended on his performance would be too much pressure. If this was how Mike behaved while relaxed, who *knew* what would happen if he was under the gun?

"I'd love to not worry, Mike," she told him, working to inject some serenity into her voice. "Really. But I need your help here. *Please.*"

She handed him the oxford and began hunting for its mate. He wheeled out one of the conference-table chairs and began swapping his grungy footwear for the spiffier stuff Amanda had unearthed.

"Look, I've had a hard week," he said as he tugged on the gray socks, not looking at her. "Somebody like you probably wouldn't understand."

"Somebody like me? What does that mean, somebody like me?" At his blithely-said words, all her pent-up fears and frustration boiled over. "Somebody who has a responsible job instead of a part-time, whenever-I-feel-like-it joyride opportunity? Somebody who plans for the future versus somebody who doesn't give a damn? What, Mike? Explain to me."

He was silent, his lips pressed together as he laced his shoe. He seized its mate from the tabletop jumble, sat down again, and rammed the shoe onto his other foot.

"I thought we'd made progress together!" Amanda cried, driven to get a reaction—any reaction—from him. Maybe then he'd take this seriously. "I thought you'd changed."

"I didn't need to change." Mike looked up, forearms resting on his thighs. His expression was dark, his gaze intent, and for the first time, Amanda wondered if she'd overstepped the boundaries between them. "I was fine just the way I was. *I still am.*"

Amanda gaped at him, dumbfounded. In all her years of coaching, she'd never encountered this. It was practically un-American not to yearn for self-improvement. She hardly knew how to respond.

"But you . . . but the résumé writing and the questionnaires . . . the fitness tests," she stammered. "The makeover. What about—"

"I did it for you. All for you."

That was encouraging, right? Momentarily bolstered, Amanda stepped toward him. He stopped her with a look.

"I thought it was temporary," Mike said. "I thought, after all this time, that you'd seen past all that. To the real me."

"I think I know you pretty well. Geez, Mike, I—" *I've fallen in love with you,* she thought, but couldn't squeeze the words past her constricting throat. "I've spent almost every waking moment with you for the past month."

Mike shook his head. "You don't know me. If you did, you wouldn't be pushing this star-chef routine on me."

He was disagreeing with the career portion of her life-coach plan *now?* Now, at the last possible minute? Amanda paced the length of the conference room, trying to understand how things could have possibly gotten so mixed up between them.

Wasn't she an excellent coach? Didn't she have satisfied clients all over the Valley? Surely she knew what she was doing, Amanda reminded herself. Mrs. Neubaum with her piano, Mr. Waring with his meditating—both of them were proof of her expertise. Weren't they?

Sure. Of course. "This is just last-minute jitters," she said, stopping in front of Mike's chair. "That's all. You've never been on TV before, and you're getting close to achieving your goals, and that's why you're saying things you don't mean."

"No. That's not it."

It has to be it, she wanted to yell. Because otherwise her world was seriously falling apart.

Amanda made herself draw in a deep, yoga-style calming breath. Her heart was racing, and she felt light-headed, and worst of all, the teasing light had gone from Mike's eyes, and she didn't know how to bring it back.

"Okay. Whatever is bothering you, we'll talk about it after the taping, all right?" she asked. Amanda picked up a black patterned necktie and slung it around his collar, preparing to knot it. "But now is the time—now is the time to buckle down and get to work. This is business."

"Is that all it is?" Mike grasped her hands in his, stilling her motions. His straightforward gaze broke her heart. "Just business?"

She knew what he wanted her to say. That it was more, so much more, than that to her. That it was love, that it could be forever. But unless she made the Lotto work, unless she gave Mike the life he deserved, Amanda couldn't promise him any of that. How could she, when everything was still so uncertain?

So instead, Amanda only disentangled herself from

his grasp and went on working her Windsor knot, and she tried to keep her voice steady when she said, "Right now, it's just business. It has to be."

Otherwise, there would never be a future for them. Without career success to assure her independence, Amanda just couldn't be with Mike. He deserved more than a needy, down-on-her-luck woman who couldn't pull her own weight. And, more importantly, he deserved the chance to fulfill his potential—in every way. She meant, no matter what, to make sure that happened.

She only wanted what was best for him. If the Life Coach Lotto didn't succeed, if her business bombed and she and her employees were out on the streets, what was best for Mike would not—could not—be Amanda.

For a long time, Mike only looked at her. Then, when she'd finished knotting his necktie and had stepped nervously backward, he lowered his head. Rubbed the back of his neck.

"I'm a regular guy with regular dreams, Amanda," Mike said quietly. "And I'm never going to be that star chef you're hoping for. I'm never going to wear designer suits and get my hair color touched up once a month. I'm never going to jog every night, practice yoga, and express my innermost feelings. I'm not the kind of guy who lives on pretending. And if that's what you want—"

"Mike—" Desperately, she needed to stop him. Suddenly, this had the feeling of a good-bye, and Amanda didn't know how they'd gotten from discussing when he'd last shaved to this. "Please understand. I only want what's best for you. I know you came to me because of a mistake—"

His lips quirked, faintly. "I can't believe you admitted that ticket wasn't mine."

"—but we can accomplish wonderful things together. I just know we can. I promise!"

That ghost of a smile disappeared as quickly as it had come. "I don't want to do wonderful things," Mike said. His voice was husky with some emotion she couldn't label. "I only want to be with someone who thinks *I'm* wonderful. Just the way I am."

"Oh, Mike. I don't know what—"

His dark gaze pierced her. Silenced her. "That someone isn't you, Amanda."

She was stunned. Disbelief poured through her with all the chill of lost hopes. "Please, don't do this," she whispered. "Not here. Not now."

"Not when your job hangs in the balance, you mean?" He looked disappointed. "I thought we'd come farther than that."

No, not when I'm so close, Amanda thought. *Not when I only just realized how much I need you.* But she couldn't find the words to say any of those things. Not when her heart was breaking as she sat there, and Mike only looked on with those sad, dark eyes.

"I don't understand," she said, clasping her hands on the table's edge behind her so Mike wouldn't see her trembling. "I didn't even see this coming."

"You were busy," he said. "Turning me into someone I'm not."

"That's not fair! You knew what the Lotto was about going in."

"You're right." Mike held up both hands and got to his feet. "I did know. And I should have bowed out then. Before I fell for you. Now it's too late."

Fell for her? Maybe there was still hope! Quickly swiping tears from her eyes, Amanda went to him. "You never know what might happen," she said hurriedly. "Things could still—"

He shook his head. "I can't be with someone who

doesn't believe in me. Not the 'potential' me—the real me. The me on the inside.''

"I *do* believe in you! Otherwise I never would have gone for any of this." Amanda's outflung arm indicated the conference room and all its pre-show disarray. "I do!"

"No." With a solemn expression, Mike raised his hand to her cheek. He stroked her once, twice, his thumb sweeping away still more tears. "You believe in *you.* In your ability to give me something I don't want. I'm sorry, Amanda."

"How can you not want what's best for you?" she cried, desperate to make him understand. "How can you just walk away from everything we have together?"

"I can because I have to," Mike said. For an instant, his expression turned compassionate, a glimpse of the easygoing man she knew and loved. "Don't worry, though. I'm a stand-up guy. I'll see the Lotto all the way through."

"But I don't—"

"Of course you care about that," he interrupted, his mind-reader's smile wavery through her tears. "And that's why I'm doing it. Send me wherever you want, put me on every morning show in town, pick me the chef's job of your dreams, whatever will make the Lotto work. I'll do it. For you. For six months, guaranteed. Okay?"

Pushing her hair back, peering into her face with well-meant masculine concern, Mike obviously expected that that would be enough. That his cooperation was all she wanted. And given the way things stood, Amanda knew she couldn't ask for more.

"Okay," she sniffed. "But afterward—"

A knock on the conference-room door made them both jump. "Five minutes till taping," said a voice on the other side.

"Afterward?" Mike looked steadily at her, his voice tender. That tenderness did nothing to dispel the impact of his next words, though. "Afterward, it will be good-bye."

Chapter Twenty-one

Three days later, Mike dragged himself through downtown Phoenix's Kugelhoff gallery, a hole-in-the-wall place dedicated to showcasing the latest in up-and-coming modern art. The walls were white, the ceilings were white, the floors were white (presumably to show off the artwork to its best advantage), and the crowd was eclectic. Well-heeled seniors, college students, couples, and groups of suburban mothers pushing strollers ambled through the gallery, today featuring the sculptures of debut artist Howard "Snake" Bulowski.

Mike was standing in front of an original Bulowski creation featuring a bumper, a Chevy logo, assorted hubcaps, and a lot of twisted baling wire, morosely trying to psych himself into appreciating the imagination involved, when Curly nudged him.

"Hey," Curly said, his pomade-shellacked hair gleaming in the track lighting. "Check it out."

He nodded toward the entrance to the display room. A skinny man wearing sunglasses, black jeans, a black Harley-Davidson logo T-shirt, and a canvas raincoat slouched into the room, looking furtively right and left. He yanked his leather newsboy-style cap low over his face and sidled up next to the first sculpture. As they watched, he thrust his hands into his pockets and pretended to view the chicken-wire-and-car-battery Bulowski creation . . . but his attention was all for the man and woman beside him.

"Look," Bruno said, having made his way over to his friends after striking out with the redhead in the Works on Canvas section. He pointed to raincoat man. "He's leaning so far over to listen to their conversation, he's practically horizontal."

"Yeah," Curly agreed. "Bizarre."

The man moved on to the next sculpture, his face shadowed by his cap and the turned-up collar of his raincoat. There he repeated his performance, this time listening in on a group of tattooed and pierced college students.

"He's not even checking out the redhead," Bruno observed, sounding surprised, "and she's right next to him."

Mike had to agree. The man only seemed interested in hearing what people had to say about the Bulowski sculptures.

Suddenly, a glint of gold caught the light. The man was smiling, and he apparently had a gold tooth. He also had the craggy skin of a man who'd spent a lot of time out in the sun—an ex–Triple A baseball player, for instance—and a suspiciously familiar look.

"It's Snake!" Bruno and Curly said in unison.

At the sound of their voices, the man jerked. He looked straight at them. Then he hustled their way, his coat swishing as he came.

It *was* Snake. "Shut up, you guys!" he hissed when he'd reached them. "I'm incognito, dammit."

"What for?" Mike asked.

"To find out how my exhibit is going. So far, it's a beautiful thing. Those two over there"—Snake gestured toward the couple he'd originally eavesdropped on—"are talking about buying the *Give Me More Juice* piece."

Bruno and Curly mumbled something encouraging. Mike couldn't muster more than a halfhearted "Good going." Since his showdown with Amanda at Channel Six earlier in the week, everything had seemed to require way too much energy.

Beside them, Snake looked jubilant. Rubbing his hands together, he said, "Whaddya say we all go back to Marvin's for a celebration after the—" He broke off and lowered his sunglasses. "Jesus, Mike. You look like you've been dragged down the street backwards with barbed wire for bumpers. What the hell happened to you?"

Barbed wire. Ha. What did Snake know? Just because Mike had started growing his beard back, was wearing his most holey jeans (strictly for the comfort factor) and a ratty T-shirt, and hadn't bothered to shower this morning didn't mean something had happened to him. Stone-faced, he crossed his arms and decided to try glaring Snake's intrusive question away.

It didn't work. "I mean, seriously," Snake went on. "You were looking pretty sharp for a while there. Sounding better, too. Like you were ready to whup ass on those April Fools' Day bastards, and—"

"He broke up with Amanda," Curly said.

"Yeah." Bruno's accusatory stare left no doubt what *he* thought of the whole affair.

Mike took one look at the trio of disapproving faces surrounding him and decided that his initial urge to support his buddies had been overrated. They obviously had no concept of friendship if they could give him a hard time about this. He turned his back and

strode to the next steering-wheel-and-radio-antenna
Bulowski on display.

"We had to drag him out of his house this morning," Curly offered, his voice carrying as the three
men followed Mike. "Once we'd fought our way
through the empty pizza boxes, piled-up Budweiser
bottles, and dirty laundry, that is. We found him in
a corner of the couch, crashed. Mouth hanging open
and all. With a video of *The Great Escape* still playing
on TV."

They all looked at him with pity. "Whoa," Snake
said.

Mike turned away, folding his arms over his chest.
So what if he hadn't been able to sleep very well
lately? So what if his bed reminded him of Amanda,
making it too painful to bunk down between the
sheets and comforter they'd shared and would
never share again? So what if he'd needed a little
bit of guy-only movie viewing to salve his battered,
postmakeover self? That didn't mean they all had
to feel sorry for him.

"Cupcake was so desperate for a walk," Bruno put
in, "that she scaled a mound of sweat socks with her
leash in her teeth, begging one of us to rescue her."

"The hell she did," Mike said. He hadn't amassed
a whole *mound* of sweat socks in only three days. And
Myrna Winchester, having mysteriously learned about
his breakup with Amanda, had stopped by to help
out with Cupcake when she could. "My dog is fine.
I'm fine. So you three can just butt the hell out."

"No way, man," Curly said loyally. "We're here for
you. When I was getting ready for my stage performance"—his posture straightened at his mention of
his songfest at Gemma's parents' anniversary party—
"Amanda told me that having a strong support network is really important to—"

"Go away." Being alone with his misery was sounding better and better. Mike moved on to the next sculpture, telling himself that he'd probably miss Amanda a lot less if these bozos would quit talking about her all the time.

"Hey, how'd that go, anyway?" Curly asked, momentarily abandoning his harassment of Mike to question the new singing star in their midst. "When I stopped by Amanda's office for advice about my new diet, she said you were a big hit."

At the mention of "diet," Mike remembered the Twinkies he'd stuffed into his jeans pocket. They were a little squashed, but it still gave him a juvenile sort of defiant thrill to bite into them. *Try and change me,* he thought as he chewed. *Ha!*

"Yeah. I guess I was," Bruno said. Beaming, the burly ex-Marine went on to describe the songs he'd sung, the appreciative hollers of the ladies in the audience, and the four curtain calls he'd taken. "I was nervous, but in the end, Amanda was right about me. I've got potential."

Mike couldn't take it anymore. "Potential, schmential," he said, crumpling up his Twinkie wrapper and tossing it into a nearby bin. "You were fine just the way you were, Bruno."

"But I'm happier now. Singing."

"And I'm happier sculpting," Snake agreed. His sunglasses winked in the artsy lighting, lending him an air of flamboyance. "Mr. Kugelhoff is already talking about booking my next show."

"And I'm happier with my hair under control." Curly ran a hand over his brilliantine-glossy red hair, the waves subdued beneath the styling products his life coach had recommended. "I've been fighting it ever since the kids in kindergarten started calling me Corkscrew Head."

"*Awww,*" Snake and Bruno chimed in sympathetically.

Bonded together in joint Amanda worship, the three men slung their arms around each other's shoulders and started comparing notes. Amanda was brilliant, they said. Insightful. Compassionate. And really generous with the hints of leg and cleavage she kept throwing them while she—

"Knock it off!" Mike yelled, driven to distraction by their over-the-top rah-rah session. If anybody knew how amazing Amanda was, it was him, dammit. And he didn't want to be reminded of it, either. Not now that he knew they couldn't be together.

How could they be when she was more interested in the potential him than the real him? When her efforts to "improve" him were costing him his team *and* his peaceful Cavaco family get-togethers?

When he'd dropped by his parents' house the day after the Channel Six morning-show taping, even his father had stooped to nagging him about "not growing back that godforsaken beard." And his sister-in-law had spent half her time pestering him about having taped a TV appearance without letting the family be at the studio. The fracas that had resulted when he'd admitted that he didn't think they'd be comfortable at his charity appearance at AJ's, either . . . well, it hadn't been pretty.

And now Bruno, Snake, and Curly were getting on his case, too. It was more than he could stand.

"What?" His buddies blinked at him, glaringly innocent.

"Enough about Amanda, already," Mike said, casting a scowl toward his would-be 'support network.' "I did the right thing with her." Maybe if he said it enough, he'd start to really believe it was true. *"She wanted to change me."*

A moment passed. The three men unslung their arms and looked at each other.

Then Curly blinked. "So?"

"Maybe you needed changing," Bruno offered.

"Hell, man." Snake whapped Mike on the back, man-to-man style. "Changing their boyfriends is the female national sport. Sort of like football, without the dirt and the penalties."

"Yeah," Curly and Bruno agreed. "Big deal."

"Big deal?" Mike gaped at them. "What do you mean, 'big deal?' A man's got to have principles. Self-respect. Boundaries."

"He's gotta have a little snuggle now and then, too," Bruno opined, his gaze earnest beneath his crew cut.

Curly nodded. "Whoopee on call doesn't hurt, either."

"Somebody to stand by him," Snake said, looking suddenly downcast. "Man, I wish I had a nice girl with me right now, to share all this with." His outspread arm encompassed the gallery and all the Bulowskis within it.

Mike couldn't believe it. Another minute and they'd all be bawling about not having embraced their inner emotions, or some crap. What was the matter with all of them?

Maybe his buddies had changed, given their contact with Amanda and her hoity-toity, touchy-feely life-coach ideas, but *he* hadn't. He was going to stick with what he believed in: himself. And if that wasn't good enough for Amanda, he was better off without her.

Right. It had all been there, right from the beginning, Mike realized. In the macho creed he'd thought of while first ferrying Amanda around town: A man didn't back down. He didn't take advice. And he didn't show weakness, no matter what.

With a disgusted wave to his buddies, Mike gave up on the remaining Bulowskis and headed toward the exit. Right now, a return to his old, familiar routine— a Big Mac, a supersize Coke, and no "meaningful" conversations while he couch-potatoed in front of ESPN, *alone*—was sounding pretty damned good.

Amanda was in her office at Aspirations, Inc., when it happened. She was surrounded by the evidence of three days' hard work designed to make her forget all about her confrontation with Mike at the Channel Six offices and in mid-conversation with a culinary contact at the time, but that didn't make any difference. Her destiny caught up with her, all the same, in the form of Gemma, Mel, and Trish.

They marched into her office commando style. First, Gemma picked up Amanda's handbag from the credenza. Then she forcibly wheeled Amanda's chair away from her desk. Unfortunately, Amanda was still sitting in it at the time. Her attempts to stay right where she was—*working*—had no effect at all, though. With the strength born of carrying twin toddlers around, Gemma easily evaded her friend's attempts to anchor herself by hooking her feet onto the bottom edge of the desk.

Trish swooped in next. Schedules, résumés, and other bits of paper swirled as she stacked and sorted, rearranging all the things Amanda had spent the past two days working on. With a determined look, she wrenched the Rolodex from Amanda's startled grasp, stacked it atop the files and papers she'd gathered, and then carried everything out of the room.

Still on the phone, Amanda tried to sound as though she weren't being hijacked as she spoke. It wasn't easy, since Gemma had unearthed a tube of L'Oreal Colour Riche from Amanda's handbag and was headed toward her with the obvious intent to give her a fresh, cheery coat of Drumbeat Red, whether she liked it or not.

"You're absolutely right, Norm," Amanda said hur-

riedly into the phone, sensing that her conversation
with the new-in-town restaurateur might be coming
to an untimely end. She made a face and puckered
for Gemma, giving in to the inevitable. "I do think
there's room in Phoenix for your concept. In fact,
there's someone who may be perfect for—"

Suddenly, Mel yanked the phone from Amanda's
hand. "Norm, she'll have to call you back," she said
into the receiver.

"No! Wait!" Amanda cried, grappling for the
phone. The notes she'd been taking fluttered from
her lap onto the floor as she stood. "I haven't finished—"

Waving away her protests, Mel went on talking into
the phone. Casually, she tucked the receiver between
her chin and shoulder, then reached forward and
fluffed up Amanda's hair. That done, Mel assured
Norm that Amanda would, indeed, call him back,
yammered for a bit about workaholics, and then hung
up with a grin.

"I think she's ready," Mel said to Gemma.

In the brief silence that followed, Amanda could
only gape at her two friends. They looked back at her
with inexplicably self-satisfied expressions on their
faces.

Well, she wasn't standing still for this! Lunging
forward, Amanda dove for her cell phone. Norm's
business wasn't launched yet, but she'd written his
contact number in her notes. If she could just—

Gemma beat her to it. Evidently, chasing after two
toddlers all day had left her with superhumanly fast
reflexes.

Still determined, Amanda made a move for her
Palm Pilot. If she couldn't actively call her clients and
contacts, at least she could do some—

Mel got there first. With frustration, Amanda

watched her friend seize the handheld computer and wink.

Amanda threw up her hands. "What is going *on* here? I have work to do!"

"It's an intervention," Mel said. She came forward and took Amanda's arm gently in hers. "You've got to stop doing this to yourself."

"Huh?"

Gemma grasped the other arm. "We're on your side, Amanda. We're only doing this for your own good."

This was too much. "You guys! I've got to get back to the—" Amanda broke off and gestured toward her confiscated phone. "And the—" Her desk, piled high with things that Trish hadn't seen fit to carry off, mocked her. "I have to work."

She struggled against them. Her friends held tight.

"We know what happened with you and Mike," Gemma went on. "Bruno told my mom about it when she called to ask him to sing at my cousin's wedding this fall."

"Your mom and Bruno are discussing my love life?"

"We only want to help."

"It's obvious you need it," Mel said. She gave some sort of signal to Gemma, and the two of them began briskly marching Amanda out of her office. "We're taking you away from here, and you can't come back until you've straightened things out with Mike."

"Mike?" Even saying his name hurt, but Amanda was determined not to let that show. "What's my . . . my client got to do with this?"

"Everything," Mel and Gemma said in unison.

"That's ridiculous." The office reception area whisked past, complete with a head-shaking Trish, who promised to hold down the fort while Amanda was away. "I have clients who are depending on me. I'm simply trying to stay on top of things!"

"Nope. You're burying yourself in work," Gemma said. "And we won't let you."

"Right," Mel agreed. "You're trying to fix a broken heart by phoning, faxing, and scheduling yourself to death. Even I know *that* doesn't work."

They reached the parking lot and marched right past Amanda's trusty Tercel. Blinded by the strong sunlight after two days spent inside from dawn to dark, Amanda squinted longingly at her car and the freedom it represented. If she could get behind the wheel, she could retrieve the case files for Mr. Waring and Mrs. Neubaum she'd left in there and spend another few hours blissfully distracted from missing Mike.

Mike, Mike . . .

Amanda shook the memories away. "Look, I'm not brokenhearted over Mike," she lied. Maybe if she said it enough, she'd start to really believe it was true. "Things didn't work out, but what could I have expected? We're two completely opposite people. He's sneakers; I'm slingbacks. He's *Monday Night Football;* I'm *Meet the Press.* He's Oscar; I'm Felix."

Mel raised her eyebrows. "Kinky."

"The Odd Couple!" Amanda cried in explanation.

"You've got us there." Unconcerned, Gemma shoved Amanda into the backseat of her suburban-mommy SUV, then she and Mel got into the front. "You two *were* an unlikely pair. Unlike me and Tom, for instance, who were perfect for each other, right from the—"

"Yada, yada, yada," Mel griped. "Enough about you and Mr. Perfect! I swear—"

"Hey, you two. Cut it out," Amanda said, automatically trying to keep the peace as she grumpily situated herself among the sippy cups, animal-cracker crumbs, and Happy Meal–type toys surrounding her. "Opposite corners."

Mel and Gemma looked at each other and grinned. Frowning, Amanda realized she'd been set up.

"Fine," she said. "Now that you've got me in your evil clutches—"

Their grins intensified. Traitors. Didn't they know she *needed* the busyness of work to keep her mind off what had happened between her and Mike?

Afterward, it will be good-bye.

Squeezing her eyes shut while the intervention-mobile lurched through traffic with Gemma at the wheel, Amanda concentrated on drawing in a deep breath. Letting it out. And not falling to pieces just because the man she loved didn't want her in his life.

"—where are you planning to take me?" she finished.

Maybe once they were there, she could sneak away and find a phone. She'd spent much of the past few days networking with foodie types, trying to nail down a good job placement for Mike. The least she could do for him was make the rest of his life—or at least the next six Life Coach Lotto–enhanced months of it—as wonderful as possible.

She'd already had a fabulous offer from a local luxury resort. The management was interested in revamping their image and had promised to give Mike free rein in the kitchens. And then there was Norm. His concept for a restaurant was unlike anything she'd ever seen before—a retro diner atmosphere with new twists on home-style cooking and a kid-friendly chef's bar where children could actually work with the chef on their meals. Given Mike's affinity for his nieces and nephews, he'd be a natural for such a post.

Of course, the resort would be the perfect culmination of all her life-coach plans for Mike. The resort paid more. Much more. It was also more prestigious, better reviewed, and had the advantage of a twenty-year history in the Valley.

Norm's start-up, on the other hand, would pay less, at least at first. The prestige factor was zero. The usual food-and-travel magazines wouldn't give it so much as a look-see for several months (if ever), and it had the disadvantage of being a less-stable, brand-new company.

Mike might enjoy working with either company. However, only *one* of the placements she'd been considering for him would impress Evan and the Channel Six execs enough to cement Aspirations, Inc.'s hoped-for featured spot on the news: the resort. Which meant the choice should have been a no-brainer. So how come Amanda was having so much trouble making it?

"Where are we planning to take you?" Mel stopped midway through the zippered pouch of music CDs she'd found in Gemma's console and looked over her shoulder at Amanda. "Easy. To my place."

Getting an idea what they were up to, Amanda held up her hands. "No, you guys. No. Not Mel's place."

"Yes. My place." Mel flipped past a hip-hop CD, raised her eyebrows at Gemma, and moved past it. She selected a different piece of music and inserted it into the CD player. "Everything's all set up."

"Oh, no," Amanda groaned. "You didn't!"

"We did," Gemma said, nodding. "We made an entire Face the Truth afternoon just for you."

The opening notes of a sappy love song wafted from the car stereo speakers. Recognizing it, Amanda sank deeper into her seat. *A Face the Truth afternoon.* Why hadn't she seen this coming?

Actually, she had. That was why she'd been saving the news of her and Mike's breakup until later. Until she was strong enough to withstand—

"We've got *An Affair to Remember* in the VCR," Mel

said, "sad songs for the stereo, a bottle of Mike's aftershave—"

Strong enough to withstand *this*.

"You stole his aftershave?" Amanda cried.

Mel snorted. "No, we found out from Bruno what kind he uses and bought some. Duh."

"We also have a bunch of other love stories on video," Gemma said, "several pints of Ben & Jerry's, pictures of you and Mike together—"

"How did you . . . ?"

"The Channel Six camera crew."

Amanda buried her head in her hands. The whole *world* was in on this.

"—and lots of other things," Gemma finished cheerfully. Her gaze met Amanda's in the rearview mirror. "It's for your own good, you know. You can't keep burying your head in the sand forever."

"Wanna bet?" Amanda asked.

"See?" Mel nudged Gemma. *"That's* why we had to do the intervention. I told you so."

Gemma sighed and glanced at Amanda again through the mirror. "We know you. You're pretending this doesn't mean anything to you, but that's not true. We've got to get through to you somehow. Otherwise, you won't deal with this until it's too late."

Too late. Her words echoed what Mike had said on that last day together. *I should have bowed out then. Before I fell for you,* he'd said. *Now it's too late.*

No. Remembering what had happened between them hurt, and Amanda refused to do it. She planned to stick with her strategy-in-progress: namely, work as hard as she could until Aspirations, Inc., was secure and give Mike the chance of a lifetime in the process. Any . . . complications that had come about as a result of pursuing that goal had to be set aside. There was no other way.

Crossing her arms over her chest, Amanda sat up

straighter and looked at her friends directly. "Go right ahead," she said. "Take your best shot. But nothing's going to change my mind this time."

"Nothing?" Mel looked over her shoulder. Raised an eyebrow. "Not even a twelve-hour marathon of the most romantic movies of all time, interspersed with poetry readings and frequent displays of Mike's picture?"

From somewhere she produced a newspaper clipping showing a surprised Mike when he'd brought in the winning Life Coach Lotto ticket. She waggled it in front of Amanda.

The image called forth a million memories, all of which Amanda would do better to forget. Staring at the grainy black-and-white image of the man she loved, she wavered. Inwardly. Outwardly, she miraculously managed to bluff her way through.

"Bring it on," she said recklessly.

But she had to look away as she did, and Gemma pounced on that weakness. "You're not as tough as you think you are, Amanda. You love Mike. Admit it."

"No."

"Admit it and go work this out with him! You'll both be happier."

"No." Stubbornly, Amanda looked out the window and girded herself for the challenge to come. No matter what happened, she had to think with her head, not her heart. She couldn't give in to the despair sloshing through her, not while there was still work to be done. "Mike and I are finished, and no amount of playing Face the Truth is going to change that."

Up ahead, Mel and Gemma only sighed . . . and prepared to prove her wrong.

Chapter Twenty-two

"Hey, Mike!" Marvin said. "Heads up!"

He slid a bottle of Budweiser across the bar toward Mike's stool. Automatically, Mike caught the bottle and added it to the two already in front of him. Their dark glass reflected the Happy Hour neon signs surrounding him and—if he cared to look closer—his unshaven, scruffy-haired image.

Mike didn't care to look closer.

Since leaving Snake's gallery exhibit, he'd spent the afternoon alone, exactly as he'd planned. In open defiance of life coaching in general, he'd wallowed in every bad habit he'd ever had ... and some he hadn't. Junk food. Nail biting. Mindless channel surfing. He'd done it all, and exactly as he was now, too—sloppy, badly dressed, and belligerent.

He should have reveled in the freedom. Rejoiced in not being expected to jog around the block, make job-hunting networking calls, or work on inner tranquillity. But somehow, as Mike picked up a greasy, cheese-covered tortilla chip from the plate in front of him, he knew he hadn't. Hadn't reveled, hadn't rejoiced, hadn't done much but mope. Which was what had brought him here, to Marvin's, in a last-ditch effort to enjoy himself.

After all, he was a wild-and-crazy bachelor, right? And the place for a guy like him on a Friday night was out on the town, meeting women. Speaking of which . . .

"Compliments of the lady at the end of the bar," Marvin said, nodding in the direction of a scantily-dressed blonde.

"Thanks, Marvin." Mike raised his newly acquired Bud toward his dolled-up benefactress and mouthed a thank-you, trying to work up some interest in her spandex-and-vinyl-covered charms. Oddly enough, he couldn't.

Well, she just wasn't his type, that was all, Mike reassured himself. He preferred his women tall, classy, and talkative, with a penchant for clipboards and a take-charge attitude. He preferred . . . he preferred *Amanda.*

With a jolt, Mike realized the direction his thoughts had taken. Staunchly, he turned them back toward his surroundings. Marvin's was packed tonight, and any red-blooded male would have found plenty to interest him. Redheads, blondes, *other* brunets. With a deliberate gesture, he surveyed the room.

Thirty seconds later, he was slumped over his nachos again. Worse, Mike found himself fighting a weird urge to shove the whole plate away and go home to fix a nice salad for dinner—something with plenty of veggies from Amanda's recommended healthy-food list. Scowling, he purposely ate a jalapeño-embellished tortilla chip.

He glanced in the direction of the blonde again.

She caught him looking and smiled. The old him, the non-life-coach-enhanced him, would have gone over and started a conversation, Mike knew. *Go on,* he urged himself. *She's cute.* But somehow he seemed to have lost his taste for women who weren't Amanda, the same way he'd lost his appetite for nachos and Twinkies and all the other nutritional nightmares he'd indulged in today.

Mike put a hand to his stomach, feeling vaguely queasy. Maybe it hadn't been such a brilliant idea to follow the pork rinds with the Big Mac, the triple brownie, and the nachos. His body suddenly seemed pissed at him for the whole rebellion-inspired extravaganza, and he suspected that his lack of a shower wasn't improving matters any.

Once he'd had a few days to let things sort themselves out in his head, he'd be fine, Mike told himself. Surely being around Amanda hadn't spoiled him for *everything* in his old life. But as he looked around Marvin's once more, his gaze fell on the pool table he and Amanda had used in that first outrageous match against Bruno and Curly, and he knew it was a lie.

Memories assaulted him, of his buddies hefting the pool table to make all of Amanda's wobbly shots go in. Of her face when she'd tasted her first Marvin-Burger. Of her smile when they'd won the match together and he'd promised to go on working with her.

The plain truth was, he'd liked his life better when Amanda was in it. So why couldn't he just knuckle down and make the changes she wanted?

It wasn't that easy. Mike still had his pride, and he still had his convictions that certain parts of his life didn't need fixing—his professional culinary ambitions, for instance. But spending time alone had gotten him one step closer to finding the solution he needed, and as Mike waved good-bye to Marvin and headed for the door, he knew that his insistence on staying the same was really just keeping him stuck.

He stepped outside into the cool, head-clearing night air and got into his cab. There was a compromise in here someplace. All Mike had to do was find it.

At Mel's apartment, everything had been exactly as Mel and Gemma had promised—decked out in full Face the Truth mode. And Amanda, even dressed in her Breakup Bolstering Ensemble (a comfy cotton-knit skirt and sweater set with take-charge boots), wasn't sure how she was going to handle it.

She made it as far as watching Gemma fiddle with the VCR and turn on the TV in preparation for *An Affair to Remember*. Then, having watched approximately twenty seconds of what was on the screen, Amanda broke down.

She was still sniffling nearly two hours of conversation later.

Gemma handed her a tissue. "Feeling any better now?"

Nodding, Amanda blew her nose. "A little."

"*Sheesh,* you're a lightweight," Mel complained, a teasing note in her voice. "We didn't even make it to the movie, kiddo."

Amanda gave her a weak smile. "You've got to admit, that wedding-band commercial was a real killer."

She'd watched, helplessly ensnared, as the TV-commercial couple frolicked on a beach somewhere, laughing and happy. She'd watched, increasingly dis-

traught, as their jewelry-company-sponsored romance
had progressed over candlelit dinners and comical
encounters with the in-laws, overlaid with the swelling
strains of heart-wrenching orchestra music. Then,
when the commercial groom-to-be had gotten on
bended knee and proposed to the commercial bride-
to-be (to the tune of a special-financing voice-over),
Amanda hadn't been able to take it anymore.

"I'm going to be alone forever!" she'd wailed, and
since that moment, her friends had stood by her with
reassurances and encouragement.

"I know what you mean," Mel said now. In her
arms she stacked videotapes, the unnecessary accoutrements of her and Gemma's plan, in preparation for
returning them to the rental store. "It's the greeting-
card commercials that get to me. One look at that
Mother's Day card spot and I'm on the phone to
my mom, apologizing for not appreciating the Rice
Krispies treats she made for me to take to school on
my ninth birthday."

Gemma nodded and sniffled. "Me, too. Except for
me, it's the Father's Day card commercials. I still feel
bad for my dad. He used to take me on these father-
daughter fishing trips, and I drove him crazy by being
too squeamish to put the little worm on the hook."

She looked sheepishly at them over her pile of
unneeded love-song CDs, as though waiting for the
inevitable censure. Amanda and Mel looked at each
other.

"Gross," Mel said. "No way."

"Of *course* you didn't squish those poor worms."
Amanda shuddered.

Gemma grinned with relief. Suitably united, the
three of them put all their things aside and huddled
together on the couch, laughing and hugging.

"You guys were right about me," Amanda said after a while. "I love Mike. *I do.* I was just in denial."

"Deep denial," Gemma agreed.

"Deep, *deep* denial," Melanie said. "Near as I can tell, you'd actually convinced yourself that the connection—and the amazing sex life—you had with Mike was less important than taking care of your clients' snoring problems, debt reduction issues, and QVC shopping addictions."

"Hey!" Amanda paused in the midst of gathering her mound of used tissues and throwing them away. "I never told you about my sex life with Mike!"

"A friend knows." Mel's grin was impish. "A friend sees the hickeys."

Amanda slapped a palm defensively over her neck before remembering that it had been days since she'd last seen Mike. Odds were good that any heat-of-passion love bites she'd received had long since faded. That didn't, however, prevent her friends from exchanging a meaningful look at her gesture.

"And besides," Amanda said, hoping to change the subject, "my clients' problems, and their goals, *are* important."

Without looking up from her pile of CDs, Gemma spoke quietly. "Important to them . . . or to you?"

Shocked into stillness, Amanda could only look at her. Then she found her voice. "Well, well—of *course* they're important to me. And to my clients. I only want what's best for them," she sputtered. "I—I believe in them!"

Mel looked at Gemma. They both shook their heads. Amanda had the feeling something important was eluding her, but she couldn't tell what it was. And then something Mike had said to her on that last fateful afternoon returned to her.

You believe in you, he'd said. *In your ability to give me something I don't want.*

Holy smokes, was it true? Mike had thought so. Her friends seemed to think so. And she . . . well, all of a sudden, Amanda wasn't sure of anything anymore.

She really hadn't listened to her clients' needs, she realized. In her eagerness to make great things happen for them, she'd leaped light-years ahead of them on the goal-setting scale, transforming their initial modest goals into tremendous accomplishments.

She'd turned Mrs. Neubaum's desire for clean closets and an organized canasta schedule into full-time piano lessons. She'd turned Mr. Waring's interest in nabbing a promotion into a full-fledged quest for personal serenity. And she'd transformed Mike's simple kindhearted gesture—helping her out of a jam with the Life Coach Lotto—into an all-out transformation fest. She, Amanda understood with growing comprehension, was a less-than-stellar life coach and an even worse listener. No wonder her business was in shambles!

It wasn't because she needed publicity—at least it wouldn't have been if she hadn't let things go this far. No, the troubles she was facing with Aspirations, Inc., were because of *her*, Amanda realized. She'd been so dead set on giving people wonderful lives, lives they didn't even necessarily *want* but which might be good for them, that she'd ignored everything else in the pursuit of it. Maintenance payments to Louie. Regular scheduling with all of her clients. Decent housekeeping at her apartment.

The revelation was an astounding one, and it took Amanda a while to get a handle on it. Fortified with cartons of Chunky Monkey and Phish Food and with a probably-unwise quantity of strawberry wine coolers, she talked the whole thing over with Mel and Gemma, telling them about the conclusions she'd reached . . . and about the decision she had to make tomorrow, the day of Mike's first Life Coach Lotto personal appearance.

"Everything starts with this one decision," Amanda said earnestly. She licked marshmallow nougat from her spoon and chased it down with a swig of wine cooler. Her head spun, and she felt a little dizzy, but she couldn't let that deter her. "I can't choose both restaurants. It's either the resort or the diner, and only one of them will make Mike really happy."

"The diner, right?" Gemma asked.

Amanda nodded.

"That makes it easy, then. Pick that one."

"Nothing's easy," Mel cautioned. With a sharp look at Amanda, she pointed her ice-cream spoon. "What's the catch?"

Amanda drew in a deep breath. "Well, the catch is that the resort would really be better for him. I believe that."

"That's a delusion, not a belief," Mel scoffed.

Gemma chided her. "It's true, though, Amanda," she added. "You can't be sure what would be better. Although the resort would seem to be a better career move for Mike—"

"See?" Amanda told Melanie. "If I want to do what's right . . . *arrgh!* I have to know what it is first! And the worst thing is, only one of the choices will satisfy Channel Six. If I don't choose the resort, I'm sure Evan will ax my Life Coach Lotto idea altogether."

"But you already have footage!" Gemma protested. "Tomorrow will be the grand finale! Surely he won't pull the plug now?"

"He wants drama. Ratings. Success. And a happy ending." Amanda sighed. *She wanted a happy ending, too.* "Packing Mike off to work in an upscale greasy spoon does *not* qualify."

"Tough choice," Mel observed. "But we know you'll figure out the right thing to do, right, Gemma?"

"Sure." Gemma nodded. "Absolutely. You'll figure it out somehow."

Amanda dropped her spoon into the Phish Food, suddenly without an appetite. "I hope you're right," she said. "I really, really do."

Chapter Twenty-three

On Saturday morning, Mike was in the midst of getting ready for his personal appearance at AJ's gourmet food store when his doorbell rang. *Great,* he thought, jerking on a pair of jeans over his Scooby-Doo boxers to go answer it. *Just what he needed when he was already running late. Company.*

He opened the door, wincing at the early-morning sunlight shafting through the Victorian buildings surrounding his carriage house near Heritage Square. On his front porch stood Myrna Winchester, and with her was—

"Mom! What are you doing here?"

Carla Cavaco stepped over the threshold, a plastic-wrapped bundle in her hands. "What? You think I'm going to let my son go on TV looking like *that*?"

Her disapproving gesture pointed out his jeans, his lack of a shirt, and the unruly hair Mike hadn't quite managed to subdue with the styling products Frederick had sent him home from Rosado with. She shook her head over the pieces of tissue glued to the nicks he'd given himself while shaving.

"I'm not going like this, Mom," Mike said. He stepped back to invite Myrna inside, and Cupcake bounded up to the two women, tail wagging. "I have my chef's jacket to wear, and—"

"Not anymore! Surprise!"

His mom thrust her package toward him. Opening it, Mike discovered a brand-new double-breasted chef's jacket in soft white cotton lined with black, with black piping, black stud buttons, and tailored French cuffs. There were natty-looking black-and-white striped pants and a designer-style toque to match. Smiling over the formal chef's wear, he glanced up to see his mother all but blushing with pride.

"Awww, Mom. You shouldn't have."

"We wanted you to have nice things, son," she said, and he could have sworn she teared up at the words. "Your family is proud of you. Proud of everything you've accomplished."

Crouching down, she hid her sniffles by petting Cupcake. Left standing there, Mike experienced a sudden attack of conscience. His family was proud of him. Could he really go on misleading them, not sharing any of the details about the April Fools' Day incident?

"Thanks, Mom." He hunkered down, rolling his eyes at his tongue-lolling dog, who liked nothing better than three cooing humans making a fuss over her. "And now that you're here, there's, uh, something you ought to know. . . ."

Mike went on to tell her and Myrna the whole story, Linguine Alla Kiss-me-o, Nick "Nicky" Nickerson's clown-nose-and-pink-toque plans, and all. By the time he'd finished, he was running later than ever, but

he'd finally stopped running away from being fired
from Cucina Amore, and in a weird way, it felt good.

"But my buddy's broken leg is almost healed,"
Mike finished up, "and he'll be able to take over his
taxi again any day now. So it's the end of the line for
me and my Twizzlers."

"Amanda will find you something better," Carla
said, patting him on the shoulder. "She's a nice girl."

"That she is," Myrna Winchester agreed, nodding.
"A little squeamish in the passenger's seat, reluctant
to flirt with the fellas, but very, very nice. You could
do worse, sonny."

"I already have done worse." Mike straightened.
"We're not seeing each other anymore."

His mother and Myrna exchanged a look. "What?"
his mother asked. "Now you're not seeing each other?
Now, when you'd just started to act like yourself again,
with your hair combed and those holey jeans in the
rag pile where they belonged?"

"Wait a minute." Mike glanced down at his jeans.
They weren't holey, but they were far from Sunday
best. "You *liked* the changes in me? The new hair?
The new clothes? The"—ah, but the embarrassment
of it was going to kill him—"the manicure?"

"Of course." With a beaming smile, Carla walked
toward him and enveloped him in a big, perfumy
hug. She patted him on the back and released him.
"No matter what you look like on the outside, you're
still you on the inside, Mike. Didn't you know that?"

"Sure, Mom," Mike said. "Sure. I do now." And,
grinning, he went to finish getting ready for the personal appearance that would change his life.

He hoped.

"Where is he?" Evan asked, his voice booming over
the melee at AJ's gourmet foods. "He's late."

Amanda jumped. The Channel Six producer had practically materialized at her elbow, and she nearly brained him with her clipboard.

"Mike will be here," she assured Evan, hoping she sounded more certain of that fact than she felt. She gave a little wave to the representatives from the Scottsdale resort who'd offered Mike full reign of their kitchens, then turned to supervise the finishing touches on the parking-lot grandstand where the Life Coach Lotto final segment would be taped. "He's very dependable."

"He's very *late*. I'm telling you, Amanda, if this thing goes south, your weekly feature spot does, too." Evan scowled, watching as a helium-filled balloon came loose from the array surrounding the grandstand and floated into the bright Arizona sky. "The resort people are very interested in working with us at the station, and this placement will be a good first step."

"Mike's placement hasn't been announced yet," Amanda reminded him, careful to sound objective. "There's always a possibility that the nouveau-diner concept will be a better match."

"Norm's restaurant?" Evan chuckled and shook his head. "I think I know you better than that, Amanda. You won't jeopardize your business for the sake of some start-up restaurant."

Amanda hoped she wouldn't have to. But if it came down to that . . .

A few minutes after Evan had finished growling warnings, Norm himself emerged from within the growing crowd of camera operators, sound people, newspaper reporters, and curious onlookers. Amanda smiled and waved. Then, from behind the restaurateur, another movement caught her eye, this one more deliberate, more familiar, more . . . *Mike!*

She was dying to talk to him. Before she could make

it so much as halfway toward him, though, Amanda was waylaid by Channel Six employees needing information, the AJ's manager wanting to discuss crowd control, and Norm. By the time she'd finished with everyone, Mike was gone.

She'd hoped to have a chance to explain to him before making her big announcement. Now she'd simply have to move ahead as she'd planned . . . and hope that in the end Mike would understand.

At the rear of the grandstand, Mike waited for his cue, dressed in his fancy new chef's gear and trying not to forget everything he'd ever learned about making profiteroles, which were to be his opening dish. Despite his Le Cordon Bleu training, he'd actually learned how to make the cream-filled puff pastries at his grandma's deli, and he'd thought it would be a nice Cavaco-family tribute to share them with the crowd.

Now, though, listening to the Channel Six announcer drum up enthusiasm for the "sexier, hotter, new-millennium Galloping Gourmet," all Mike could do was hope he survived the morning.

He craned his head, looking for Amanda. He'd spotted her once and then lost track of her. The glimpse he'd had of her all-business, clipboard-toting demeanor hadn't given him much hope for patching things up between them . . . but a guy had to keep the faith, right?

"Yo, Mike," Snake said, jabbing him in the ribs. "How's it going?"

"Fine. For a mob scene."

Snake chuckled. Then he leaned closer. "Listen," he said, speaking quietly. "There's something I've been meaning to tell you."

"You want to give me a commission on all those

Bulowskis you sold at the gallery?" Mike joked. "I did introduce you to Amanda, after all. A finder's fee wouldn't be out of line."

"No, it's not that." Suddenly, Snake's voice turned unusually somber. "It's about this Lotto thing. See, uh, that winning ticket was mine. I left it in your cab. On purpose."

Mike turned to look at him. He was serious!

"I thought I oughtta come clean. You know, seeing as how you're probably worried the real winner will turn up and wreck everything."

"I'm not worried about that." *I'm incredulous that you're telling me this now, but I'm not worried about that.*

"Hell, Mike. You can't fool me. You're as jumpy as a nun on a Harley."

He was. Because of wondering about Amanda. Because of needing, desperately, to work things out with her.

"It's okay, Snake," Mike said, nodding to his friend as the music swelled over the increasingly packed parking lot beyond the grandstand. "You've put my mind at ease."

"Whew. Glad to hear it, man."

Minutes after Snake had vanished into the crowd to try to score a free sample of imported German Terminator beer, Rico edged nearer.

"Hey, dude." He waved a hand in greeting, then shoved his fists in his jeans pockets and ducked his head. Rapidly, he said, "I gotta tell you somethin', Mike."

Mike went on searching the crowd, hoping for a glimpse of Amanda. Occasionally, he'd catch sight of her upswept dark hair as she moved among the attendees, but that was it. "What's that?" he asked absently.

"The winning Lotto ticket? It's mine, dude. I left

it in your cab on that day you drove me to CheapCuts. Remember?''

Mike nodded. Now Rico was the one who owned the winning ticket? Unbelievable.

''But I don't want it, you know? I left it there for you on purpose. So don't worry about it.'' Rico's cheerful, pockmarked face loomed up beside him. ''Okay?''

''Okay.''

''Right on.'' Rico paused. ''Are you sure you're okay with this? Because you look kinda worried.''

''I'm not.'' Was he sweating bullets or something? Surely he didn't look *that* anxious about reconciling with Amanda.

''Okay. Cool.'' Rico went to chat up a cute lighting girl.

Next came Myrna Winchester. ''Listen here, sonny,'' she said as she sidled up beside him. ''I didn't want to say anything while your mother was around, but I've got to confess before this goes any further.''

Mike could guess what was coming by now.

''I bought three of those Life Coach Lotto tickets and left them all in your cab, that day you drove me to the park to feed the ducks. I'm pretty sure that winning ticket of yours is really mine, but since I was only trying to keep you from turning into some kind of loser when I left it for you, I'm going to let you have it. It'll be our little secret.''

Trying hard not to grin, Mike met Myrna's earnest gaze. ''Thank you very much, Mrs. Winchester,'' he said.

''Don't mention it, sonny.'' And then she delved into the crowd, intent on getting the phone number of the AJ's butcher who was, Myrna informed him, ''a real silver fox.''

In the course of the next several minutes, Bruno, Curly, Doris, Tracy, and Jake all came forward to confess that (confidentially) the winning Life Coach Lotto ticket *really* belonged to them. Each was willing—no, dead-set on letting Mike keep his prize, though. Evidently, his friends and team members had wanted him to get back on his feet so much, that most of them had *planted* Lotto entries in the back of his cab with hopes that he'd emerge with the winning ticket. It was incredible.

And, Mike had to admit, it was a little heartwarming, too. Not that a diehard macho guy like himself planned to say so out loud, of course.

He didn't have much time to contemplate his friends' kooky brand of generosity, though, because suddenly the music swelled again, he heard his cue, and it was time to go onstage.

He bounded onto the grandstand, barely aware of the cheers and applause that greeted his appearance. His body vibrated with adrenaline, the bright lights and even brighter sunlight made him sweat, and he'd only just gotten himself situated behind the working-kitchen set when she emerged.

Amanda. Holding a microphone, she joined him on the grandstand, looking vibrant and professional and every bit as . . . dressed in gray summer-weight wool as he remembered?

Mike blinked and looked again. Yes, he realized, it was true. Amanda appeared to be wearing a tailored-to-fit version of the suit she'd had on in the Robinson's-May dressing room the first time they'd kissed. *The lucky suit.* Could that mean what he thought, what he devoutly hoped, that meant?

While Mike attempted to quit having first-kiss flashbacks and ogling Amanda in her surprisingly sexy getup, she explained the Life Coach Lotto program and summarized some of the steps she and Mike had taken together. Most of the words flew past Mike's head, chased by memories and followed up by hope.

All he wanted was to take her in his arms, kiss her into silence, and admit that she'd been right about him, all along.

Well, mostly right. Ninety percent right. Maybe ninety-five. Aww, hell, Mike decided, feeling a stupid grin break over his face at the possible significance of Amanda in that lucky suit. One hundred percent right. He needed to change. A little. And she was just the woman to help him do it.

"So now," Amanda was saying, discreetly wiggling her fingers in welcome to the Cavacos, who were making their way to the front of the crowd, "we come to the final portion of Mike's personal-growth program: announcing which local restaurant will enjoy the benefits of the hottest new chef in decades. The demand for a skilled professional like Mike Cavaco has been overwhelming, but in the end, we've narrowed it down to just two terrific contenders."

She paused, following instructions from Evan Krantz to wait while the cameras panned over the people assembled at one end of the grandstand— representatives of the competing restaurants, Mike guessed. In the interval, Amanda drew in a breath and looked directly at Mike for the first time, and he was struck with the intensity of her expression.

Her face was filled with longing, Mike saw. And love. The same longing and love he'd felt every moment they'd been apart. His pulse began to race.

"These are both wonderful opportunities for Mike," Amanda went on to say, turning back to the crowd again. "The first, with one of the Southwest's premier resorts"—she named the well-known resort, and the crowd applauded—"and the second, with an up-and-coming restaurant whose unique, family-friendly dining experience will be the talk of the town as soon as it's open this fall."

At the edge of the grandstand, Evan Krantz

frowned. Mike caught the producer's expression and knew, all at once, what was behind it. Channel Six wanted an alliance with the resort. The other restaurant choice—spearheaded by a restaurateur named Norm somebody, Amanda was explaining now—was nothing but a decoy. If Amanda didn't choose the resort, Mike was suddenly certain, her business-building opportunities at Channel Six would be finished.

He wanted to catch her attention. To let her know that he didn't mind if she chose the resort, that he'd work through it somehow, for her sake. But before Mike could do more than start to walk toward her, Amanda was making her announcement.

"I'm happy to announce that the choice is," she was saying, gesturing with a flourish as the crowd noise drowned out some of her next words, "Phoenix's newest nouveau diner, BeeBop!"

Pandemonium erupted. The crowd applauded, cameras flashed, and from the corner of his eye, Mike saw the Channel Six producer hurry to the resort representatives, his mouth moving rapidly as he soft-pedaled this unexpected development. A robust, gray-haired man came forward and shook Mike's hand, introducing himself as Norm, the owner of BeeBop, and even as Mike did his best to say a few coherent words to his new boss, all he could think about was Amanda.

And what she'd done, what she'd sacrificed, for him.

She came toward him too slowly, an instant-replay moment he knew he'd remember for the rest of his life. The brilliance of her smile reached him first, then the fresh, subtle scent of her perfume, and finally—*finally*—the woman herself. Amanda squeezed both hands on his biceps and leaned forward to whisper to him.

"Norm is staffing from the ground up," she said

quickly. Bravely. "I've already talked to him, and your whole team is in. Everybody. From Rico to Jake, and no clown suits, either."

Mike was overwhelmed.

"Why?" he asked, bringing his hands to her cheeks and tilting her face upward. Tears shimmered in her eyes, and he couldn't stand to see her sad. "Why throw away everything you've worked for, Amanda?"

"Don't worry about me," she told him, her expression reflecting a bravado Mike was all too familiar with. "Please. I'll be all right. I'm pretty resilient, you know."

"But you didn't have to do this. Your company, your clients, your employees—"

"They don't mean as much to me as you do, Mike," Amanda said, her voice husky with unshed tears. Her hands trembled where she touched him, and her eyes begged him to understand. "They never did. I'm so sorry. Please forgive me for trying to turn your life into something you didn't want. I'm going to do better from now on, I promise. I never meant—"

"Only if you'll forgive me for being a stubborn, sloppy pain in the ass," Mike said, brushing back a strand of hair from her face. "I never meant to hurt you."

"I do! Oh, Mike, I missed you so much."

"Hey, you two." Beside them, Norm nudged Mike. He nervously cleared his throat, looking out at the intensely interested AJ's onlookers and the still-rolling Channel Six camera crew. "Ixnay on the big reunion. The show must go on, remember?"

"Oh!" Laughing, Amanda raised her microphone. Her breath shuddered through the speakers, all the pent-up emotion in her face released and amplified through the crowd. "I'm sorry, everyone. We've, um, prepared a special preview of the Life Coach Lotto winner's experiences, and we want to show that to you today while Mike sets up for his first gourmet dish."

Shakily, she gestured toward the middle of the grandstand, where a multimedia screen behind them began to play footage of Mike turning in the winning ticket, walking into Rosado, and beginning his whole-life makeover. The crowd yelled their appreciation, but Mike had other ideas . . . and now was the time to use them.

He took Amanda's hand in his, then nodded toward the microphone. "May I?" he asked.

Looking confused, she handed it over. Nervously, Mike juggled the mic in his hands, and then brought it up to his mouth.

"I don't know how many of you realize what's happened here today," he said. Feedback squealed. Keeping Amanda's hand in his, he squeezed her fingers and gave her a reassuring smile. "And I don't know how many of you will have the privilege of working with this brilliant, generous woman at her company, Aspirations, Inc., in the future—"

A hush fell over the crowd, and Amanda grinned self-consciously at his mention of her and her business.

"—but I hope it's most of you. Because Amanda Connor has changed my life. She's made an amazing difference to me. That's not the reason I fell in love with her, of course—"

The crowd gasped. So did Amanda. Feeling himself relax, Mike grinned, and spared a moment to look back at the multimedia screen behind them. As he'd suspected, somehow the technical wizards at Channel Six—the same people who had trailed him for a month and played poker in every possible location— had switched the input. Now the screen showed him and Amanda, together onstage. Live.

"There are lots of other reasons for that. But it is

the reason I'd trust her to do the right thing no matter how tough it was." With difficulty, Mike suppressed the glare he wanted to give Evan Krantz for putting this pothole in Amanda's future. "And it *is* the reason that I'm going to do this."

With suddenly shaky fingers, Mike gave the microphone to Norm. Amanda gaped at him, wide-eyed, as he pulled up the leg of his new chef's pants and, still holding her hand, lowered himself onto one knee before her.

"Amanda," he said, then paused. It was hard work speaking past the lump that was rapidly forming in his throat. "I've loved you since you hijacked my taxi and made me wear pink. Since you shaved my beard—"

Mike waggled his eyebrows, remembering the risqué circumstances in which she'd done so.

"—and adopted my hopeless frou-frou runt of a dog. Since you made me do yoga and since you laughed at all my jokes. There's nothing I'd rather do than be with you, forever, and I can't believe I've waited so long to ask . . . will you marry me?"

Breath held, Mike looked up at her. Amanda's eyes filled with tears, her face suddenly crumpled, and all at once he was certain she was going to refuse.

Time slowed to an agonizing crawl. Norm held the microphone higher, poised to broadcast Amanda's eventual answer to the entire crowd.

"She cries when she's happy," Mel yelled helpfully from the sidelines. A weepy Gemma agreed. Mike wasn't sure he believed something so nutty, but a moment later . . .

"Yes!" Amanda shouted, laughing and crying and trembling beside him. Her knees knocked against his upraised forearms. Her tears dripped onto his painstakingly styled new haircut. And Mike didn't care a bit. "Yes, I'll marry you!" she said.

Relief flooded him. Happiness swamped him. And everything would have been perfect, except for the nagging feeling that he had forgotten something, somehow.

A ring. He'd forgotten to get an engagement ring! Wanting to smack himself on the forehead for his own oversight, Mike scanned the crowd in a panic. Maybe Snake had some kind of spare circular car part he could substitute for the time being? Maybe the sous chef who'd volunteered to help him had twisted a tinfoil ring on the spur of the moment?

"Mike!" The voice came from the front of the crowd. His mother pushed to the edge of the grandstand and held up a ring. "Here—your grandmother's!"

Norm—helpful, wonderful Norm—hurried to her and retrieved the ring. In disbelief, Mike felt it being pressed into his free hand.

"You hadn't brought a girl home in months," Carla said with a shrug. "We all knew it must be true love, so I came prepared." Then she clasped her hands together, gazed at her son and his bride-to-be, and burst into happy tears.

"It *is* true love, you know," Amanda said when Mike raised the antique pearl-and-diamond ring and prepared to slip it onto her finger. "I love you like crazy, Mike. Let's never be apart again."

"Then you'd better come over and help me make the profiteroles," Mike said, sliding the ring onto Amanda's finger and then getting to his feet. "But first . . ."

He lowered his mouth to hers, and the crowd went wild. Heedless of their cheers and wolf whistles, Mike drew the woman he loved still closer and lost himself in the sense of belonging that engulfed him whenever Amanda was near. He kissed her thoroughly, and he kissed her leisurely, and when it was over with, he took a minute to give her a wink and a whispered compliment.

"Nice suit," he said. "I remember it. And I can't wait to get it off you."

Amanda blushed and laughed and gave him another kiss. "I was hoping you'd say that," she murmured, her lips close to his ear now. "I don't have a stitch on underneath it."

Surprise thrummed through him—surprise and something a little spicier, too. Mike raised his eyebrows. "Is that so?"

"Sure is."

"Hubba, hubba."

Leaving the microphone behind for the announcer who was scheduled to narrate the cooking segment, they walked hand in hand to the kitchen set up on the grandstand. Norm had left the stage, but sometime during the last few minutes, Evan Krantz had managed to station himself beside the six-burner professional range, and he plucked at his tie, scowling as Mike and Amanda approached.

Spotting the producer, Amanda looked at Mike. She gave him a carefree grin. "I hope you don't mind the fact that I'm about to be unemployed," she said to her new fiancé, her tone offhanded.

"Not at all." Mike said just as casually. "In fact," he teased, "I'm pretty sure I can get you a bang-up job if only you'll follow my point-by-point instructions. I learned them from this life coach, whom I absolutely *love*."

"Hmmm. I'll consider it. Since my company won't possibly survive without the Lotto—"

Evan cleared his throat and interrupted. "Actually, Amanda, about the Lotto . . . I may have been too hasty."

"May have been, Evan?"

"Yes. Er—" He shot a glance at the departing resort

contingent, then continued. "Judging by the crowd response here, I'd say your Lotto is a huge success! Dramatic, romantic, unpredictable. It's fabulous. Everything I wanted. The news-feature spot we discussed is yours if you're still interested."

"Still interested?" Arm in arm with Mike, Amanda gave him a speculative look. She pursed her lips thoughtfully. "I'm not sure. What do you think, Mike?"

"I think it's completely up to you." He kissed her.

"In that case . . ." Amanda smiled and hugged Mike closer. "I'll take it, Evan. *After* the honeymoon—"

"The very *long* honeymoon," Mike added.

"—is over with, that is."

Then she and Mike tied on coordinating chef's aprons, picked up their whisks, and got down to the *really* serious business at hand—cooking up their very own, utterly delicious, happily-ever-after.

Dear Reader,

Sometimes stories come from the funniest places—an overheard comment, an oddball news item, a chance meeting. Mike and Amanda's story was the result of a passing thought I had: what if an utterly macho guy found himself unexpectedly in the midst of a frou-frou makeover and wanted to stick with it, for the sake of the woman he was instantly smitten with? The comedic possibilities grabbed me right away, and I was off and running with *Making Over Mike*.

I hope you had fun reading about Mike and Amanda's wacky (and sometimes bumpy) journey toward true love. I couldn't wait to share their romance with you, and I hope you've had a few laughs, some sighs, and a few hours' worth of romantic escape.

I'm currently working on my next contemporary romance, which will be published by Zebra Books in 2002. Until next time . . . I'd love to hear from you! Please write to me c/o P.O. Box 7105, Chandler, AZ 85246-7105, send e-mail to *lisa@lisaplumley.com*, or visit my website at *www. lisaplumley.com* for previews, reviews, my reader newsletter, sneak peeks of upcoming books, and more.

In love and laughter,

Lisa Plumley

Complete Your Collection of
Fern Michaels

__Dear Emily	0-8217-5676-1	$6.99US/$8.50CAN
__Vegas Heat	0-8217-5758-X	$6.99US/$8.50CAN
__Vegas Rich	0-8217-5594-3	$6.99US/$8.50CAN
__Vegas Sunrise	0-8217-5893-3	$6.99US/$8.50CAN
__Wish List	0-8217-5228-6	$6.99US/$8.50CAN

Call toll free **1-888-345-BOOK** to order by phone or use this coupon to order by mail.

Name _____

Address _____

City _____ State _____ Zip _____

Please send me the books I have checked above.

I am enclosing $_____

Plus postage and handling* $_____

Sales tax (in New York and Tennessee) $_____

Total amount enclosed $_____

*Add $2.50 for the first book and $.50 for each additional book.

Send check or money order (no cash or CODs) to:

Kensington Publishing Corp., 850 Third Avenue, New York, NY 10022

Prices and numbers subject to change without notice. All orders subject to availability.

Visit our web site at **www.kensingtonbooks.com**

Stella Cameron

"A premier author of romantic suspense."

__**The Best Revenge**
0-8217-5842-X $6.50US/$8.00CAN

__**French Quarter**
0-8217-6251-6 $6.99US/$8.50CAN

__**Key West**
0-8217-6595-7 $6.99US/$8.99CAN

__**Pure Delights**
0-8217-4798-3 $5.99US/$6.99CAN

__**Sheer Pleasures**
0-8217-5093-3 $5.99US/$6.99CAN

__**True Bliss**
0-8217-5369-X $5.99US/$6.99CAN

Call toll free **1-888-345-BOOK** to order by phone, use this coupon to order by mail, or order online at **www.kensingtonbooks.com**.
Name_____
Address _____
City_____ State _____ Zip _____
Please send me the books I have checked above.
I am enclosing $_____
Plus postage and handling* $_____
Sales tax (in New York and Tennessee only) $_____
Total amount enclosed $_____
*Add $2.50 for the first book and $.50 for each additional book.
Send check or money order (no cash or CODs) to:
Kensington Publishing Corp., Dept. C.O., 850 Third Avenue, New York, NY 10022
Prices and numbers subject to change without notice. All orders subject to availability.
Visit our website at **www.kensingtonbooks.com**.

Romantic Suspense from
Lisa Jackson

__Treasure
0-8217-6345-8 $5.99US/$6.99CAN

__Twice Kissed
0-8217-6308-6 $5.99US/$6.99CAN

__Whispers
0-8217-6377-6 $5.99US/$6.99CAN

__Wishes
0-8217-6309-1 $5.99US/$6.99CAN